WHEN Doves LAMENT

KATIE EAGAN SCHENCK

Faery Whisper Press
Pasadena, MD

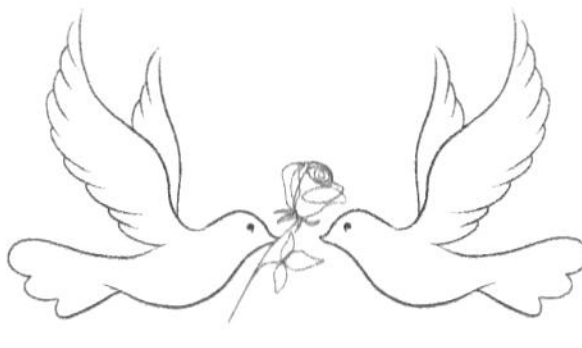

Dedication

To my father and his "love" of brown pasta.
And to my stepmother who indulges his preferences.

Contents

Epigraph

"As when the dove laments her love
All on the naked spray
When he returns, no more she mourns
But loves the live-long day"
— Aria from Acis and Galatea
by Handel George Frideric

Chapter One

WHOEVER SAID IT WAS better to have loved and lost than never to have loved at all had clearly never been divorced. The moment Max McAllister signed the divorce papers his ex-wife's lawyer had drawn up, he'd sworn off love for good.

Well, romantic love at least. His love for his children was apparent in the way he hoped each of them would have a more successful marriage than he'd had. As his son danced with his new bride, Max sent up a short prayer that the next generation of McAllisters wouldn't screw things up the way he had.

"Your mother would have loved this," he whispered to his daughter, Lanie, as they stood on the sidelines.

"I'm sure she's here in spirit." Lanie's hazel eyes glistened.

It'd been over a year since his ex-wife had died. Despite being divorced for more than a decade, he'd been by her side at the end.

"And I'm sure she's anxious to see you join your brother in marital bliss." Max slid his arm around his daughter and squeezed her shoulders. Her eyebrows rose in apparent surprise, and he pulled away gruffly. He supposed he deserved her reaction. They'd never been particularly close, a reality he was working to rectify since she'd moved back in with him. Besides, as far as affectionate parents went, that had been more Melody's area than his.

"What about you, Dad? Are you sure you don't want to give marriage another try?"

He snorted. "Definitely not. Once burnt twice shy, as they say."

"I believe the saying is once *bitten*."

"Sentiment's the same," he grumbled.

"The bride and groom invite everyone to join them on the dance floor," the DJ announced.

"Want to practice for the father–daughter dance?" Lanie lifted her arms, but Max waved a hand.

"I don't need to practice. I've been dancing since before you were born." As he spoke, his daughter's fiancé, Nate, walked up behind them. "This one, on the other hand, could probably use all the help he could get."

"Thanks for that," Nate muttered, pushing his dark-brown hair out of his face.

"You're better company, anyway," Lanie stage-whispered as she slid her hand through Nate's arm and led him away.

Max crossed his arms and leaned back against the pillar, surveying the reception. The wedding almost hadn't happened. His son, Steven, had suffered a heart attack a few months before. The doctors and Steven's nurse fiancée, Rose, had warned him to take it easy, but Steven hadn't heeded their advice. When he ended up back in the hospital, a frustrated Rose had broken their engagement.

Thankfully, Steven had seen the light and made choices that saved not only his relationship and the wedding but also his life. While he still had a long road to recovery, Max trusted his son would get there in the end.

Watching his children dance with their partners took him back to his own wedding. He and Melody were barely more than children themselves, having married when they were only nineteen. They'd been together since they were thirteen and hadn't seen the point in waiting any longer. But on reflection, he wished they had. Maybe if they'd left the small town of Cedar Haven and gone away to college, gained more life experience, things might have been different.

Well, no point dwelling on it now. Max ordered a soda at the bar. The bartender raised an eyebrow.

"Not much of a drinker," Max said, though he wasn't sure why he felt the need to explain himself. Still, he was probably the only person at the wedding who wasn't imbibing.

Drink in hand, he headed to his seat. Steven and Rose had opted for a sweetheart table, which meant Max had been seated with Nate, Lanie, and—his jaw clenched—that blasted wedding coordinator, Carissa. But as he approached his chair, he breathed a sigh of relief at the sight of the empty table.

If he never saw *that* woman again after the wedding, it would be too soon. After she'd vetoed every one of his suggestions for a rehearsal dinner spot, he'd appealed to his son in hopes that someone would be on his side. In the end, they'd compromised on an elegant restaurant on the edge of town. The cost was more than Max had expected to pay, but he was glad a local establishment had won over one of the many overused chains Carissa had suggested.

He checked his watch, relieved it was half past seven in the evening. About an hour to go before the bride and groom would make their grand escape, then he hoped to make his own. Weddings weren't really his thing, and he was already dreading going through it all over again in a couple of months with Lanie. Two kids married. Who would have thought he would be the only parent to witness it?

"Ah, Melody," he whispered. "They've done you proud."

A few hours later, the hall was clean. Max and Lanie walked outside, and Max took a deep breath of late-August evening air. Soon, the torturous hot and humid days typical of a Maryland summer would give way to the crisp, cool autumn he preferred.

When they reached the car, Max handed Lanie the keys. At her questioning look, he shrugged. "I'm too tired to drive."

She climbed into the driver's side. As they drove home from the church, he glanced at her out of the corner of his eye. In a few months, she would be married as well and leave his home for good. Despite his love of solitude, he wasn't sure what he might do with himself when he was alone again. She'd been living with him for about six months, since her mother's house had sold in March, and he'd gotten used to having her around.

"I can practically smell the smoke from whatever has your head spinning," she joked, turning down Main Street and passing Bea's Diner.

He laughed. "Nothing in particular." The last thing he wanted to do was make her worry about him. Besides, she would only be moving a few streets over. Much better than across the country to California, which was where she'd originally planned to go after settling her mom's estate.

"Could have fooled me," she murmured as she pulled into his driveway.

With a sigh, he unbuckled his seat belt. "I'm going to miss your cooking when you move out." He gave her a wry smile. "Stouffer's has nothing on you."

"I'm sure Nate and I will invite you over all the time." She climbed out of the car, opened the trunk, and grabbed her suitcase after spending the night before with Rose. "And it's not like you don't know how to cook."

"Nate told me you called my burgers hockey pucks once."

A laugh bubbled out of her throat. "Well, he's one to talk. His cooking isn't much better than yours."

"But it is better?" Max followed her up the driveway to the house.

"Only marginally." With a wink, she unlocked the front door and flicked on the light. They both sighed simultaneously, relieved to be home.

"I'm glad that's over." Lanie kicked off her shoes and flung herself into a recliner. "Now, I understand why people only get married once." Realizing what she'd said, she bit her lip and glanced at him. "Er, I'm sorry, Dad. I didn't mean—"

He waved a hand. "Bah, don't worry about me." After sinking into his chair, he propped his feet up. "Besides, I did only get married once."

"Thus far." She nudged his foot with her toe.

As if she hadn't spoken, he asked, "How are the plans going for your wedding?"

"Better now we've switched the date to around Christmas."

"I never saw you as a Christmas bride."

"I didn't expect to be one either," she admitted. "But we wanted to get married by the end of the year."

"Why the rush?"

Her eyes took on a distant look, and a small smile lifted her lips. "Have you ever heard that saying, 'When you find the person you want to spend

the rest of your life with, you want the rest of your life to start right now?'"
At his head shake, she sighed. "Nate has always been my person. It just took
me a few years to realize it. And now that I have, I can't wait to make up
for lost time by building a life with him."

Max stared at his hands, unsure how to respond. It brought up memories he would rather forget, like how he'd felt much the same way when he'd proposed to Lanie's mother. How she'd enthusiastically agreed to be his wife. And how those strong feelings his daughter described had led to a marriage for which neither one of them was prepared.

But Lanie was different. For starters, she wasn't nineteen. She'd finished a master's degree, had seen more of the world than he had at her age, and unlike Max and Melody, she'd dated other people.

Still, there was a reason Melody had opposed Lanie's relationship with Nate. Her worst fear was that Lanie would follow in their footsteps, sinking into the same mistakes and patterns that led to their divorce. Melody had wanted a better life for Lanie and made her daughter promise to leave Cedar Haven and never look back.

Then Melody got sick, and Lanie dropped everything to come home to care for her. During that time, Melody had come to regret the promise she'd extracted from Lanie. It was as if the reality of her own demise had caused her to reevaluate her past choices. She'd gone so far as contacting Nate, but in true Melody fashion, she'd taken a situation that required nothing more than a simple apology and explanation and complicated it.

Max shook the thoughts from his head. "I don't want you to rush into anything. You've just started your career."

"We're not rushing into it." She tilted her head. "Like I said, we lost so much time in the intervening years after I left for college."

"But you have your whole life ahead of you."

Lanie took a deep breath, and Max started to worry he'd said the wrong thing—again. The tense silence that followed reminded him of their phone call around the same time the previous year. Lanie had told him she planned to move to California with James, her boyfriend at the time. In the heat of the moment, Max had called her decision a disappointment, which had led to a huge misunderstanding.

"I want what's best for you."

His daughter's face softened. "I know you do. I only wish you'd trust me. Nate and I have discussed the future a lot." A flush crept over her cheeks. "And the past. But, Daddy, I've loved him since before I truly understood what that meant."

It was the way she said "Daddy" that stopped Max in his tracks. She might not be a child anymore, but somehow, she would always be his little girl. Even though she was twenty-four, he still wanted to step in and protect her from the consequences of her decisions.

The conversation was getting too emotional for his tastes. "I'm going to bed." With a grunt, he hoisted himself off the chair and headed toward the stairs.

"Good night, Dad." The disappointment in Lanie's tone caused a pang in his chest.

Their relationship had never been easy. His job required him to work long hours away from home, and he'd missed a lot of her childhood. While he tried to make it up to her with extravagant gifts, making sure she wanted for nothing, his efforts never seemed to be enough.

Then their arguments over the last year about her choice to move to California had exacerbated the cracks in their relationship. He'd pushed her to her breaking point by trying to convince her to stay in Cedar Haven, not because he couldn't bear life without her but because he thought it was best for her. In the end, she'd come around but at a price. Max worried the reason she was in such a rush to marry Nate had less to do with love and more to do with desperation to get away from *him*.

The next morning, Max awoke to the delectable scent of fried bacon wafting up from the kitchen. It reminded him of Sunday mornings during his marriage, when his wife would make breakfast for the whole family. Was his daughter trying to recreate those happier days?

When he entered the kitchen, Lanie thrust a plate of scrambled eggs and toast into his hands before returning to the stove. It wasn't the warm greeting he'd hoped for, but she'd made him breakfast, so he kept his thoughts to himself. Still, he couldn't help the way his face scrunched up in disappointment at the lack of bacon on his plate.

"What are your plans for the day?" He pulled out his chair at the end of the table and sat, subtly reaching for the salt shaker.

But Lanie got there first and replaced it with pepper. "Don't even think about it. Your blood pressure can't handle it."

With a harrumph, he sprinkled pepper on his eggs. Maybe her moving out wouldn't be so bad after all. At least then, he could eat whatever he wanted in peace.

"That's the last time you accompany me to a doctor's appointment." He scooped up a bite of eggs and closed his eyes. At least she'd added cheese and a dash of hot sauce, just the way he liked them.

To his surprise, she laughed. "You forget, you signed a HIPAA waiver for me to view your medical records. And I already told Dr. Carson to keep me informed if your blood pressure continues to skyrocket." Before he could respond, she added, "Anyway, to answer your earlier question, Nate and I are meeting with a potential caterer this afternoon."

That caught his attention. He'd been trying to figure out a way to discreetly become more involved in her wedding and thus spend more time with her, but she'd resisted his help. "Mind if I join you?"

She turned from the stove with a raised eyebrow. "Are you only going for the free lunch?"

"Of course not," he retorted, though as he thought about it, that sounded a lot more appetizing than trying to find anything edible on the special diet his doctor had recommended.

"Mm-hmm," Lanie muttered, clearly not convinced.

"I want to make sure you're getting your money's worth." He took a bite of his toast. "Not that you'll let me help you with that."

His daughter visibly stiffened. "Dad, we've been over this." Her voice sounded strained, and she took a deep breath. "Nate and I want to pay for this ourselves. It's important to us to have the wedding we want and remain within the budget we set."

Though she didn't say it outright, he could hear the underlying meaning in her words, and he resented them. "I know what Rose told you, but I did *not* insist their wedding had to be done my way. All I asked that crazy wedding planner for was a say in the rehearsal dinner, which is trad—"

"Traditionally hosted by the groom's family," Lanie finished in a poor attempt at imitating him as she glanced over her shoulder. "And in their situation, I understand why you stepped in. After Steven's accident, they needed the financial assistance. We don't."

Apparently, he'd made that argument too many times before. Perhaps he needed to try a different tactic. He scooped up another mouthful of eggs and chewed to buy him time. When he failed to come up with anything she wouldn't immediately counter, he decided to try honesty.

"Look, I want to spend some time with you. You've been gone for most of the last six years, and even when you were home with your mother, you were busy taking care of her. I barely saw you."

"Okay, you can come today." Then she pointed the spatula at him. "But you better behave."

"I'm not a child," he protested.

As she slid an omelet onto her plate, she mumbled something that sounded suspiciously like she was asking whether he was sure about that.

Chapter Two

CARISSA OWENS HAD BUILT her business from scratch. After planning her own nuptials over thirty years ago, she fell in love with everything wedding planning had to offer and wanted to give brides the same joy she'd had on her special day. But despite her best efforts, she'd never been able to branch out beyond Southern Maryland or into other types of events like corporate retreats or even retirement parties.

Still, she considered her work a moderate success, and she had her late husband, Chuck, to thank for that. He'd supported her through those early years of barely making it to her becoming the main breadwinner when he was diagnosed with cancer five years ago. Her work allowed her the flexibility of caring for him during those final months while still providing enough income to replace his when he could no longer work.

As she was fast approaching her sixtieth year on earth, she was faced with a decision: keep trying to break into other markets or throw in the towel and sell her business to enjoy a well-deserved retirement. Chuck would have encouraged her to retire, as he'd always had his eye on traveling the world before they were too old to enjoy it. But without him, she wasn't sure there was much point. Her business was all she had left of the life they'd built together, and she wasn't sure she was ready to give it up.

Thankfully, it wasn't something she needed to worry about yet. Her client for that day had been the maid of honor at the last event she'd planned. After the setbacks with Steven and Rose McAllister's wedding, she hoped Steven's sister, Lanie, would have an easier time. She and her fiancé were planning a Christmas wedding, and Carissa hoped it would be the key to breaking her out of her usual holiday funk. After all, nothing looked quite as beautiful as a snow-white dress against the deep green of a Christmas tree covered with sparkling lights.

But when she entered the door of the caterer, her excitement deflated. There, sitting beside the bride-to-be, was Carissa's least favorite person in the world: the bride's father, Max McAllister.

He'd been a thorn in her side during his son's wedding, and she'd hoped he would be less involved with Lanie's. From what Carissa had seen, Max didn't have a close relationship with his daughter, but she supposed it'd been too much to hope that would apply to wedding planning as well. Usually, it was the mothers of the engaged pair who bickered over the wedding details, but Lanie's mother had passed away the previous year. Carissa reminded herself to tread lightly with her new client. She could only imagine how hard it must be to plan a wedding after such a major loss.

Still, Carissa's job would be difficult with Max around. Part of her wished she could view it as a blessing that a father was involved, and had it been any man other than that one, she might have been able to. He was, without a doubt, the most stubborn, pigheaded man she'd ever met.

Pasting a smile on her face, she sashayed up to the table. Lanie turned just as Carissa reached them, and she jumped up and greeted her.

"Carissa! Thank you for fitting us in on such short notice." She pulled Carissa into a hug.

Nate stood and shook her hand, but Max didn't move. His expression had changed from one of genuine surprise to a cold fury, the warmth in his deep-brown eyes frosted over like a window on a snowy winter day. The feeling was mutual.

"Max." Carissa tried to keep her tone even.

Unfortunately, he didn't repay the favor. "What are *you* doing here?"

She opened her mouth to respond, but Lanie beat her to it. "Dad! You said you were going to behave."

"I didn't know *she* was coming," he replied without a bit of remorse.

Nate pulled out a chair for Carissa, and she gave him an appreciative smile, choosing to ignore Max's less-than-welcoming reception. *You're not here for him*, she reminded herself. It was a mantra she'd developed for the more difficult family members of her clients, but somehow, it had never worked with Max. Something about that man got under her skin.

"It's nice to see you too," Carissa said, surprised by how calm she sounded.

Before Max could insult her further, Nate cleared his throat. "We've been looking over the menu, and we have some ideas of what we want to serve at the reception."

Grateful for his intervention, Carissa nodded. "That's great! Tell me what you envision, and we can look at how it works with your overall theme."

"It's food," Max said, his eyes narrowing at her. "Food doesn't need a theme."

Carissa was tempted to laugh. How little people understood the way weddings worked. From the venue to the decor to the meal, everything needed to fit in with the overall theme of the wedding. Most food was versatile enough to work with any theme, but there were certain ways to finagle dishes to support the overall vision.

But that would be lost on someone like Max McAllister. She'd learned that lesson while planning his son's wedding. Instead of engaging Max, Carissa decided to do what she'd done the last time she'd had to deal with him: ignore him entirely. Nate slid over the printout the caterer had provided, and Carissa's eyes flicked over the choices they'd circled.

"You're going with the traditional Christmas dinner." She pursed her lips. "That's wise, but we need to be careful not to veer too close to Thanksgiving." Her finger slid down the page to the options for sides. "I would forgo the cranberry salad and try for something heartier. How do you feel about squash?"

Lanie and Nate looked at each other and shrugged.

"Depending on how it's cooked, we're fans," Lanie said.

"Good. A maple-glazed butternut squash would offer something colorful and different but still appeal to most of your guests." Something at the bottom of the page caught Carissa's eye. "We could have holiday cookies in addition to your cake." At their dubious faces, she continued, "Having alternative desserts often helps reduce the cost of the cake, as we can make a smaller cake due to the variety of options."

"Who has cookies at a wedding?" Max scoffed. Without waiting for Carissa to reply, he gestured to Lanie. "If the cost of the cake is a problem, I'm happy to pitch in."

A red flush stole over Lanie's cheeks, leading Carissa to believe that was not the first time Max had offered to pay for something. "We've got it covered, thanks."

"Should we add some pies as well?" Nate asked, clearly trying to prevent an argument between father and daughter.

"It's an idea," Carissa said. "But the point of including a variety of cookies would be to reduce the overall cost. If you start adding a bunch of other desserts, you risk paying more than you would have if you just made a cake large enough for all your guests."

"That makes sense." Nate looked at Lanie. "What do you think?"

"I like the idea of having cookies, but I was wondering if we could save even more money by baking them ourselves," Lanie said.

Carissa bit her lip. On the one hand, she didn't want to discourage her client, but on the other... "That's a lot to take on the week of your wedding."

"Oh." Lanie's face fell. "I didn't think about that."

"But if it's something you want," Max said, "I'm sure Rose, Steven, and I can help bake them."

Nate coughed loudly, and Lanie covered her mouth with her hand. An amused glance passed between them.

"No, that's okay," Lanie replied quickly. "I wouldn't ask that of you."

Carissa kept her eyes on the menu to keep from laughing. From what she'd heard, Max didn't have many culinary skills.

His eyebrows pulled together. "You didn't ask. I offered."

"Perhaps you should talk to Rose and Steven before you offer their services," Carissa said with as much tact as she could muster. "Besides, isn't Steven still recovering? I thought the doctors had encouraged him to continue to take it easy. We wouldn't want to add more stress to his plate."

"And perhaps you should keep your nose out of my family business," Max retorted.

"Dad!" Lanie pushed her chair back and stood. "If you don't knock it off, I'm going to have to ask you to leave."

"Me?" he demanded. "I'm not the one pooh-poohing every idea you have."

If looks could kill, Lanie's furious glare would have slain Max long ago, but luckily for him, Nate intervened. "It's Carissa's job to give her opinion of our ideas. That's why we hired her. She's planned more weddings than any of us, and we trust her."

Carissa's heart warmed. When she'd first spoken to Nate and Lanie, he'd resisted the idea of hiring a wedding planner. They'd originally hired her only for the day of the wedding, but as they'd started putting things together, Lanie had convinced him they were in over their heads.

"Fine." Max crossed his arms like a petulant child. "I'm sorry." But his tone and lack of eye contact suggested he didn't mean it.

Stifling a sigh, Carissa continued to peruse the side-dish options. For a Christmas wedding, she wanted food that embraced the spirit of the season while also providing guests with a hearty meal before they ventured out into the cold at the end of the night.

"What if we did a play on classic Christmas carols for some of the food options?"

Lanie cocked her head. "What do you mean?"

"For instance, they have a fig-and-prosciutto appetizer, which could be a fun play on the line from 'We Wish You a Merry Christmas' about figgy pudding."

Lanie's hazel eyes lit up. "Oh, I see! We could serve roasted chestnuts and maybe have little nutcrackers on every table as a decoration."

"Exactly," Carissa said. "Or we could serve the chestnut-and-rice pilaf as a side dish."

"So more of a subtle nod to the songs than a direct correlation?" Nate asked. "I like this idea."

She braced herself for Max to make a comment, but he didn't seem put off by the plan, even though it was her idea. If she didn't know any better, she would almost think he liked it, though he'd probably never admit that.

"They have towers of garlic bread." Lanie pointed at the option on the menu. "Maybe they can make it look more festive, like a Christmas tree."

"I'm sure we can find a way to make that happen." After pulling out a notebook, Carissa jotted down their ideas, more excited to plan their wedding than she'd been for any event in some time.

⁕

Later that evening, Carissa arrived at her home in Hidden River City, a few towns over from Cedar Haven. She'd shared the house with her late husband, and since his death, it'd become both sanctuary and prison. While the house still looked the same as it had when he was there, sometimes, she wished she could bring herself to make it more her own. The constant reminders of his presence weren't helping her to move on, but at the same time, she couldn't bear to give them up.

Setting her bag on the kitchen table, she breathed a deep sigh. "You would love this wedding, Chuck." Her voice seemed to echo off the walls. "Christmas was always your favorite time of year."

Unfortunately, since he'd been gone, it'd become her least favorite holiday. Despite trying for years, they'd never had children, which meant she often spent Christmas alone. Her family had scattered across the country like fallen autumn leaves. Every year, she received invitations to go to her siblings' houses, but she preferred her own company. Instead, if she wasn't working, she blindly picked a place on the map and booked a solo vacation. If she was working, she was usually too busy to notice the holiday.

"This year, I won't be alone," she told the empty house.

In some ways, working with both McAllister children had made her feel like a part of their family—minus their father. She shook her head in bewilderment. Those kids must have taken after their mother because neither one was anything like their dad. Grumpy, pigheaded, and intolerable were just a few of the words she would choose to describe him, and those were the nicer ones that came to mind.

That's how he presents himself, she could almost hear Chuck saying. It was something he'd repeated throughout their marriage whenever Carissa complained about a difficult client or, worse, one of their family members.

15

Chuck believed that everyone had a mask they wore before the world, and his favorite part of getting to know a person was watching that mask fade as the person grew more comfortable with him. Her husband had studied to be a psychiatrist, though he ended up teaching instead of opening his own practice. Still, he'd had a knack for putting people at ease.

If that man has a mask, he's worn it so long he doesn't know how to live without it. She could almost see Chuck's weathered face break into a smile and the way he would shake his head, admonishing her for not looking deeper. Her heart panged at the image, and she closed her eyes.

But her thoughts were interrupted by the shrill ring of her cell phone. Without looking at the caller ID, she answered. "Carissa Owens."

"Hello, Carissa. It's Max."

Closing her eyes, Carissa stifled a sigh. Had her thoughts conjured the phone call? *I thought the saying was* speak *of the devil and he shall appear.* But perhaps thinking about someone was close enough.

"Max, what a surprise. Miss me already?"

A snort sounded on the other end of the line. "Hardly. I spoke to Rose and Steven, per your suggestion, and they're more than happy to help Lanie and Nate bake cookies for their wedding."

She rolled her eyes and was thankful she wasn't on a video call. "Don't you think there will be enough to do for the wedding without adding baking to the list?"

"McAllisters always rise to a challenge."

Pinching the bridge of her nose, she struggled to keep her voice even. "That may be true for you, but I'd prefer to confirm this with my *client* before we make any definitive plans."

He scoffed. "You don't think I discussed it with my own daughter? She does live with me, you know?"

"Not for much longer," she muttered under her breath.

"What was that?"

"Max, I'm in the middle of something right now," she lied. "Don't do anything until I've consulted with the bride." Without waiting for a response, she tapped the button to end the call and tossed her phone onto the counter.

"It's going to be a long four months," she grumbled. First, she'd endured his behavior toward her at the caterer, then came his discussion with Steven and Rose without Lanie's knowledge. It appeared Max was going to be a thorn in Carissa's side once more.

Chapter Three

WHEN MAX WENT OUT to refill his bird feeder the next day, a sole mourning dove perched on the porch railing, cooing softly. As he approached, the bird fluttered its wings but didn't move, its gaze trained on the ground. Peering over the edge, Max groaned. A pile of feathers was all that remained of the dove's mate.

"I understand how you feel," he said. After descending the stairs, he looked around, trying to determine what had happened. "Must have been a predator of some sort." He glanced up at the dove and found it watching him. "Looks like he put up a hell of a fight, though."

The screen door opened, and Lanie popped her head out. "Who are you talking to at this hour?"

"Myself," Max replied. It probably sounded less crazy than to tell her he was talking to a bird. "Don't come out here. There's a dead bird."

"Aw, poor thing." Ignoring his warning, she stepped onto the porch and approached the dove, which was still perched on the railing. "Was that your mate?"

The bird cocked its head and stared at her before flapping its wings and taking to the sky. Max envied the bird's ability to easily escape uncomfortable conversations.

"Now you've scared it off."

Lanie shrugged, unconcerned. "I seem to have that effect on birds. I had a frequent cardinal visitor when I stayed at Mom's. Whenever I got too close to it, it flew away." Her eyes searched the sky. "I'm sorry for that poor dove. I've heard they mate for life."

"I'm sure it'll find a new mate soon," he said, but it was a sobering sentiment. Humans could learn a lot from birds. He would hazard a guess that divorce didn't exist in the animal kingdom. The animals that chose new mates each year were unlikely to experience jealousy either.

He gestured for her to return to the house, following closely. There wasn't much point to cleaning up the feathers, as they would likely blow away. As he closed the sliding glass door, the lonesome dove returned to its perch on the railing. It glanced at him before bowing its head as if sending up a prayer for its lost mate.

His daughter slid into a chair at the kitchen table and sipped a cup of coffee. She looked exhausted, and he couldn't help wondering if she'd bitten off more than she could chew. Between planning her wedding and beginning a new school year, she had a lot on her plate. It didn't help that it was her first year of officially teaching students with disabilities.

"Got any plans for the day?" he asked.

"Nate and I are meeting to start building a registry, and then I've got lesson planning to do." Her voice lacked its usual enthusiasm.

"You don't sound excited."

"I could use another week or two off," she admitted. "The summer was a whirlwind, between Steven's recovery, helping to plan the wedding that almost wasn't, and now trying to plan my own." She shook her head. "I'm exhausted."

"Maybe you could push your own wedding back a bit." *And find yourself a new wedding planner in the process.* He was still irritated with the reception he'd received from Carissa when he called her last night. The nerve of that woman to suggest she knew his own daughter better than he did. They might not have the best of relationships, but he and Lanie *had* discussed his idea about doing the baking themselves before he contacted Carissa. So what if Lanie had been half asleep when he suggested it? She'd still nodded, sort of. The argument could be made that she'd nodded… off.

She rolled her eyes. "We'll manage, especially with Carissa's help."

"Some help." With a harrumph, he grabbed his mug. The last thing he needed was a third cup of coffee, but maybe it would help spark some idea of how to reach his daughter. If he could convince her to find a new wedding coordinator, or better still, nix that expense entirely, his life would be a lot easier.

"I don't get why you don't like her," Lanie continued. "She was instrumental in getting Steven and Rose down the aisle, and she's been a godsend with finding vendors that were available on such short notice."

"Maybe if you had a longer engagement, she wouldn't be necessary," he muttered under his breath.

Lanie rubbed her temples and took several deep breaths.

A quiet voice inside told Max to drop it. *Change the subject.* Whatever it took to keep his daughter from pulling even further away from him.

"She's too pushy," he said, trying to steer them back to Carissa. "It's as if no one else's ideas are ever good enough for her."

"Well, she has been doing this for her entire adult life."

"But everyone can learn something new," he pressed.

Lanie quirked an eyebrow. "Even you?"

Instead of answering, he drank his coffee to hide his scowl. It wasn't that he *couldn't* learn new things. It was more that he didn't see the point in bothering.

"I'm retired. I don't need to learn anything new."

She laughed. "Learning isn't limited to work. It's something we should strive to continue doing at any age, whether through formal education or not."

He grimaced at her authoritative tone, the one she usually used on students. "I don't need a lecture."

She sighed. "I'm not lecturing you." Tapping her fingers on the table, she appeared to consider a different approach. Before he could redirect their conversation to Carissa, her eyes brightened. "What about woodworking?"

"What about it?"

"You used to want to build furniture. There were several unfinished pieces at Mom's house that we moved here. Wouldn't you like to learn more about that? Develop that skill?"

He didn't have the heart to tell her that his dream had died with his marriage, which was why all his pieces had stayed at the house he'd left behind. Melody had been a staunch supporter of his work, even begging him to refinish the kitchen cabinets and build a matching set of nightstands for the master bedroom. The thought of going back to that, without her encouragement, was one he couldn't quite swallow.

"Woodworking is a young man's business." He drained his coffee cup then stood, hoping that would signal the end of the conversation.

"No, it's not," she countered, not taking the hint or perhaps ignoring it entirely. "And if furniture is too much to start with, you could try whittling."

"I'm no sculptor."

"My point," she said with a sigh, "is that you don't have to have a job to find something worth learning about. Studies show the best way to counteract mental deterioration and prevent illnesses like dementia and Alzheimer's is to continue engaging our brains through learning."

"I'm not *that* old."

She crossed her arms. "You're the one who said woodworking was a young man's business. I was pointing out how hobbies can help avoid the diseases old people such as yourself"—her lips twitched as if she was fighting a smile—"are at risk of developing."

"We're getting off the subject." He waved his hand. "*My* point is Carissa doesn't know everything, and she should listen to her client's ideas with care and consideration."

"Seeing as I'm the client, I'd say she *is* listening to *me*."

"I've invested in this wedding too." He folded his arms on the table. "I paid for your dress."

That was the wrong thing to say. Lanie's eyes darkened, and her lips pressed into a thin line. "I let you pay for *one* thing and only because you kept *insisting* on it. As I've told you several times, Nate and I are perfectly capable of paying for the rest of the wedding ourselves."

"Lanie, I didn't mean—"

"I'd better get moving, or I'll be late to meet Nate." Her eyes flashed to his before dropping to the floor. "We can discuss this later."

Max sank back into the chair at the kitchen table with a sigh. *Strike two.*

Try as he might, Max couldn't get Lanie's suggestion out of his head. It'd been years since he'd done any woodworking. The half-finished pieces were moved to his garage after Melody died, in preparation for selling the house. They'd been sitting there gathering dust. His drive to build and create things had dissipated with the smoldering ashes of his marriage.

It wasn't like the divorce was a shock. He and Melody had been having problems for years before they finally called it quits. While they'd gotten married young, they'd waited to have children. But after they had Steven, things started falling apart. He'd taken on more hours at work to support their growing family, which meant Melody often spent time with the children alone without a break. His absence led to resentment, not just with Melody but with his children as well.

In a last-ditch effort to save his family, Max had planned a trip to Disney World when Lanie was twelve. The trip hadn't gone as expected, as everyone had gotten sick from the heat, and they'd spent a couple of days recovering in their hotel room. Despite the illness, those had been such happy days. Spending time as a family, playing board games, talking and laughing—it felt like things were going to be okay. But once they'd recovered, the bickering started again, and he and Melody knew it was time to let go.

He entered the garage, preparing for an onslaught of unhappy memories as he removed the sheets covering the unfinished furniture. To his surprise, the sad memories didn't come. Instead, as he inspected his handiwork, he realized he was a lot closer to finishing the pieces than he'd originally thought. The intricate designs he'd started would be easy to replicate with practice.

Leaning against the wall, he surveyed his options. He could sell the unfinished furniture or give it away to Goodwill. Maybe someone who had more interest and drive could finish what he'd started. Alternatively, he could buy some scrap wood and retrain his hands, rebuilding his carving skills to what they'd been when he was younger.

A part of him wondered what the point was. His house was fully furnished. Granted, most of it, he'd put together himself with frustrating instructions written in broken English by a Swedish company. But it held together just fine. Why did he need to finish that furniture? Why bother doing all that work when the person it was meant for would never enjoy the completed product?

But another part of him, the part that still loved his late wife, sparked to life at the thought of doing one last thing for her as a tribute to her memory and the love they'd once shared. A love they'd rekindled briefly, only to be snuffed out by a disease that even the strongest of bonds couldn't overcome.

"You look like you're trying to work out a tough math problem," a voice said from the open garage door.

He jumped and banged his knee on a nightstand. As he rubbed the sore spot, he frowned when he met a familiar pair of blue eyes. "What are you doing here?"

Unperturbed by his demanding question, Carissa sauntered into the garage, running a finger over the nightstand. "I came to speak to Lanie." Her forehead creased as she examined the rest of the items surrounding him. "Is this a furniture graveyard?"

He bristled. "No, they're not decrepit. Just unfinished."

"Why did you buy a bunch of unfinished furniture?" Her half smirk gave her a more youthful look. If she hadn't been making fun of him, he might have found the expression attractive.

"I didn't *buy* this stuff," he retorted. "I made it." A rush of satisfaction went through his veins on seeing her obvious surprise.

"You made these?"

The admiration in her voice made his chest swell. "A long time ago."

"Why didn't you finish them?"

That question deflated his ego—and his mood. "They were a gift for my ex-wife. When she served me with divorce papers, it became a moot point."

Her eyes widened. "Oh, I see." Her teeth chewed on her lower lip, and he found the action disturbingly distracting. "Well, they're quite beautiful." She met his gaze head-on. "You should finish them. They'd be a lovely wedding present for Lanie and Nate."

Now, why hadn't he thought of that? Probably because he was so focused on their original intended recipient that he hadn't even considered his daughter might like them. But it made sense. She'd been the one to suggest he return to his former passion, so why shouldn't she be the beneficiary of him doing just that?

"That's a great idea," he said.

His sincerity seemed to catch Carissa off guard. They stared at each other, and his heartbeat quickened. But she broke eye contact first, clearing her throat. The sound brought him back to reality.

"What'd you want with Lanie?" he asked, trying to refocus the conversation.

"To talk to her about the idea you called me with last night." She wore a hint of a smile.

He avoided looking at her directly, fearing a repeat performance of whatever had happened between them minutes before. No way was he attracted to that woman. She was his polar opposite in every way and a real thorn in his side about his children's weddings. Still, he could acknowledge she was pretty. Her ocean-blue eyes were framed with dark lashes, and her silver hair gave her a sophisticated air. He wasn't blind, after all, but that was as far as his attraction went.

"You mean to convince her not to go along with it," he replied, unable to keep the frustration out of his tone.

"Not necessarily." She stepped forward as if she wanted to reassure him. "I want to make sure she understands what an undertaking that would be before she makes a decision." When he didn't respond, she sighed. "I'm not your enemy, Max."

The way she said his name did strange things to his insides. "Oh, really? Is that why you've shot down every idea I've had?"

Her face fell. "I understand why you feel that way, but I assure you, it's not on purpose. I've been doing this a long time, and I know what works and what doesn't."

"That's what Lanie said."

"But I thought about what you said last night, and the fact that Steven and Rose are willing to help with the baking…" She shrugged. "Lanie and Nate are on a budget. If they're on board, then so am I."

A home run! With a nonchalant shrug, he tried to temper his joy at winning. "Glad you're finally seeing the light."

She scoffed. "I wouldn't go that far."

"I'll tell Lanie you stopped by and that we finally agreed on something."

"I bet if you weren't so pigheaded, you'd see there is a lot we agree on."

The way she said it almost sounded like a challenge, and Max straightened his spine, pulling himself up to his full height. "Is that how you always talk to your clients?"

"I thought I made it clear last night you aren't my client," she said, completely undeterred by his attempt at intimidation.

They'd moved subtly closer to each other until they stood a hair's breadth apart. Her flowery perfume filled his senses, intoxicating and infuriating all at once. She lifted her chin. Whether that was a further challenge or an invitation, he couldn't tell. And he wasn't brave enough to find out.

Taking a giant step back, he breathed deeply, relishing the fresh air that wasn't polluted by her scent. As he did so, his senses cleared, and he glared at her. "If there's nothing else you need, I have work to do."

An emotion that resembled disappointment flickered across her face, but before he could fully register it, it was gone.

"Tell Lanie to call me." Then she spun on her heel and stomped down the driveway.

Once he was alone, Max leaned against a half-finished table and ran a hand through his hair. He had no idea what had just happened, but he couldn't help hoping that whatever it was, it might happen again.

Chapter Four

A FEW DAYS LATER, Carissa had mostly put her strange encounter with Max McAllister out of her mind. She'd spoken with Lanie via phone, not trusting herself to meet in person again and risk seeing Lanie's father. The McAllisters were set to bake the cookies themselves, and Lanie had even invited Carissa to join them. But she'd declined, stating she wasn't much of a baker.

Truthfully, her husband had been the kitchen wiz. He loved trying new concoctions, and she'd been a willing guinea pig. Nowadays, she avoided the kitchen like the plague, choosing instead to order takeout and eat on her couch. Her oven probably had cobwebs in it.

Besides, the idea of working in such close quarters with Max wasn't a welcome one. She could only imagine how he would criticize her lack of culinary skills. The last thing she wanted was to derail Lanie's plans for homemade sweets by bickering with Max. If it were up to her, their interactions would be limited to only those necessary.

Unfortunately, she couldn't avoid him forever. In fact, she was preparing for yet another encounter that evening. Lanie and Nate wanted to check out a local band, and they'd invited both Carissa and Max to join them.

A double date, she mused, remembering the way they had inched closer to each other until the scent of his cologne had flooded her senses. That close, she could see the flecks of gold in his brown eyes. Funny how she'd never noticed them before, though she supposed fielding his sarcastic barbs had kept her distracted enough. But for a moment, his eyes had filled with an unfamiliar warmth that made her weak in the knees.

She stopped that thought train before it ran away from her. Or worse, derailed completely. Whatever had transpired between her and Max was fleeting. She needed to focus. Tonight was about her clients and nothing else.

And that became her mantra as she entered Seabreeze, a cheesy tiki bar on the outskirts of Cedar Haven. Lanie, Nate, and Max had already arrived and were sitting at a table near the stage. Max wore a Hawaiian shirt for the occasion, which normally would have looked out of place on him. Somehow, in that bar, with its fake palm trees, tiki torches, and other themed decor, it fit. He appeared less grumpy than normal, and she paused in the doorway to drink him in. Were he not such a grouch, she might even say he was handsome.

"Carissa!" Lanie called when she spotted her. "Come join us."

Shaking off her fascination, Carissa made her way to the table. To her dismay, Lanie indicated the seat between her and her father. Carissa supposed there weren't many options. After all, it would be weird to sit between the bride and groom.

As she took her seat, Max glanced up and met her gaze. Something like electricity went through her, and she quickly broke eye contact.

"What are you drinking?" Max signaled to the waiter to come take her order.

"I'm not sure," she said, grateful for a chance to look at the menu, though the options were disappointing. While she'd been there once or twice before, it wasn't her scene. A classy bar with a piano in the corner and a glass of Chardonnay was more her style. *When in Rome, as they say.* "I'll have a piña colada."

The waiter nodded before heading to the bar. Max was staring at her with the strangest expression. At first, she tried to ignore him, but after a few minutes, she couldn't take it anymore.

"What?" she asked, exasperation coloring her tone.

"You don't strike me as the fruity-cocktail type."

Her face heated, but she kept her tone cool. "Shows how well you know me."

He raised an eyebrow but didn't say anything else. The tightness in her chest eased as the band came onto the stage, and he turned away.

Lanie leaned toward her. "I hope you like these guys. Nate and I saw them all the time when we were in high school."

"You came to a bar when you were in high school?" Carissa frowned.

"Oh." Lanie laughed. "No, they played at the local dances."

"That makes much more sense." Carissa gazed at the stage. The men setting up looked like they hadn't changed much in the intervening years since the two had graduated. "Do they play outside of Cedar Haven?"

"Mostly locally," Nate replied. "They've done a few larger shows throughout the state, but they haven't made it big quite yet."

"Which is why we're hoping they'll do the wedding," Lanie said. "And then if they do become famous, we can say we knew them when."

As the band began to play, Carissa struggled to place their genre of music. It had a pop feel with a slight country twang. She had her suspicions about why they hadn't been able to move beyond the local bar scene, but she understood why Lanie and Nate thought they would work for the reception. They played some of their own songs as well as a few good covers.

She glanced over and was surprised that even Max was tapping his toes to the beat. When he caught her staring, he shrugged.

"I may not get out much, but I can enjoy a good tune as much as the next guy."

"Is this your usual type of music?"

He shook his head. "Not really. I'm more into country and old-school country at that. Alan Jackson, Garth Brooks, and even some Dolly Parton."

"So you won't be suggesting the McAllisters could form a band and play instead," she said dryly, unable to help herself.

"Lanie's about the only one with any musical talent, but she's more into singing than playing an instrument."

"That's right." Nate smiled. "She sings at karaoke sometimes."

Lanie's face flushed, and she mock punched Nate in the arm. "Not now."

Carissa exchanged a puzzled look with Max. It was clear this was some sort of private joke between the engaged couple. For the first time ever, Carissa was grateful Max was there. Were it not for him, she would start feeling like a third wheel.

Though if she were honest with herself, that was a given in her profession, especially since her husband had passed. When she'd first started out, she spent most of her time with the bride. The groom often just showed up to the wedding, happy to have everything planned for him. But the current generation of men was different. Even though Steven had joked that he needed only to show up to say his vows, he'd gone out of his way to make the day special for Rose. And Nate had attended every meeting Carissa had had with Lanie, providing his opinion and brainstorming ideas on his own.

Max's interest in the wedding was a surprise, too, though often more of an annoyance than a blessing. Normally, if the father was paying for the wedding or even a portion of it, he was content to hand over his credit card. It was the mothers who insisted on inserting themselves into every detail. But since Lanie didn't have that option, Carissa assumed Max had stepped in to soften the blow.

Carissa's heart went out to Lanie. She couldn't have imagined planning her wedding without her mother's help. It was a rite of passage for mothers and daughters to have that time together. Between the bickering over every little detail and the tears when they found the perfect dress, it often strengthened that mother–daughter bond.

The band took a break, and Lanie jumped up to seize the opportunity. She grabbed Nate's hand, and they raced to the stage, leaving Carissa and Max alone.

"Any idea what they might expect for compensation?" Carissa inclined her head toward the lead singer, who had jumped off stage to better hear Lanie.

"I doubt it'll be cheap. Don't we have to feed them too?"

"Yes, although we do get a discount from the caterer for vendor meals."

"I suppose that's something," he muttered. At Carissa's questioning look, he sighed. "I tried to convince her to hire a DJ. Figured one person with a sound system would be easier, and then you can hear any song you want." His eyebrows pulled together. "But I suspect you're going to tell me you prefer a band."

"Actually, I agree with you. DJs are less expensive and provide a much smoother experience."

He smirked. "Well, whaddya know? Something else we agree on. What are the odds?"

"As I told you the other day, I expect we have more in common than you think." She laughed, nudging his leg with her knee as she sipped her cocktail.

His eyes widened, and she realized a moment too late what she'd done. *Why am I* flirting *with him? It must be the alcohol.* Her cheeks warmed, and she pushed her chair back.

"I should, uh, go see if they've made any progress on convincing the band." Without waiting for his response, she hurried away.

Ugh, what the heck was that? It didn't make any sense. Just the other day, they were hurling insults at each other and bickering over the wedding. Not to mention, the last thing she needed was to complicate her business with a client's father. She glanced over her shoulder and almost tripped over her own feet when she found Max's eyes on her, watching her every move.

Focus, she commanded herself. When she reached Nate and Lanie, she pasted on a smile and tuned in to their conversation.

"That would be great!" Lanie was saying, her hazel eyes lighting up.

"It sounds like we've got a deal," Carissa said.

Three heads turned in her direction.

"Oh, Dan, this is our wedding coordinator, Carissa," Lanie said.

Dan stuck his hand out. "Nice to meet you."

After accepting it, Carissa raised an eyebrow at Lanie. "So, what did you decide?"

"We'll do the wedding." Dan beamed at Lanie and Nate. "Can't disappoint our biggest fans."

"Thank you!" Lanie gushed. "We haven't talked about compensation, but—"

"Don't worry about that." Carissa handed Dan her card. "Call me tomorrow, and we can discuss terms."

"Sounds great." Dan tucked her card into his pocket. "Now, if you'll excuse me, I need to grab some water before our next set."

Lanie practically skipped back to the table with Nate following closely. Their excitement was contagious, but Carissa dreaded sitting beside Max again. Why had she made things awkward by flirting with him?

But when they got there, he paid her no mind, instead focusing on Lanie. "How'd it go?"

Lanie smiled as she slid into her seat. "They said they'd do it, and Carissa gave them her card."

"That's great," Max said. "One more thing off the list." He took a sip of his beer. "Aren't you going to sit?"

Swallowing her apprehension, Carissa made a show of checking her watch. "Now that everything's settled with the band, I should go."

Lanie blinked. "So soon? But they've only played one set. You should stay and listen to the rest of their stuff."

"Yeah," Nate agreed. "It'll give you a better feel for what to expect at the reception."

Just as Carissa was about to decline, Max pulled out her chair. "I ordered you another drink while you were gone."

With a sigh, she sank into her seat in defeat. Perhaps it wouldn't be as bad as she feared. Max was acting as if nothing had happened, so she could do the same.

"I suppose I shouldn't leave you to third wheel it all on your own," she murmured to him as he moved back to his chair.

He laughed. "I appreciate the sacrifice, but I'm rather used to it."

"Not dated much since your divorce?" Carissa couldn't stop herself from asking. She immediately regretted it. *What is* wrong *with you?*

Max shrugged, clearly not bothered by her impertinence. "I haven't dated at all."

For reasons she couldn't quite articulate, his admission pleased her, but before she could say anything else, her drink arrived—a glass of Chardonnay.

Her lips twitched as she tried to hide her smile. She lifted the glass and swirled the golden liquid before bringing it to her nose. Hints of mango and peach filled her senses, and she sighed.

"How'd I do?" Max arched his eyebrow.

"Not bad." She took a sip, eyeing him over the glass. "Lucky guess."

He shrugged. "Maybe. Or maybe I know your type."

"My type?"

"You don't strike me as someone who gets out much unless it's for work."

Instead of answering, she took another sip of wine and savored the buttery, citrusy flavor. The band was coming back on stage, and Max had returned his attention to the front of the room. She snuck a glance at him. His salt-and-pepper hair was parted to the side, and even in his ridiculous Hawaiian shirt, he had a certain brooding presence. Were he not such a thorn in her side, she would almost call him attractive. Almost.

Chapter Five

THE NEXT MORNING, MAX came downstairs with more pep in his step. He hummed a song he couldn't get out of his head, one that he also couldn't quite place. As he entered the kitchen, he once again found his daughter already there.

She greeted him with a knowing smile. "You're in a good mood."

"Can't a man be happy in the morning?"

"Most men, yes, but you usually don't even crack a smile until you've had at least three cups of coffee."

He harrumphed as he set a coffee cup in the Keurig and pressed the button to brew. While he waited, he grabbed sugar and cream. The whole time, he could feel Lanie's eyes boring a hole in his back.

"So, you and Carissa seemed to be getting along last night. At least, better than usual." Lanie's voice sounded conversational, but Max heard the barely suppressed curiosity.

"I promised you I would be on my best behavior," he mumbled. After his coffee was ready, he searched the cabinets for something to eat. But really, he was stalling.

His daughter snorted. "You've promised that before and not delivered. What was different last night?"

When he could no longer avoid it, he sighed and took his coffee and a bagel to the table. After setting a container of cream cheese out, he sank into his chair and prepared for the Spanish Inquisition.

"I know how important the wedding is to you and how instrumental she has been in helping you to plan it." He slathered cream cheese onto his bagel and took a bite. "So I'm making an effort."

"That's uncharacteristically selfless of you." Lanie peered at him over her cup of coffee.

"Ouch," he muttered into his mug. When Lanie gave an unapologetic shrug, he grimaced, unable to articulate why he'd had a change of heart toward Carissa. It definitely had nothing to do with the fact that he'd briefly thought she was flirting with him. First, that wasn't possible. Carissa had made her dislike of him perfectly clear over the few months they'd known each other. And second, when she returned to the table, she'd acted as if nothing had happened. Clearly, he'd imagined the way her knee grazed his or the way her eyes sparkled when she teased him.

"No offense, Dad, but you've never exactly been one to care what other people think of you." Lanie shook her head. "If I didn't know better, I'd wonder if you were interested in her."

Max choked on his bagel, and he quickly downed the rest of his coffee, ignoring the way it scalded his tongue. *Interested in Carissa? Ludicrous.*

"Hardly," he scoffed.

"You sure?" Her lips quirked into a smile. "You hesitated. Almost like you were debating how to respond."

He scowled. "I figured it would be easier to be nice to her, for your sake." After finishing his bagel, he smacked his hands together to remove the crumbs. "But if you'd rather I continue to fight with her at every meeting, that's fine with me."

Lanie rolled her eyes. She stood and carried her coffee mug to the sink. After rinsing it out, she leaned against the counter and studied him.

"Just... promise me that if you do have any interest in her, you won't pursue it until after the wedding. The last thing I need is her to quit in the middle of planning the event after you break her heart."

"That's the easiest promise I'll ever make," he said, forcing a laugh. But an ice-cold weight settled in his chest, and he struggled to swallow. He cleared his throat before continuing. "You have nothing to worry about. There is not and never will be anything going on between Carissa and me."

"Good. I appreciate that." Lanie's shoulders relaxed. "I've got enough to worry about as it is." She pushed off from the counter. "Though you should consider dating again. I hate the idea of you being alone in this big house by yourself after I'm married.

Lifting a finger, he wagged it at her. "Why don't you focus more on your own relationship and stay out of my love life?" *Or lack thereof.*

Lanie raised her hands in surrender. "I'm just saying it's something to think about." She left the room, calling over her shoulder, "After all, you're not getting any younger."

⁓ℓℓℓ⁓

Once Lanie had left for work, Max headed into the garage. The more he thought about Lanie's suggestion to resume work on the unfinished furniture, the more he wanted to try his hand at woodworking again.

But first, he needed to update his tools. Some of them needed sharpening, but most needed to be replaced. Once he made a list, he headed to the store.

After visiting the hardware store and a few other places in town, he had most of what he needed. The rest, he hoped to find online. But instead of going home, he stopped in at Bea's Diner. He hadn't been in a while, and he had a hankering for her chicken-fried steak.

"Max McAllister, as I live and breathe," Bea called out the moment Max entered the diner. Her white hair was covered in a black hairnet, and she wiped her hands on her apron as she approached. "I haven't seen you in a month of Sundays."

"Afternoon, Bea. Been busy with the kids and their weddings." Max gave Bea an awkward hug. "Good to see you."

"Grab a place wherever," she said. "Coffee?"

"Please." Max surveyed the diner. It was a bit early for lunch, and the rush hadn't started yet. Just as he was about to slide into a chair at the breakfast bar, he caught sight of a familiar head of silver hair.

"Hello, Max," Carissa said. "Would you like to join me?"

His first instinct was to decline. After his promise to Lanie, it seemed prudent to avoid Carissa unless it was for something wedding-related. But she had that monstrosity of a binder on the table before her, which meant she was working. Surely, they could get through one lunch without bickering. Besides, he hated to eat alone in public.

"You don't mind?"

Her lips curled in a sardonic smile. "I wouldn't invite you to join me if I minded."

Fair enough. Max walked to her table and slid in across from her. The binder was opened to Lanie's wedding, and he could just make out some calculations on the corner of the page Carissa was studying.

"I'm glad I ran into you," Carissa said, covering the page with her napkin. "I've been struggling with something, and I could use some advice."

He leaned back, crossing his arms. "I would have thought I was the last person you would ask for advice."

"It does concern your daughter, and as you keep reminding me, I shouldn't assume I know her better than you."

Her words surprised him, but he worked to keep his expression neutral. "All right. What's going on?"

"Let's order first." Carissa grabbed two menus from the stand on the table and handed him one. "You strike me as a black-coffee kind of guy."

"I like a little cream and sugar," he said. "But none of that pump of this, sprinkle of that, extra whip stuff they serve at Starbucks. I prefer coffee that tastes like coffee."

Her smile faltered, and he realized a moment too late he'd put his foot in his mouth. Again. "N-not that there's anything wrong with that. It's just not for me."

"I like a sugar rush with my caffeine," she said in an attempt at a joke. It fell flat.

He shifted uncomfortably and was relieved when the server came and took their order. Once they were alone again, he leaned forward and gestured for her to begin.

"So, I spoke to the band this morning, as I'd promised Lanie," she began.

"And?" he asked. "Is there a problem?"

"They're asking for a lot more money than I was anticipating. It's going to blow up the budget Lanie and Nate set."

That didn't surprise him. He still thought a DJ would be the better option, but Lanie had her heart set on a band, that particular band. She would be devastated to learn she couldn't afford it.

He studied Carissa across the table. "Why are you telling me this? As you love to remind me, I'm not your client."

To his satisfaction, her face flushed scarlet. "That's fair, and to be honest, I probably shouldn't be talking to you about this." She pushed a lock of hair behind her ear, which he'd learned was a nervous habit. "But I hate disappointing my clients. I also prefer to offer them options for solutions to problems rather than simply presenting the problems themselves." Her blue eyes bored into his, and the intensity caught him off guard. "You know Lanie better than I do. Would she be content with a DJ instead or even a less-expensive band? Or is this a priority for her? If it's the latter, I can investigate making cuts elsewhere in the budget."

He sighed. "She has her heart set on this band. Beyond the fact she likes their music, they have sentimental value for Lanie and Nate."

With a nod, Carissa moved her napkin and flipped through the binder again. "We could potentially reduce the catering budget by removing one of the entrée options. We've already reduced the cost of the cake because of the cookies you plan to make." She tapped her pen against her lips. "But I'm still not sure it'll be enough."

"What about the photographer?" Max asked. "Could we reduce the number of hours they have to cover? For instance, Lanie's cousin had a photographer for the ceremony and the first hour or so of the reception. They were able to get the formal photos done and several candid photos before the photographer left."

"It's an idea," Carissa said, though she didn't sound convinced. "But we've already signed a contract with them, and I'm not sure we can alter it at this point."

An idea formed in his head, but he pushed it away. After the many fights he and Lanie had had, the last thing he wanted to do was go behind her back and offer to pay for the band. If she found out, she'd be furious, and it would only cause more damage to their already tenuous relationship.

That's assuming she finds out. Max gazed at Carissa, assessing her. Could he trust her to keep a secret from Lanie?

"What would you say to me covering the difference for the band?" When she opened her mouth as if to respond, he hurried on. "That way, I'm not paying for it outright, just the portion that falls outside of their budget."

She chewed on her bottom lip, and he found the action more distracting than he wanted to admit. Shaking his head slightly, he forced himself to focus.

"We should talk to Lanie about it—"

"She'll say no." He sighed. "She's been refusing my assistance from day one."

"Then what are you saying?" Carissa raised an eyebrow. "That we don't tell her you're footing the difference?"

He lifted his shoulders in what he hoped came off as a nonchalant shrug. "What is that saying? 'What she doesn't know can't hurt her'?"

"And if she finds out?"

"We'll blow up that bridge when we get there."

Carissa's lips twitched. "I believe the saying is 'cross that bridge.'"

"Sentiment's the same," Max grumbled, waving his hand.

"I'm uncomfortable lying to a client."

"It's not exactly lying. It's…" Max searched for the right word. "Fudging the numbers a bit. I'd be paying what? A few hundred dollars? That's a drop in the bucket of the overall cost for this wedding." He hoped he sounded more confident about the plan than he felt.

At first, Carissa didn't respond. She seemed to be performing calculations in her head and weighing the pros and cons of his suggestion. Part of him hoped she would refuse. After all, Lanie had made it clear she and Nate wanted to pay for the wedding themselves. And she might be willing to sacrifice in a different area to afford the band.

On the other hand, Max didn't want her to have to sacrifice at all. She'd been through hell, first in caring for her mother during her illness then in learning the truth about what had actually caused her initial breakup with Nate. If anyone deserved to have the wedding they wanted, it was Lanie.

"Look," Max said, breaking the silence. "If Lanie finds out, I'll take the blame. She can add it to the list of things I've done wrong." The last sentence came out more bitterly than he'd intended.

Carissa met his gaze, and curiosity danced in her eyes. But she didn't press. "All right. I'll iron out the details with the band and send you the invoice."

"And you won't tell Lanie?" Max asked.

"I promise, this will stay between you and me."

"Thank you."

Their food arrived, and Max was grateful for the distraction. He hoped the meal would smother the nagging feeling in his gut that he shouldn't be making decisions about the wedding behind Lanie's back, regardless of how well-intentioned they were.

"I'm surprised you didn't tell Lanie about your preference for a DJ," Carissa said a few moments later, breaking the silence.

He shrugged. "I didn't want to dampen her mood, and the band isn't half bad."

Her lips curved into a smile. "I'm surprised you're capable of such restraint."

"Shows how much you know about me," he retorted. After he finished his meal, he paid the bill. "I should get going."

"Hot date?" Despite a teasing lilt to her tone, her blue eyes burned with an emotion he couldn't quite place.

He snorted. "I don't date."

"Ever?" She cocked her head.

"Not recently, anyway," he admitted. "I tried after the divorce, but it didn't take."

Her expression softened. "I understand that more than you know."

That's right. She lost her husband. "Have you dated anyone since your husband...?"

She shook her head. "For a long time, I wasn't ready, and then business picked up." Clearing her throat, she forced a smile. "And now, I'm looking to expand."

"How do you expand a wedding-planning business?" he asked, genuinely curious. "Or do you mean you're expanding to neighboring counties?"

"No. Actually, I'm trying to branch out into corporate retreats." She sighed. "But it's not as easy as I had hoped. Somehow, knowing the perfect color coordination for a specific theme doesn't translate well to team-building activities and seminars. It's been a struggle to even convince a company to give me a chance. That said, I do have a meeting tomorrow with a corporation in DC."

"That's gotta mean something, right?" He leaned forward, folding his arms on the table.

"Yes and no. The client was an acquaintance of my late husband. So he's doing me a favor."

"Maybe he'll pass on your information to other business owners."

"That's the goal."

The server arrived. "Did y'all want anything else?"

Carissa looked at Max. "Do you need to go? I don't want to keep you."

They'd finished eating, and there wasn't anything else to discuss about Lanie's wedding. Yet while he had no reason to stay, he also wasn't quite ready to leave.

"I'd love another cup of coffee."

Carissa smiled. "Me too." After the server left, she placed her elbow on the table and rested her chin on her hand. "What about you? Now that you're retired, do you do any work on the side?"

"Not really." Worried his response would cause the conversation to die, he hurried on. "But as you saw the other day, I'm getting back into woodworking."

Her eyes lit up. "Oh, right. The furniture in your garage. The designs you've carved are beautiful. I'd love to see the finished product."

"Then you'll have to come by when I'm done."

She smiled shyly. "I'd like that."

To his immense surprise, he realized he liked that idea too.

Chapter Six

Carissa didn't stop smiling the rest of the day and into the next morning. Part of her couldn't believe she'd spent an hour talking to the same man who had driven her crazy only a month before about his son's rehearsal dinner. But she knew him better now, and it was clear from their conversation he deeply cared about his children, even if he sometimes had a strange way of showing it.

Stop thinking about Max and get your head in the game. The potential client she was meeting provided the perfect jumping-off point for her new work planning corporate events. They were interviewing several companies for their annual retreat, and she was determined to win the contract. Her desire to expand beyond weddings was twofold. First, she wanted to prove to herself she could plan more complicated events. Second and most important, her wedding clients had dwindled over the last few years.

Some of that was due to technology. Modern brides and grooms had greater access to venues and caterers than they'd had in the past. They could also host smaller gatherings while sharing their special day with friends and family abroad thanks to livestreaming services. The accessibility of technology and direct communication had made Carissa's job almost obsolete. Often, as Lanie and Nate had initially done, couples would contact her for her "day of" package, which consisted of a few brief meetings before the big day and coordination of the festivities. Though the package was popular, it wasn't as profitable as Carissa's more traditional service offerings.

Her location also limited her ability to attract new clients. Southern Maryland had built up in recent years, but it was still mostly rural with a few small towns sprinkled between vast farmlands. Clients in DC and Baltimore were less likely to hire her because of the distance, and though she'd considered moving, she would rather give up her business than the home she'd shared with Chuck.

For all those reasons, she'd decided to expand to corporate events, and she was excited for her first opportunity with Imaginavigation Enterprises in DC. Of course, driving into the city meant lots of traffic and parking, but she'd built in extra time just in case. The parking price tag was difficult to swallow, but she promised herself it would be worth it if the meeting went well. After leaving her car, she headed to the restaurant.

As expected, she was the first to arrive. She gave the hostess the reservation name and was led to a small table in a back corner. Not wanting to waste a moment, she removed her laptop from her bag and set it up. Then she placed the packets of printed slides at each table setting.

A few minutes later, the hostess approached with three men trailing her. Nervously pulling on her suit jacket, Carissa plastered a smile on her face.

"Carissa, so lovely to see you." Jacob, the CEO of Imaginavigation Enterprises, held out his hand.

She'd perfected her firm handshake after her father had forced her to practice it for years in her youth. He believed the secret to any successful business transaction was in the handshake. In his mind, it could make or break every deal.

"You as well," she said before turning to the other gentlemen who had accompanied him.

"I'd like you to meet Mr. Anthony Westman, our chief financial officer, and Mr. Colin Fields, our activities coordinator."

After shaking both men's hands, Carissa gestured to the table. "Shall we sit?"

The men filed into the three seats opposite her. Colin began flipping through the slide deck while the other two picked up their menus.

Jacob took the slides from Colin and set them on the table. "Let's order first before we get down to business."

Following Jacob's lead, Carissa picked up her menu, though she'd decided before arriving what she would have—a simple chef's salad and a glass of water. Her stomach was churning too much to eat anything heavy, and the water would help counteract the dry mouth she always experienced when nervous.

"Did you have any trouble finding the place?" Jacob peered over his menu at Carissa.

"Not at all. Your directions were thorough, and I used GPS."

He smiled. "I'm glad. The city can be hard to navigate when you're not used to it."

His condescending tone wasn't lost on her, and she gritted her teeth. Part of her wanted to remind him that as someone who had lived in the area for most of her life, she'd visited the city on many occasions. But her father's favorite quote went through her mind: "Better to remain silent and be thought a fool than to speak and to remove all doubt." Besides, she hoped that by the end of the meeting, she would prove not only her competence but also her talent at bringing a vision to life.

"What are you having, Jacob?" Anthony flipped his menu closed.

"A steak, of course. My wife won't let me eat red meat at home. Too worried about my cholesterol."

The other men laughed, and Carissa forced yet another smile, but inside, her heart cracked. How she wished she still had Chuck around to nag about his diet. She swallowed the urge to defend Jacob's wife, but she couldn't blame the woman for wanting to keep her husband around as long as she could.

After the server had taken their orders, Carissa cleared her throat. "Would you like me to get started while we wait for our food?"

Jacob waved a hand. "I don't like hearing a pitch on an empty stomach." He leaned forward. "Besides, I'd like to get to know you a bit better before we get into the business side of things. Have you lived in Maryland long?"

"Most of my life," she said. "My husband was in the army when we first got married, but as soon as he was honorably discharged, we came back to Maryland." She looked over at the other men. "What about you all?"

"Anthony's from New York, and Colin's from Boston," Jacob answered. "I've been in DC most of my life, though I was born on the West Coast." As he took a sip of water, he gazed at her over the rim of the glass. "You've been planning weddings since you moved back?"

"It started as a hobby when we were stationed in North Carolina."

"A hobby?" The skepticism in his voice was unmistakable.

"Quite a few of my friends were getting married at the time, and I had a knack for taking their visions and bringing them to life."

"And you think that'll translate to the corporate world?"

His expression had changed to almost a sneer, though she suspected he was trying to hide his true feelings. *So much for saving the business until after lunch.* But she squared her shoulders and looked him directly in the eye.

"I believe my experience would be a valuable asset for any event planning. Not only am I able to take an idea and turn it into a well-executed event, but I'm also used to working with people in highly stressful situations."

Jacob didn't hide his disdain as he snorted. "Weddings are highly stressful?"

Carissa took a deep breath. She would bet her right arm that Jacob's wife had done all the legwork for their wedding and he'd just shown up, probably drunk, to say his "I do." It was too bad his wife wasn't the one she was pitching to.

"They can be," she said sweetly, forcing a smile. "Especially if there's any rift in the family."

Their food arrived, and Carissa gave the server a grateful smile. Maybe once he had some food in his belly, Jacob would be more amenable to listening to her full presentation instead of degrading her experience. But she had to admit, things weren't off to a great start.

The conversation shifted to a situation the men had experienced in the office, which left Carissa mostly to her own devices. She ate her salad in peace, clicking through her presentation while tuning in every now and again to what was being said in case it might help her pitch.

As soon as Jacob had finished his meal, he pushed his plate away and folded his arms on the table. "All right, Carissa. Let's hear your pitch."

Taking a deep breath, she launched into her presentation. The men were silent as she spoke, flipping through the slides and jotting notes in the margins.

"I believe I can take your ideas for your corporate retreat and create an experience that focuses on team building that's fun and rewarding."

She sat back in her chair and looked at each of the men in turn. For a moment, nobody spoke, and her confidence faltered.

"How much would something like this cost?" Anthony asked.

"That would depend on a few things, such as how soon you want to hold the retreat, if you have a specific location in mind, and how long you want it to last. But I have several contacts throughout the area, which would provide cost savings to the company. Those details can be found on slide fifteen."

"Are your contacts familiar with the corporate world, or are they more geared toward social events like weddings?" Colin leaned forward with a raised eyebrow.

"I have several contacts that work with both social and business events. For example, I often work with local hotels for weddings and parties, but I have seen them host professional conferences." She cleared her throat and snuck a glance at Jacob. "That's why I feel I'm uniquely qualified to do this event because I would come at it with a different perspective."

But Jacob didn't seem impressed by her statement. "We're not planning a party."

"I understand that," she said carefully. "But there's no reason a professional retreat can't include some fun, is there?"

"She's got you there, Jake." Anthony slapped Jacob on the back.

Jacob frowned at his colleagues' antics and flipped through the slides. She held her breath. When he glanced at Colin and nodded, her heart jumped in her throat.

"As I'm sure you're aware, we've been listening to multiple pitches over the last week," Colin said. "We've asked a couple of them to prepare a proposal of three different options for the retreat with a detailed itinerary that includes information such as location, activities, theme, and the like. If you're still interested in working with us, we'd need you to submit your proposal in three weeks."

The tension in her shoulders eased. "That sounds amazing. Thank you for the opportunity."

Jacob signaled to the server to bring the check. "Colin will send you the details for what needs to be in the proposal via email this afternoon."

Her hands shook with excitement, and she tucked them under her thighs before anyone else noticed. She was one step closer to achieving her dream of expanding her business. With a lot of hard work and a little luck, it might be the start of a whole new life for her. And she couldn't wait.

⁓ℓℓ⁓

As soon as Carissa arrived home, she got to work, hunkering down in her kitchen to brainstorm ideas for her detailed itinerary. Relying on her experience in planning weddings, she believed she could come up with a unique offering others wouldn't think to include.

She thought of how family oriented both Steven and Lanie's weddings were turning out to be. Some of that had to do with Max's insistence that he be involved, but a lot reflected the desires of the bride and groom in each instance. Corporations were always throwing around words about how they saw themselves as "one big family," but what if she could create an event that backed up that statement?

She suspected most of her competitors would focus on the typical corporate week away, one where the company forced its employees to leave home and family to travel to some big city with mandatory participation in team-building activities. Sure, they'd have some social and networking options, but in her experience, it wasn't something the employees looked forward to.

But most people liked going to weddings and parties. How could she bring that fun mindset to a boring corporate event? And was it possible to do so without breaking the bank?

About an hour later, her phone vibrated beside her. She jumped then glanced at the caller ID. "Hi, Max," she answered a little breathlessly.

"Hey, are you okay? You sound like you've been running."

"Sorry. I was in the middle of something, and the phone surprised me."

"Oh, is this a bad time?"

"No, no, it's fine. What's up?"

"I wanted to hear how your pitch went."

She blinked. That was unexpected. Since when did Max McAllister care about her professional life?

"Uh, it went well, actually." She bit her lip. *Should I say more?*

"And?" he pressed. "Did you get the gig?"

A laugh bubbled up in her throat. "I wouldn't call it a *gig*, and I didn't get it. At least, not yet." With a smile, she told him about the meeting and the proposal she had to put together.

"Wow, that sounds like a lot of work. Three different ideas for one event? Are they paying you for this?"

"No." She sighed. "But that's how this industry works. It's highly competitive, and I need to make sure my ideas are top-notch if I have any hope of branching out."

"What do you have so far?"

The blank screen stared back at her. Glancing at the pad of paper on the table in front of her laptop, she pursed her lips. "Fragments of ideas, but nothing that's remotely ready to present."

"Okay." He drew out the word. "Tell me the fragments."

She leaned back in her chair and frowned. "Why do you care?"

After a beat of silence, she wondered if she'd been too abrupt. Still, she couldn't wrap her head around why he'd called her. While she'd enjoyed having coffee with him the other day, she wouldn't exactly call them friends.

"I'm sorry. I don't mean to pry. You sounded excited yesterday about the meeting, and the plans for your company intrigued me."

He's being nice. Why are you giving him a hard time? "No, I'm the one who should be sorry." Their rocky start had put her on edge whenever they spoke, and apparently, even a phone call made her suspicious.

After another awkward silence, she cleared her throat. "But if you're interested in hearing my scattered brainstorming, I'm happy to share."

"Share away," he said.

"I have a few locations in mind, mostly local, but it might be fun to do a more rugged retreat. Like a trip to the mountains, where the participants could go hiking, whitewater rafting, or even rock climbing."

"That sounds… adventurous." He seemed to stumble over the word. "Were you thinking West Virginia? Isn't that kind of far for the DC businessmen?"

"More like Deep Creek Lake," she said. "It *is* quite a drive from DC, but I hear it's beautiful in the autumn." After putting her phone on speaker, she set it on the table and scribbled a few more notes on the page. "I'm hoping for something refreshing and different while still being fun."

"It sounds like you're off to a good start," he said, and his sincerity caught her off guard. "If there's anything I can do to help, let me know."

She smiled. "I appreciate that, and I will definitely take you up on it." Her phone beeped in her hand. "Oh, I've got another call. Can I call you back?"

"I don't want to keep you from your work. I'm sure we'll see each other soon for some other wedding-related event."

Her chest tightened, and she almost ignored the incoming call to stay on the line with Max a moment longer. But Lanie's name was flashing on the screen, and she couldn't ignore her client.

"Thanks for calling, Max."

"Anytime."

⁓ ℮ℓℓ ⁓

Lanie's call had been a request to meet the next evening. As Carissa headed into the school where Lanie worked, she spotted Max crossing the parking lot. His brown eyes crinkled as he smiled at her.

"Fancy meeting you here," he joked as he opened the door.

"Any idea what this is about?"

"I'm as clueless as you."

When they got to the classroom, Lanie was at her desk, poring over papers, and Nate was at a bulletin board, stapling colorful construction paper that had been cut into the shapes of autumn leaves. He glanced up at the sound of their footsteps and waved a leaf at them.

"Thanks for coming. You can sit in the back corner at the table." He pointed toward a small conference table set up with four chairs.

Carissa sat across from Max and pulled out her planning binder. A moment later, Nate joined them and sat beside Carissa, leaving the seat next to Max for Lanie.

"Do you know why we're here?" Max asked Nate.

"Lanie had another idea for the wedding she wanted to run by both of you."

Another one? Carissa pressed her lips together. If Lanie had many more ideas, the wedding was going to get out of hand.

"How much is it going to cost me?" Max grumbled.

"She plans to pay for it herself," Nate said, and Carissa didn't miss the way his jaw clenched. She wondered why they had invited Max if they didn't need him to pay. Surely, this was something they could resolve between the three of them.

"Hi, everyone." Lanie slipped into her seat. "I'm glad you could make it." She placed a collection of Popsicle sticks, construction paper, and string on the table.

Max and Carissa exchanged a look. Were they supposed to do an art project? She'd seen her share of strange ideas but none as odd as that one.

"So, since we're having a Christmas wedding, I thought it would be fun if we gave the kids at the wedding the option to make their own favors." Lanie gestured to the materials she'd laid out. "We could bring a bunch of crafting supplies, and they can make their own ornaments."

At first, nobody said anything. Carissa hoped someone else would chime in. She hated to rain on her bride's parade. When no one did, she squared her shoulders.

"Who would be supervising the children during this activity?" She tried to keep her tone gentle. In her line of work, she'd found the best way to lead someone away from an idea was to have them explain their thought process. Often, they realized they hadn't considered all the work that would go into implementing the idea.

"I would assume their parents would," Lanie said, though her forehead wrinkled.

"But isn't one of your bridesmaids a mother?"

"Trudy has a baby, but he's not old enough to do a craft like this."

"It's a nice idea," Max chimed in. "Though I'm not sure it's the best option to keep the kids busy during the reception."

Lanie sucked in her cheeks. "Why not?"

"Crafts are messy," Max said.

Carissa shuddered as she imagined sticky children with glue on their fingers touching the decor or, worse, Lanie's beautiful dress.

Her client's face fell. "That's true."

"But Lanie thought it would be a nice thing for the families to have." Nate took his fiancée's hand. "Something unique that would allow them to remember our wedding for many Christmases to come."

As much as Carissa disliked the idea, she tried to find a way to salvage it that would keep the spirit of Lanie's desire alive without causing irreparable damage to any aspect of the wedding. She met Max's gaze and raised her eyebrows as if to ask if he had a way to preserve his daughter's vision.

"What about if we have holiday-themed stained glass window kits?" Max asked. "You remember, don't you, Lanie? You used to get kits like that for your birthday, and you'd make one for everyone else."

"Are those less messy than glue?" Carissa asked, hoping to mask the skepticism in her tone.

"They have stickers that fit into the different panes of the design, so it should be." To her surprise, Max winked at her. But thankfully, neither Nate nor Lanie appeared to notice.

"That could work," Lanie agreed, but everyone could hear how half-hearted she sounded.

"Let's keep brainstorming ideas," Carissa suggested. "And I'll research the stained glass things Max mentioned."

"That sounds good." Nate gave Lanie's hand a squeeze.

"Was there anything else you needed to discuss with me?" Carissa asked.

"Where are we on planning? I want to make sure I'm staying up to date on deadlines."

Carissa flipped her binder open. "We're doing fine. I've sent the contract to the band we saw the other night, and we have the cake tasting next week. The wedding invitations should arrive at the beginning of October. We'll need to set aside some time to get those addressed and mailed. But otherwise, we're right on schedule."

Her client sagged into her seat with apparent relief. "Thank you. I'm always afraid I'm going to forget something."

"No worries. That's why you hired me." Carissa made a few notes about Lanie's latest idea in her binder then closed it. "If there's nothing else, I will see you next Wednesday for cake!"

She stood and made her way to the door. A moment later, heavy footsteps sounded behind her, and she turned to find Max hurrying after her. Her eyes narrowed as he neared. "Did you need something?"

He flushed. "Uh, Lanie asked me to walk you to your car since it's starting to get dark earlier."

"Oh." Carissa frowned as Max opened the door. Her gaze strayed to the setting sun in the distance. "That was kind of her but completely unnecessary."

"And I, uh, might have wanted a moment alone with you," he continued.

She cocked her head. "Why?"

If she didn't know any better, she would say he almost appeared nervous. But that didn't make any sense. What would Max McAllister have to be nervous about?

He opened his mouth then closed it as if unsure of himself. Then he sighed. "I was curious about how things were progressing with your proposal for the corporate event."

Although she got the feeling that wasn't why he'd wanted to speak to her, she didn't press. "It's coming along well. I've started to put together the different ideas."

"That's great."

They'd reached her car, and he stood awkwardly beside it as she put her binder and purse into the passenger seat. When she emerged, he ran a hand through his hair.

"I'd love to hear your pitch when it's ready. If you wanted to practice on someone, I mean."

"That'd be really helpful, actually," she said, still unsure why he was acting strangely.

Though the summer humidity was hanging on, it was only a matter of time before the brisk chill of autumn would set in and the trees would begin to put on a colorful show. She shivered both at the thought and at his close proximity. The scent of his woodsy aftershave tickled her nostrils.

"I love the autumn," she said suddenly, hoping to break the weighty silence that had settled between them.

"Me too." He cleared his throat and took a step back as if he, too, had realized how close they were standing. "People hate it because everything is dying, but it's nature's reminder that even death can be beautiful."

In another life, she might have thought his statement morbid, but having lost her husband, she recognized the truth in his words. She felt the loss in every fiber of her being, but she'd come to accept that death was just the final stage of life. And her husband had lived a beautiful life with her.

Nonetheless, an errant tear slipped out of her eye and down her cheek. She turned her head but not before Max saw. With one finger, he traced the trail of water the tear had left. His touch caused an unexpected warmth in her chest, and she leaned closer to him. He cupped her cheek in his hand and leaned toward her.

"Dad?" Lanie called from across the parking lot. "Are you still out here?"

Max and Carissa jumped apart with wide eyes. Without a word, Carissa hurried to the driver's-side door, thankful they had been partially hidden by an SUV. When she was safely ensconced in her vehicle, she pressed her hand to her cheek, which still burned from the warmth of his touch. She didn't know what had happened between them, but she couldn't help wondering what else might have occurred if they hadn't been interrupted.

Chapter Seven

IT TOOK EFFORT, BUT Max managed to keep his expression blank as he walked back to his daughter, but his insides were a turbulent storm. He could still feel the softness of Carissa's skin on his fingers.

"I'm here," he said when he reached Nate and Lanie. "What did you need?"

"Nate and I are getting ready to leave. We wondered if you wanted to join us for dinner."

"No, you two kids go have fun. I've got a steak with my name on it marinating in the fridge."

Lanie raised an eyebrow. "Marinating? Since when do you marinate anything?"

"From what I've heard, you put some butter and pepper on it and call it done," Nate said with a grin as he left the school.

"Oh, ha ha." Max glared at both of them. "Go have your dinner and leave this old man in peace." Without waiting for their response, he stalked off to his car.

The truth was, he'd been making an extra effort to improve his cooking ever since Lanie had set her wedding date. He knew his days of eating well were numbered. After spending the better part of ten years getting his dinners from the frozen food section, he was in no hurry to return to it.

Homemade meals. That was one of the many things he missed about Melody. She'd been a spectacular cook, which had clearly rubbed off on Lanie.

When he arrived home, he sat in the driveway for a moment, staring at his dark, empty house. Since his divorce, he'd thought about dating every now and again but had tried only a few times before swearing it off for good. A part of him was afraid he liked his own company too much to share it with someone new. But he had to admit that ever since he'd started spending time with Carissa, his perspective had shifted.

Climbing out of his truck, he trudged up the stairs to his home and unlocked the door, flipping light switches as he made his way to the kitchen. As he gathered the ingredients, he found himself wishing he and Carissa hadn't been interrupted. Something had clearly changed between them, but he wasn't sure where it was all leading... if it was leading anywhere.

He opened the sliding back door and stepped onto the porch. Evening was rushing in, casting his backyard into shadow. After setting his lone steak on the small table by the railing, he fired up the grill. Once it was hot enough, he set his steak on the grate and closed the lid. Soon, the delicious scent of roasting beef wafted through the air, and he inhaled deeply.

Part of him wished he'd invited Carissa over. The steak was a decent size, and they could have split it. Maybe opened a bottle of wine, though he wasn't sure he even *had* wine in the house. He had a couple of russet potatoes he could have thrown on the grill to make it more of a meal.

Actually, that's not a bad idea. He slipped into the house and grabbed a potato then wrapped it in aluminum foil before placing it toward the back of the grate, away from the flames. His stomach growled. He didn't usually eat that late, but it'd been worth it to spend some extra time with his daughter and to see Carissa again.

In his mind, he replayed the moment the tear had appeared on her cheek. He'd acted on pure impulse, wanting to comfort her in what was clearly a moment of pain. While he and Melody had been divorced for years, it hadn't lessened the pain her death had caused. And yet he could still only imagine how much harder it was for Carissa.

Shaking the thoughts from his mind, he flipped the steak and the potato. He needed to focus, or else he would give Lanie another reason to make fun of him.

Later, he'd finished his dinner and cleaned up the grill and the kitchen. The night was still young, and he had a lot of pent-up energy after his daughter had interrupted him and Carissa earlier.

"Might as well get some work done on that furniture," he told the empty house. He headed into the garage and flipped on a light.

After running into Carissa at the diner the other day, he'd set aside some spare pieces of wood to practice on before he began carving the real thing. He was honestly afraid he wouldn't remember how to maneuver his tools in the delicate way he used to. It took the better part of an hour for him to find his rhythm again, but once he did, he was pleased with what he produced.

A knock on the wall broke his concentration, and he glanced up, irritated. "Don't you know not to sneak up on people wielding a knife?"

Lanie leaned against the doorframe, unperturbed. "I've been calling your name since I got back. Didn't you hear me?"

He shook his head, turning his attention to his work. "Did you have a nice time?"

"Always." She moved into the garage and picked up a piece he'd finished earlier. "Looks like you haven't lost your touch."

"Still rusty but improving with practice."

With a nod, she set it down. "Steven's here."

Max peered toward the door. "He's not coming out?"

"We were hoping you'd come in. He brought you something."

After wiping his hands on his pants, Max headed into the house. His son hadn't come by often since his accident, and truthfully, Max was surprised he was there then. But he took it as a good sign. Steven had continued to improve every day since the wedding, but his doctors were still recommending he take it easy.

He was sitting at the kitchen table with Rose behind him when Max walked in. They smiled at him and gestured to the chair at the end.

"We brought you dessert," Steven said, sliding a plastic container over to him.

Inside was a small piece of chocolate cake. Max raised his eyebrows, but Steven just grinned. Apparently, his son didn't care as much about his diet as his daughter did.

"Did you go out together?" After grabbing a fork, Max dug into the cake. It wasn't as good as a homemade one, but it would do.

"Yeah, we met Lanie and Nate at The Muddy Oar. And then I thought we'd stop by and bring you their cake since I know how much you like it."

"Thank you. I appreciate it." Max took another bite. "How's married life?"

Steven took Rose's hand and kissed it. "Amazing. Rose is almost all moved in, and we're talking about going away to Mexico in the new year."

"Assuming Steven gets the all clear from his doctor," Rose added.

Lanie came in from the garage and shot a look of disapproval at Max's cake. "Steven and I were talking about going apple picking this weekend."

"Apple picking?" Max leaned back in his chair. "I can't remember the last time we went."

"Probably about a decade ago," Steven said. "Before..."

The words he hadn't said hung in the air between them. Before the divorce, before their family broke apart. Max swallowed thickly. They never really talked about those years, and he wasn't about to start.

"Sounds like fun, though I'm not sure the weather will be great. Were you thinking Saturday?"

"Or Sunday," Lanie said. "We wondered if you might want to join us."

Traipsing through an orchard wasn't exactly his idea of a fun time. In the past, he'd only gone because Melody made him in the name of "quality family time." Then again, as he looked at his children, he realized maybe she'd had a point. After all, nobody had known back then how fleeting that time was.

"Sure, I'll go," he found himself saying. "We used to take you kids in October, as there was usually a greater variety of apples ripening with the cooler weather."

Lanie frowned. "If the weather doesn't cooperate this weekend, maybe we can plan for October instead."

"Sounds good." Max stood and stretched. "I don't know about the rest of you, but I'm beat." He slapped Steven on the back. "Tell me what you decide about apple picking."

"Will do, Dad. Good night."

"Night," Max said.

As he headed up to his room, he had the strangest desire to invite Carissa to go with them. She'd said she loved autumn, and it might be a welcome distraction from the stress she was under with the proposal.

Almost as soon as the thought came to him, he dismissed it. Running into Carissa in town was one thing, but inviting her out with his family would send the wrong message. The last thing he wanted to do was break his promise to Lanie. How strange that when he'd made that promise, not dating Carissa had seemed like the easiest thing in the world. But he couldn't deny his attraction to her.

It won't last, he promised himself. After all, until recently, they'd barely been able to stand being in the same room together. His interest in her was fleeting and would fade in time. Once the wedding was over, they would go their separate ways, and he'd probably never see her again.

The weather that weekend was atrocious. They postponed apple picking until later in the season. Max spent the time holed up in the garage instead. By the time Wednesday rolled around, he had almost finished one of the nightstands. As he stepped back to scrutinize his work, he wondered what he would do with the finished piece. Perhaps he could give it to Lanie as a wedding present. The matching set would look great in a master bedroom.

At the same time, Nate had a fully furnished house, and as far as Max knew, Lanie planned to move there after the wedding. While the newlyweds might make some adjustments to better make it their home, he wasn't sure refurnishing it was in the cards.

He crossed his arms and sighed. Maybe he should buy her something off the registry. That was why people made those lists, but that felt impersonal and detached.

Since he wasn't a man of many words, making something with his hands might be the key to showing Lanie how important she was to him. He regretted not making her a larger priority when she was a teen. His initial bitterness over the end of his marriage had caused him to distance himself from his children. By the time he realized how much he'd hurt them, the damage had already been done. Steven was more willing to forgive him, but Lanie... Since Melody had passed, it felt like almost every conversation Max had with his daughter became a battle. No gift, no matter how much time and effort he put into it, would heal the broken parts of their relationship, but it was a start.

After checking his watch, he dusted off his clothes and headed into the house. He didn't have much time before he was supposed to meet Lanie, Nate, and Carissa at the bakery. His stomach flipped at the thought of the wedding planner. They hadn't seen each other or spoken since that moment in the parking lot.

He laid out a fresh set of jeans and a button-down shirt then hopped into the shower. As he rinsed off the sawdust and sweat, he tried to allow the warm water to calm his nerves. Unfortunately, it didn't help. By the time he shut off the water, he was even more wound up than before.

He dressed quickly before moving to the sink to comb his hair. The reflection staring back at him appeared calmer and more collected than he felt.

"You're being ridiculous," he told himself as he combed his hair. "She's just the wedding planner. In a few months, you'll never see her again, and that moment or whatever it was will be a distant memory."

Despite the conviction in his words, he didn't believe a thing he said. Whether Carissa had felt something in that parking lot or not, *he* had. And since then, he hadn't been able to get her out of his mind. He could only imagine what seeing her that day was going to do to him.

Part of him wondered if he should make an excuse, but then he would miss time with Lanie. Besides, he was no coward. He straightened his shoulders and grabbed his jacket, wallet, and keys. Then, taking a deep breath, he headed to his car.

Lanie and Nate had both worked that day, so he was meeting them and Carissa at the tasting. Rose had promised to try to stop by, but with the hospital even more short-staffed than usual, they knew it wasn't likely.

When Max pulled into the parking lot, he saw no sign of Lanie's car. Carissa, on the other hand, was standing by the entrance of the bakery, armed with her *War and Peace*–sized binder. She saw Max and waved before crossing the street.

"Hey," she called as he climbed out of his car. "Looks like you and I are the first to arrive."

Great. He really didn't want to be alone with her again, especially as the cool late-September wind picked up and whipped her hair forward, dousing him in the tantalizing scent of her perfume. Without thinking, he leaned closer to her and closed his eyes.

"Max? Are you all right?"

The confusion in her voice was like having a bucket of ice-cold water dumped over his head. He straightened up and cleared his throat, desperate to find some clean air that didn't fill his head with thoughts he shouldn't be having about his daughter's wedding planner.

"I'm fine," he said, though the words came out strangled. His eyes met hers, and he thought he saw something there beyond the concern. But then she blinked, and it disappeared.

"Lanie texted she's going to be a bit late." Carissa brushed her hair back from her face as the wind picked up again. "If you want, we can get out of this wind and wait."

He led the way to the door. Once he was clear of her scent, he regained control of his emotions. Though that didn't last because he stupidly opened the door for her, and the breeze as she passed made him lose his head all over again.

Get it together, McAllister. It would be a long evening if he couldn't focus.

They headed toward the kitchen, where a large table had been set for the tasting. Carissa gestured to a seat on one side, and she sat across from him. For a moment, he was relieved to have some distance between them, then he realized he would essentially be able to stare at her all night.

While she busied herself with her binder, he did just that. Her graying hair was tousled around her head from the wind, making her appear more relaxed than usual. She shrugged out of her jacket, and beneath was a deep-blue sweater with a V neckline. As she scribbled notes, her small nose bunched up in an adorable way. Then she pulled her bottom lip between her teeth, and suddenly, he could barely breathe.

The sound of his daughter's voice broke through his thoughts, and he jerked his gaze away from Carissa. He stood to embrace Lanie, grateful for the distraction.

His daughter immediately engaged Carissa in a conversation about the wedding plans, and he looked around the bakery. The dining area was small, with only a few tables and chairs set up opposite the counter. It wasn't crowded, but he suspected they did most of their business in the early morning.

On the wall opposite the counter was a cute imitation of the game Candyland but with baked goods instead of candies. Cupcakes, cookies, fudge, muffins, and other pastries were painted in an assortment of colors to bring the mural to life.

A moment later, Nate arrived, and Carissa went to fetch the baker. Max breathed a sigh of relief. The sooner they started the tasting, the sooner he could get some distance from Carissa.

"Welcome to Bakeryland." A woman with short brown hair and green eyes appeared beside Carissa. "I'm JoAnne, the owner of this establishment." She glanced at Lanie with a warm smile. "And I assume you are the bride-to-be?"

Lanie nodded. "And this is my fiancé."

JoAnne took Nate's hand and squeezed it. "Wonderful to meet you both." She turned to Max. "And you are the proud father of...?"

"Lanie." He inclined his head to his daughter. "But I'm mainly here to eat."

Lanie, Nate, and JoAnne laughed politely at his poor attempt at a joke. Carissa gave a tight smile but didn't meet Max's eyes. Perhaps he'd imagined the moment in the parking lot.

"All right. Well, I've spoken at length to Carissa, and I have an idea of what flavors you're considering, but do you have a certain style you want?"

JoAnne set a few photos on the table in front of Lanie and Nate. "We can go as fancy or as simple as you like, though keep in mind, we are on a bit of a time crunch."

"We'd like to keep it simple," Lanie said quickly with a glance at Nate. "We definitely want festive colors like red and green to match the Christmas theme."

"So maybe something like this." The baker laid out a photo of a tiered white cake with red and green flowers and other embellishments. "This is a rather simple design that is enhanced with edible flowers." She set down another photo. "If you want a little fancier, we can create a gingerbread house cake with gingerbread cookies and candies as the embellishments. Or we can do something like this"—she laid down one last photo—"where the tiers themselves are either red or green and the embellishments are in other holiday colors."

The photos were stunning. Max had had no idea how beautiful baked goods could be. Then again, he'd never admired a cake for its beauty, as he was more interested in its flavor.

Lanie and Nate exchanged a glance. "And how much would each of these cost?"

"It depends on how many layers you want and the number of guests," JoAnne said. "If budget is a concern, it's also possible to have what we call a dummy tier. It's basically a fake, nonedible cake layer that's used to make the cake seem larger than it is. That's one way to save money on the cake."

"Money isn't a concern." Max waved a dismissive hand.

"Um, yes, it is," Lanie protested without looking at Max, but her hand clenched the photo she'd picked up. "Nate and I have a very specific budget."

Max opened his mouth to interject, but Nate shook his head. "Please don't start."

Carissa cleared her throat. "JoAnne is aware of the budget. We're still hashing out the guest list, but I would assume it would be between one hundred and one hundred fifty people. Right, Lanie?"

"That's correct."

With a nod, JoAnne pointed at the simple tiered cake with the red and green embellishments. "This is going to run you about four hundred dollars for the higher end of your guest list. The fancier cake will be closer to a thousand dollars. If you like the colored tiers, you could save money by having one dummy tier." She smiled. "I've also worked with brides who used two dummy tiers and only had the top tier as a real cake for their first anniversary. Then we had a sheet cake in the back for the guests, which is the least expensive option."

For a moment, Lanie's gaze strayed longingly to the photo with the red bottom tier and the green and gold embellishments. But then Nate picked up the simpler design.

"How about this one?" he asked.

Although Lanie smiled, Max couldn't help feeling it seemed forced. "But that's not the one you really want, is it?"

Lanie shot him a warning look. "This cake is beautiful. It'll be perfect for our wedding."

"Sounds like a good plan. I'll go get the flavors you've requested for tasting." Without another word, JoAnne headed to the kitchen.

"I saw the way you looked at the other cake," Max said the moment JoAnne was out of earshot. "If you'd prefer that one, I'm happy to pay the difference."

Nate glanced at Max with a frown before addressing Lanie. "Is he right? Do you like the other cake better?"

Instead of responding, Lanie took a deep breath and whispered something that sounded suspiciously like she was counting down from ten. Then she turned to Nate with a smile. "All of the cakes were lovely, but it's important for us to stay on budget."

"You wouldn't have to worry about the budget if you let me help you," Max muttered under his breath.

Carissa raised her hand. "Why don't we—"

"Seriously, Dad?" Lanie's eyes narrowed. "Since when do you care how pretty a cake is?"

"I simply want you to have the wedding of your dreams." Max leaned back in his chair. "What's the big deal? I'm helping to pay for the band. Why can't I pay for the cake as well?"

From the corner of his eye, Max saw Carissa drop her head into her hands with a groan. *Oops.* He remembered a moment too late that Lanie didn't know about the band.

"What does he mean he's helping to pay for the band?" Lanie whirled on Carissa. "I thought you said the band was willing to work with our budget because we're such big fans."

Before Carissa could respond, JoAnne returned with an assortment of different cakes. She set them on the table, oblivious to the tension growing by the minute.

"This is our red velvet cake. I also have a vanilla, a regular chocolate, a peppermint chocolate, which is a seasonal favorite, and a few other options I thought might work with a Christmas wedding." JoAnne beamed at each of them as another woman passed out forks and plates. "Please try all of them and tell me which ones you like best. Depending on how many tiers you get, you can have a different flavor for each tier. Enjoy!"

The moment they were alone again, Lanie opened her mouth to start in on Carissa, but Nate put a hand on her shoulder. They engaged in a silent conversation. Then Lanie nodded, and he cut her a piece of red velvet cake.

For the rest of the evening, they ate the cakes in a mostly tense silence. Only Lanie and Carissa voiced their opinions of the different flavors. Nate seemed to enjoy every flavor and had no preference. Meanwhile, Max kept his thoughts to himself. Apparently, he'd done enough damage.

As the tasting drew to a close, Lanie and Nate chose a more traditional vanilla cake for one tier and the peppermint mocha flavor for another to fit the theme of their wedding. They didn't decide on the third layer, though it was clear they were leaning toward using a dummy tier to save money. It took effort, but Max held his tongue.

Once the cakes were cleared, Lanie grabbed Carissa's hand and dragged her outside. Max slumped in his chair. It seemed no matter what he did, his relationship with Lanie would take one step forward and a hundred steps back.

Nate leaned forward. "You need to stop doing this."

"I'm trying to help."

Nate stared at him. "It's not particularly helpful when you cause Lanie more stress by constantly undermining her. If she wants you to help her out with the wedding, she'll ask."

"You didn't see her face," Max said. "She looked so wistful at the cake with the red bottom tier." He sighed. "I want to make her happy."

"If you want to make her happy, you might try listening to her."

"I do listen to her."

Nate studied Max. "Has it ever occurred to you why she doesn't want you to pay for the wedding?"

"Because she's stubborn?"

To Max's surprise, Nate laughed. "While that's true, that's not the reason."

"Then why?"

Nate folded his arms on the table. "Because she doesn't want the wedding to be another problem you throw money at."

"What is that supposed to mean?" Max demanded.

Instead of responding, Nate pushed back his chair and stood. "I'm going to go try to calm Lanie down. You have a good night."

Alone at the table, Max tried to push Nate's words out of his mind. But they played on repeat as if to torment him. *Is that what Lanie thinks I do? Throw money at my problems?* Then an awful thought occurred to him. *Is she right?*

Chapter Eight

With growing anxiety, Carissa followed Lanie through the bakery and out the door. *I should never have trusted Max to keep a secret.*

As soon as they were outside, Lanie crossed her arms and leaned against the building, clearly waiting for Carissa's explanation. Carissa stopped, surprised by how much Lanie resembled her father in that moment. The way her eyebrows pulled down over her hazel eyes only added to the stark similarity between father and daughter.

Here goes nothing. "I'm sorry for lying to you about the band." Carissa took a deep breath and launched into the story of what had happened. How she and Max had run into each other at Bea's Diner and started talking about the expense, including whether there were places in the budget that could be cut.

"Your father offered to pay for the band outright, but I knew how you felt about him pitching in with the wedding. So we developed a compromise where he would only pay the difference, and..." She sighed. "We agreed not to tell you, which I acknowledge was wrong and unprofessional of me."

"Why didn't you come to me first?" Lanie asked.

"I suppose I hoped I could come up with a solution that would allow you to keep your dream band without going over budget. And when I ran into Max, it seemed like the best option, and I thought, since he was just paying the difference, it wouldn't be that big of a deal. He is paying for your dress and alterations, after all." Carissa shook her head. "I realize now I was wrong. I'm sorry for not telling you the true cost and for going behind your back with your father."

At first, Lanie didn't say anything. She stared across the parking lot as if gathering her thoughts. Carissa braced herself for the consequences of her actions. While she didn't fully understand why Lanie insisted on paying for the wedding herself when her father was willing to help, Carissa also understood that Max and Lanie had a complicated relationship. Besides, Lanie's reasons didn't matter. Carissa had betrayed her client's trust, which was in direct contradiction to how she'd set up her business.

If Lanie fired her, she would understand. She hoped it wouldn't come to that, though. And she promised herself she wouldn't allow whatever was happening between her and Max to jeopardize her business relationship with Lanie.

Finally, Lanie took a deep breath. She looked calmer, and she even smiled. But Carissa didn't let her guard down.

"I guess I can't blame you for not understanding my insistence on not allowing my dad to pay for things. I don't know that I've ever explained why we have such a turbulent relationship. The truth is it wasn't always this way. Before my parents got divorced, I was very much a daddy's girl. While his work schedule made it difficult for us to spend much time together, we relished the time we had." Lanie's expression darkened. "But after the divorce, he shut down emotionally. Steven and I were supposed to visit with him on the weekends, but half the time, he had to work. And when we did visit, he seemed to think he had to make up the lost time by buying us things." She sighed. "Sometimes, it feels like that's his solution to everything in his life—just throw money at it."

Carissa's heart went out to both of them. "I'm sorry. I had no idea."

Lanie shrugged. "Why would you? We're not exactly known for talking about our feelings in the McAllister clan. That said, I've made a lot of progress with my therapist. She's given me coping mechanisms to help me avoid lashing out at Dad every time he tries to throw money at a wedding problem, but it's not easy."

"Especially since he does it so often," Carissa murmured, earning a laugh from Lanie.

"You have no idea." Lanie sighed. "He means well, but sometimes, I wish he would listen to me." She cleared her throat. "Anyway, how much does the band actually cost?"

Carissa bit her lip. "Uh, around five thousand dollars."

Lanie's eyes grew wide. "No wonder you didn't want to tell me." Her face fell. "There's no way we can afford that. Even if we tried to cut something like the floral budget, it wouldn't be enough."

"Exactly. A DJ is only about a thousand, which is more in line with your budget."

"I see." Lanie ran a hand through her blond hair.

"At this point, it'd be cheaper to keep the band than to find an alternative." Carissa kept her tone gentle but firm. "You'll lose your deposit if you cancel now."

"I suppose you're right." Though Lanie didn't sound happy about that. "Please promise me you'll come to Nate and me first about any future budgetary issues." Lanie leaned against the brick wall of the building. "It's times like these I wish I had my mom as a buffer."

Me too. But Carissa kept that to herself. "I promise to be up front with you in the future about the costs of things."

"Thanks." Lanie pushed herself off the wall and opened the door. "Let's gather the guys and get out of here. Want to grab some dinner?"

Carissa shook her head. "The cake samples were pretty filling, and I've got a lot of work to do for other clients." She followed Lanie into the bakery. Nate was waiting for them on the other side of the door. "I'll be scheduling your dress fittings soon, and we'll have another tasting at the caterer, but otherwise, we're in a good place. Let me know if you need me in the meantime."

"Sounds good. Thanks, Carissa," Nate said as he slid an arm around Lanie.

"See you later." Carissa grabbed her things from the table and spun on her heel, determined to put as much distance as possible between herself and Max.

"Wait!" he called, but she didn't turn.

Her pace quickened when she heard his heavy step behind her, and she practically ran to her car. But she wasn't fast enough. As she reached her door, he put a hand on her shoulder.

"Hey, stop. We need to talk."

She whirled around and glared up into his stupid handsome face. "Haven't you said enough? Why couldn't you keep your mouth shut?"

At least he had the good sense to look chagrined. "I'm sorry. It slipped out." He slid his hands into the pockets of his jeans. "What did Lanie say?"

"She asked that in the future, I talk to her about the budget and leave you out of it." A feeling of satisfaction swelled in Carissa's chest when Max looked as if she'd slapped him. "And I promised to alert her to any more of your shenanigans."

"*My* shenanigans?" Max retorted. "You weren't exactly refusing my offer to pay the difference. We were in on this together."

She hated that he was right, but she wasn't about to admit that. "Be that as it may, I thought I could count on your discretion. Apparently, I was mistaken." Without another word, she sidestepped him and opened her car door. "Now, if you'll excuse me, I have work to do."

"We're not finished here."

"I have nothing further to say to you." After climbing into the driver's seat, she reached for the door, but he blocked her from closing it. "Please let me leave."

Although he stepped back, he put his hand on the door. "I'm sorry for getting you in hot water with Lanie. I didn't mean to mention the band, but if it's not clear, her happiness is important to me." His head dipped, and for reasons she couldn't explain, her heart went out to him. "I don't want her to settle for less than she deserves."

Carissa sighed and leaned back in her seat. "I understand that. Your heart is in the right place, Max, but your methods could use some finessing."

He raised his head with a wry smile that took her breath away. "Ya think?"

Her lips twitched, but she fought to keep the grin off her face. "Maybe try asking your daughter what she wants and how you can help, then actually *listen* to her response. There might be more you can do that doesn't involve solving her problems by throwing money at them."

His eyebrows pulled together as he appeared to consider her words. "That reminds me. I wanted your opinion on a wedding present for Lanie and Nate. I've been working on carving designs into the nightstands in the garage, but Nate has a fully furnished house. I don't want to give them something they don't need."

Her earlier aggravation evaporated as she imagined Lanie's face on receiving such a beautiful gift. His thoughtfulness also surprised and touched her. *Perhaps there's hope for him after all.*

"Are you kidding? I can't imagine a more wonderful gift than something you made with your own hands." Impulsively, she sat forward and cupped his cheek. "I bet she'll love it."

His expression changed as he leaned into her hand. An emotion she couldn't place stirred in his gaze before it dropped to her mouth. Her heartbeat picked up its pace as she struggled to keep breathing.

Is he going to kiss me? More importantly, did she want him to? She blinked at the thought and dropped her hand. As quickly as it'd come on, the moment passed, and Max shifted away from her car.

"Have a good night," he said, his voice hoarse.

Her stomach flipped, and she hurried to close her door. As she drove away into the sunset, she could no longer ignore the attraction between them, but she had no idea what she was going to do about it.

⸎

"So, you're planning a June wedding?" Carissa began typing notes into her computer. *So much for Sunday being a day of rest.* "Have you booked anything yet, like the venue for the ceremony or the reception?"

"Not yet," the quiet voice on the other line replied. "We got engaged last week, and I'm already overwhelmed."

"No worries. That's what I'm here for." Keeping her voice professional, Carissa clicked over to her calendar. June was already almost full, but she could squeeze in one more bride. "I'm sorry. I didn't quite catch your name."

"It's Meredith."

Moving the phone to the table and putting it on speaker, Carissa frowned. The woman sounded like she was barely eighteen, but then, most young people sounded like children to her.

"Well, Meredith, I do have an opening for June. If you'd like to meet in person with your fiancé so we can discuss logistics, I'm happy to get started right away."

"Oh, really?" The high-pitched voice let out a squeal that reminded Carissa of a dog whistle, and she was glad she'd put the phone down. Even from the table, the noise made her wince.

Once they'd agreed on a date and time to meet, Carissa assured Meredith she would send over the details in a reminder email, then she hung up the phone. Sagging against her chair, she stared at the ceiling. *Another quick wedding?* As much as she loved new business, she hated short engagements. Steven and Rose had planned a wedding over two years, and she'd relished spending that much time with them. It'd given her a chance to really get to know them and what they wanted. In contrast, Lanie's wedding seemed to age Carissa by the day and not just because of the weird dance she and Max found themselves in.

Any new clients are better than no new clients, she reminded herself. But shorter engagements made her job that much harder and added unnecessary stress. Venues and vendors booked up well in advance, which left few options for those who wanted to get married quickly. Besides, part of her wondered if she wasn't funneling clients to Steven so he could act as their divorce attorney. While she wasn't aware of many clients who had gotten divorced a few years after their marriage, there were enough to almost make her lose faith in the whole idea of love... at least for the new generation.

With a sigh, she pushed away from the table to grab a glass of water before diving back into her proposal. She'd been working diligently on it all morning before the latest call, and she returned to it with renewed purpose. Maybe once she had a few corporate events under her belt, she could be more choosey about what weddings she worked on in the future. Being in high demand would be nice, and it would allow her to focus on events she actually wanted to do instead of working with whoever happened to call that month.

A few hours later, she'd created a decent first draft of her three event ideas, but she couldn't decide how to present them. Should she start with her favorite then go through to the one she liked least? Or was it better to start with expectations low so she could wow them at the end? She drummed her fingers on the table. Humans had short attention spans. It might make more sense to end with the option she hoped they would choose, to keep it fresh in their minds.

She glanced at her watch and was surprised to find she'd lost the whole day. *I'll work on my slides tomorrow.* Though it was late in the afternoon, she needed to go to the grocery store before it closed.

After compiling a small list of items, she rushed out the door. Sundays in Cedar Haven meant everything closed early, and she had just over an hour to get her shopping done. The store was empty save for a handful of people at checkout. She needed to hurry.

She grabbed a cart and headed to the produce section. The other problem with shopping so late on a Sunday was that everything was picked over from the weekend rush. Perhaps she should have waited until the following day, when things would be restocked, but she had several appointments with her brides, and a presentation to finish.

Her aggravation grew with every aisle she went down. She was about halfway through the store, and they were missing a quarter of the things she needed. At that rate, she would have no choice but to make two shopping trips during the week.

"This is ridiculous," she grumbled as she searched for her favorite spaghetti sauce and then her second-favorite one.

"I've heard spaghetti sauce described as many things," a voice said behind her, "but ridiculous is new."

She spun around and flushed as her eyes met Max's. His amused expression did little to help her bad mood.

"They're out of everything I need." She waved the sauce she'd picked up, the generic store brand that always seemed overly salted. "That's what's ridiculous."

"Ah, I feel your pain. I should have gone out this morning, but it slipped my mind." He shrugged. "It just means another trip later this week."

"Some of us don't have that luxury," she muttered. Her next item was chicken broth, which, mercifully, was well stocked.

"If you want, I'm happy to pick up whatever you can't find when I come back."

Her eyebrows shot up. Max McAllister was offering to do her a favor? "I wouldn't want to put you out."

"You wouldn't. I've already accepted I'll be back here soon. It wouldn't be any trouble to pick up some things for you." His lips curved into a genuine smile, which caused her heart to flutter.

Though she tried not to, she found herself returning his smile. "I must admit, it's tempting to accept your offer. I've got so much going on this week, I'm not sure when I'd have time to come back."

"Then accept it." He gave a playful shrug. "After all, bringing you groceries is the neighborly thing to do."

"Uh-huh." She crossed her arms on the handle of her cart. "We're not actually neighbors, though."

His face broke into a broad grin. "Details."

She studied him as she considered his offer. It *would* help her a lot, but the last thing she wanted was to be indebted to him. "Does your delivery service include no-contact drop-off, or do I actually need to answer my door?"

"Hmm." Tapping his chin, he stared at the ceiling. "I wouldn't want to risk any of your perishables going bad. It's best if I not only confirm you're home but carry the groceries in for you."

A laugh bubbled up in her throat. "Are you planning to put them away as well?"

"That one might cost you."

Is he flirting with me? "Ah, there *is* a fee for your services."

He winked, and her breath caught in her throat. "Not for pickup and delivery, but putting them away, well, that's asking a lot. I mean, I don't even know where you keep all your items. It'd take me a while to figure it out on my own."

They had moved closer to each other, and the warmth from his body poured over her in waves. She tilted her head back to get a better look at him, and his gaze drifted to her mouth. For the second time in a week, she wondered if he might kiss her.

"So," she said, her voice breathy and soft. "Are you expecting a tip, or is it included in the cost?"

His expression changed, and his eyes filled with hunger. "My terms are negotiable."

She pursed her lips. "Fine. What's your starting offer?"

"Have dinner with me," he blurted out.

Did he... Did he just ask me out? She swallowed, but Max looked as shocked by his question as she was.

"I mean, er—" He stared at his feet, avoiding her gaze. "Not like a date, exactly. More... a meal, uh, between friends?" His voice rose on the last word like a question.

The *yes* was on the tip of her tongue, but she hesitated. Besides the fact that she and Max could hardly get through a conversation without bickering, he was her client's father. Her number-one rule was not to mix business with pleasure. And she'd already jeopardized her relationship with Lanie once because of Max. Although, he'd said it would be as friends...

"It may sound crazy," Max continued when she hadn't responded, "but I feel like we've been getting along better, and well, I, uh, don't get out much, as you can imagine." He chuckled nervously. "Besides, I'm sure it would take a load off Lanie if we were friends, and you keep saying we may find we have more in common than we think." He shrugged. "Why not find out?"

The idea of getting to know Max both thrilled and terrified her. Her attraction to him seemed to grow each time they met, and she wasn't sure she would be able to resist acting on it if they were alone together. On the other hand, he had a point. If they could discover more things they had in common, they might butt heads less often. And once the wedding was over...

Don't go there. Allowing herself to even consider Max in that way would only make it that much harder to keep things between them strictly platonic.

Before she could answer, someone came down the aisle. She took advantage of the interruption to search for the next item on her list, a box of wheat pasta. But her emotions were all over the place, and she couldn't seem to focus. Just when she was about to give up, he bent beside her and pointed.

"Is that what you're looking for?"

After grabbing the box, she stood and stared at him. "How'd you know?"

Moving around her, he plucked her list from the seat of her cart. "I read it right here." His eyebrows pulled together. "Though I can't say I'm much of a fan of brown pasta."

Despite the chaos swirling inside, she laughed. "It's good for you."

"If you say so," he said, clearly unconvinced.

"I-I need to go," she said, turning her cart in the opposite direction. "They're going to close soon."

"Carissa." The way he said her name sent shivers down her spine.

She glanced at him over her shoulder. "Let me think about it."

He opened his mouth, then he nodded. "All right. Text me with what you can't find, and I'll stop by the store on Wednesday."

With a tight smile, she hurried out of the aisle. Thankfully, the next one was empty, and she leaned against her cart while taking deep breaths.

What is this man doing to me? The way he made her feel like some lovestruck teenager. The last time a man had made her feel that way was...

"Chuck," she whispered, surprising herself. But that was crazy. What she and Chuck had was that incomparable, soulmate, once-in-a-lifetime love. She'd considered herself lucky to have found it once, but there was no way it could happen twice, right? And especially not with someone like Max McAllister.

As she finished her shopping and checked out, she kept expecting to run into Max again. But he must have left, because she saw no sign of him in the store. Her emotions swung between relief and disappointment. She only hoped she would have an answer to his invitation by the time he showed up on Wednesday.

Chapter Nine

THE NEXT MORNING, MAX woke with the taste of bitter disappointment on his tongue. No matter how much he tried to wrap his head around Carissa's refusal to answer his question, he couldn't understand why she hadn't agreed to join him for dinner. Perhaps his delivery could use some work, but he'd made it clear that the dinner was a friendly invitation and not a date.

Though deep down, he wished he was free to ask her out. His promise to Lanie had seemed trivial at the time, but as his interest in Carissa grew, so did his desire to spend more time with her.

A realization hit him. *Maybe she feels the same and was hoping for more than just a friendship.* He would have to explain about Lanie, but he was sure Carissa would understand. She was a businesswoman, after all.

When he came downstairs, he found Lanie in the kitchen and at the stove. The scent of fried bacon wafted toward the doorway, and he inhaled the delicious smell. He hurried to the table and slid into his seat.

A moment later, Lanie placed two plates on the table. His anticipation of a hearty breakfast diminished when he was greeted with an egg-white omelet and a dry piece of wheat toast. Meanwhile, Lanie's plate had two pieces of bacon and scrambled eggs.

"What gives?" he demanded with a frown.

She rolled her eyes. "You can't eat bacon. You're lucky I let you have all that cake at the tasting."

"Lucky," he muttered as he cut into his omelet with a fork. "Like I'm a child instead of a grown man."

"So, how was your evening?" she asked in a falsely cheerful tone. After grabbing the salt, she sprinkled some on her food.

He held out his hand for her to pass it, but she placed it out of reach and handed him the pepper instead. At his scowl, she simply shrugged.

"Nothing of interest to report. I went grocery shopping." He cleared his throat. "I saw Carissa while I was there."

"Oh? How is she?"

Max shrugged. "Fine, I guess. We didn't talk much." That was the understatement of the year, but he had to tread carefully where Carissa was concerned. The last thing he needed was for Lanie to worry he was breaking his promise.

"I'm glad you're at least able to exchange polite pleasantries. A few months ago, that didn't seem possible."

He shifted uncomfortably in his chair. "I'm trying to be on my best behavior. Anyway, how was your night?"

"Nate and I had a good time, though it's always hard to leave him at the end," she said, her face taking on a wistful look. Then she blinked, and it was gone. "He's coming over this evening after work to go over the guest list for the wedding. Oh, and we're planning to go apple picking on Sunday. The weather looks great."

"Who's driving?" Max asked.

"We could all ride up in your truck if you're still coming."

"Just you and Nate?"

"And Steven and Rose."

"I'm not sure I can fit everyone."

She frowned. "Maybe Steven and Rose can drive up separately. His car is a bit more rugged than mine."

"That sounds more doable, but we can figure it out when we get closer to the day."

"I was also thinking," she continued with a quick, almost guilty glance at him, "maybe you could invite someone."

He almost dropped his fork. Tightening his grip, he shoveled another bite of eggs into his mouth to buy him some time before answering. After washing it down with coffee, he raised an eyebrow. "Why would I invite anyone?"

"I don't want you to feel like a fifth wheel."

He scoffed. "I'll be fine. It's not like I haven't gone out with the four of you before."

"True." Lanie placed her elbow on the table and rested her chin on her hand as she studied him. "But don't you ever get lonely?"

The piece of toast seemed to lodge in his throat, and he coughed violently. Lanie rushed to get him a glass of water, and he downed it in a few gulps.

"I'm not lonely, and as I said before, I'm too old for dating."

"No, you're not. That's why they have those dating apps for people your age. Isn't one of them called, like, Our Time or something?"

As much as he hated to admit it, he'd heard of that particular app. But the idea of meeting someone that way didn't sit right with him.

"Or if you don't want to go on an app," Lanie continued when he didn't respond, "you could ask out one of the women in our community."

"You sound like you have a list." A queasy feeling in the pit of his stomach told him she probably did.

"I have a few suggestions." Lanie grinned.

Despite his better judgment, curiosity got the better of him. "Who's on this list of yours?"

Lifting her mug, she regarded him over the rim. "Our old neighbor Cassandra, Bea, and Mrs. Carlisle."

Max's mouth dropped open. "Bea and Mrs. Carlisle are both at least ten years older than me."

"And?" Lanie asked, unperturbed. When he glared at her, she sighed. "Fine. What's wrong with Cassandra?"

"She's too eccentric."

"Or you're too picky." She carried her dishes to the sink. "I'm not saying you have to marry any of them, but it wouldn't kill you to put yourself out there. I haven't seen you go on one date since Mom."

"I don't need to date," he protested. "I have you and Steven."

When she leaned against the table, her eyes filled with concern. "It doesn't hurt to have friends your own age."

"I have friends." He dumped his plate on the counter. "And I don't need my daughter meddling in my love life or lack thereof."

"I'm not meddling. I'm trying to help—"

"Well, don't!" he shouted. "It's not your problem nor your business."

The hurt look on Lanie's face filled him with remorse, but before he could apologize, she grabbed her bag and ran out of the house. He considered going after her, but he knew it would be a futile attempt. With a defeated sigh, he began washing the dishes.

ele

After his argument with Lanie, Max was in no mood to work in the garage. He needed something that required more physical labor than carving. As he glanced out the back door, he debated cutting the grass. It would probably be the last time that season he needed to mow, as October was right around the corner.

He slid the door open and stepped out onto the back deck. The cool September air greeted him, and he closed his eyes. Just being outside lifted his mood. A soft cooing sound caught his attention, and he opened his eyes to find a mourning dove perched on the railing.

"Shouldn't you be flying south for the winter?" His knowledge of birds was limited, but there didn't seem to be many species that stuck around for the cold, snowy months.

The bird cocked its head, and for one crazy moment, Max wondered if it actually understood him. It cooed again, a mournful, poignant sound that tugged at Max's heart. He understood in that moment where the bird got its name.

"Are you the same one that lost your mate?" He moved closer to the bird, careful not to scare it away. Unfortunately, all doves looked the same to him, but it wouldn't be a stretch to think it was the one he'd seen before. Max searched the trees for a nest. Perhaps the bird didn't understand its mate was gone.

"If you're hoping your mate will return, I'm afraid you're out of luck." He sighed. "You should go find someone new."

As the words left his mouth, he had to wonder which of them he was addressing, the bird or himself. The thought brought him up short. But before he could spend too much time brooding over it, his phone beeped.

Does the offer to pick up my groceries still stand?

A smile tugged at Max's lips as he sent a confirmation message to Carissa. That was a good sign. Even if she didn't accept his offer for dinner, at least she seemed more open to him than she had before.

About an hour later, he arrived at her house with several bags of groceries. He gathered them into his arms, trudged up her front stairs, and rang her doorbell.

"Special delivery," Max said, lifting the bags.

"My hero," Carissa teased as she took one of the bags. The warm grin on her face caused his heartbeat to stutter. She'd never looked more beautiful.

He followed her into her house. It was a cozy ranch-style home with an open floor plan that led directly into the dining room. A large bay window jutted out above the kitchen sink with a gorgeous view of her backyard. The marble counters were an eye-catching contrast to the white cabinets.

"You have a lovely home." He marveled as he set the bags onto the small island in the center of the room.

"Thanks." She began to unload them. "And thank you for picking up my groceries. You're a lifesaver." As she put away the groceries, she hummed a merry tune.

Since he didn't know where anything went, Max stood on the other side of the island, out of her way. "What's got you in such a good mood?"

She shot him a smirk over her shoulder. "I finished polishing up my presentation."

"Oh?" A laptop was perched on the dining room table with a pad of paper and a pile of notecards beside it. "Want to practice it on me?"

When she turned toward him, her eyebrows pulled together. "Um, no. That's okay." His face must have given away his disappointment because she hurried on. "I don't want to jinx anything."

"Fair enough." He wouldn't press, though he was dying to know what options she'd put together.

"Thank you again for doing this. I really didn't have time to get back to the store this week."

"Happy to help. Not much else on my plate these days anyway." Try as he might, he couldn't quite keep the edge out of his voice.

"How's Lanie?"

"Busy with school, so I haven't seen much of her." He turned away from Carissa to hide his face.

She laid a tentative hand on his arm. "Are you going to tell me what's wrong?"

"I'm not sure I should."

"Why?"

Running a hand through his hair, he huffed a breath. "It's complicated and embarrassing."

"This is a judgment-free zone," she said. "But I won't twist your arm. Do you want something to drink?"

"Water, please."

She indicated he should take a seat at the table. A moment later, she returned with two glasses and set one in front of him. He wrapped his hands around it and stared at the wall.

Her eyes seemed to search his face. "I'm here if you want to talk."

Instead of responding, he took a sip of water. He wasn't sure he wanted to tell anyone about what had happened with Lanie, least of all Carissa. At the same time, he hated that yet another thing had sprouted between him and his daughter.

With a sigh, he leaned forward. "Lanie has been on my case to date." His eyes flicked to Carissa then back to the wall. "While she's made me promise not to date you, she has offered up other... unappealing options."

"Lanie asked you not to date me?" Something in her voice caught Max's attention. Her eyebrows were pulled together in a concerned frown.

"She didn't want it to complicate things," he said.

"I suppose I should be flattered you find me to be an appealing option," she teased. When he didn't laugh, she cleared her throat. "Sorry, that was in poor taste. Who else has she suggested?"

"Bea, Mrs. Carlisle." At Carissa's bewildered expression, he clarified, "The teacher who Lanie was hired to replace after she retired last year and my old neighbor, Cassandra Winters."

Despite her attempts to disguise it as coughing, Max knew when he was being laughed at. He glared at her. "It's not funny."

"It's sweet she cares so much about you. And the options she gave aren't bad. Cassandra is pretty. Bea and Mrs. Carlisle are a little old for you, but—"

"A *little* old for me?" he growled. "Bea is seventy-two!"

Carissa covered her mouth with her hand to hide her laughter, but her shaking shoulders gave her away. The sound caused his anger to dissipate, and before long, he found himself joining in.

"She means well," Max said. "But sometimes, she's like a dog with a rare steak. She sinks her teeth into it and won't let go."

Tears streamed down Carissa's face from laughing so hard, and she wiped them away. "What did you say to her suggestions?"

"Some things I regret, honestly." His expression sobered. "She caught me off guard, and like I said, her suggestions left a lot to be desired."

"Oh no."

"Yeah, 'oh no' is right." He slid his head into his hands. "I blew up at her. Told her to stay out of my love life."

"I bet that didn't go over well," Carissa said.

"She stormed out of the house, and I don't know if she's going to come home or go stay with her brother." He leaned back in his chair and stared at the ceiling. "It seems like every time I take a step forward with her, I screw something up and end up five paces back."

"But this wasn't your fault." At his incredulous expression, she hurried on, "I mean, yes, you shouldn't have blown up at her, but your reaction is justified. It's not her business whether you date or not."

"She wants me to be happy."

Carissa pursed her lips. "I'll allow that her intentions are honorable, but you know what they say, the road to hell and good intentions."

"Fair." He shifted in his seat. "So, what do I do now?"

"She's at school, so hopefully, being away from you will give her time to cool off. And if she does stay with Steven, don't try to force her to talk to you. Eventually, she'll come home, and you can apologize for your outburst while also making it clear you don't appreciate her meddling."

"Easier said than done."

Carissa's lips twitched as if she were fighting a smile. "I imagine admitting you were wrong is rather difficult for you."

Max scowled. "I'm not *that* stubborn."

"I appreciate the qualification." She bit her lip. "Though now, I understand why you asked me out to dinner as friends."

That caught his attention. He leaned forward, his eyes searching her face. *Is she disappointed it wouldn't be a date?* "Is that why you said no?"

"I didn't say no." Carissa tilted her head. "I didn't really say anything other than to let me think about it."

"And?"

"Dinner is still too..." Her eyebrows pulled together as if she was searching for the right word. "Intimate. I want to respect Lanie's wishes, and dinner would feel like a date."

"Well, how about this?" Since Lanie had already suggested he bring someone, inviting Carissa seemed a safe option. And as it was a group outing, Lanie couldn't accuse him of breaking his word. "We're going apple picking this weekend. Why don't you join us? We can spend some time together socially but without the pressure or intimacy of a solo dinner."

"I wouldn't want to intrude on your family time."

"You wouldn't be," he insisted. "Bringing someone was actually Lanie's idea." He laughed. "She didn't want me to feel like a fifth wheel."

"In that case," Carissa said, her face brightening, "I'd love to."

<hr>

Max hadn't heard from Lanie by the time school was letting out. But per Carissa's advice, he didn't text her. If she needed space, he would give it, and in the meantime, he would rehearse what he wanted to say to her.

Since he didn't know whether he would be alone for dinner, he decided to prepare something that would make decent leftovers. It also happened to be one of Lanie's favorite meals, or perhaps the better description was that it was one of the only meals he made that she enjoyed. Meat loaf, but not the run-of-the-mill dry meat loaves portrayed on old sitcoms. His included a special sauce that gave it a spicy kick. And he didn't just pour the sauce on top. He mixed it in by hand, which kept the meat from drying out in the oven.

The whole process took a half hour, and it was already after five by the time he slid the loaf into the oven. To his surprise and relief, the front door opened, and his daughter's heels clicked over the linoleum in the hallway.

She entered the kitchen without a glance his way. After removing Tupperware from her lunch box and setting it in the sink, she put the lunch box away. Finally, when she had nothing else to do to avoid him, she faced him. Sniffing the air appreciatively, she met his gaze. "Smells good in here."

"It's meat loaf."

The anxious crease in her forehead disappeared as a small smile tugged at her lips. "My favorite."

"It's going to be about an hour." He shifted from foot to foot. "Gives us time to talk."

Taking a deep breath as if to steel herself, she pulled out a chair. He followed suit, and for a moment, neither of them said anything. But Carissa had told him to start with an apology.

"I'm sorry for blowing up at you this morning," he began. "I didn't mean to react that way, and I know you believe you're helping me."

He hesitated, unsure whether he should wait for her to say something or continue with Carissa's other suggestion. If the conversation turned into a lecture, Lanie might tune him out or walk away before he got through it, but if he could engage her, she might be more receptive.

"I'm sorry too." Her face flushed. "Nate said I needed to butt out of your love life."

Not for the first time, Max sent up a prayer of thanks that Lanie had found her way back to Nate. That man understood him more than most, and Max appreciated how Nate was able to get through to his daughter when he couldn't.

"I understand that you want me to be happy and that your concern comes from a place of love." Max took a deep breath. "But I'm not unhappy. If someone comes along and things happen organically, then I'm open to it." He raised an eyebrow. "Besides, after all the meddling your mother did in your love life, you should be more wary of interfering in others' relationships."

The flush on her face deepened as she dropped her gaze to the table. "That's fair. Though I hate the idea of you being alone again when I move in with Nate."

He waved his hand. "I was alone before your brother came home to start his business, and I was alone before you moved back after your master's." He shrugged. "While I'll miss your cooking, I can get by on my own."

"But I finally got you to stop using paper plates all the time." Her hazel eyes danced with mischief.

"Paper plates conserve water," he retorted. He went over to the oven to check on dinner's progress.

"And clog up landfills."

"Well, I guess no matter what I do, I hurt the environment." As he returned to the table, he raised an eyebrow. "So, are we agreed, then? No more meddling?"

She bit her lip. "Will you at least try going on a dating app? Or maybe joining some local groups?"

"No to the dating app, and maybe to the groups thing." As her face broke into a smile, he waved a finger. "But no promises. I'm not exactly the most social of people."

She burst out laughing. "Understatement of the century."

"Ha ha." His voice dripped with sarcasm. "Still, if it'll make you feel better and convinces you to stop suggesting women almost twice my age, I'll consider it."

"That's all I ask."

Once that was settled, he decided to change the subject to something less uncomfortable. "How was your day?"

That was all the prodding Lanie needed to launch into a lively one-sided conversation detailing what had happened. It sounded like she had a good class, with some of the same students from the year before. Because Cedar Haven was such a small town, they didn't have a lot of options for students with disabilities. Most of them ended up attending the program at the middle school for much of their lives.

"I'm hoping, once I get my bearings, to petition the board to expand the program to allow the students to continue their education with their peers. It's especially hard for the high school–aged students to be stuck in a classroom with the younger kids. I'd like to change that, but I know right now, the budget isn't there."

"Sounds like you need another fundraiser."

She blew out her breath. "I can't fundraise an entire program." Shaking her head, she grabbed a glass from the cabinet then filled it with ice water. "The school system can't support it, and some of the parents end up putting their children into private school when their kids become teenagers because there are more opportunities there." She took a sip of water and sank into her chair. "Mrs. Carlisle and I talked about it at great length before she retired. Apparently, she's been petitioning for the same thing for years to no avail. So now, it's my turn to take up the banner."

"What would the program entail?" Max felt like he was missing something. "Couldn't they hire another teacher and find space at the high school?"

"If only it were that simple. But even if it were, there's no place to put the class at the high school or any of the elementary schools. That's why it's at the middle school. It was the only place with room." Rubbing her temples, she stared at the table. "And as far as hiring someone, well, consider how much it took to convince me to give up that job in California and stick around. And I have family and a fiancé here. There's not much to entice someone who doesn't have roots in this town."

He bristled. It'd been a point of contention between them when she'd come home to settle her mother's estate with the express intent on leaving ASAP. Her view of their little hamlet was in direct contrast to his. She'd insisted there was a whole wide world out there waiting for her, but he struggled to understand why she couldn't go experience the world then return home. Sometimes, he wondered whether she would have ended up in California after all if it weren't for Nate.

"Don't look at me like that," she said when she caught him staring at her. "I'm happy to be home, and I love this town, but even you have to admit it doesn't have much to offer. Sure, cost of living is lower than some places, but the salaries barely cover it. If I hadn't moved in with you, I'm not sure I could afford my own place, even if I subsidized my salary with my inheritance."

"I don't know why you say that. We're not far from DC, and there's plenty to do here."

She raised her eyebrows. "Karaoke nights at Seabreeze and endless town events aren't likely to entice people from my generation."

"Okay," he said, keeping his thoughts about her generation to himself. "Why not hire someone older?"

"Because they'll retire sooner, and we'll be back in the same position we are now." After draining her glass, she shrugged. "Besides, like I said, there isn't any room in the budget even if we could find someone to hire."

For once, he found himself completely devoid of any advice to give her. He knew little of the town budget, having worked as an electrical lineman for a private company for his entire career. The only time he cared about the government's budget was when it came time to pay taxes, and usually, he grumbled about it.

"Anyway"—she waved a hand—"that was my day. How was yours?"

"Uneventful," he said, choosing his next words carefully. "Went grocery shopping, did some woodworking in the garage, and then started dinner."

She smiled. "Sounds like a relaxing day of retirement."

The oven timer beeped, and he took the meat loaf out of the oven. After setting it on the counter, he grabbed a bag of frozen vegetables and popped them into the microwave. Lanie sighed, and he hid a grin. She'd been on his case to use fresh vegetables since she'd been home, saying they were better for him. But he'd gotten into the habit of keeping things simple, and he figured produce in any form was better than nothing.

Once dinner was on the table, the conversation died as they both dug into the meal. He snuck a few glances at his daughter and couldn't help noticing how tired she looked.

"I'd say a penny for your thoughts, but I expect they're worth more."

Though she smiled, it didn't quite reach her eyes. "I'm worried about the wedding."

That wasn't what he'd expected her to say. "Don't you and Carissa have everything under control?"

"We do, but it's come at a price. And I can't help wondering if I made a mistake picking a date so soon after the engagement."

"What does Nate say?"

A bitter laugh. "He'd be just as happy to elope." Her eyes flicked to Max then back to her plate. "He's like you in that way. Doesn't need or want the pomp and circumstance."

"Hey, now, your mother and I had a big wedding."

"Which I would bet good money was more her idea than yours."

Instead of responding, he harrumphed and focused on his meal. Thinking back, he couldn't remember ever suggesting to Melody that they elope. For one thing, his Catholic mother would have murdered him. But for another, he'd wanted to crow to the world how happy he was that someone like Melody had agreed to marry someone like him.

"I'm sure if you wanted to push the date, Carissa would be willing to work with you," he finally said.

"I don't want to postpone it," she replied, her voice determined. "But I wish there were more months between now and December."

"If there's anything I can do to help, let me know."

"Well, I could use your advice on one thing…" She bit her lip and avoided his gaze.

"Which is?"

Her breath came out in a huff. "Carissa isn't open to the idea of using silk flowers, even though Rose and Steven used them in their wedding. I helped Rose put together her bouquets, and I liked how they turned out."

"What does she have against silk flowers?" Max suddenly wished he hadn't been so willing to help. The last thing he wanted to do was get between Carissa and Lanie when he and Carissa were finally connecting.

"She thinks they're tacky." Lanie rolled her eyes. "But it depends on where you buy them. Some of them are so realistic, you can't tell the difference." She finished the last bite of her dinner and washed it down with some water. "Besides, the flowers I want are expensive. If we did them ourselves, it would save on the cost, *and* I would have something I could keep forever."

"Your mother dried her bouquet and preserved it that way," he said, though he doubted his suggestion was helpful.

"I know that's an option, but it doesn't alleviate my financial concerns."

"All right." He stifled a sigh. "What do you need me to do?"

Her eyes widened. "Do? I don't need you to do anything. I'm planning to talk to Carissa about it again the next time I see her, and I'd love some advice on how to approach it."

"I'm not sure the approach is the problem. It sounds like she's not listening to you."

"For the most part, she does. It's just..." Lanie leaned her chin on her hand. "With her experience, she encourages me to do certain things her way."

That didn't sound right. While Carissa had proven how good she was at her job, what Lanie was saying reminded him of the many arguments he'd gotten into with Carissa during Steven and Rose's wedding. Back then, he'd thought she didn't like him or that she assumed he knew nothing about weddings. But now, he wondered how often Steven and Rose had been pressured to do something that didn't match their vision or budget. "When are you next seeing her?"

"I'm not sure, but probably sometime this week."

"Well, I'm happy to tag along." No matter how he might feel about Carissa, Lanie was his daughter, and he would do whatever it took to make sure she got the wedding she wanted. Especially if doing so helped him build the relationship he wanted with her.

Chapter Ten

CARISSA NERVOUSLY TAPPED HER index finger on the steering wheel. She was having dinner with the Imaginavigation Enterprises CEO in DC that evening. It wasn't her official pitch yet, but he wanted a preview before she presented to the board the following week. Although it seemed odd, she assumed that was how things worked in the corporate world and decided to go with it.

Which was why she found herself driving to the city on Wednesday evening. Traffic was light since rush-hour commuters were heading in the opposite direction. She hoped parking would be cheaper outside of office hours as well.

When she arrived at the same parking garage as before, she took her time getting out of the car. She'd left earlier than needed, hoping driving would distract her from thoughts about Max. Ever since he'd asked her to dinner, she'd been unable to get him off her mind.

"Buck up, Carissa," she told herself. "Max doesn't matter right now. This meeting could change the course of the rest of your life. Stay focused."

The words sounded empty, but she pretended to believe them. As she climbed out of her car, she straightened her spine and tried to look more confident than she felt.

The restaurant was rather run-down, especially compared to the place they had met for lunch previously. It had a small storefront she almost walked by, and when she entered, she was directed to a dark set of stairs into the basement below. The space was small, with only a few high-top tables and a bar along the length of one bright-green wall. The other walls sported similar bright colors—orange, yellow, and pink.

Jacob waited for her at the bar. His tie was loosened, and he appeared to have been sitting there for some time. Steeling herself for more condescension, she took a deep breath and marched over to him.

"Mr. Mikelson," she said.

As he glanced at her with a flushed face and bloodshot eyes, he swayed precariously on his stool. "Carissa, you made it. Please, call me Jacob." His words were slightly slurred.

I'd rather call you a cab. How were they supposed to have a meeting with him in that state? Would he even remember her pitch?

"Is this a bad time?" she asked, choosing her words carefully.

"Of course not." He gestured to the stool beside him. "Please have a seat."

"Oh, I thought we were having dinner."

After lifting his glass, he toasted her before draining it. "We are, but eating at the bar is less formal." He signaled to the bartender for a refill. "Plus the service is faster."

Stifling a sigh, she hoisted herself onto the stool and shifted uncomfortably. That wasn't at all what she'd had in mind for that night. Without another word, she picked up a menu and resigned herself to what was sure to be a miserable dinner.

But she'd barely even opened the menu before he snatched it from her hands. "You don't need that. Let me order for you." When the bartender arrived, Jacob continued, "I'll have a medium-rare steak, the most expensive one you've got, and she'll have a salad." A smirk crossed his face as he glanced at her. "Water again as well, or did you want to be more adventurous?"

Swallowing a retort, she forced a smile. "Water is fine."

"Unsurprising," he muttered. Then he shook his glass at the bartender. "And keep these coming."

"About my presentation," she began, hoping to turn the evening around. "I brought my tablet to show you my slides and to go over my ideas at a high level. I wasn't sure if—"

He waved his hand. "No shop talk."

Frowning, she stared at him. "I thought you asked for this dinner because you wanted me to go over my presentation before I meet with the board."

"Wow, you really bought that."

To her horror, he laughed.

"I just wanted to see you again."

Her heart pounded, and her palms grew sweaty. "Why? Aren't you married?"

"I am, but my wife and I have an... agreement." He gave her a once-over.

Repulsed, she leaned away from him. *Is your wife actually aware of this agreement, or is it all in your head?* She pressed her lips together so she wouldn't say anything she might regret, a courtesy she wished Jacob would bestow on her as well.

"I'm sorry, Mr. Mikelson, but I'm not looking to date a married man."

"Perfect." His smirk slipped into a sneer. "Because I'm not looking to date either."

"Then what—"

"Oh, come on, Carissa," he slurred, sliding an arm around her shoulders. "Don't play coy. You were flirting with me throughout our entire last meeting."

She blinked rapidly and pulled away. Was he serious? "I was being polite and professional. I'm sorry if my behavior came across as anything else, but I assure you that wasn't my intention."

Thankfully, she was saved from having to hear his response by the bartender returning with her water and another glass of whatever alcohol Jacob had ordered. In the few seconds it took for the bartender to set down her drink, she debated her options. She could stay there and try to redirect the evening to her proposal, or she could leave and kiss the chance of a lifetime goodbye.

"Excuse me," she said before hurrying off to the ladies' room.

When she got there, she stood in front of the sink and stared at the mirror. She'd been on her share of bad dates before finding Chuck. Back then, she would have suffered through the experience, but she wasn't young and naive anymore. And besides, it wasn't a date. It was supposed to be a business meeting.

The door opened behind her, and a black-haired woman wearing a uniform in bright colors similar to those of the restaurant entered. Carissa dropped her gaze, but to her surprise, the woman walked right up to her.

"Excuse me, ma'am. The bartender sent me in here. That guy you're with was thrown out."

Carissa spun around, her mouth falling open. "He *what*?"

The woman shrugged. "I don't know exactly what happened, but I heard shouting, and then two off-duty cops dragged him outside." She glanced toward the door then back at Carissa. "If you want to catch him, he probably hasn't gone far, but Ricky, our bartender, got the feeling you weren't entirely comfortable with him."

"I wasn't." Carissa exhaled heavily, leaning against the counter for support.

"In that case, it's probably safe for you to leave." The woman searched her face. "Do you need me to call you a cab?"

"No. I drove myself into the city, and I haven't been drinking." Carissa forced a smile. "But thank you."

After the waitress left, Carissa splashed cold water on her face and took several deep breaths. She had no idea what the evening's turn of events would do to her relationship with Jacob's corporation—or her career.

❦

When Carissa woke up the next morning, she groaned. She'd hoped last night had been a bad dream. Jacob hadn't contacted her since he'd been kicked out of the restaurant, and she'd waited a half hour before leaving just in case he was lurking, hoping to catch her. By the time she left, there was no sign of him, and she drove home without incident.

Thankfully, she didn't have any client meetings until that evening, and she relished the time to recover from her experience. She couldn't explain why she was shaken by Jacob's behavior. He'd shown how condescending he was at that first lunch, and he probably figured he was doing her a favor by propositioning her like that. Still, it'd been a long time since a man had behaved that way toward her. Even Max, with his grumpy antics during Steven's wedding planning, had never acted inappropriately.

After dragging herself out of bed, she went through her usual morning routine and decided to take a trip to Bea's. It might do her some good to be in a familiar place, surrounded by other people.

When she entered the diner, she caught sight of Max in a booth toward the back of the restaurant. Her first instinct was to avoid him. While Max and Jacob were nothing alike, she wasn't sure she could stomach sitting in close proximity to another man right then. But then he saw her, and the way his face lit up touched her heart.

"Fancy meeting you here," he said as she sat down. "What'll you have?"

"Coffee, black," she said. *Like my mood.*

Max raised his eyebrows and signaled for the server. Once they were alone again, he leaned back and assessed her. "Are you okay?"

"I will be." A moment later, the server returned with her coffee, and she took a sip, savoring the bitterness.

"I'm actually glad I ran into you," Max said when she didn't elaborate. "I wanted to talk to you about the flowers for Lanie's wedding."

Where did that come from? Frowning, she folded her arms on the table. "What about them?"

"Lanie wants silk flowers, but she says you told her they're tacky."

Carissa stared at him blankly. "And? I meant what I said."

His eyes narrowed, and he leaned back, crossing his arms over his chest. "But it's what she wants."

"I understand, but—"

"No 'buts.' If that's what Lanie wants, then that's what she gets. Besides, they're on a budget."

She raised an eyebrow. "You're not supposed to be meddling in Lanie's wedding anymore."

His face flushed, which told her everything she needed to know. "She was upset last night and told me all about it. I had planned to join her the next time she met with you, but since you're here, I figured I'd bring it up now."

This man can't help himself. Taking a deep breath, Carissa wrapped her hands around her mug. "I'm familiar with the wedding budget, and I've given Lanie several suggestions on how to save on the flowers."

"And I assume none of them included silk substitutes?"

"No," she admitted. "They did not." He opened his mouth to respond, but she held up a hand. "Look, I appreciate Lanie's concerns, but she's not my first bride with a small floral budget. I've suggested cheaper versions of the flowers she wants in her bouquet."

"Like what?"

Pursing her lips, she studied him. Would he understand the different types of flowers if she described them? Somehow, he didn't strike her as the type, but since he'd asked, she couldn't see any way around it.

"Gardenias are much like roses and smell just as good." She began ticking off the rose alternatives she'd used in the past. "Camellias are so similar, you almost can't tell the difference, and like roses, they come in many different colors. Ranunculus would work as well."

As his eyes began to glaze over, she gave up trying to explain. Hopefully, he would realize he was out of his element and let it go. The last thing she wanted to do was go back to the days of fighting with Max over his children's weddings.

"So, let me get this straight. You're willing to use some cheap imitation flower in her bouquet but not an exact replica that happens to be fake?"

She bristled at his characterization. "First of all, they are less expensive, yes, but I would hardly call them 'cheap.' And secondly, have you seen the fake flowers they sell at craft stores? They don't hold a candle to any real flower, regardless of whether it's a rose."

"But Lanie isn't planning on buying flowers at a local craft store. She's ordering them special online."

"Which is more expensive than a craft store," Carissa pointed out.

He frowned. "Is it more expensive to buy silk flowers online than real flowers from a florist?"

"Again, it depends on the flower. Roses would likely be more expensive from a florist, but the less expensive alternatives I—"

"Then you've proved my point," he cut in.

Heat rose up her neck, and she glared at him. "Why do you care so much?"

His mouth turned down. "I'm trying to rebuild my relationship with Lanie. If this matters to her, it matters to me."

Of course. With a sigh, she tried seeing things from his eyes. When Lanie had told Carissa she wanted silk flowers, she'd said she wanted something she could keep forever. If she'd told her father the same thing, Carissa could understand why he was fighting for her.

"You're right. I'm sorry." She took a sip of coffee. "However, there would still be an added cost to have a florist design the silk flowers, just like there would be if they designed real ones."

"What if we did them ourselves? Didn't Rose and Steven do that?"

With Lanie's help. Thankfully, they'd put together the bouquets and boutonnieres before Steven's accident. There wouldn't have been time otherwise.

"They did, but they also had more time to work with than Lanie does."

"What if we all pitched in to help?" Max's voice held a note of pleading.

Wow, he really would do anything for her. A strange feeling of longing welled up in Carissa's chest, and she wondered if that willingness to help applied to everyone he loved. Before that train of thought could derail her, she pushed it out of her mind.

"Are you sure you have time for it? You're already planning on baking cookies for favors."

Max squared his shoulders. "We'll make it work."

Stifling another sigh, she nodded in defeat. "Fine. I'll make the arrangements to get the flowers and assist with making the bouquets. I'll also talk to Lanie about canceling our meeting with the florist."

The slow smile that came over his face took her breath away. Despite the rocky start to their conversation, she was happy to have run into him. Something about him seemed to make all her cares disappear.

"How was your meeting last night?" he asked, and just like that, the night before came back to her in a blinding flash.

She grimaced. "Not great."

His smile faded, and his eyebrows pulled together as if he were concerned. "What happened?"

Squeezing her eyes shut, she counted down from ten to calm the anger that began to rage inside her belly. It wasn't the time or the place to have that conversation. She wasn't sure she ever wanted to talk about what happened with anyone, least of all Max.

"Hey," he said, and when she opened her eyes, he was standing. After tossing a few dollars on the table, he held out his hand. "Let's go for a walk."

She allowed him to lead her out of the restaurant and down the street. Already, the leaves on the tops of the trees had turned bright colors. Reds, oranges, and yellows dotted the otherwise green trees towering over Main Street. A slight breeze brought enough of a chill to remind them autumn had arrived.

Normally, the change of the seasons brought her peace, but instead, it was another reminder of how much her own life hadn't changed. In the five years since her husband had died, she'd lived each day pretty much the same. Wedding planning for several hours, updating her business profile, and grabbing snacks from the fridge. She couldn't remember the last time she'd cooked a decent meal.

Expanding her business would change all of that, but after last night, it felt like a pipe dream. While she could explore other avenues to break into corporate event planning, the idea of canceling her pitch meeting to the board hurt her heart. She'd worked day and night on her proposal, and she was confident in her ideas. To tuck her tail between her legs and admit defeat was too much to bear. She wasn't sure where she would find the energy to start over from scratch. Her husband's name had gotten her the meeting with Imaginavigation Enterprises in the first place. Unfortunately, his contact there had since retired, which was why she was stuck dealing with Jacob.

Max took her hand and settled it in the crook of his arm, drawing her back to the present. They strolled toward Nate's mechanic shop, taking in the sights and sounds of downtown Cedar Haven. Part of her wondered if that was a smart move, walking arm and arm in public like they were, but then she decided she didn't care. The pressure of his arm around her hand helped to center her and made last night feel like a dream... or a nightmare.

But Max, seeming to read her mind, took her to a small street that led to a quiet park. A few children ran and laughed around a playground, but he led her toward a set of picnic tables where they could be alone. When they reached them, he sat on one of the table benches, facing the playground. She settled beside him with a contented sigh and rested her forearms on the table.

"So, do you want to talk about it?" He nudged her with his shoulder.

"No," she whispered, but that wasn't true. She needed to get it out before it could fester, and she could use some advice on what to do.

"Okay, then." His response was simple, so *Max*, that a laugh bubbled up in her throat.

"I don't *want* to talk about it, but I *need* to."

He didn't say anything, clearly letting her take her time. It was weird to think how much his stoicism used to frustrate her. At that moment, she found it comforting.

"The CEO was already drunk when I arrived," she began. "And things went downhill from there."

In painstaking detail, she relived the night before. Max kept silent, but his muscles grew tenser the more she said. When she finished, she took a deep breath and let it out slowly, surprised by how much lighter she felt. She hadn't realized how the events had been weighing on her.

"What a jerk." The phrase was said in a way that was meant to be offhand, but Carissa could hear the edge in his voice. "Someone needs to teach him some manners."

"It's a bit late for that." Impulsively, she leaned against Max, relishing his warmth and strength.

"Are you still planning to pitch his company?"

She picked at her fingernails as she debated her response. "I don't know. I mean, on the one hand, I feel like I shouldn't. The last thing I need is to work with some cheating, entitled creep."

"And on the other hand?" His voice sounded strained, like he was holding something back.

Lifting her head, she gazed up at him. His jaw was clenched, and he stared straight ahead.

"Hey." She squeezed his arm. "I'm okay now."

A flush crept over his face as his eyes narrowed. "Yes, *now*." Shaking his head, he finally met her gaze, and his dark eyes burned with barely controlled fury. "But if you hadn't been in a public place, if he hadn't been thrown out of the bar..." His hands clenched into fists. "He better hope I never meet him."

Max's anger surprised her. Sure, he was protective of his children and their desires. But his reaction then, like he wanted to protect *her*... Well, it was new and different and surprisingly attractive.

She wasn't usually into the overly protective type of guy. Her late husband had always respected her ability to stick up for herself. But she couldn't deny there were times she'd wished he would step up for her. Like when the father of the bride or even a groomsman would get a little rowdy and she'd have to put them in their place. Although Chuck would listen to her rant about the experience and took care to make sure she was okay, he'd never said or done anything that made her feel like he would set the world on fire to keep her safe.

Seeing Max angry on her behalf gave her a heady feeling that both exhilarated and scared her. Max was intense, and she wondered if that intensity was part of what had led to the end of his first marriage. Maybe Melody couldn't stand the heat.

Placing a cautious hand under his chin, she pulled his face around to hers. "I appreciate your concern, but I promise I can handle myself."

Slowly, the angry red color faded from his cheeks, and the fire in his eyes dimmed. "I'm sorry. Just... the thought of someone treating you that way." His hands clenched again. "It makes me see red."

"I didn't love it either." Her hand cupped his cheek. "It's over now, and I'm okay."

He lowered his gaze. "But you're still planning on pitching your proposal to him."

"To be fair, I'd be pitching the *board*, not him. Or at least not *only* him." She searched his face. "But I understand your concern."

"You understand it, but you don't share it?"

"Oh no, I share it." Tilting her head back, she closed her eyes as the warmth of the sun caressed her skin. "I worry that if I don't go through with it, then he wins. I mean, who knows, maybe last night was part of his attempt to convince me I need to stay in my lane and stick to wedding planning. His condescension at our lunch meeting gave me the impression he doesn't think I have what it takes."

Max frowned. "Was it all an act?"

Though she hadn't considered that, Carissa doubted that was the case. "He doesn't strike me as that good of an actor, and I can't imagine he'd purposefully get drunk to sabotage me."

"When is your meeting with the board?"

"Next week on Wednesday."

Max didn't speak as he digested her words. Part of her wondered if she shouldn't have told him, but the relief she experienced on getting it off her chest overcame any misgivings she had. Besides, he'd asked. If he didn't want to know, he would have said.

"While it doesn't sound like a good idea, I understand it's a huge boon for your career. Just... Promise me you'll be careful and you won't allow yourself to be alone with him."

She raised three fingers of her right hand. "Scout's honor."

His lips pulled into a soft smile, and he took her hand, brushing her fingers against his lips. Her heart stopped then raced in her chest. But before she could say or do anything, he stood.

"We should go before I do something reckless." He held out his hand to help her off the bench. Then he took her back to the diner.

For a moment, she thought he might kiss her by her car, but unlike the times before, there was no doubt in her mind she wanted him to. Instead, he squeezed her hand.

"I'll see you Sunday."

Chapter Eleven

THE DOORBELL RANG AS Max finished lunch. He tossed his paper plate into the trash then went to answer it. His future son-in-law stood on the porch, dressed like a lumberjack—flannel button-down shirt, cargo pants, and work boots with a fleece jacket thrown over his arm.

"It's a bit warm for that, isn't it?" Max nodded to the jacket.

Nate shrugged. "It's colder up in the foothills." He gave a sheepish grin. "But it's more for Lanie. She gets cold easily."

"That makes more sense." Max motioned for Nate to come in. "Lanie's upstairs getting ready. Did you want something to drink?"

"No, thank you. I'm okay."

They went into the living room and sat down to wait. Neither of them spoke, but the silence wasn't awkward or uncomfortable. The one thing Max had always liked about Nate was he was also a man of few words. In that respect, they were cut from the same cloth.

But they weren't alone for long. The front door crashed open, and in walked Steven and Rose. Steven had brought his cane, likely more to help him navigate the rough terrain than because he really needed it.

"Glad you're coming with us, Dad." Steven plopped onto the couch beside his father.

"Where's Lanie?" Rose flipped her black hair over her shoulder. "I'm anxious to get my basic white girl on."

"I heard that!" Lanie called from upstairs. She scampered down and glared at her sister-in-law. "There's nothing wrong with apple picking."

"Of course not," Rose said. "But it is one of those overrated traditions people prop up as the epitome of autumn. Like PSLs."

"Whatever." Lanie rolled her eyes. "It's still fun, and I'll be putting them to good use in several desserts that I bet you gobble up." Turning her attention to the men in the room, she gestured to the door. "Are we ready to go?"

"As soon as we figure out who's driving." Steven pushed himself off the couch.

"Nate and I were planning to ride with Dad," Lanie replied. "We thought you and Rose could come up in your SUV since it's a bit more durable than my car or Nate's Camaro."

Steven grimaced. "I'm still not fully comfortable driving long distances yet."

"Could you drive his car?" Lanie asked Rose.

Pursing her lips, Rose shook her head. "I've not driven it often, and I prefer smaller cars. SUVs make me anxious."

"We're actually waiting on one more person." Max kept his gaze on the floor.

Steven frowned. "Who else is coming?"

Before Max could respond, a tentative knock sounded at the door. He rushed over to answer it, wondering if he should have warned his family prior to Carissa's arrival.

"Carissa," Rose called out, her brown eyes widening. "You're joining us today?"

After a quick glance at Max, Carissa nodded. "If you'll have me."

Max held his breath as he finally risked a look at Lanie. His daughter seemed more surprised than angry, though she did raise her eyebrows at him.

"The more the merrier," Lanie finally said with a tight smile. "Though that does complicate the driving situation a bit more."

"No it doesn't." Max gestured to Nate. "You can drive my truck with Lanie, and I'll take the rest of us up in Steven's SUV."

Lanie looked at her fiancé. "Is that okay with you?"

"If your dad trusts me with his truck, I'm game."

They filed out of the house. Max handed Nate his keys before heading to Steven's car. Steven started to climb into the passenger seat, but Rose stopped him with a meaningful look at Carissa.

"I'm happy to sit in the back with you, Rose," Carissa called.

"Nonsense," Max grumbled beside her, taking her hand. "You're sitting up front with me."

"But Steven might be more comfortable—"

"He'll be fine." Max opened the passenger door. "You're my guest, after all."

Rose and Steven settled into the back as Max closed the door and headed to the driver's side. Once he was buckled in, he started the engine then gestured for Nate to pull out first. Although he'd plugged the address into the GPS, he preferred to follow Nate because he wasn't as familiar with the area where they were headed.

A few minutes into the trip, he started to regret his insistence that Carissa sit up front. Her intoxicating perfume filled his senses, and he struggled to concentrate on the road. He needed a distraction.

"How's work going?" he asked Steven, glancing at his son in the rearview.

"Good. Mr. Willoughby's divorce is finally going to trial."

"Which I hope he loses," Rose quipped.

"That's not very supportive of your husband's hard work," Steven retorted.

"Perhaps not, but that man deserves it."

"Back me up here, Dad," Steven pleaded.

Carissa glanced at Max with an amused smile, and he rolled his eyes. For a couple who'd just had their wedding a little over a month ago, they fought like they'd been married for years.

"I'm afraid I'm with Rose on this one." At Steven's harrumph, Max amended his statement. "But I'm sure you've done a good job of painting what happened in a much different light. It'll probably result in some sort of compromise where neither party is completely happy."

"That's typically how divorces end," Steven agreed with a sigh. "It's not for lack of trying, though. He would have gotten a better deal if he'd listened to me instead of fighting everything I suggested tooth and nail."

"Like I said, I hope he gets what he deserves," Rose said again.

"How's your physical therapy?" Max asked, hoping to change the subject.

"It's... going." Frustration colored Steven's tone. "There are still times where it seems like my legs and brain aren't making the connection, but I'm able to move around without the cane most of the time."

"That's good news."

"Although long trips like this tend to make me stiff."

"If you need me to stop for a break, let me know."

"You? Stop for anything aside from gas or food?" Steven laughed. "Who are you, and what have you done with my father?"

Max scowled. "People can change."

"Can they?" Carissa whispered. At his grimace, she giggled. "To be fair, your father has been somewhat more agreeable the last few weeks."

"Which I'm sure is owing more to your influence than anything else," Steven said.

"Sitting right here," Max muttered. He was grateful when Nate flicked on his turn signal, confirming they were almost to their destination. Maybe for the ride home, he could convince his future son-in-law to drive Steven and Lanie. Somehow, he expected he would have a more peaceful ride without either of his children.

The road into the farm was bumpy, though Max tried to alleviate the jostling as much as possible. Still, by the time they pulled into the parking lot, Steven's face was a mask of pain.

"Do you want to rest for a minute?" Max asked.

"I'll be all right." Steven rubbed his back. "Honestly, getting out and stretching will probably be better than rest at this point."

Max nodded. "If you're sure."

"I have some ibuprofen in my bag if it'll help," Carissa offered.

"Thanks, but I took some before we left."

Lanie and Nate had already headed up to check them in and get the bags for the apples. It made more sense to hang out by the car while Steven stretched than to make him walk all the way up the hill. Rose stepped behind Steven and rubbed his back, which seemed to help with the pain.

"Maybe you shouldn't be pushing yourself." Her eyebrows pulled together as he completed a series of movements.

"Dr. Myers cleared me to come today."

"I know, but—"

"Here come Nate and Lanie now," Max interrupted, hoping to stem another argument.

"We got two pecks." Lanie handed one of the bags to Rose. "Four people can pick a peck." She turned to Max and Carissa. "Did you two want to come with us or go with Steven and Rose?"

After finishing one last bent stretch, Steven straightened up. "Hey, that's not fair. You'll have more people on your team."

Lanie scoffed. "Not everything has to be a competition."

"What are we picking today?" Carissa asked, and Max gave her a grateful look for the distraction.

Lanie lifted one shoulder. "It's whatever you want." Gesturing with the bag, she explained the different types of apples available that day and where they were located. Max hid a smile. She sounded like a walking apple encyclopedia.

"Why don't Rose and Steven pick the Pink Lady and Stayman Winesap, since those trees are right here? Then the rest of us can go up the hill to pick Crispin, Ambrosia, and Jonagold."

"That sounds like a plan," Rose said. "Meet you back here in about half an hour?" Without waiting for a response, she linked arms with Steven, and they set off into the trees.

The rest of their group headed up the hill. Quite a few people were at the farm, enjoying the cool October day. Several visitors had filled their bags to the brim with apples. Others were sneaking bites between the trees.

"I can't do that," Max murmured to Carissa, pointing at a young boy who had already eaten half of an apple.

"What?" Her eyebrows pulled together. "Eat apples?"

"Not with the skin on," he said. "I'm allergic."

Her eyes widened. "Can you pick them, then?"

"Oh yeah. The skin doesn't bother me unless I ingest it. I have to peel the apples first."

She wrinkled her nose. "That's the weirdest allergy I've ever heard of."

Lanie spun around, a wide grin on her face. "And one he was kind enough to pass on to me. Though at least I can eat strawberries."

"You can't eat strawberries?" The way Carissa looked at him made him feel like an alien. "Do you know exactly what you're allergic to?"

He shrugged. "It could be the pesticides, but I've never been brave enough to try organic."

"What happens?" she asked. "Do you go into anaphylactic shock?"

Despite the fear on her face, Max couldn't help but laugh. "No, nothing that serious. I break out in hives."

"My mom thought it was chicken pox," Lanie said, linking her arm with Nate's. "Which I honestly would have preferred."

"Well"—Nate bent and kissed the top of her head—"at least it's an easy allergy to avoid."

By that point, they had reached the top of the hill. Nate and Lanie took the row of Jonagold while Carissa and Max slipped into the row of Ambrosia. Max had hoped to spend some time alone with Carissa, but as his wish came true, he couldn't think of anything to say.

"Thank you for inviting me," Carissa said. "I can't remember the last time I went apple picking."

His shoulders sagged in relief. "It's been a while for me as well, but we used to go often when the kids were little." He waved a hand. "Nothing wears a kid out more than physical labor."

She laughed. "I can imagine." They walked farther into the row of trees. "What do you do with the apples?"

"It depends. But Lanie loves to bake. I imagine she'll be making all sorts of desserts. The school is having a bake sale soon."

"You don't bake?" Carissa asked, a hint of amusement in her blue eyes.

He grimaced. "Baking was more Melody's area. And as I'm sure Lanie's told you, my cooking leaves a lot to be desired."

"She might have mentioned it."

The conversation died as they focused on picking apples. Max kept track of the number they were picking, as he didn't want to overload the bag with just one type. They each had their arms full when they met up with Lanie and Nate at the end of the row.

After a quick assessment, Lanie nodded. "We've got about ten of each, which means there should be room for a few Crispins. Hopefully, Rose and Steven tried to keep things even on their end as well."

Together, the four of them headed into the last row of trees. The Crispins must have ripened earlier than the rest, as they were pretty picked over, but they each managed to find a couple in good shape.

As they traveled down the hill, Max's body felt heavy. He'd hoped for more time with Carissa, but the activity hadn't taken nearly as long as he'd remembered. Though he supposed that made sense. The kids were young then and had needed a lot more direction and attention.

"How'd you all do?" Steven asked when they met up by the check-in tent.

"Pretty well." Lanie held out their full bag.

"Nice." Steven gestured to the bag in Rose's hand. "Looks like we'll need to find some ample storage space."

"They should fit in the garage," Max said. "And I'm sure Carissa would like to take some home as a reward for her hard work."

"Oh, I wouldn't know what to do with them."

"We should have a baking day," Rose suggested. "Lanie can teach us."

"I volunteer Dad's kitchen," Lanie joked. With a smile, she lifted her bag of apples and gestured to the car. "Shall we go?"

"Are we going home already?" Max asked.

His children glanced at each other, and Lanie shrugged. "The farm has a store not far from here. We could check out what other apple varieties they have."

"If I remember correctly, they have a fall festival as well. We could hang out there for a bit, maybe grab a snack," Steven said.

"Sounds like a plan!" Max could hardly contain his enthusiasm. Spending more time with Carissa was exactly what he'd hoped for, and who knew? Maybe by the end of the afternoon, she would take him up on his offer to go to dinner. The only problem was, he wanted more than a platonic outing, and he had no idea how to reconcile that desire with his promise to Lanie.

Chapter Twelve

CARISSA LOVED THE FARM store with its homemade décor and desserts, farm-raised meat, and assorted fresh vegetables. While the young couples checked out the festival, she and Max perused the many offerings inside. At first, Max held her growing pile of purchases until an employee quietly offered him a cart.

"Sorry about that." Carissa nibbled her lip. "I wasn't paying attention."

He shrugged as he placed her items in the cart. "It's fine. I was happy to continue carrying everything, but this makes it easier."

They wandered through the store, admiring the various baked goods. Carissa wasn't much of a baker, but she did have a sweet tooth. It was difficult not to put every item into their cart.

Once she was satisfied with her lot, she and Max got in line at the checkout. She looked over her items with a smile. When she glanced at Max, she noticed he hadn't picked up anything for himself. "There's nothing you wanted?"

He shook his head. "I only decorate for Christmas these days."

Lifting a pie, she held it out. "You don't like pie?"

"I do, but Lanie makes the best apple and pumpkin pies. I'm sure she's going to make a ton of delicious desserts with all the apples we picked."

A twinge in her gut caused Carissa to turn around. What she wouldn't give to be able to share a pie with Chuck and his family. Her parents had passed many years ago, but Chuck's parents were still around. While they'd always been kind to her, she wouldn't say they were close. Ever since the funeral, she rarely saw any of his relatives. At first, it had hurt too much, then so much time passed that it didn't seem appropriate to reach out.

"Next!" a cashier called.

Carissa and Max wheeled her cart over to the lane and began removing the items. It took longer than she expected, and she worried she'd gone overboard.

It'll brighten up the house, she told herself. Her home could use it. Returning home alone after spending time with Max and Lanie made her rather lonely.

After she finished checking out, Max helped her carry her bags to Steven's SUV. Steven, Rose, Lanie, and Nate were heading down the sidewalk toward them, each carrying a cup of warm apple cider.

"We grabbed you guys one too." Lanie held out a Styrofoam tray holding two additional cups.

"Thank you," Carissa said, lifting one of the cups and wrapping her hands around it. The sun was lower in the sky than she'd expected, and a chill was in the air.

"We should get back." Max accepted his cup and took a sip.

"You good with me driving your truck again?" Nate asked Max.

Max nodded. "I'll follow you out."

Carissa, Max, Steven, and Rose headed to the SUV while Nate and Lanie went to the truck. When Max opened the passenger door for her, Carissa couldn't help noticing he seemed disappointed, though she couldn't imagine why. The ride home was much quieter than the trip to the farm had been. She hid a smile. It appeared apple picking had had the same effect on Max's adult children that it had when they were little.

When they arrived at Max's house, Carissa felt a pang of regret. She wasn't quite ready for the day to end. Max helped her transfer her purchases from Steven's vehicle to hers, then Steven and Rose headed home.

"Nate and I are going to dinner if you'd like to join us," Lanie said as Nate handed Max the truck keys.

Carissa exchanged a glance with Max and shook her head. "I need to get back. I've got some work to do this evening."

Something flashed in Max's eyes, but before she could decipher the emotion, it was gone.

He nodded to Lanie. "You go have fun. I've got some leftovers calling my name."

"I'll see you for your dress fitting next week," Carissa called as Lanie and Nate walked away.

When she was alone with Max, she smiled. "Thanks for inviting me."

"I'm glad you came."

They stood in an awkward silence as she debated what to say. While she did have work to do, she wasn't quite ready to leave. Deep down, she hoped he would ask her out again.

"So, how'd I do?" Max finally asked.

She cocked her head. "What do you mean?"

"This was our trial run, wasn't it? Sort of a preview before you'd agree to have lunch with me."

A laugh bubbled up in her throat. "Ah, right." His nearness made it difficult for her to think. "And this outing, it would still be just friends, right?"

"I—" Max began then closed his mouth. His eyebrows pulled together.

"What's wrong?"

He ran a hand through his salt-and-pepper hair. "I know that's what I said, but..."

"But?" she asked breathlessly.

"I want... more."

Her heart skipped a beat. "Like a real date?"

"Exactly." His gaze swept over her hungrily before his frown deepened. "But I promised Lanie."

And just like that, the warmth that had been building in her chest vanished. "Right." After such a wonderful day, she'd almost forgotten she was still planning his daughter's wedding. "She didn't seem to mind me tagging along today."

"I'm not sure what she felt," Max said. "But I'm sure if she wasn't happy about it, I'll get an earful later."

Carissa sighed. "She's right to be concerned. If we start something and it doesn't go well, it will make the wedding awkward."

"I suppose we could wait until after the wedding." From Max's tone, Carissa gathered that wasn't what he wanted. In truth, it wasn't what she wanted either, but it seemed their only option.

"It's only a few months away," she agreed reluctantly.

"Or..." He took a deep breath. "We could keep it a secret."

She burst out laughing. "Because that went so well last time."

His harrumph only made her smile wider. "It was an accident. I wasn't thinking." He placed his hand on her shoulder. "This is different. It's not wedding-related, which means I'm less likely to slip up again."

"If she found out, you're not the only one who'd be in hot water. My reputation, my business could be tarnished." Her heart hammered in her chest, both from his proximity and a real concern for what that might mean for her livelihood. Her eyes searched his face. *Is he worth the repercussions I could face if this ends badly?*

"I know, and I hate the idea of sneaking around, but waiting until after Christmas is worse." His fingers tucked a lock of hair behind her ear, and her skin heated where he touched her. Part of her wondered if he would kiss her, and she feared she wouldn't be able to resist him if he did.

Words failed her. Her heart wanted to throw caution to the wind and see if her growing feelings might develop into something real. But as her mind played out the worst-case scenarios, it put a damper on her passion. A cool breeze blew past them, causing her to shiver.

"Do you want to come inside?" Max gestured to the house. "I don't want you to freeze."

"I should go." His face fell, and she hurried on. "But let's plan to grab lunch this weekend."

He smiled. "Saturday?"

"Saturday sounds perfect."

"Until then," he said.

They walked to her car, and he opened her door. She buckled herself in and backed out of his driveway. When she glanced in the rearview, he was still standing outside, watching her leave.

The whole way home, she was on cloud nine. As she gathered her bags and carried them into the house, she practically floated to the door. After Chuck had passed, she never expected to feel this way again and certainly not about Max McAllister. But so much had changed between them in the last month, and she couldn't wait for Saturday.

First, she had to get through her pitch.

When Wednesday finally arrived, Carissa was a bundle of nerves. She drove into the city and parked in the garage under the building where Imagi-navigation Enterprises was headquartered. As she took the elevator to the lobby, she kept smoothing her hair and her clothes to keep her hands from shaking.

The receptionist took her name and showed her into a large conference room. A table in the center had somewhere between twenty to thirty chairs stationed around it, though she wasn't sure how many people from the board would be in attendance. A large screen stood at one end, and she decided to set up there.

After plugging in her laptop, she clicked through her slides to make sure everything worked. Once she was ready, she took a seat and sipped from the provided water bottle, trying to calm her nerves.

To her chagrin, Jacob was first to arrive. She kept a neutral smile on her face while she shook his hand and prayed he wouldn't recall their encounter from the other night.

"Carissa, glad you were able to come today." His eyes swept over her body, and she resisted the urge to pull away from him. "I was disappointed our date the other night was cut short."

Bile rose up in her throat, but she swallowed it. "It was unfortunate you had to leave our business meeting so abruptly."

His face darkened, and he opened his mouth to respond, but she was saved from whatever he was going to say by the door opening and the board members filing in. One by one, they shook her hand and introduced themselves before taking their seats.

After everyone was seated, Jacob stood and gave a small introduction. "Now that we've all met Carissa, let me tell you about our lunch meeting last month to give you a sense of what she has to offer. Carissa owns a little wedding business in southern Maryland and has recently sought to branch out into corporate events, including holiday parties and team-building retreats."

She bristled at the description of her business as "little" but worked to keep her smile on her face. As Jacob continued, he couldn't seem to resist firing a jab at her here and there, but thankfully, his remarks mostly went unnoticed by the rest of the board. When he was finished, he sat down with a satisfied smirk.

Determined not to let him rile her, she took a deep breath and mentally counted down from ten before she began. He was one of many who would decide which event coordinator would get the company's business. If she could win over everyone else in the room, she could not only realize her dream but also make him eat crow. The thought thrilled her, and a genuine smile tugged at her lips.

"Thank you for having me today. I've enjoyed learning more about your company." She cleared her throat. "I was asked to present three different options for events that I think will help strengthen the cohesiveness of your company through team building, but first, I'd like to tell you more about me and how I got started in event planning."

Clicking to the next slide, she began the speech she'd rehearsed over the last several days. Her confidence grew as she finished her introduction, and several board members leaned forward, clearly interested.

"The first option I have for you is a trip to a local winery." The next slide showed a beautiful landscape of rolling hills against a deep-blue sky. "For the first night, a wine tasting will be provided for an icebreaker. Then you'll take a horseback ride through the countryside, followed by a special dinner pairing each course with a different wine. Other activities will include a cooking class, a soccer game, and a tour of the winery, during which you will be provided an overview of the wine-making process."

She saw a few nods in the audience, but overall, the reaction wasn't positive. But Carissa had expected that. The winery was her least favorite of her three ideas, and she'd decided to start small and work her way up to the best one, which she hoped would win them over.

Her next slide showed the National Harbor lit up at night. "For the next option, we have a long weekend in the National Harbor. One of the benefits is it's not far from the city. Folks can go home at night to their families or choose to stay in the lovely Gaylord Hotel. The first night will have a welcome dinner cruise. One of the team-building activities will be an escape room. There will also be a rowing contest on the Potomac River."

After she gave a few more details about the second option, she glanced at the board members to gauge their reactions. Some maintained eye contact, but most were losing interest. She started to wonder if she should have presented her ideas in reverse order or discussed her favorite option in the middle to keep their attention.

Quickly clicking to the next slide, she squared her shoulders and paused dramatically. The sudden silence had the desired impact, as many people put aside their phones and focused on her once more.

"And last but certainly not least, the third option is a trip to Deep Creek Lake. As with the second option, there will be an opportunity for water sports but also mountain climbing, biking, hiking, and sightseeing. There are several cabins that can be booked for a week, allowing a perfect getaway with a rustic backdrop while still incorporating modern conveniences like Wi-Fi."

As she finished her presentation, she put her hands behind her back and gazed at the board members expectantly. "Any questions?"

Hands shot up around the room, and her earlier fear about the order of her presentation melted away. She was so busy fielding the questions they fired at her she barely noticed Jacob scowling from across the room. Though her confidence soared, her stomach did a little flip. She worried that even if the board voted in her favor, Jacob would find a way to quash the opportunity.

Chapter Thirteen

THE JOY MAX HAD experienced after making plans with Carissa dissipated as he considered the logistics of getting out of the house without Lanie learning of those plans. While he and Carissa had agreed to keep things platonic for the time being, it would still seem odd to Lanie that he was having lunch with Carissa on his own. He'd yet to think of a good excuse, and he hoped to avoid the topic entirely by slipping out of the house unnoticed.

Unfortunately, dodging Lanie proved to be more difficult than he'd expected. With it being Saturday, he assumed she would have plans with Nate, but she seemed perfectly content lounging around the house. She'd staked out the living room for the day. When he came downstairs, she already had papers stacked around her and the television tuned to some sappy Hallmark movie.

"What's all this?" He gestured to the mess.

She pointed at the piles one by one. "Lesson plans. Worksheets. Individualized Education Programs, or IEP, I need to review." Her eyebrows pulled together as her hand hovered over the last pile. "Papers to grade." She shrugged. "The work of a teacher never ends."

"Oh, you don't have plans with Nate?" He tried to hide his disappointment.

"Not until later." She cocked her head. "Why? Trying to get rid of me?"

"Of course not," he retorted, turning to the kitchen. But he stopped and glanced back. "Uh, what time is Nate coming?"

Her eyes narrowed. *Wrong question.* If he'd hoped to keep her from becoming suspicious, he was off to a bad start.

"I want to make sure he doesn't block me in," he said, keeping his voice neutral.

Lanie didn't appear to buy his lame excuse, but she didn't press. "Probably not until this evening."

He went to get a cup of coffee. His plan wasn't going to work. He needed to leave by noon to pick up Carissa, which meant he would have to sneak out of the house without Lanie seeing or concoct some plausible excuse for where he was going. And he'd have to give up any hope of dressing nicely for the occasion because that would surely raise her suspicions.

He'd have to make do with something he normally wore. He rolled his eyes. Because that was going to be easy. Maybe he should cancel. Carissa would understand.

But he didn't want to cancel. He'd been looking forward to their lunch all week. Part of him almost wished Lanie had never moved in with him, but he immediately regretted the thought. If she hadn't moved home, he wasn't sure he would ever have the chance to make amends with her. Besides, she'd probably be happy he was putting himself out there again were it not for the person he had chosen to spend time with.

After finishing his coffee, he wandered into the garage. If nothing else, he could make some serious progress on the remaining unfinished furniture. With luck, Lanie would finish her school stuff before lunch and vacate the living room. He crossed his fingers.

As he worked, he tried to get into his normal rhythm. Usually, woodworking helped him to clear his head, but that day, he couldn't seem to concentrate.

Maybe it was because the last time he'd worked on those pieces was before his marriage imploded. Or perhaps it was the fact that autumn always reminded him of Melody because her birthday was in November. Whatever the reason, his mind kept replaying their last argument.

"You need to work on your relationship with Lanie," she'd said. Despite how much the cancer had already eaten away at her, she still had a fierceness he admired, except when she aimed it at him. They were on the front porch of the house they had once shared. Melody sat in a wicker chair in the corner while Max was perched on the stairs.

"Lanie and I are fine," he retorted. "You worry too much."

She raised an eyebrow. "I won't be around to manage your relationships for you. And one day, you may wake up to find yourself cut off from her life."

He snorted. "You're one to talk."

"What's that supposed to mean?"

"Don't think I don't know what you and Nate talked about the other day. Jesus, Melody, you can't put a promise like that on that kid."

Her eyes narrowed. "He's not a kid. He's a grown man. And don't change the subject. We're talking about *your* relationship with Lanie, not mine." Unshed tears glimmered in her eyes as she turned away. "It's too late for me to fix things."

"Don't say that." He stood, hoping to put an end to the morbid conversation.

"It's true, and it's about time you faced it." She sighed. "Let me say my piece, and then I promise not to bring it up again."

"Fine." Leaning against the porch rail, he crossed his arms.

"You've always had an easier relationship with Steven. The two of you are a lot alike in many ways." Her teeth worried her lower lip. "But with Lanie, it's different. When she was younger, she was such a daddy's girl. Since she grew up, it's like you've held her at arm's length."

"It certainly didn't help that she went to college on the other side of the country."

"That was my fault." She stared at the ground. "I leaned on her after the divorce, and I pushed her to get out of this town. I wanted something better for her."

He shifted uncomfortably. Melody had told him about forcing Lanie to promise she'd leave Cedar Haven and never look back. When she'd first told him, he hoped she'd learned her lesson and would make amends before... His mind tripped over the words. Then she'd extracted a very different promise from Nate, and Max wondered if she understood the destruction she'd caused.

"If Nate can't get through to her..." She swallowed. "Then you have to."

"I thought you liked her current boyfriend."

"James is a good guy, and there was a time I believed he was perfect for her." Her eyes misted again. "But I know my daughter, and she's not happy with him. She'd never admit it, but she stays with him to fulfill her promise to me."

"I'm not sure she'll listen to me any more than she would Nate."

She raised an eyebrow. "I wonder where she got that stubbornness from."

His lips twitched as he tried not to smile. "'Cause you're not stubborn at all, right?"

Her answering smile caused his heart to skip a beat, just before a knife twisted in his stomach. They'd lost so much time, and now, she was dying.

"Promise me you'll fix things with Lanie. She's going to need you when I'm—" Her voice cracked.

In an instant, he'd knelt beside her and grabbed her hands. "I promise."

Lanie's laugh floated out into the garage from the living room, interrupting his thoughts. He stared at the wood shavings peppering the floor. What was he doing out there, hiding from her, when he had such precious time left? The wedding was in less than three months, then she would move in with Nate. Had he done enough to fix things with her? Or would she stop by only for the obligatory get-togethers on major holidays?

He didn't want to find out. After putting his tools away, he grabbed a broom and swept the garage. As soon as he was finished, he headed into the house.

Lanie sat in the same spot, but she shifted the papers around her. It appeared she'd made a lot of progress. She looked up and smiled as he came into the room.

"How's the furniture coming?"

"Not bad. I'm still rusty, but I'm getting the hang of it again." He cleared his throat. "I was going to get some lemonade. Did you want some?"

She blinked, seemingly surprised by his offer. "Um, sure?"

Her reaction grated on him, and he hurried into the kitchen before she saw his face. When he returned with two glasses, she accepted hers and patted the empty spot beside her, which he slid into. For a moment, they sipped their drinks in silence as yet another Hallmark movie started.

"How do you watch these things?" He tilted his glass toward the screen. "Aren't they basically the same plot?"

She laughed. "Yes and no. It's the same structure, but the plots and characters are different." His doubt must have been clear on his face because she shook her head. "Okay, sometimes they run together, even for me." She glanced at the screen. "But I like predictability. No matter what's going on in my life, I can watch one of these movies and be guaranteed a happy ending."

"Sounds boring to me."

"Besides," she continued as if he hadn't spoken, "they're easy to follow, so I can focus on something else and have it on in the background."

"I suppose that's true."

After draining her glass, she set it on the small table beside the couch. "Are you planning on working in the garage all afternoon?"

He shook his head. "I'm done for the day. Thought I'd come in and see how you were getting on."

"I've got a few more things to do, but I should finish soon." Her eyes strayed to the papers in her lap, and she picked up her pen.

Normally, he would take that as his cue, but he didn't want to leave. The whole point of him coming in early was to spend some quality time with her, but he didn't want to disrupt her work.

"If you want to change the channel, you can." She nodded toward the remote on the coffee table in front of them.

"Oh, that's okay. There's nothing I want to watch."

Another beat of silence, then she shifted on the couch to face him full-on. "Is something wrong?"

Great. She'd noticed he was acting weird. "No, why?"

"Just... You don't usually hang out here during the day." She shuffled her papers. "If I'm in your way, I can go to my room—"

"No, no, you're fine." *Why is this so difficult?* "I was hoping to spend some time with you."

Her eyebrows shot up, and he wished he'd found a better way to word it. Ah, well, he'd done it. He took another sip of lemonade to buy himself some time.

"Oh," she finally said.

Her teeth worried her lower lip, and it pained him to realize how much she looked like her mother when she did that. "I'm not sure I'll be much company until I finish this stuff."

"That's okay." He peered over at the paper on top of the pile. "So, does the school provide you with a personality profile on every kid?"

She laughed. "You make it sound like the FBI." Then her face grew serious. "It's their school record, with report cards, IEPs, and other pertinent information. I don't have to go through it like I'm doing, but some of these kids were with the last teacher for years. I only spent a little time with them before she left, and I want to make sure I'm meeting their needs."

"You always were a planner," he replied with a wry smile.

"I believe I get that from you," she murmured.

"Me?" He blinked. *When have I ever planned anything?* "I'm not sure I follow."

With a sigh, she set aside the pile and faced him. "I suppose it's not that you're a planner, but you always seem to try to have a firm grasp on any situation."

"Is that a bad thing?"

Her lips twisted as she appeared to consider his question. "Not exactly bad, but it can be frustrating."

His heart sank. "In what way?"

"For starters, you always think you know what's best for everyone. While I'm not saying you're wrong in every instance, it's frustrating because when you're convinced you're right, you don't listen to anyone else's opinion."

"That's not true."

She raised an eyebrow. "Isn't it? You were convinced I belonged in Cedar Haven. You practically badgered me into staying."

"Are you saying I was wrong?"

"No," she admitted. "But I *am* saying you went about it the wrong way." He opened his mouth to protest, but she held up her hand. "Let me try to put it in a perspective you'll understand. Ever heard the saying 'You'll catch more flies with honey than vinegar'?"

He crossed his arms. "In the version I'm familiar with, it's manure, not vinegar."

"Of course it is," she muttered, rolling her eyes. "Anyway, my point is I might have been less resistant to the idea of moving back home if you hadn't continued to undermine my choice at every turn. For example, perhaps instead of calling my decision a disappointment, you could have simply said you wished I would reconsider but you respected that it was my life to do with as I wished."

"Would that have convinced you to stay, though?"

"I didn't need you to convince me to stay, Dad. I needed you to listen to me as an adult and stop treating me like a child."

He scowled. *When have I ever treated her like a child since she's been home?* "I don't do that."

Her lips curved in a sad smile. "Not always, but you often seem to underestimate my capabilities."

The conversation was starting to hit the point where he usually shut it down and left, but something told him he needed to hear what she had to say, regardless of how much it hurt. With a deep breath, he swallowed his retort. "How so?"

A surprised glint lit her hazel eyes. "Take my wedding, for example. You keep offering to pay for things, even though I've told you Nate and I have it handled. Then, to back up your offer, you read into any expression that crosses my face." She raised an eyebrow as if daring him to counter it.

"But you did seem to want that other cake."

"It's a lovely design, but I don't need it." Her mouth turned down. "Sometimes, it feels like you equate money with true emotional connection."

Ouch. He ducked his head to hide how much her words had hurt him. *Is it wrong to want to provide for your children even when they're grown?*

"I'm sorry," Lanie said, clearly realizing her statement had cut deeper than she'd intended. "I shouldn't have said it like that."

"It's okay." He waved a hand and tried to play it off as no big deal, but the words still stung. To give himself a moment to recover, he checked his watch. It was already after eleven. If he had any hope of being on time for lunch, he needed to get ready.

He stood and stretched, ignoring the frown that crossed Lanie's face. As much as he hated to cut their conversation short, he needed some time to process everything she'd said.

"I'm having lunch with an old friend." He headed to the stairs. "We can talk more about this later."

"Okay," she called, her tone dejected. "Have fun."

His chest tightened as he climbed the stairs to shower and change. While he'd known fixing things with Lanie wouldn't be easy, he'd never expected that hearing how she felt would wound him. His mixed-up emotions were only exacerbated by the lie he had just told her. The last thing he wanted to do was cause more issues between them, but he suspected the truth would upset Lanie more.

Chapter Fourteen

CARISSA EXAMINED HER APPEARANCE for the hundredth time. Nothing had changed, but somehow, noting her makeup hadn't smeared and her hair wasn't out of place calmed her.

Why am I nervous? It was just lunch between friends. Or at least, that was what she kept telling herself. While they might not be calling it a date, it certainly felt like one. Which meant so much could go wrong. If things didn't work out, the next few months would be awkward until after the wedding. Or if Lanie found out, she might not like the fact that Carissa was mixing business with pleasure.

Carissa was thankful Max didn't have any more children. As happy as she was to have snagged two clients from the same family, she doubted she would survive another McAllister wedding.

The doorbell rang, and her heart leaped into her chest. Taking a deep breath, she swallowed her nerves and opened her door.

Max's eyes traveled down her body, and she bit her lip to hide her smile. The blue long-sleeved dress she wore had been sitting in her closet, gathering dust. She was thrilled to not only have a reason to wear it but also that it still fit.

"You look..." He stopped as if he couldn't find a word that quite fit whatever he saw.

"So do you." Her voice came out much more breathless than she'd intended, but it was true. He wore a leather jacket over a dark-blue button-down shirt, which went nicely with his black trousers. Normally, she wasn't into such dark colors on a man, but somehow, on Max, it fit.

He cleared his throat. "Shall we go?"

After grabbing a light trench coat, she nodded. He held out his arm, and she took it, feeling her fingers warm where they brushed his leather jacket.

When he opened the passenger door, she smiled. "How chivalrous."

He grinned. "What can I say? I'm old-fashioned. Or, you know, just old."

She laughed as she climbed into the truck. The cab was nice and toasty, a welcome change from the chill.

"Won't be long now before we'll be wearing coats and scarves all the time," Max said a moment later, buckling his seat belt.

"Mm, don't remind me."

"Don't you like autumn?"

"Oh, I do." She turned toward him. "But it means we're running out of time to get everything set up for your daughter's wedding."

He scoffed. "If she'd stop coming up with these harebrained schemes, we'd be fine."

"She's excited."

"I'm glad she's happy." As he drove toward the highway, he glanced at her. "But enough about weddings. How did your pitch go? We haven't had much of a chance to talk about it."

"Eh." She closed her eyes, trying to push away the memory of how condescending the CEO had been. "The board seemed interested in the Deep Creek idea, not so much the other two."

"You don't sound very enthusiastic."

"To be honest, I'm not." At his frown, she sighed. "It's not that I don't want the opportunity anymore, but part of me wonders if it's worth it."

"What do you mean?"

"I'd hoped the CEO would have been too drunk to remember our aborted dinner the other night. Unfortunately, he was the first person in the room after I got there, and then during his introduction, he couldn't seem to resist making a few jabs to throw me off my game." She chewed her lower lip. "If I get the event, I may have to work with him directly, and I'm not sure I can handle it."

"Any idea what he has against you?" He glanced at her before returning his gaze to the road.

"I'm sure it has a lot to do with the fact he thinks I'm not qualified for the job." She rolled her eyes. "He keeps referring to my business as 'a little wedding planning.'"

"Which just goes to show he doesn't have a clue about what goes into a wedding. He probably showed up on his wedding day drunk and forgot his vows."

She laughed. "That wouldn't surprise me, but I'm trying not to let his behavior color my perception of the company. While yes, he's the CEO, the event I'd be planning is more focused on his employees. And he doesn't make the ultimate decision. The board does."

"I suppose that's something." A few minutes later, Max pulled into a parking garage. "Still, I'd hate for your first experience in planning corporate events to be with someone who doesn't respect you."

"I've dealt with worse." She raised an eyebrow and patted his hand.

His deep laugh sent butterflies fluttering through her stomach. "I deserve that." Then he climbed out of the truck and came around to her door. When he opened it, he offered her his arm. "Shall we?"

He led her through the busy streets toward the river. Her eyes lit up when she recognized the restaurant they were heading to.

"Oh, McCormick and Schmick's! I do love this place, though it's been years since I've been. Not since—" She stopped herself as a wave of sadness washed over her. The last time she'd come was with Chuck for their anniversary.

"Not since...?" Max paused at the door to the building and searched her face. Understanding dawned in his eyes. "You came here with your husband."

Unable to speak, she nodded once then stared at the ground, taking deep breaths until she'd regained control of her emotions. It had been five years, and still, little things like that could trigger tears.

"It's okay." Max wrapped his arms around her. "I get it. Grief is an unpredictable animal. Just when we think we're moving on and letting go, it jumps up and bites us in the rear."

Despite being on the verge of crying, she burst out laughing at his crazy analogy. As she raised her eyes to meet his, she realized that was his goal.

"We can go somewhere else," he offered. "There are plenty of other restaurants nearby."

"No, I want to go here. It's one of my favorites as well, and it'll be nice to make some new memories."

He stared at her for a moment as if debating whether she was lying to him, then he shrugged and opened the door. The place was busy, and she wondered if they would even be able to get a table, but Max walked up to the host stand with confidence.

"Reservation under McAllister," he said.

She blinked. It hadn't occurred to her to make reservations. So many places didn't even accept them anymore. But the host confirmed the reservation and gathered menus before leading them to a back-corner table with a spectacular view of the Potomac River.

Max pulled out a chair for her on the side of the table closest to the wall. "So you have the best view while we eat."

Her surprised smile coaxed a shy grin from him as he sat opposite her. If someone had asked her months ago how to describe Max, she would have said he was arrogant, stubborn, and overbearing. But in the last few weeks, he'd proved to be thoughtful, understanding, and kind. She began to understand that his gruff exterior was a hard outer shell he'd created to protect his soft heart.

Her eyes swept the room. The walls were covered with dark-wood paneling, with beautiful red flowers adorning each table. When she turned to the window, a large Ferris wheel stood in the distance, just before the rippling water of the Potomac River. "This would be a nice place for a wedding."

His gaze followed hers, and he pursed his lips. "Bit too fancy for me. But maybe an idea for your corporate event."

Tapping her fingers against her chin, she considered that. "It's a bit more expensive than I would like, but I bet the CEO would love it. While the board loved the idea of Deep Creek, he didn't seem as enthused. I imagine he'd prefer to stay close to the city."

"No team-building exercises on a local working farm?"

She snorted, trying to picture any of the men she'd met mucking out a barn, their designer trousers drenched in mud. "I'm afraid not."

"What would a corporate retreat look like in a place like this?" He crossed his arms on the table and leaned forward.

"Probably a lot of boring presentations about how to lead from the bottom." Her smile faded. "Which is exactly like every other retreat they've probably done." She sighed. "I want to stand out, do something unexpected, while still incorporating learning and team building."

He furrowed his brow. "What about sailing? That's a great way to learn teamwork."

"Do you sail?"

"I used to when I was younger. Not so much these days."

The server came and took their drink orders. While Max was giving his, Carissa mulled over what he'd said. Sailing would be a good team-building exercise and something the corporate employees might enjoy. And Maryland was practically surrounded by water between the rivers, the Chesapeake Bay, and the Atlantic. Although it was too late to pitch another location, she could keep that in mind for any future retreats. *Assuming I get another shot at a corporate event.*

"I can practically see the wheels spinning in your head," Max said when they were alone again.

"You've given me ideas for future events."

He raised his eyebrows. "Are you planning on pitching other companies?"

"Maybe. But if I do, it'll be in the new year." She pulled out her phone and typed into her Notes app, where she kept her ideas so she wouldn't forget them.

"Anyway," she continued, "enough about business. Tell me what you've been up to since our trip to the orchard."

"Not much. I did some woodworking this morning, and then I watched a Hallmark movie with Lanie."

She raised an eyebrow. "*You* watched Hallmark?" Shifting forward, she put her hand on his forehead. "Maybe I should take you home. You're clearly feverish."

"Ha ha." His voice dripped with sarcasm. "I didn't say I *enjoyed* the movie."

His expression changed, and he looked so vulnerable, she wished she could take back her joke. "She also said some... things." He cleared his throat, clearly not in the mood to elaborate. "I loved spending that time with her. I don't have much of it left."

Though curiosity burned in her chest, Carissa didn't push him about his conversation with his daughter. Instead, she gave him a gentle smile. "She's not dying."

"No, I know." He sighed. "But she is going to move out as soon as she's married, and, well, we don't have the greatest relationship, as I'm sure you're aware."

Her heart went out to him. "She does seem to have been closer to her mother."

"Yeah, that's my fault." He pushed his hair off his forehead. "I don't know what happened, really. With Steven, it was easier. We're a lot alike, and he's... simpler, I guess." Running a hand over his face, he shook his head. "I'm not making any sense."

"I get it. I mean, I don't have any children of my own, of course, but I can certainly understand the struggle. Every child is different, and I suppose it's natural Lanie gravitated to her mother, especially as she got older. And then, with caretaking, that can forge an even stronger bond."

"If the caretaker and the person being cared for don't kill each other first," he grumbled.

She pressed her lips together to hide a smile. "That's also a possibility."

"Anyway, I promised my lat—er—ex-wife I'd work on rebuilding a relationship with Lanie." He stared at his hands. "And I guess I promised myself that too."

Impulsively, she covered his hand with her own. "You can call her your late wife."

"We weren't married at the—when she—"

"Did you love her?" she asked, her voice soft.

"Of course."

"Then that doesn't matter."

The slow, shy smile that blossomed on his face took her breath away. But the moment was soon interrupted by the arrival of the server with their drinks. They flushed and pulled away from each other.

"Are you ready to order?" the server asked.

After exchanging a look, Max nodded. "Ladies first."

"I'll have the seafood pasta, please," Carissa said.

"And I'll take the crab cakes."

"How very Maryland of you," Carissa teased when they were alone again. "Though I don't recall Steven or Lanie mentioning any crab feasts this summer. Is that because of Steven's accident?"

"No." His eyes darted around the room, then he leaned closer. "I'm not actually into the whole crab-picking thing," he stage whispered.

Her hand flew to her mouth in mock shock. "Isn't that like sacrilege here?"

"The only foods I like to eat with my hands are burgers, hot dogs, and french fries." He shrugged. "Picking crabs is too much effort. But the kids normally do it for the Fourth of July. After Steven's accident, nobody was interested in upholding summer traditions."

"He looked like he was doing well on Sunday."

"He's doing a lot better, though he's still having some balance issues." Max smiled at her. "I'm glad you joined us. I had a really nice time."

"Me too." She smiled in return.

"Maybe we can do it again sometime. The town's fall festival is coming up in a few weeks."

Her heart leapt at the thought, but she took a deep breath to calm her emotions. "I'm not sure that's such a good idea."

The warmth in his eyes dimmed slightly. "Right. While Lanie seemed okay with you coming with us apple picking, two events back-to-back might make her think I'm breaking my word."

"Exactly. Besides, we're just getting to know each other." She took his hand. "Let's take our time and enjoy it."

He lifted her hand and brushed his lips across her knuckles. "Sounds like a plan."

Butterflies exploded in her stomach, and she ducked her head to hide her smile. If she wasn't careful, she might fall for the softer, happier side of Max. And she wasn't sure if she was ready for that.

ell

By the time they finished lunch, it was late afternoon. The sun glinted off the stream of cars on the Woodrow Wilson Bridge, signaling the beginning of rush-hour traffic. Carissa lingered over her glass of wine, savoring the evening and wishing it didn't have to end.

"Did you want dessert?" Max asked, breaking into her reverie.

She shook her head and grinned. "I can't eat another bite."

After signaling for the check, he leaned back in his chair. "This was nice."

"It was," she agreed, trying to hide her disappointment with how quickly the time had passed.

"What's on your agenda for the rest of the day?"

The question surprised her. "Um, I've got a few wedding details to work on for my other brides."

"So..." He hesitated.

"Yes?"

"You don't need to hurry back?"

Where is he going with this? "No. Why?"

"Since we've come all this way, maybe we could check out the harbor."

Her heart skipped a beat, and she nodded enthusiastically. "That sounds good to me."

"Great." He paid their bill. "Let's see what this little city has to offer."

The late-afternoon air was much cooler, though the lingering humidity kept her from being cold. They walked toward the pier, away from the hustle and bustle of the downtown area. As they meandered down the narrow docks, the sound of water lapping against the wood helped soothe Carissa's butterflies.

But the afternoon was starting to feel like déjà vu. She and Chuck had spent a night eating at the restaurant then lingering in the city afterward. It had been their twenty-fifth wedding anniversary, and she'd joked they should rent the private room at McCormick & Schmick's for their fiftieth.

Chuck had smiled and told her he wasn't sure it could fit all of their friends and family.

"I'd prefer a more intimate gathering," she'd said.

His arms encircled her waist, and he kissed her cheek. "A big party is more appropriate for such a milestone, don't you think?"

"Fine." She'd relented. "A big party, so long as for our fifty-first, we stay in and have a quiet evening at home."

"Deal," he'd promised.

Her heart ached at the memory. They never celebrated another anniversary. Seven months later, he was gone.

"I'd offer a penny for your thoughts, but I get the feeling they're worth much more." Max had stopped a few feet back and watched her.

"Sorry. I was remembering the last time I came here."

"With your husband?"

She nodded, swallowing the sob that threatened to escape her throat. "For our twenty-fifth wedding anniversary."

"Quite a milestone," he murmured.

If they kept on that track, she was going to lose the thin control she had over her emotions. She changed the subject. "How long were you married?"

"Almost thirty years."

"Really?" She cocked her head, doing some quick math. "How old were you when you got married?"

"Nineteen." His lips pressed into a grim line. "I don't recommend it."

"Still, you lasted longer than most people who marry that young."

"I guess," he said, shifting uncomfortably. "Come on. Let's go check out the Capital Wheel. I'll bet you get amazing views up there."

"Um, I'll pass." She pressed a hand to her stomach as it flipped at the thought.

His eyebrows shot up. "Why? You afraid of heights?"

"A little." That was a lie. She was terrified of them, but she didn't want to tell him that.

"Then what?" His face fell. "Unless... Do you want to go home?"

"No," she said, quicker than she'd intended. "Let's check out some of the shops instead."

"It's too nice out to be cooped up in a shop," he countered. Grabbing her hand, he pulled her toward him. "Come on. It'll be fun." He had a gleam in his eye. "And if you happen to get scared, I'll be there to keep you safe."

The words both frustrated and thrilled her. It was clear he hadn't bought her declaration that she wasn't afraid of heights, but the idea of being in his arms, even if she was terrified, was enough to coax her to go with him.

That was, until they were actually sitting in the gondola, or cage as it seemed to her. What she'd initially believed was excitement soon revealed itself to be paralyzing fear as she gripped the edge of the bench. The ride had no bar or seat belt, and Max sat on the opposite side.

"Where's the safety bar?" She tried to keep the panic out of her voice.

He gave her a weird look. "There isn't one. It's not like a Ferris wheel at the county fair." Her face must have betrayed her fear because he took both her hands. "Keep your eyes on me and take a deep breath."

The first instruction was easy to follow—she'd barely taken her eyes off him all day. But the second... Suddenly, the air seemed too thick, and when she tried to breathe, she started choking on it.

The operator shut the door, and they began to move. She squeezed her eyes shut and bit her tongue to keep from crying out. Max's hands tightened around hers, and he took several loud breaths. After a moment, it dawned on her that he was breathing that way in hopes she would mimic him. She focused on his breathing and matched it, and soon, her fears began to subside.

When she opened her eyes, Max was staring in wonder off into the distance. Then he turned to her and smiled.

"That's better." He nodded to the view. "I can describe what I see if you're too afraid to look."

"Just... give me a minute," she said, still sounding breathless. Her stomach had tied itself in knots, but otherwise, her heart rate was slowly returning to normal.

"Take all the time you need," he said, giving her hands another squeeze.

Chapter Fifteen

As color returned to Carissa's face, a stab of guilt hit Max's gut. He shouldn't have forced her to go. He'd known she'd been lying about not being afraid of heights, but he hadn't imagined her fear ran that deep. Though his hands ached because of how hard she was squeezing them, he never let go, silently pledging to hold on until they were safely on the ground or until Carissa was comfortable, whichever came first.

A moment later, her grip relaxed, and she turned her head the slightest bit. Her eyes widened, taking in the view.

"Wow, you were right. This view is spectacular."

He smirked. "Told you so." At her glare, he ducked his head. "Though I wish I hadn't forced you up here. I had no idea you were that scared."

"I'll be fine."

Her face was still pale, but they'd almost reached the apex of the wheel. Perhaps knowing the ride was about half over was encouraging to her.

They sat in silence, enjoying the breathtaking views. The sun had sunk low over the western shore of the river. It glinted off the buildings and the cars going over the bridge.

Once they were on the ground, the operator stepped forward and helped Carissa exit the gondola. She immediately went to a bench nearby and sat down. Max scrambled out after her.

"Are you sure you're okay?"

She nodded, staring at the ground and taking deep breaths. "I also hate flying. Being up in the air is okay, but the takeoff and the landing are my least favorite parts."

We weren't going that fast. But he kept the thought to himself. Instead, he offered his hand and helped her up.

"I'll take you home," he offered half-heartedly.

Her smile was apologetic. "Yes, please."

His heart sank, but he reminded himself they had a long ride home. At least she didn't seem upset at him, just out of sorts and probably nauseated.

"I promise for our next date, there won't be any heights."

She glanced at him. "Our next date?"

"Er... outing. Friendly lunch?"

Carissa laughed as she stood, still wobbly on her feet. Taking her hand, Max led her to the truck.

As they drove home, he rested his hand on the gear shift. At some point, Carissa trailed her fingers down his arm until she found his hand and curled her fingers over his. Her skin was warm and soft.

"I had a nice time today."

He squeezed her hand. "I did too." Taking a deep breath, he continued, "I meant what I said. I'd like to take you out again and soon."

From the corner of his eye, he could make out a faint blush tingeing her cheeks. She didn't immediately respond, and he tried not to let that bother him. Besides, he had a bigger question weighing on his mind.

In his day, it wasn't necessarily expected to receive a kiss on a first or second date, but times had changed, and he and Carissa weren't a couple of nervous teenagers finding their way through their first romance. Still, they'd agreed it wasn't a date, and he didn't want to pressure her. But the thought of what it would be like, what it would *feel* like, occupied his mind for the rest of the drive to her house.

When he pulled into her driveway, he put the truck in park and climbed out to open her door. She accepted his hand, and he pulled her to her feet. After tucking her hand into the crook of his arm, he led her to her door.

Then, they stood there, the awkward moment growing until he wondered if he should say goodbye and go. He squared his shoulders and met her gaze, but before he could speak, she lifted her hand and cupped his cheek.

"Thank you for lunch."

"My pleasure," he said, his voice hoarse with emotion.

She leaned forward, closing her eyes, and his heart pounded as he closed the distance between them. He could feel her breath on his face as he moved slowly toward her.

Ping.

The sound of his cell phone made them jump. He removed it from his pocket and rolled his eyes.

"Just Lanie checking up on me." He gave Carissa a rueful smile. "Guess she's not used to me being gone so long."

Instead of laughing, Carissa bit her lip. The mood seemed to shift, and he held his breath.

"Max, I had a wonderful time with you."

His stomach flipped, and he braced for whatever she was about to say. "But?"

She sighed. "We're moving into dangerous territory. The apple picking was one thing, though I'm still not sure how Lanie felt about it. Lunch today was wonderful, but we shouldn't be sneaking around behind Lanie's back like this. She made it clear she didn't want you and me to date, and we should respect her wishes."

"We can certainly slow things down until the wedding is over," he said, searching her face. "But why can't we keep seeing each other casually in the meantime?"

"And if she finds out?"

As much as Max wanted to respond with a careless shrug, he knew Carissa wouldn't buy it. Quite frankly, he was terrified of what would happen if Lanie discovered he'd broken his word. While he and Carissa might tell themselves they were just friends, the fact they'd almost kissed proved Carissa's point.

At the same time, he was feeling things he'd never expected to feel again after Melody. Her death had taught him how short and precious life was. Despite how much he didn't want to hurt Lanie, he hated the idea of missing out on whatever was blooming between him and Carissa.

"Maybe she won't mind now that the wedding is mostly planned," he said meekly.

She raised an eyebrow. "You don't believe that's true any more than I do."

"What if I promise not to let our relationship interfere with the wedding?"

"You can't make that kind of a promise." Lowering her head, she stared at their hands. "And it's not just about making things awkward with one client. Wedding planning is my livelihood. And if the corporate gig doesn't work out, I don't want to do anything that risks my professional reputation."

"I understand." For a moment, he wasn't sure what to say. Emotions warred within him. On the one hand, he didn't want to cause her any hardship, financial or otherwise. But was it that selfish to want to be happy?

He ran his hand through his hair. "Listen, if you want to take a step back until the wedding's over, then that's what we'll do." At her growing smile, he held up a hand. "For the record, I don't like it, but I don't want to do anything that will jeopardize your business or my relationship with my daughter."

She searched his eyes. "I'm not saying never. Just maybe not now."

He nodded, though it killed him to do so. It figured that the first time he'd developed feelings for someone since his marriage, it was complicated. Nothing in his life was ever as simple as he wanted it to be.

"So where do we go from here?" he asked, unable to keep the disappointment out of his voice.

"We can still text and maybe meet for coffee," she said. "And of course, we'll see each other for wedding-related events."

"What about after?"

She leaned forward and kissed his cheek before unlocking the door. Glancing over her shoulder with a sly smile, she winked. "I guess we'll have to wait and see."

As he walked to his truck, his emotions were all over the place. On the one hand, he wished December would hurry up and get there so he and Carissa could give their relationship a real shot. But on the other hand, the sooner the wedding arrived, the sooner Lanie would move away and start her new life. His time with her was running out.

He climbed into the car and stared at his reflection in the rearview mirror. "Keep your head in the game, McAllister. Lanie is the priority. Carissa can wait."

Chapter Sixteen

Carissa's phone rang bright and early Tuesday morning, waking her up. Rubbing her bleary eyes, she answered it on speaker. "Hello?"

"Carissa, hi. It's Colin Fields, the activities coordinator at Imaginavigation Enterprises. How are you?"

Her early-morning brain fog dissipated, and she sat up. "Oh, hello, Mr. Fields. I'm well, and yourself?"

"Very well, thank you." He cleared his throat. "Listen, I wanted to call and thank you for your presentation the other day. The Deep Creek idea you had was a huge hit with the board."

"Does that mean—" She took a deep breath. "That is to say, I'm glad you enjoyed it."

"We did indeed, but we were wondering if you would be willing to allow us to move forward with your idea internally."

She blinked. "Excuse me?"

"We loved your idea, and we're willing to offer you a contract as a consultant."

It took significant willpower to keep her tone even. "Let me see if I have this right. You liked my idea enough to use it but not enough to hire me as the actual planner?"

"Oh, well…" The cool and confident tone vanished. "Um, you see, we don't believe you have enough experience to pull it off. I'll be leading this event, and Jacob thought you might be willing to collaborate with me."

I bet he did. Her heart pounded, and she glared at the opposite wall. *The nerve.* "I'm sorry, Mr. Fields, but I'm afraid I'm not interested in acting as a consultant. While I can't stop you from planning your retreat in Deep Creek based on my recommendation and pitch, I've no reason to assist you in bringing it to fruition when I'm perfectly capable of leading such an event on my own."

"But you would profit too. Albeit less than you would have if we awarded you the contract outright."

"And that is precisely why I'm not interested in your offer."

"Carissa." Another voice, gratingly familiar, came over the line. "You're making a mistake. This is a way for you to get your foot in the door and gain some experience so that the next time an opportunity like this arises, you'll have this event in your portfolio."

Closing her eyes, she ground her teeth in frustration. Jacob was right. No matter how much it hurt her pride, consulting on the event would give her the experience she needed to break into corporate event planning. Her previous attempts to expand into that world had not panned out, and the only reason she'd had the opportunity to pitch Imaginavigation Enterprises was her husband's acquaintance with the former CEO.

She sighed. *I could end this call right now and never have to deal with this jerk again.* But doing so would mean starting over from scratch, and she was tired of having doors slammed in her face. Besides, she wouldn't put it past Jacob to blacklist her to every other corporation in the DC metro area.

"I'll consider it and get back to you," she finally said as she swallowed her pride.

"You have twenty-four hours," Jacob replied, and she could practically hear his smirk.

The phone beeped three times, confirming they'd disconnected. She put her head in her hands, and tears pricked her eyelids. She'd been confident that she'd nailed the presentation, and she'd hoped her experience in event planning in general would have compensated for her limited knowledge of corporate retreats.

Consulting would help her garner that experience but at a price. She expected she would be working closely with Jacob, and the idea made her skin crawl.

She needed advice, but she wasn't sure who to turn to. Max was the first person she wanted to talk to, but she'd just told him that she should take things slowly, and she didn't want to send mixed messages. Unfortunately, she hadn't told many other people she was pursuing the venture in case it didn't work out.

I need to get out of the house and clear my head. She dressed quickly and headed into the chilly autumn air. The sky was filled with ominous dark clouds that seemed to match her mood. She drove aimlessly until she found herself turning onto Main Street in Cedar Haven and heading toward Bea's Diner.

When she walked in the door, she saw Max sitting at a booth near the back. His eyes lit up at the sight of her, and he waved her over. A warmth blossomed in her chest as she made her way toward him.

"Fancy meeting you here." He lifted his mug in salute. "Care to join me?"

Carissa bit her lip. As happy as she was to see him, they shouldn't be spending time alone together in public.

"I promise I won't bite." A smirk pulled up one side of his mouth, and she couldn't help smiling.

"All right." She slid into the booth across from him. "But just for a minute."

"What brings you out here? Do you have a meeting with a bride?"

Before she could answer, the server came to take her order. She selected a chai tea, hoping the spices would lift her mood.

"No meeting," she said once they were alone again. "I went for a drive to clear my head and ended up here."

He tilted his head. "Something wrong?"

Once again, she hesitated. She'd meant what she'd told him the other day about keeping their distance, but right then, she could really use a friend. "I didn't get the corporate event gig."

His eyebrows pulled together in concern. "Did they tell you why?"

"Apparently, I don't have enough experience." Her hands clenched into fists on the table. "And that's not even the worst part." She proceeded to tell him about the consulting offer and Jacob's smug attitude.

"He knows he's got me. His company only offered me the opportunity to pitch on the recommendation of their former CEO. If I refuse, I'm back to square one."

"If I were you, I'd start over and hope to find someone who isn't such a jerk."

"It's not that simple." She rubbed her temples. "Companies like Imaginavigation Enterprises talk. A lot of event coordinators work on referral. This was supposed to be my ticket into that world. Even if I try to start over, Jacob could blacklist me."

"But why? You've done nothing wrong."

"It doesn't matter. I refused his advances at the restaurant. Men like him have done much worse for less obvious slights."

"Then you should file a harassment charge against him. Or at the very least, report what he did to the board."

"It's my word against his, and they have a relationship with him. Besides, if I reported him now, it would look like I was retaliating for not getting their business."

Max was quiet, and she took a sip of her tea, hoping it might make her feel better. It didn't. The drive hadn't helped either. Perhaps she would have been better off staying home and wallowing for a bit.

"Why not start with local businesses? Planning holiday parties and the like?"

Max was doing that thing Chuck used to do, trying to fix things instead of letting her vent. Was that just a habit with men from her generation?

"I already plan holiday parties for some local businesses. Corporate retreats are a whole different animal because you're not just booking a location and entertainment, you're planning an entire week of activities as well as lodging, food, and the like."

"What about—"

She held up a hand. "I know you're trying to help, but I didn't come here to brainstorm my next move. I wasn't planning on talking about it at all, but you asked. Let's change the subject, okay?"

It came out harsher than she'd intended, but she didn't have the energy to manage anyone else's feelings that day. A pained expression crossed his face. He gave a gruff nod and stared at the table.

Great. Now she'd upset him too. The day was off to an amazing start. "I'm sorry. Maybe I should go. I don't want to take it out on you."

"No, please stay." He blew out his breath. "Melody used to complain about the same thing. I do better when I have a tangible problem I can fix. But I'm trying, and if you want to vent, I'm here to listen."

"Thanks," she said, and she meant it. But suddenly, all the fire had gone out of her. She was not in a good place for company, and she didn't want to risk taking her frustrations out on Max any more than she already had. "Actually, I'm going home."

He blinked in surprise. "Already? But you just got here."

"I need some time to process this and make up my mind about what I'm going to do." She downed her tea. "Thanks for letting me vent, and I'm sorry I intruded on your breakfast."

He stood and pulled her into his arms before she had a chance to stop him. "I'm here for you. Anytime."

Plastering a smile on her face, she extricated herself from his embrace and waved goodbye. Once she was in her car and driving home, she let the reality of the situation hit her full force. She barely made it home before she fell apart in her car, leaning against the steering wheel and letting the tears fall.

"What am I going to do?" she whispered.

That question haunted her for the rest of the day, and by the evening, she still wasn't sure. She vacillated between taking the consulting gig to garner experience and telling Jacob where he could stick his offer. No matter how hard she tried to convince herself, she wasn't sure she could stomach the idea of working with him.

But the idea of going back to the drawing board and trying to figure out her next plan of attack gave her a headache. She feared her lack of experience would continue to be a barrier, even if her ideas were well received. And if she couldn't expand her business, she wasn't sure what she would do with it when she was ready to retire. She'd hoped integrating corporate retreats into her business would make it a more attractive sale. Without that expansion, she wasn't sure how enticing the business would be to potential buyers.

Her phone rang, and irritation boiled in her belly when she recognized the number. She debated ignoring it, but that wouldn't be professional. With a groan, she picked it up and answered. "Hello, Jacob."

"Actually, it's not Jacob. It's Colin."

"Oh, hello, Mr. Fields."

"Listen, I know Jacob gave you twenty-four hours to decide, but I wondered if there was anything I could do to sweeten the deal to convince you. The position isn't what you want, but it would be a foot in the door with not only our company but the larger corporate world at large."

"Believe me, I'm aware," she said, unable to keep her aggravation out of her tone. "And it's not that I'm averse to coming on as a consultant." Even if it still grated on her nerves that they were more interested in her idea than her ability to implement it.

"Then what's holding you back?" When she didn't immediately respond, he added, "If you don't mind my asking."

She bit her lip. What she wanted to say warred with what she *should* say. Was there a tactful way to tell the activities coordinator that her main aversion was working with his boss? Probably not. And anything she said would likely be relayed to Jacob, which would put her in an even worse situation.

"I'm concerned there will be friction between Jacob and me." Her anxiety eased a little. That sounded vague enough to explain her hesitation without saying anything directly negative about the CEO.

A nervous chuckle came over the line. "I can understand why you'd say that about Jacob." He cleared his throat. "How about this? We can meet outside of the office to limit your interactions with Jacob. I'm happy to set up working lunches at restaurants or even come down to your neck of the woods to discuss things. We can even do virtual meetings if that's easier for you."

He had a hint of desperation in his voice, which only confirmed that he was in over his head. She felt bad for him, and she had to admit his offer was enticing. She could still garner the experience she needed to pitch other companies while maintaining a positive business relationship with Imaginavigation Enterprises. And if she could do that and avoid Jacob, all the better.

"All right," she finally said. "I'll do it. But I want a contract drawn up detailing my consulting fee and terms allowing for that amount of flexibility." Chuck had always insisted she get everything in writing.

"I'll get our legal team on it first thing tomorrow," Colin promised. "And then I'm hoping to get started as soon as the ink is dry."

"That works for me."

After they hung up, the joy she normally felt after closing with a new client didn't come. She was still too anxious. Even if she never set foot in the offices of Imaginavigation Enterprises again, she doubted she could avoid Jacob altogether. But she'd made her bed, and all she could do was hope Colin was true to his word and kept his boss as far away from her as possible.

Chapter Seventeen

Max spent the next several days working in the garage in the futile hope of keeping his mind off Carissa. It didn't help that he hadn't heard from her since they left Bea's. He wanted to give her space, and if he was honest with himself, he wasn't ready to put it behind him. Her reactions had reminded him uncomfortably of many similar arguments he'd had with Melody. Listening without offering suggestions of how to fix things wasn't how he was wired, but he'd tried, and he wished that counted for something.

Their break from each other would be coming to an end soon. They were supposed to meet for the final caterer tasting that evening, and Lanie was excited about it.

He'd considered not going. It would make things a lot less awkward if he stayed home. But over the summer, he'd made such a fuss about being a part of things that a sudden change of heart would raise his daughter's suspicions. Besides, he wanted to go if for nothing else than to spend more time with Lanie.

As he finished up in the garage, the door to the house swung open, and Lanie came in. Her face was lit up with an exuberant smile he tried and failed to return.

"Are you about done?" she asked as she admired his handiwork.

"Yeah. Just need to clean up the dust and debris, then I'll change, and we can head out."

To his surprise, Lanie grabbed a broom and started sweeping. "I can't believe how fast time is flying. Next week is the middle of October."

"We'll need to pull out the Halloween decorations soon," he said.

"About that." She stopped sweeping and rested her hand on top of the broom handle. "Steven and Rose invited us to the town's fall festival this weekend. In addition to the hayrides and pumpkin patch, I heard there's going to be a haunted house. Would you want to go?"

To buy some time, he busied himself with putting away his tools. Ever since Carissa had turned him down for that very festival, he'd been determined to avoid it. Thinking about it, then, only added to his miserable mood, and he wasn't sure he could muster up the enthusiasm to go in time. The last thing he wanted to do was ruin his children's fun with his sour attitude.

"I'm not sure. When do you need an answer?"

Her smile faded, and she returned to sweeping. "Um, tomorrow, I guess?" She glanced at him. "Maybe you could bring someone." A shadow passed over her face. "But maybe not Carissa."

His heart seemed to stop. "Did it bother you that I brought her apple picking?"

She kept her eyes on the floor. "I suppose I was more surprised. On the one hand, I appreciate that you're trying to get along with her, but on the other…"

"We're not dating." He forced a laugh to disguise the bitterness in his tone.

"Good." Her answering chuckle sounded hollow. "I appreciate you keeping your word."

Instead of responding, he focused on putting away his tools. How would Lanie feel if she learned he and Carissa had had lunch together? Would she believe it was an innocent outing? He shook his head. *I don't even believe that.*

Once Lanie finished sweeping, she helped him cover his pieces. They went into the house together, and he headed upstairs to change.

He stepped into the bathroom and turned on the shower. As he waited for the water to warm, he mulled over his conversation with Lanie.

"What else can I do?" he asked his reflection. "Carissa already said no, and Lanie just reiterated she doesn't want me to date her wedding planner."

Of course, things were already awkward between him and Carissa. He sighed as he climbed into the shower. The tense silence he'd felt since she'd left Bea's would likely get worse once they were in the same room together. Perhaps he should open the lines of communication before he left.

As soon as he was out of the shower, he typed a quick text. He kept it simple since he had neither the time nor the wordsmithing capabilities to make it more detailed. After he hit Send, he dressed and made his way downstairs.

His phone pinged, and he checked the screen. *We're good. Sorry I haven't been in touch. Decided to consult on corporate retreat.*

He frowned. She'd taken the consulting gig after all? Well, he wouldn't ask her about it that night. But he hoped they could get together soon to talk more. He wondered what had made her choose to go forward with it after everything that jerk CEO had put her through.

"Ready to go?" Lanie came into the hallway with her coat hanging over her arm.

With a curt nod, he grabbed his coat and opened the door. They climbed into his truck, and he drove to The Muddy Oar. If nothing else, he had a delicious piece of chocolate cake to look forward to.

When they arrived, Carissa and Nate were already there. The hostess took them to a back room with a private table, where they would have the final tasting. Several hors d'oeuvres were already laid out on the table.

"Help yourselves," the hostess said. "The chef will be with you momentarily to discuss the options he has prepared."

Lanie and Nate sat together on one side of the table, leaving Max to sit next to Carissa. His stomach knotted at the sight of her, but she acted like everything was fine.

"I'm sorry I haven't called," she said in a low voice. "But I have a lot to tell you."

"Maybe we can meet up for coffee tomorrow."

"I was actually hoping you'd be able to stay after and have a drink with me."

"What are you two whispering about over there?" Lanie's eyes narrowed with suspicion.

"Nothing of importance," Carissa said quickly, leaning away from Max.

Before Lanie could press the issue, the chef returned carrying a tray. Max pushed his concerns aside as the delicious scent of roasted meat and herbs washed over him.

"Good evening, everyone," the chef said. "Tonight, I wanted to start you off with lemon-and-herb-roasted turkey with a side of baked parmesan asparagus."

"Ooh." Lanie clapped. "It sounds delicious."

The chef set the tray on the table. Everyone took a generous helping, though Max tried to hide his displeasure at the asparagus.

But Carissa wasn't fooled. "Not a fan?"

"It's not my favorite," he admitted.

"Well, I love it," Lanie said, taking a bite and smiling. "And it'll be a nice change from green beans."

"I may not love the asparagus," Max said after devouring the turkey, "but the turkey has my vote and should be one of the entrees."

Nate laughed. "We still have three other entrees to try." He waved a fork at Max. "Don't fill up on the first option."

As if on cue, the chef emerged again with a tray of steak and an array of vegetables. "We have filet mignon with baked potato and a roasted vegetable medley."

Without waiting for an invitation, Max helped himself to a filet and dug in. He could get used to wedding tastings if it meant he got to eat such delicious food. Maybe he could convince Carissa to allow him to accompany her on meetings with future clients.

"Dad!" Lanie cried out. "You're not supposed to have red meat."

Max harrumphed. "The doctor said I can in moderation."

"You and I have very different definitions of what counts as 'moderation.'"

"Why can't you have red meat?" Carissa asked, her eyebrows pinching together.

Just as Max opened his mouth to respond, Lanie cut in. "Because of his cholesterol."

"It's a little high," Max replied, unable to keep the growing irritation out of his tone.

"A little?" Lanie scoffed. "If you don't get it under control, you're going to have to start taking medication, and we both know how much you hate the side effects."

"I'm fine," he growled, stabbing his fork into the thick cut of beef.

"What do you think of the options?" Carissa asked, clearly trying to prevent another argument.

"I tend to agree with Max on the turkey," Nate said. "And it fits our Christmas theme perfectly."

Lanie pressed her lips together and nodded. Once again, Max found himself silently thanking God for Nate. He only wished his future son-in-law wasn't always needed to step in and defuse the situation between Max and Lanie.

The rest of the meal passed in a tense silence. After the last entree had been served, Carissa handed out scorecards to everyone to help determine which dishes would be included in the final menu. Each card had four options: steak, turkey, crab cake, and ham.

"Rank your favorite dish from one to four, with one being what you liked best and four representing what you liked least. The two entrees with the most votes will be served along with the vegetarian dish we selected last time."

Max ranked his favorites as steak, turkey, crab cake, and ham. Although he enjoyed the crab cake, it was the most expensive option, and he wanted to be mindful of Lanie and Nate's budget. He assumed they would choose either the turkey or the ham for their Christmas theme.

"All right," Carissa said after tallying their responses. "It looks like turkey and steak received the most votes for first and second place."

The chef returned and took the cards from Carissa. After a brief conversation, he signaled for the servers to clear the table.

Carissa checked off the caterer. "We're all set! The last thing the caterer will need from us is a final head count, which is due about two weeks before your wedding. Your invitations arrived yesterday, and we need to get those out by the end of next week." Her face relaxed into an easy smile. "We're right on track!"

Lanie breathed a sigh of relief. "That's good to hear." She hugged Carissa. "We couldn't have done this without you."

"It's what I'm here for." Carissa patted Lanie's back. "Now, why don't you two kids go have some fun?"

"Sounds good to me." Nate grabbed Lanie's hand. "Thanks for everything, Carissa." Without another word, he led Lanie away.

Max stared after them, wondering if that meant he was heading to his house alone.

"How about that drink?" Carissa asked.

Max tore his gaze away from his daughter's retreating back. "Sounds good to me."

They left the small dining area and headed to the bar. The bar was mostly empty, and they had their choice of seats. After they sat near a quiet corner, the bartender came over.

"What'll you have?"

Max glanced at Carissa. "Ladies first."

"I'll have a whiskey, neat."

His eyes widened, but he ordered the same. After the bartender walked away, he stared at her. "I didn't take you for a whiskey girl."

"Normally, I don't drink hard liquor straight like that, but it's been a week, and I want something that's going to burn on the way down."

"Speaking of that," Max said, his tone betraying his hesitation, "do you want to talk about it or...?"

She nodded at the bartender, who was preparing their drinks. "Let's wait until we've had a round."

Once the drinks were in front of them, Carissa closed her eyes and took a sip. "Just what I needed."

"I half expected you to take it like a shot," he joked.

"Don't tempt me." She laughed. Her sips did become more pronounced, and soon, she was waving the bartender over for another.

"You as well?" the bartender asked.

Max glanced at his drink, which he'd barely touched. "I'm good for now."

An amused smile pulled at Carissa's lips. "You need to keep up."

"I'll get there." Max took another sip of his whiskey.

After Carissa had her second glass in front of her, she curled her fingers around it. "So, I'm sure you're wondering why I decided to work with Imaginavigation Enterprises after everything that's happened."

He nodded, saving himself from speaking by draining his glass. The bartender must have expected that because a second later, he'd poured another two ounces for Max.

"It's not as bad as I originally feared. I'd be working mostly with Colin, and I wouldn't have to go into DC unless I wanted to." She proceeded to tell him the entire conversation she'd had with Colin Fields.

When she finished, she downed half her second round of whiskey. Her eyes watered, but otherwise, it didn't seem to impact her at all.

"At least you're not working directly with the CEO." Max ran a hand through his hair. "But can you trust Colin with your idea?"

She snorted. "I can't trust him to pull it off without me, no. That guy has barely planned a birthday party, let alone something as complicated as a retreat. Still, he's given me no reason not to trust him to serve as an intermediary between Jacob and me. Besides, as I told you the other day, this is the first real chance I've had to branch out and expand my business."

Max twirled his now-empty glass on the bar in front of him. The last thing he wanted to do was discourage her dream, but he couldn't quite shake the bad feeling swirling around in his stomach. From everything she'd said about Jacob, he sounded like bad news, and Max couldn't see any good coming from the job.

But he forced a smile and kept his opinions to himself. "It sounds like you've put a lot of thought into this, and it does seem like a good opportunity."

"I hear a 'but' in there somewhere." Carissa raised an eyebrow.

Biting back a smile, he cleared his throat. "Just... Be careful. Jacob sounds like a real snake."

Her eyes softened, and she took his hand. "I appreciate your concern, and I promise to take it to heart."

"That's all I ask."

"I want to apologize," she continued, running her thumb over his knuckles. "I shouldn't have left so abruptly from Bea's."

"It's okay. I'm sorry I tried to fix it when it was clear you needed to vent."

"I know you meant well." She took a deep breath. "And I'm sorry I've been MIA the last few days. Between receiving the news I wasn't chosen and starting to work with Colin as a consultant, I've had a lot going on lately, and it's important to me to keep my work life separate from my personal life." Her smile faded. "I'm usually better about maintaining a balance."

"It's a new venture for you. It's understandable that it's going to take up more of your time."

"But I'm glad I got a chance to see you again."

"Yeah?" His chest filled with warmth.

"I've missed you."

Impulsively, he lifted his hand and cupped her cheek. "I've missed you too."

Her eyes widened, and her gaze darted nervously around the bar. As it was a weeknight, there weren't many other patrons around. Still, he didn't want to make her uncomfortable. He lowered his hand and shifted away from her.

With a sigh, she placed her glass on the bar and signaled to the bartender. "It's getting harder and harder to keep my distance from you."

"I know what you mean." His voice came out huskier than he intended. "But the wedding is in just over two months."

Her lips quirked up. "I've never been so ready to be done with an event I was planning."

They paid for their drinks and left the restaurant. He walked her to her car and tried to ignore the familiar pull that seemed to draw them together like magnets.

"Will Lanie still be against us dating after the wedding?" she asked as she unlocked her car door.

"Why would she?" Max frowned. "Her fear seems focused on how our relationship might make things more stressful for her if we broke up before the wedding."

"I hope that's the case."

He stepped back to allow her to climb into the car, and once she was settled, he closed the door. As he walked to his truck, he sent up a small prayer that things would work out with her new business venture. But deep down, he feared it was all going to blow up in her face.

Chapter Eighteen

The next day, Carissa had her first virtual meeting with Colin. He warned her Jacob would be sitting in, but she felt confident she could handle it. At least they weren't in the same room, and she wasn't above pretending to have connection issues if he tried to derail the meeting.

She was the first to sign in, and she made sure her audio and video were working well. A few minutes later, Colin popped onto her screen, and she could just make out Jacob in the back of the room. His feet were propped on the conference table, and he scribbled away at a notebook in his lap.

"Good morning, Carissa," Colin said.

"Morning, Colin. How are you?"

"Doing well." The pleasantries out of the way, he got right to business. "So, according to your proposal, we need to contact the cabin rental office to determine when would be the best time for our retreat. Are you able to work on that this weekend?"

Carissa drummed her fingers on her desk. Working weekends was quite normal for wedding planning since most events occurred on Saturdays, but she'd hoped to keep the corporate retreat to normal business hours. While she'd told Max she wouldn't join him for the fall festival in town, she still hoped to go on her own. It was one of the highlights of the season.

"I can give them a call today to set up a meeting for either Saturday or sometime next week, but Sunday, I am unavailable."

Jacob's feet disappeared from view, and he leaned toward the camera. "What do you mean, you're 'unavailable'?"

Before she could answer, Colin intervened. "Now, Jacob, we have a contract with Carissa for a certain number of hours, but there is no stipulation of when those hours must occur. If she doesn't want to work Sundays, that's perfectly fine."

"Says you," Jacob retorted. He moved directly behind Colin. "We need to get this booked ASAP. Whatever weekend plans you have can be canceled, at least until we're further along in the process."

Her mouth fell open. "You can't be serious."

A sinister smile came over his face. "Unless you're not up to the task. I'm sure we can compensate you for the idea, and Colin can handle things."

Colin paled. "Sir, with all due respect, an event this large is beyond my capabilities."

"Then perhaps we need to replace you as well," Jacob said.

At least it's not just me. Jacob had made it clear he didn't see wedding planning as a real business, but watching him interact with Colin, Carissa suspected he was simply a jerk to everyone.

"Excuse me," she called, hoping to regain control of the situation.

Both men turned to the screen but with very different expressions. Colin gave her a pleading look, while Jacob's furrowed brow almost felt like a challenge. Carissa squared her shoulders.

"You're not even planning to host this event until sometime next year," she began, strategically sidestepping the question of her schedule. "While it's important we book the location as early as possible, a few days won't make that big of a difference."

Jacob opened his mouth to respond, but she continued before he could. "I will contact the rental office today and set up a conference call Colin can attend. In the meantime, we should brainstorm a list of ideas for activities we'd like to plan. That way, we are not only fully prepared to discuss our needs with the rental office, but we can also ask if they have suggestions of places to contact."

It was the men's turn to gape at her. Colin appeared impressed, but Jacob's expression was a mixture of annoyance and uncertainty. She smiled pleasantly at the camera, but inside, she was dancing a jig.

Clearly, this man has never had someone tell him no and stick to it. "I'm going to share my screen now and show you what I've been working on over the last few days."

The rest of the meeting went smoothly, in large part because Jacob appeared too dumbfounded by her standing up to him to say anything. After they said their goodbyes, Carissa signed off and pumped her fist in the air. *Carissa: 1, Jacob: 0.*

True to her word, she called the rental office as soon as she finished celebrating. The last thing she needed was for Jacob to start harassing her for updates the moment he recovered from her taking control of the meeting.

"Good morning, The Lodges at Sunset Village, Kevin speaking."

"Hello, Kevin. My name is Carissa, and I'm coordinating a corporate retreat on behalf of Imaginavigation Enterprises. I was wondering if we could set up a call to discuss our options for renting several cabins from you sometime next year."

After a moment of silence, Kevin responded. "Sure thing, Carissa. Let me check my calendar." The clacking of keys wafted over the phone. "I can meet anytime Monday morning between the hours of nine and eleven or Wednesday after one in the afternoon."

Apparently, she wasn't the only one who didn't want to work weekends. "Let's do Monday at nine. Can you provide me with an email address so I can send you the details?"

When she got off the phone, she sent the appointment to Kevin with a carbon copy to Jacob and Colin. Her smile was smug as she closed her computer.

And I thought working with Jacob was going to be hard.

By the time Sunday rolled around, Carissa was desperately in need of a break. Despite her prompt scheduling of the appointment to discuss the cabin rental, Jacob had been blowing up her phone for the last few days with the most asinine requests. From an updated list of potential activities, most of which he ended up rejecting, to insisting she put together a detailed itinerary, his demands were beginning to make her regret taking on the project. Ignoring the fact they hadn't even determined the season for the retreat, let alone set a date, she did the best she could with the information she had. Her updated itinerary accounted for things like not being able to take a boat ride in the middle of December or an inability to ski down a mountain in July.

But she wasn't going to let Jacob interrupt her fun-filled day at the festival. She put her phone on do not disturb with a voicemail stating she was unavailable for the day and would respond Monday morning. Although she suspected her decision would backfire and she'd have a million voicemails and texts to deal with, that was a problem for future Carissa.

Her doorbell rang unexpectedly as she was getting ready to head to the festival. When she opened it, Max stood on her front porch with a bouquet of flowers in lovely autumn colors. Red roses, orange lilies, and a couple of sunflowers were interspersed with gold and purple chrysanthemums.

"Well, this is a nice surprise." She accepted the flowers and breathed in their sweet scent.

"I saw these as I was walking past the florist shop on my way to the fall festival, and I thought of you." He shifted his weight to his back foot. "Though now that I'm here, I'm wondering if this is too forward."

"Perhaps, but they're beautiful, so I can't quite bring myself to be cross with you." She smiled and glanced behind him. "You're going to the festival alone?"

"I told the kids I'd meet them there."

A stab of guilt hit her stomach, but she nodded. "Would you like to come in for a moment? I'm going to put these in water."

It took longer than she wanted to find a vase. The last time she'd received flowers was from Chuck for their wedding anniversary. After he died, she'd packed her vases into boxes, not wanting the constant reminder.

The vase she chose was dusty and had a small crack at the top, but otherwise, it appeared in good shape. While she washed it, Max set to work trimming the flowers. When the vase was clean and dry, she began arranging the blooms. Her fingers moved with the familiarity of someone who had successfully avoided bouquet catastrophes at many a wedding. Once she was satisfied, she set the vase near the window.

Chuck would never have gotten her an assortment like that, preferring the traditional dozen roses. But somehow, the arrangement fit Max and their blossoming relationship. The riot of color had a complicated beauty that drew the eye and delighted the senses.

Max placed a hand on her shoulder and gently turned her toward him. "I should get going. I promised Lanie I'd be there for lunch."

"Thank you for the flowers. They're lovely."

His lips lifted in a grin. "Lovely flowers for a lovely lady."

Her face warmed, and she dropped her gaze. "Perhaps I'll see you at the festival."

When he didn't immediately respond, she looked up. A dozen emotions seemed to dance across his face.

"You're going?"

"Of course. I love the fall festival. It's my favorite event of the year."

A muscle feathered in his jaw. "I see."

Too late, she realized he was hurt. "Max, it's not that I don't want to go with you. I do. It's just—you promised Lanie we wouldn't date, and this would be the second outing with your children that I crashed."

"I invited you to go before Lanie brought it up to me. I could have told her..." He appeared at a loss for words.

"Exactly. There's nothing you could have said that wouldn't have made it sound as if you'd broken your word." She smiled sadly. "But if we run into each other there, then it's less suspicious."

The light returned to his brown eyes. "I hadn't considered that."

She touched his arm. "Go meet up with your kids. I'll head over in a few minutes."

After he'd backed onto the street and driven away, Carissa went into her house. She found herself drawn to the flowers like a moth to a flame. Part of her wondered if she shouldn't have refused them. As she'd told Max the other night, it was getting more and more difficult to be around him and not act on her feelings.

At the same time, if she hadn't accepted the flowers, it would have hurt Max, and she didn't want to do that either. She sighed. She was walking a fine line between protecting her business relationship with Lanie and trying not to fall head over heels for Max, and it was getting exhausting.

When she arrived at the festival, the town square was packed. The familiar scents of funnel cake and hot cocoa filled the air. Carissa closed her eyes, remembering the last time she'd come to the festival with Chuck. It was the last big outing he'd had before he got too sick to leave the house.

She opened her eyes as a stab of pain hit her chest. Though she stood in a sea of people, she'd never felt more alone. Perhaps she should have stayed home.

But then, through the crowd, she saw Max, and her heart skipped a beat. She wouldn't approach him yet, as it might look too coincidental. Just knowing he was there helped ease the ache in her heart, and she forced herself to put one foot in front of the other.

"Carissa!" a familiar voice called. She turned to find Rose and Steven coming up behind her.

"It's good to see you both," Carissa said, pulling Rose in for a brief hug. Her gaze swept over Steven. "No cane today?"

"The doctor said I should try to get around without it." He nudged Rose with his elbow. "And she promised not to let me fall flat on my face."

"Provided you behave." Rose's dark eyes glinted with mischief.

"I'll do my best, but no promises," Steven teased, sliding his arm around her shoulders. He nodded to Carissa. "Are you meeting someone?"

"Nope, I'm here by my lonesome." Carissa's voice cracked on that last word, and she forced a smile to cover it.

"We're meeting up with Lanie, Nate, and Dad. You're welcome to join us."

"Oh, I wouldn't want to intrude," Carissa protested, though deep down, she couldn't help feeling a little thrill. Her plan to make it look as if she and Max had bumped into each other was going better than she could have imagined.

Rose scoffed. "There's no intrusion. After working with us for two years, you're practically part of the family." She took Carissa by the hand and led her to the ticket booth.

A moment later, they joined Lanie, Nate, and Max at the entrance. Lanie was purchasing wristbands for the rest of the group.

"Look who we found," Rose said with a smile.

Lanie glanced over her shoulder. When she saw Carissa, her forehead creased, but the frown disappeared before Carissa could decipher it.

"Make that six wristbands, please," Lanie said. Once she completed her order, she stepped out of line and handed them each a band. "This allows you to enter the festival. Everything except food is included."

"Thanks." Carissa put the band on her wrist. "I can pay you back."

"There's no need." Lanie led the way into the festival.

As she followed the group, Carissa's eyes widened as she took in the plethora of activities awaiting them. The entire town square was closed to traffic. The festival offered pumpkin-carving stations and pie-eating contests, hayrides, a petting zoo, a small carnival with questionably safe rides, and even a few demonstrations scheduled throughout the day. Though overwhelming, it was exactly the distraction she needed after dealing with Jacob all week.

"Let's go sign up for a hayride before they're booked up," Lanie suggested.

Carissa swallowed. Hay wreaked havoc on her sinuses, and the last thing she wanted to do was spend the day sneezing and sniffling. "Oh, um, you go on ahead. I'm happy to watch your things."

"Are you sure?" Lanie raised an eyebrow. "The hayrides are a lot of fun, and they take you to a farm not far from here with a pumpkin patch."

"Positive," Carissa said.

"Count me out as well," Steven chimed in. "Not sure I'd be able to haul myself up into that wagon."

His sister's face fell. "Oh gosh, I hadn't even thought of that." She bit her lip. "Maybe we should pick something else to do."

Stepping forward, Max pointed at Lanie. "You, Nate, and Rose can go on a hayride, and Steven, Carissa, and I will scope out the food options for lunch."

"All right," Lanie said, though her disappointment was palpable. "Meet back here in a few?"

"Unless there's a hayride available before then. Just text us if that's the case, and we'll meet you afterward."

After they split into two groups of three, Carissa breathed a sigh of relief, though she worried Max had given up something he might have enjoyed to stay with her and Steven.

"You could have gone," she murmured.

He grunted. "I'm not much into hayrides myself." Leaning closer, he whispered, "Besides, I haven't seen much of you with this new project you've got going on. I want to make the most of the time we have."

"Should I leave you two alone?" Steven asked.

They turned to find him leaning against a light pole, crossing his arms. Warmth spread over Carissa's cheeks, but Steven appeared more amused than annoyed.

"Let's go check out the food stands. I've been smelling funnel cake since we arrived, and I've got a hankering for it now." Max headed toward the food trucks.

"Isn't it a bit early for that?" Steven asked.

"It's a festival," Max replied. "There are no rules."

Several food trucks were parked in a semicircle on the edge of the festival. A funnel cake truck was toward the middle of the semicircle, and Max made a beeline for it, stopping only when his phone vibrated.

"Lanie said they're catching the next hayride and will be about a half hour. I figure we can grab a couple of funnel cakes now for a snack"—Max slipped his phone back into his pocket—"and then make our way over to the petting zoo. Then later, there's a woodworking demonstration I'd like to check out."

Carissa smiled. "You could probably teach that."

"Not quite." Max laughed. "I'm still a bit rusty, but I've about finished all of the furniture I had started before my divorce."

"I'd love to see it sometime."

After glancing back at Steven, who had snagged a picnic table, Max continued in a low voice, "Maybe you can come over for dinner tonight. The kids are going out, but I'm making spaghetti, and I have enough for two."

A laugh bubbled up in her throat. "I've heard horror stories about your cooking."

"Lanie talks too much," he muttered. "Besides, it's hard to burn spaghetti."

"Somehow, I think you could pull it off."

He glared at her. "Now you have to come to dinner so I can prove you wrong."

"That sounds too much like a date." She frowned. "And I don't want to upset Lanie. What if I come by tomorrow while she's at school? You could cook me lunch instead."

Part of her hoped he would insist on dinner. Even burnt spaghetti sounded better than spending yet another evening eating a microwaved meal in her living room. It'd been years since she'd had a home-cooked meal.

But they shouldn't risk it. What if Lanie came home early? How would she react to Carissa having dinner with her father? Carissa snuck a glance at Max. *And how can I resist kissing him if we're alone together?*

"All right," Max said, though she could hear the reluctance in his voice. "How about I make some fried chicken and potato salad?"

Carissa smiled. "That sounds delicious."

Chapter Nineteen

MAX COULDN'T REMEMBER THE last time he'd had so much fun. After Lanie, Nate, and Rose returned from the hayride, they met the rest of the group at the picnic tables. Lanie and Nate each carried a pumpkin because Lanie had insisted they needed to carve at least two for Halloween. While she'd chosen a taller pumpkin with a more oval shape, Nate's choice was short, squat, and fat. Or as Carissa said, "pleasantly plump."

"We should pick up those pumpkin-carving kits at the store before we go," Lanie said, setting her pumpkin on the table before sliding onto the bench and helping herself to some funnel cake.

Max raised an eyebrow. "You never said anything about carving some intricate design."

Her lower lip pushed out in a pout, and he was reminded of when she was younger and could convince him to do anything she wanted. He could already feel himself caving. Clearly, not much had changed in the intervening years.

"But the triangle eyes and nose with a mostly toothless grin is overdone," she whined.

"Are you kidding?" Steven asked, admiring the pumpkin Rose had gotten for the two of them. "It's a classic."

As his children continued to bicker over the best pumpkin design, Max whispered to Carissa, "Either way this goes, I'm betting I'll be carving all of the pumpkins."

Her eyes twinkled in amusement. "You could have said no."

He sighed. "True." But then he waved his hand. "I'll do anything to see her happy, though."

"Who knew you were such an old softy?" Carissa teased.

"Keep that to yourself," he grumbled. "I've got a reputation to protect."

"So, who's up for the pie-eating contest?" Steven asked as he clambered over the picnic table bench.

Max patted his stomach. "I'm still full of the funnel cake, but you go on ahead."

Rose and Lanie exchanged a look. "How about we cheer you on from the sidelines?"

"Aw, come on," Steven said, his face falling. Then he turned to Nate. "What about you? Are you game?"

Though it was clear from his expression that trying to quickly eat a pie was just about the last thing Nate wanted to do, he gave a reluctant nod. "Sure, I'll give it a go."

"Awesome!" Steven pumped his fist in the air, which almost caused him to lose his balance. Nate, Lanie, and Rose followed him toward the tent where the contest was being held, leaving Carissa and Max alone.

"What would you like to do?" he asked her as he offered his arm.

"Let's visit the petting zoo."

He steered them in that direction. It was one of the more popular attractions, especially among the children. They bought some feed and took it to a couple of goats hanging out near the edge of the pen.

"I've always wanted a goat," Carissa said with a happy sigh.

"That's an unusual pet."

Her eyes remained on the goats. "It is, but they're more than pets. You can milk them, and they can be like miniature lawn mowers, if you think about it."

Max laughed. "I suppose that's true." He cleared his throat. "Chuck didn't want them?"

"He did, but we didn't have the room or the time it would have taken to care for them." She raised her face and met his gaze. "Our retirement plan was to buy some land for goats, a garden, and maybe even a horse."

"Oh," he said, unsure of what else to do. Internally, he cringed. It seemed like one of those moments where he should either say something comforting about her late husband or maybe even change the subject so she didn't have to dwell on the loss. But he'd never been especially good at knowing what to say or do in such situations.

"Anyway, I doubt I could afford something like that on my own," she continued, turning back to the goats.

He shifted uncomfortably. Was she hoping he would offer to help fulfill that dream? Wouldn't that be awkward, since she'd planned to do it with another man? It felt too soon to be talking about the future in that way.

"Did you have a plan like that with Melody?" she asked when he didn't say anything.

"Uh, not really. I looked forward to the day when the kids were grown and it would just be the two of us." He shuffled his feet. "But she was hoping to travel more, and it's not my thing."

Standing, she brushed her hands on her pants. "Well, you're retired now and soon to be an empty nester. Have you made any plans for after Lanie is married?"

He didn't want to talk about how much he was dreading it. When Lanie had announced her engagement, he'd expected the planning to take at least a year. After all, Rose and Steven had taken two years to plan their wedding. Then, Lanie had initially planned to get married on her mother's birthday, which hadn't gone over well. When Rose had recommended December, a part of Max died. So little time left before she would be too busy for her old man.

"I haven't given it much thought," he finally admitted. Forcing a smile, he gestured to the goats. "But I'm not opposed to trying out life with goats." Her face contorted, and he worried he'd said the wrong thing.

"We should probably get back to the others," she said before she walked away.

Stifling a sigh, he trudged after her. *Way to ruin an otherwise perfect day.* Though he wasn't sure exactly what he'd done wrong. Was it the combined future that scared her off or his attempt to co-opt a plan she'd had with her late husband? He supposed either could have caused her negative reaction.

He hurried to catch up with her. "I'm sorry if I came on too strong back there."

"It's okay. You were mostly joking." Her eyes met his briefly before refocusing on the path before them. "It hit a little close to home because I haven't given up on the dreams I had with Chuck, but I'm also not sure I'd want to share them with someone else."

"I understand," he said, and he did, even if it hurt. "Maybe we can come up with some new dreams of our own."

A small smile lit up her face. "I'd like that."

~ ❧ ~

The next day, Max was in the kitchen, putting the breaded chicken in the fryer, when the doorbell rang. He hurried over to let Carissa in.

"Welcome to my humble abode," he said with a smile as he took her coat. His heart stopped as he took in her outfit. Her blue sweaterdress seemed to hug every curve, and it matched the deep blue of her eyes. "You look beautiful."

Her cheeks flushed pink as she stepped around him into the kitchen. "Can I help?"

"The potatoes should be cool enough to mix with the rest of the ingredients." He gestured to the colander in the sink.

She shook out the colander to rid it of excess water before dumping the potatoes into a bowl. Then she mixed in the rest of the ingredients of the potato salad. They worked together in comfortable silence.

Max realized that was something he and Melody had rarely done. When the kids were young, Melody stayed home with them and cooked dinner around Max's shift work as an electrical lineman. When she went back to work, he took over the cooking whenever he was home. Their schedules didn't allow them many opportunities to cook together. An ache developed in his chest as he supposed that fact basically summed up their marriage. Like their schedules, they were never in sync.

"It's been a long time since I cooked with someone," Carissa said as if reading his mind.

"Oh?" He checked the chicken. "You and Chuck cooked together often?"

"Sort of. He did most of the cooking. I was relegated to side tasks like chopping or putting together a salad." She smiled wistfully. "But I loved spending time with him in the kitchen. It was our way of realigning after being away from each other all day."

The ache in Max's chest grew. From the way Carissa talked, he could tell hers had been a happy marriage, and he envied her. Though he and Melody had parted on good terms, they'd managed to reconcile only right before they'd run out of time.

"But it also caused most of our fights," Carissa continued, a hint of amusement in her voice.

"Fights?" Max turned toward her with a raised eyebrow.

"Oh yes. He was a much more by-the-book cook than I was. If a recipe called for a pinch of salt, he would ensure it had exactly one pinch." She rolled her eyes. "It didn't matter that such forms of measurement are less than accurate or that some recipes suggested adding salt to taste."

"And I take it you were much less stringent in the kitchen?"

She laughed. "That's putting it mildly. I saw a meme on social media recently that said something about adding spices to a dish until my ancestors tell me 'That's enough, child.'" Her smile widened. "That fits me perfectly."

"I've never been much for recipes either, which has been my downfall. At least, if you ask Lanie." He grimaced. "But I've forced myself to learn average cooking times, so I don't burn things as much as I used to."

"For which I'm sure your daughter is grateful."

"I hope so," he said.

The first batch of chicken was done, and Max carefully removed the pieces from the fryer. After placing them on a paper towel to soak up the excess grease, he added the next batch of chicken pieces to the oil. The pan popped and sizzled with each new addition.

While the chicken cooked, he grabbed two plates and silverware before setting the table. The kitchen had warmed considerably with the heat from the stove, and he pushed his sleeves up in an attempt to cool his skin.

"Would you like some wine?" he asked with trepidation. He was more of a beer guy and had no idea what sort of wine should be served with fried chicken, but Lanie had several bottles of red and white in the small wine cabinet she'd insisted on buying after moving in.

"Mm, wine makes me sleepy. I'll stick with water."

A wave of relief flowed over him as he took out two glasses and filled them with ice and water from the fridge. He set them on the table along with the bowl of potato salad.

"The chicken is almost ready," he called. "If you want to grab a seat, I'll bring the platter over."

The sound of a chair leg scraping across the tile rang out behind him. After removing the last of the chicken pieces from the fryer, he set them on the paper towel then unplugged the fryer. Once he'd soaked up most of the grease, he transferred the chicken to a platter and carried it to the table.

They were quiet as they served themselves. Somehow, that afternoon felt different from their lunch the other day, more intimate since they were completely alone. Max snuck glances at her, marveling at the fact that a few months ago, they could barely stand to be in the same room. And yet, there they were, sharing a meal as if it was the most natural thing in the world. The thought made him smile.

"What's going on in that head of yours?" she asked, catching him staring.

"I was thinking of how much we used to hate each other."

She barked a laugh. "Hate's a bit of a strong word." She lowered her gaze then looked up at him from beneath her lashes. "But I'm much happier with where we are now."

"As am I." He cleared his throat. "After we finish up here, I'll show you what I've been working on in the garage, and maybe you can give me some advice on a wedding gift for Lanie."

Carissa cocked her head. "Oh?"

"I wanted to give her the finished pieces I've been working on, but she's moving into a furnished house with Nate. I'd prefer if my gift was both meaningful and useful."

"I'd love to see what you've been working on, though I have no idea what assistance I can provide on a gift idea." She smiled. "I usually pick something off the couple's registry."

"It needs to be special," Max insisted.

She placed a hand on his arm. "I'm sure no matter what you decide to give her, it will be."

Once they finished eating, Max cleared the table before putting the dishes in the sink. "I'll take care of those in a bit," he said as he grabbed her hand and pulled her from her seat. He was eager to gauge her reaction to the pieces he'd finished.

After flicking on the light in the garage, he removed the sheets one by one, glancing at Carissa as he did so. The nightstands were revealed first then a small chest of drawers. Finally, he revealed the table, which hadn't needed much work.

"These are amazing," Carissa said as she moved closer to the pieces.

"Thank you." He dropped his gaze, feeling suddenly shy. Her approval meant more to him than he'd expected.

"What were you planning to give Lanie?"

Stepping around her, he pointed at the nightstands. "These might work in the master bedroom at Nate's house, but he has a pair that match the bedframe and dresser."

"They are striking, but I can understand your hesitation if Nate already has nightstands." She cocked her head. "What about end tables in the living room?"

"Nate's living room is rather small. I'm not sure they'll fit."

With a nod, she turned to the other pieces. "I suspect Nate already has a table as well. The chest of drawers is small enough to be placed on a surface like a dresser or nightstand."

"It seems too small for a wedding gift."

Her head shot up. "Not if you made it. I'm sure Lanie could store her jewelry in there or something similar."

"I guess." As much as he understood Carissa's point, it wasn't enough to show Lanie how much he loved her. He wanted his wedding gift to stand out.

Carissa moved beside him and put her hand on his shoulder. "I'm sure you'll come up with something. You still have two months until the wedding."

"That's not a lot of time to come up with something from scratch."

She smiled. "I have faith in you."

Her words caused a flood of emotions to flow through him. Without thinking, Max slid his hand over her cheek and into her hair. Bending his head, he searched her eyes for a moment before tentatively brushing his lips against hers. He pulled back, afraid he'd gone too far. But before he could move away, she pushed up on her tiptoes and kissed him more fervently. Her arms wrapped around his neck, pressing her body against his.

Every inch of his body felt like it was on fire. His heart pounded as he slipped his other arm around her waist, drawing her closer.

A moment later, she took a ragged breath and stumbled back. The cool air that rushed in from her absence was like a bucket of cold water. As he came back to his senses, he struggled to think of what to say. She'd wanted to take things slowly. He'd promised Lanie they wouldn't date. And yet, there he was, practically making out with her in the middle of his garage.

But he didn't regret it for one moment. Things had changed between them over a month ago, and he'd resisted the urge to kiss her every time they were alone together. However, if he'd hoped that finally giving in to that urge would squelch the desire, he was sorely mistaken. If anything, that kiss made him want her more.

"Carissa, I—"

"Don't," she whispered. "Don't say anything."

"But—"

"School will be out soon. I-I'd better go before Lanie gets home."

Though his lips still burned from the warmth of her kiss, his heart sank. He reached for her, but she shifted away from him. "Shouldn't we talk about this?"

When she finally lifted her head to look at him, her expression seemed to change by the second. First, her eyes filled with longing, then her eyebrows pulled together in confusion. She brought her hand to her mouth.

"We shouldn't have—I mean, I wanted to, but..." She shook her head. "I have to go." Without waiting for a response, she rushed out of the room.

Max stood frozen in his garage. Part of him wanted to run after her, but he couldn't seem to convince his legs to move. The warmth and joy he'd experienced just moments before when she was in his arms felt like a distant memory. In its place was a cold, miserable emptiness. He didn't know what had happened, but he feared he'd screwed up in ways he couldn't yet fathom.

# Chapter Twenty

Carissa stared at her reflection in the mirror as she brushed her graying hair back into a clip. Her cheeks appeared permanently flushed, though that might have had something to do with the fact she couldn't get Max's kiss out of her mind.

"Lanie will be here any moment," she told herself. "Focus."

If only she'd had the forethought to postpone the meeting with Lanie, but her mind had been a chaotic mess, and she'd barely slept the night before. She feared Lanie would see right through her thin grasp on her emotions and know what Carissa and Max had done.

All day, Carissa had vacillated between calling Max and pretending the kiss had never happened. They were supposed to be keeping their distance from each other, and she'd assumed, foolishly, that lunch would be safe.

Absolutely careless. They'd had several close calls previously, but something had always interrupted them at the perfect moment. The day before, they'd been alone in Max's house with little chance of anyone or anything drawing their attention away from each other.

Talk about the perfect storm. Still, despite her fears about Lanie learning the truth and how she might react, Carissa couldn't quite bring herself to regret the kiss. She'd wanted to kiss him since things between them had started to change. *And now that I know, I want more.*

A knock at the door sent Carissa's heart racing. She took a deep breath and one last glance in the mirror. Other than the flush on her cheeks, her face didn't betray her guilt.

When Carissa opened the door, Lanie greeted her with a smile. *So far so good.* Carissa led them into the dining room, where she'd set up the piles of cardstock and envelopes that made up Lanie's wedding invitations.

"These look amazing," Lanie said as she lifted an invitation. The design was simple with a white background, dark-green lettering, and a poinsettia at the top of the card.

"I'm glad you like them. I've got my calligraphy pen set up as well as an assortment of pens for writing the addresses on the envelopes."

"Thank you for agreeing to do this." Lanie stared at the table with wide eyes. "I love calligraphy, but I lack the skill."

Carissa waved a hand. "It's no problem at all. I do this as a regular service for all my clients if they request it."

They sat down to work, and Carissa was relieved to have something to focus on. The silence made her uncomfortable, and she wished she could think of something to say.

"Did you enjoy the fall festival?" Lanie asked.

Carissa carefully wrote out a name in her fancy script before responding. "It's my favorite event of the season."

"It's one of mine too." Lanie took the finished inner envelope and slipped the invitation and RSVP card into it. "Though I haven't been in a while due to school." She cleared her throat. "I was glad my father was able to join us."

Warmth rushed to Carissa's cheeks, and she kept her eyes on the next invitation. "You two seem to be getting along better." She snuck a glance at Lanie. "At least, as long as the conversation stays far away from the wedding."

Lanie snorted. "The wedding is only one of many topics we seem to avoid. I can't wait to move in with Nate and get some distance from Dad." She gave Carissa a rueful smile. "It sounds odd, but I'm hoping not living together anymore will give us the space to improve our relationship." Her face darkened. "Though he doesn't agree."

"Why do you think it'll help?" Carissa chose her words carefully.

"I can't explain it." Lanie shrugged. "But I guess I'm hoping having my own space and not seeing him every day will give me some breathing room to come to terms with what has happened between us in the past. Sometimes, I feel like I'm suffocating in that house with him, and new resentments start to build on top of the old."

Carissa set down her pen and studied Lanie. "Have you tried to explain that to him?"

"At this point, I'm trying to keep the peace as much as possible. And besides, whenever we have a conversation that starts to get too deep, he bails." Lanie rolled her eyes. "He's not exactly the picture of emotional maturity."

A couple of months ago, Carissa would have wholeheartedly agreed, but since she'd started spending more time with Max, she'd seen a different side of him. Her heart broke for both him and Lanie. It was clear he didn't want to be that vulnerable with his daughter, though Carissa couldn't quite understand why. It seemed like the key to repairing the hurts of the past and building a strong foundation for the future of their relationship.

"He relied a lot on my mother to communicate with us kids on his behalf," Lanie continued when Carissa didn't say anything. "And I suspect it's a struggle to figure out how to connect with us, especially now that I'm an adult." Her eyebrows pinched together, and she looked so much like Max, Carissa almost laughed. "Well, I should rephrase. He connects with Steven just fine. Which means I must be the problem."

Carissa leaned across the table and put a hand on Lanie's arm. "It takes two to make and two to break a relationship. I believe you two want the same thing, but it sounds like neither of you are sure how to go about it."

"Well, I can tell you, arguing with me about every little detail of my wedding is definitively *not* the right way to connect with me."

Carissa laughed. "Agreed."

"I appreciate that you've been able to mediate between us, though I hate you have to."

A laugh bubbled up in Carissa's throat. "That's a bit of an understatement, but I've grown accustomed to telling your father no. It seemed to be my go-to word during your brother's wedding."

"Rose said as much, and to be honest, I'm amazed at your fortitude." Lanie chuckled. "It takes a strong person to put up with my father's antics."

Carissa hid a smile. While Lanie wasn't wrong about Carissa's ability to handle Max's outbursts, the method she used had drastically changed between Steven's wedding and Lanie's event. "This isn't my first rodeo, and if at any point you feel like your father is overstepping, let me know." She snuck another glance at Lanie. "Though I would like to be clear on something as well."

Lanie blinked. "Oh?"

Carissa set her pen down and folded her arms on the table. "From now on, if you have a problem with how I'm handling something, I would appreciate it if you would come to me yourself."

To her surprise, Lanie rolled her eyes. "I *told* Dad I would talk to you about the flowers myself, but in true Max McAllister fashion, he didn't listen to me."

Carissa chuckled. "Why doesn't that surprise me? Have you ordered the silk flowers yet?"

"No. I was hoping to get your opinion on them."

As she addressed another envelope, Carissa smiled. "Tell me what you're thinking."

The next day, Carissa's phone rang bright and early. Jacob's name flashed on the screen, and for a moment, she debated not answering. She'd been avoiding the men in her life since her kiss with Max, and she was in no mood to put up with Jacob's antics first thing in the morning.

But she refused to act unprofessionally despite how much the CEO deserved it. "Good morning, Jacob. How can I help you?"

"We need to get eyes on the site," he said, for once jumping right to business. "The pictures on the cabin's website aren't enough. I need someone to go up to Deep Creek this weekend and scope out the cabin."

"All right." She bit back a sigh. "I'll call Colin tomorrow. Perhaps he can meet me there—"

"Colin has other work to attend to," Jacob cut in. "Book something for yourself. Leave no later than Friday."

The phone beeped three times, indicating Jacob had disconnected. Heat rushed to her face as she tossed the phone on the bed. The nerve of that man. Who did he think he was, demanding she drop everything and drive across the state with no notice? Not to mention, it was already Wednesday. What if the cabin was already booked for that weekend? With the fall foliage reaching its peak earlier in the month, she wouldn't be surprised if they were booked solid through the entire month of October.

But what could she do? If she didn't visit the cabin, she risked him firing her. After all, she'd done much of the legwork, researching various activities and setting up the meeting with the cabin rental office. While Colin likely wouldn't fully integrate her vision, he had enough information to make the event happen with a degree of success.

Muttering, she opened her laptop and clicked through to the site. To her surprise, a couple of cabins were available that weekend. As she clicked through to book one of them, her phone rang again. Her stomach knotted as Max's name flashed on her screen.

"Not now." She hated ignoring him after what had happened between them, but she wasn't ready to discuss the kiss. Besides, until she'd established herself in the corporate world, her client had to come first.

Chapter Twenty-One

MAX SAT BACK AS he finished carving a design into his last piece of furniture. It was hard to believe he'd managed to finish two nightstands, a table, and a couple of chairs in just over a month. Retirement certainly made it easier, but he hadn't expected the skill he'd honed all those years ago to come back so easily.

But something still didn't feel right. None of the pieces seemed worthy of being a wedding gift for Lanie. For one thing, she'd seen all of the furniture in various stages of completion, so there wouldn't be much of a surprise. Then there was the fact she was moving into a furnished house. While Carissa had said the nightstands could be put to other use, Max wanted to give Lanie something meaningful to start her new life.

Carissa. Though he'd tried to sound understanding when she'd called early that morning to tell him about her trip to Deep Creek, he couldn't quite hide his disappointment. He was relieved she'd told him about her plans, but the call had been brief, and they hadn't talked about their kiss. He suspected she'd been avoiding him, and that hurt more than if she'd told him she regretted the kiss.

Shaking his head, he forced his thoughts back to Lanie's wedding gift. *Sitting here staring off into space isn't helping anything.* He headed through the house to the back porch. Perhaps he would find some inspiration in nature.

When he slipped out the back door, a mourning dove was perched on the railing again. He had no idea if it was the same one that had lost its mate, but it seemed likely. The bird cooed softly at him before spreading its wings and taking flight.

It didn't go far, just up into the branches of the tree nearest his house. He could barely make out a small nest settled between a spot where two large branches met. From his vantage point, it resembled an arch.

The longer he stared at the bird's nest, the more an idea began to form. His daughter was getting married. What could be more beautiful for a wedding than an arch for Lanie and Nate to stand under as they said their vows?

Not one of those cheap plastic arches that fell apart in a strong gust of wind but a wooden arch with hand-carved roses and vines. With the right design, he could even create notches in the sides where silk flowers could be wrapped around the wood to give the arch more color.

He closed his eyes as he tried to picture it. A deep cherrywood would work nicely in the church where they were having the ceremony. After the wedding, the arch could act as an elaborate entrance to Nate's backyard. Maybe Lanie could plant a garden using the arch as a focal point.

His excitement grew as he considered the level of detail and work that would be needed for the project. The arch had to be portable so it could be moved first to the church then to Nate's house. He could make it in two pieces that interlocked at the top to allow it to be transported more easily. *What better way to represent their new union?*

"This will require a lot of fresh-cut wood," he muttered to himself, though he would have to figure out the size of the arch and where he might obtain wood pieces that were large enough. There was a time he could have made do with whatever he found in the forest near his house, but a project like the one he was planning would need more than whatever scraps he could harvest.

With one last look at the dove in the tree, he headed into his house. An internet search might help him get an idea of where to start. Then, he would have to figure out how to hide the arch from Lanie until the wedding. Perhaps he could get Carissa involved to help him plan the surprise.

A few minutes later, he was surfing the web for places to buy wood. He found quite a few reputable sources not too far away and sent up a quick prayer of thanks that he'd had the forethought to get a custom truck with an eight-foot bed. Without it, he wouldn't be able to transport the logs easily. A few lumber yards were located not far from him along with a woodworking store that offered classes in whittling and carving. Perhaps they would have a lead on where he could get raw materials for the arch.

After contacting a few places, he leaned back in his chair. Building a wedding arch from scratch was a huge project. Halloween was less than a week away, which meant he had roughly two months to finish the piece.

Am I biting off too much? Maybe I should think smaller, like a vanity or something that would fit in a small corner of the house.

That would certainly be an easier build. But Lanie already had a vanity she'd inherited from her mother. It was old and not in the greatest condition, but she loved it. Would she be open to replacing it?

Max stood and stretched. He would pick up some materials from the hardware store to build a vanity as a backup, but his heart was set on building the arch. It would be the perfect gift—a way to feature his love for his daughter in her wedding then provide a beautiful entryway for a backyard garden.

"She'll love it," he told himself.

———————

Two days later, Max drove across the county to meet with a tree-cutting service. They were scheduled to cut down a cherry tree and had told him he could have the wood if he hauled it away.

When he reached the address, the tree service was already there. The cherry tree was in the front yard of an old colonial-style house. Its branches spread across the lawn and were filled with colorful red and orange leaves. Max took a photo with his cell phone. Later on, it might be fun for Lanie to see what her arch had looked like as a tree.

"Are you here about the wood?" asked a young man with sandy-colored hair and tanned skin.

Max held out his hand. "Max McAllister."

"Adrian Lockes." Adrian shielded his eyes from the sun as he gazed up at the tree. "Any idea how much you want?"

"As much as I can fit in my truck. I'm building an arch for my daughter, and I want to make sure I have plenty of pieces to work with."

"Makes sense. My guys are about ready to start cutting off the branches. Just hang back here, and as they bring her down, you can tell us which pieces you want."

"Sounds good." They shook hands again, and Max moved away to lean against his truck. As the men began tying ropes around the tree to hoist themselves into its upper levels, he was overcome with sadness that something so beautiful was about to be cut down. He hoped to do the tree justice with the arch he was planning.

Cutting the tree down took most of the day. After choosing from the multitude of strong branches, Max managed to fill his truck. He checked his watch as the last log was loaded into his truck bed. He needed to hurry if he had any hope of beating Lanie home. But he planned to store the branches in the shed behind the house until he figured out which pieces he would use. Since it was far from the house and filled with all manner of creepy insects, Lanie was afraid to go back there.

As he drove home, he considered calling Carissa before she left for Deep Creek. Part of him wondered if he shouldn't have offered to go with her, but that felt too forward. They hadn't even been on an official date yet, and her silence since their kiss only confirmed she wasn't ready to take their relationship to the next level. It was clearly too soon for a weekend away together, no matter how much he wished it wasn't.

Figuring it couldn't hurt to try to reach her, he slipped an earbud into his ear and pressed Call. To his surprise, she answered on the second ring, her voice a little breathless.

"Hi, Max. I'm afraid you caught me in the middle of packing."

"I won't keep you," he promised. "I wanted to hear your voice."

"It's good to hear yours too." Her tone became wistful. "I'm sorry we haven't had a chance to talk about... things. I needed some space."

"I understand, though I hope we can sit down and talk when you get back." He cleared his throat. "I wanted to tell you I've figured out what I want to give Lanie as a wedding gift."

"Oh?" Curiosity colored her voice. "Are you making her something?"

"Yes, but I'd rather show it to you when it's further along. It's difficult to explain."

"Okay…" She hesitated.

"And you can't tell Lanie. I want it to be a surprise."

Carissa laughed, though it sounded a bit forced. "Won't that be hard since she lives with you?"

"Don't you worry about that," he said as he pulled into his driveway. Lanie's school had let out, but she likely wouldn't be home for another hour. Still, he needed to hurry. "Anyway, I have to go, but I hope you have a good trip tomorrow. Text or call when you get there."

"I will. Try not to kill yourself in that garage of yours while I'm gone."

He snorted. "No promises. Woodworking is a dangerous gig."

They disconnected, and Max smiled as he climbed out of his truck. Though he struggled under the weight of the logs, he made quick work of unloading them and storing them safely in his garage. By the time Lanie came home, he had just finished sweeping out the debris from his truck.

"Hi, Dad!" she called as she climbed out of her car. "How was your day?"

Taking a deep breath, he plastered a smile on his face. *Act natural.* "Not bad. I finished the furniture from the old house the other day, so I picked up some wood for a new project."

She cocked her head. "What are you building next?"

"Maybe a dining room table. I haven't decided yet."

They fell into step beside each other as they walked toward the house. Lanie had a book bag slung on one shoulder and another bag on her arm. The plethora of papers seemed to weigh her down.

"Need a hand?"

"I've got it."

After he opened the door for her, he followed her inside. She took a deep breath, and her shoulders sagged.

"Are we not having dinner?"

Ah, crud. "No, we are. I got home later than expected. You go sit in the living room, and I'll get it started."

With a weary nod, she sank onto the couch and began removing stacks of paper from her bags. Max rushed into the kitchen and removed a packet of chicken from the refrigerator. He preheated the oven then prepared the drumsticks with various spices. It wasn't how he normally cooked, but Lanie had mentioned more than once that his chicken tended to be bland.

A half hour later, dinner was ready. He called to Lanie and set the food on the table. When she came into the dining room, her steps seemed slow and tired.

"Everything all right?"

She gave a one-shoulder shrug. "It's been a long week, and I'm ready for the weekend." After taking a sip of water, she glanced over at him. "Do you have any plans?"

"I'll probably be in the garage all weekend. What about you?"

When she didn't respond, he took a long look at her. Her arm rested on the table as if it were the only thing holding her up. And while she ate with her normal enthusiasm, she seemed to be dragging.

"Are you sure you're okay?"

She sighed. "The stress of the wedding is starting to catch up with me. Carissa and I made a lot of progress the other night, and the invitations are out, but between working all day and then wedding planning at night, I'm exhausted."

His immediate reaction was to offer help, but he didn't want to upset her. Instead, he covered her hand with his own.

"I'll be okay." She gave him a tired smile. "Especially once December has come and gone."

"I don't want to overstep or throw money at your problems." Her earlier words still haunted him. "But I'm happy to help in other ways, even if it's just running errands for you. I *am* retired, after all."

"Honestly, not having to cook dinner is a huge help." She grinned. "Even if sometimes, it's almost inedible."

He folded his arms on the table and glared at her. "I'm improving."

To his surprise, she nodded. "You certainly are. This chicken is delicious."

They fell into silence as they focused on their food, but Max didn't want the conversation to end there. He wracked his brain for something else to say.

"I realize this is probably something you would have preferred to ask your mother," he finally said, choosing his words carefully. He was completely out of his wheelhouse, but he was desperate to connect with his daughter on a different level. "But do you have any questions about, uh, well, marriage itself?"

Real smooth, McAllister. Could you be more awkward? He prepared for Lanie to laugh off his question or change the subject.

"Oh." Lanie's eyes widened. "Um, I have always wondered if there was anything you might have done differently to prevent you and Mom getting divorced."

He'd repeatedly asked himself that very question after they'd first separated. His answers were usually surface level. Perhaps they should have waited until they were older. Or maybe they should have gone off to college, dated other people, then found their way back to each other, much like Lanie and Nate had done.

But faced with the question from his daughter, he forced himself to dig deeper. She deserved more than some flippant response, especially since he could see the fear in her eyes. While he'd thought she'd accepted that Melody had made a mistake in discouraging her relationship with Nate, Max suspected that the damage Melody had done to their daughter went far deeper than even Lanie realized.

"There are many things I could have done differently," Max blurted out, unable to choose only one thing he would have changed. "But what it comes down to is I wish I had gotten out of my own way more often." Seeing her frown, he considered how to better explain himself. "You said the other day I seem to always think that I'm right, and you made it sound like I see the world through a very narrow lens. The truth is I'm so terrified of making a mistake that I stick to something that's worked in the past. With your mother, we defined our roles early on in our marriage. When we had Steven, she quit her job to stay at home, and then when we had you, it made sense to keep things as they were. But as you both got older, your mother wanted to reassess things. She wanted to go back to work, and with that, she wanted me to take on a more active role in the family, particularly with parenting you and Steven."

"Was that such a bad thing?" Lanie asked, and Max didn't miss the hurt in her voice.

"Of course not," Max replied quickly. "But I couldn't just flip a switch. I was gone often due to my job. Even once I had more seniority, I didn't take advantage of the privileges it allowed. I could have taken more vacation, switched my hours to be home more often in the evenings to help with homework or go to your extracurriculars." Remorse filled his chest. "My attitude at the time was if it ain't broke, don't turn over a new leaf."

Lanie burst out laughing. "The phrase is 'if it's not broke, don't fix it.'"

That made a lot more sense, but he waved his hand. "You know what I mean. Your mom and I had a system, and she wanted to change the system because it no longer worked for *her*." He shifted in his seat. "I wish I had removed my blinders and seen what was right in front of me. If I had given the slightest inch, we might have had many more miles in our marriage."

For a moment, Lanie didn't respond, but her eyes glistened with unshed tears.

Max wondered if perhaps he'd said the wrong thing or been too honest. He didn't usually allow his conversations with his children to get heavy, but Lanie had asked, and he would gladly lay his soul bare if it meant they found an ounce of common ground.

"Thank you for sharing that with me." She wiped her eyes. "It gives me a better perspective of what you and Mom went through." She cleared her plate, which he took as his cue that the conversation was over.

"If you want to know anything else, please ask." He stood, and when she turned from the sink, he held out his arms. "I'm always here for you, even if I'm not the greatest at showing it."

She smiled and stepped into his embrace. "Thanks, Dad. That means a lot."

After giving him a tight squeeze, she kissed his cheek and left the kitchen. He watched her go with a full heart. It felt like they had finally made a breakthrough, and he hoped it was the first of many.

Chapter Twenty-Two

CARISSA ENTERED HER CABIN and collapsed into a rocking chair near the fireplace. Traffic had been horrible on the Baltimore beltway, making her second-guess her decision to take such a long drive on short notice.

But the peace of the cabin settled over her, and she breathed in the rich, rugged scent of wood, lingering chimney smoke, and pine. The air was still and cool, as autumn's hand had snuffed out the last remnants of summer warmth there in the mountains of Maryland.

Soon, she would need to start a fire, but for the moment, she allowed the coolness to seep into her bones. It was strangely refreshing.

The cabin was a simple one-room design. To the right of the front door was a full kitchen, complete with an oven, fridge, and plenty of counter space. To the left of the door sat a small wooden table and two chairs. Behind that was a massive stone fireplace. A king-sized bed took up the majority of the center of the room, and Carissa gazed at it longingly. The rocking chair by the fire had been nice, but she was ready for a good night's sleep.

Her lone suitcase was filled with warm sweaters and jeans in anticipation of the cooler mountain air. She threw on a cozy sweater and headed out to the cabin's back deck. A large hot tub sat against the back wall.

Bed or bath? A small smile tugged at her lips. What a privilege to have such simple choices for once. After the last few hectic weeks of planning weddings and a corporate event, coupled with the delicate balance she'd tried to strike between her growing feelings for Max and her business relationship with Lanie, she ached for that simplicity.

Definitely a bath, but first... Her attention strayed to the natural wonder behind her cabin. *Well, not exactly a* natural *wonder.* It was a well-known fact that Maryland didn't have natural lakes. They were all man-made. Still, she could easily forget that knowledge when taking in the pristine view. The fall foliage had peaked there, with the rippling waters reflecting the brilliant reds, oranges, and yellows.

She headed down to the lakefront, listening to the water lapping gently along the shoreline. She tried to remember the last time she'd been up that way.

Chuck was still alive. The thought came to her, unbidden, and in an instant, the peace she'd enjoyed disappeared. He'd always loved to be in nature, and he'd requested they spend one last summer camping. Unfortunately, his illness hadn't allowed for such rugged adventures, so they'd settled for a cabin. It was rustic enough to give the feel of being in the great outdoors but with the modern conveniences his deteriorating body needed.

In that moment, she realized the memory of that trip had inspired her to pitch Deep Creek for the corporate retreat. Her eyes grew misty, and she raised her face to the darkening sky. She could almost feel Chuck with her then, and her heart ached for him.

A small pier jutted out into the lake, and she walked carefully onto its weathered surface. The wood wasn't in the best condition, but it appeared sturdy enough. She stared out across the water for a while, simply watching the few boats that braved the biting autumn wind.

Glancing down, she caught sight of a carving in the railing. Two sets of initials were crudely cut into the wood, surrounded by a heart. *T.S. + T.K.* Though it lacked his level of skill, Carissa's mind immediately went to Max.

She closed her eyes and allowed herself to remember their kiss. Though she'd chosen to avoid him for the past few days, she couldn't help missing him. Part of her had wanted to invite him with her, but it was much too soon. She hoped to use the trip to clear her head and determine what she wanted to do about their relationship. The distance might do them both some good and give them perspective. But she'd promised to tell him when she arrived, so she sent a quick text.

A million other notifications stared back at her, most of them from Jacob. She glared at the screen, fighting the irritation rising in her chest. Was it not enough that she'd come up there on barely a moment's notice? Why couldn't Jacob trust her to do the job she'd been sent there to do?

She pushed off the railing and headed to her cabin. The beauty around her wasn't enough to quell her growing aggravation, but perhaps a warm bath with a glass or two of pinot grigio would do the trick.

The next morning, Carissa woke with a dull headache. Her first instinct was to roll over and go back to sleep, then she remembered the reason for her impromptu trip. Groaning, she rolled out of bed and slipped into the bathroom. After splashing some water on her face, she made herself a cup of coffee and opened the front door. A blast of chilly air would wake her up more than the caffeine could ever hope to.

Once she was fully awake, she showered and set off to start her day. She had a list of possible venues to visit. While most of the retreat would take place either on the lake itself or near the cabins, she'd wanted to infuse some variety into the agenda.

Her first stop was a ropes course with zip-lining. The tour promised tests of agility and required teams to work together with a guide to get everyone through the challenges. As she drove around the north side of the lake, she was surprised by the number of cars she passed. Deep Creek was a perfect summer vacation spot, but the place she was heading to doubled as a ski resort in the winter. She supposed she shouldn't be shocked that other people were drawn to the area for the beautiful fall foliage.

When she reached the resort, she parked and surveyed the building. It was nondescript aside from a sign advertising the zip-lining course. She walked up to the glass door and peered inside.

"Do you have a reservation?" a deep voice asked behind her.

Spinning on her heel, she found a young man with a backward baseball cap on his head. Tufts of blond hair stuck out of the hole in the hat. His gaze traveled over her outfit. "You're not really dressed for climbing."

Straightening her suit jacket, she forced a smile. "I'm not here to climb. I was hoping to talk to someone about bringing a corporate retreat here. Are you the owner?"

"No, but I can take you to him." He moved past her and opened the glass door. "After you."

Once they were inside, the man indicated she should wait in the lobby then left to fetch the owner. While she waited, Carissa wandered around the small area. Instructions were posted in large signs over the check-in desks, and to the right were several small computers where people could view photos of themselves on the course.

Before arriving, she'd checked out their group rates. She was disappointed to learn that they limited the size of each group to eight people. Jacob wouldn't appreciate that. It would take hours to get all of his employees through the course.

"How may I help you, Miss...?" An older man with a receding gray hairline and a scruffy beard walked into the room.

"Owens." Carissa held out her hand. "Carissa Owens. I wanted to speak to you about your group rates."

He clasped her hand briefly and gave it the slightest of shakes. "Ah, do you have a large family on vacation with you?"

"I'm actually planning a corporate retreat for next autumn, and I'm scoping out potential activities to include on our itinerary."

His brow furrowed. "How many people are you expecting?"

She'd anticipated his reaction and took it in stride. "Likely around fifty people."

When his frown deepened, she hurried on. "But that's an estimate, and not everyone will want to participate in every activity. My goal is to provide attendees with a variety of options to explore."

"Well, it would depend on which course you hoped to do." He handed her a brochure. "Because of the size of the group and the time it would take for each person to go through the course, I would suggest one of our shorter courses. The challenges are not complicated, and participants are brought to the zip line portion much quicker, which is usually the appeal."

She cocked her head. "What if we offered all the courses? Could we split the group based on level of preference?"

Scratching his beard, he seemed to deliberate. "I might be able to do that, but I'd need enough notice to ensure we were well staffed."

"I should be able to provide options for dates and times by the end of this year and then numbers of participants by late spring of next year."

"Then we can accommodate you."

Relief washed over her. *One activity secured.* She handed him a card. "Here's my information. I'll be in touch."

By the end of the day, Carissa didn't feel like she'd been on a weekend getaway at all. She'd driven all over the area while checking out restaurants, local hiking trails, and even a white-water rafting company. The latter, she'd visited only on Jacob's insistence. She couldn't imagine anyone would want to risk falling headfirst into the freezing waters of a raging river in the middle of October.

All she wanted to do was soak her aching muscles in her hot tub and open another bottle of wine. Her stomach growled. But first, she needed to grab dinner.

The fast-food restaurants she'd passed on her way back to the cabin didn't appeal to her. However, a small hole-in-the-wall diner caught her eye. Its simple design and homey vibes reminded her of Bea's. A wave of homesickness came over her as she turned in to the parking lot.

The similarities to Bea's ended at the front door. Inside, the diner was decorated in a much more rustic fashion in contrast to Bea's 1950s nostalgia. There was no swaying-Elvis décor and no jukeboxes. Instead, various animal heads were mounted on the walls, and the floor was riddled with peanut shells.

"Sit anywhere you'd like," a woman said as she passed by Carissa on her way to the kitchen.

Carissa surveyed her options. Several booths sat to one side near a huge fireplace, while a breakfast bar was set up on the other side of the room nearest the kitchen. The appeal of the fire was too strong, and Carissa chose a booth closest to it. A sigh escaped her lips as she welcomed the warmth from the hearth into her old bones.

The woman she'd seen earlier stopped by and handed her a menu. "What can I get you to drink?"

"Water's fine for now," Carissa said with a smile.

After the woman left, Carissa flipped open the menu. The options were fairly standard—burgers, chicken-fried steak, and shepherd's pie—but one item stuck out to her.

"Bison burgers?" she asked as a water glass was set in front of her.

"Don't let the name scare ya. They're just like your typical beef burger, but they got a bit of a wilder edge to 'em."

Carissa shrugged. *When in Rome.* Besides, she'd already been to half a dozen fancy restaurants in the area. It would be good to include something local and original for the corporate retreat.

"I'll have that." She glanced at the menu. "And I'll take a beer from one of your local breweries. Whatever goes best with bison."

The waitress grinned as she took her menu. "I love an adventurous soul."

After she left, her words lingered with Carissa. *An adventurous soul. Is that what I am now?* Her wedding business had sometimes taken her to exotic locations when brides requested destination weddings, but the corporate world was opening many more opportunities.

Her phone buzzed in her pocket, and she pulled it out, expecting to hear from Jacob. Instead, Max's name stared back at her.

We need to talk. Dinner when you get back?

Carissa sighed and turned off the phone, in no mood to deal with Max and the repercussions of their kiss. While she knew she couldn't avoid it forever, at that moment, all she wanted to do was enjoy a nice, quiet meal and celebrate how much she'd accomplished. After her excursions that day, she deserved time to relax. Her real life could wait until she was home.

A few moments later, the waitress returned with her food and beer. Carissa took a sip from the cool glass, savoring the mellow and smooth flavor with just the slightest hint of sweetness. The burger was ginormous, which seemed fitting because of the animal it came from. Carissa opted to cut it in half but still required two hands to lift it. Her first bite oozed with delicious juiciness.

Closing her eyes, she chewed quickly before devouring the first half of the sandwich. It was the best burger she'd ever had, and she was ravenous after rushing around all day.

A soft chuckle caught her attention, and she opened her eyes to find the waitress hovering nearby. Carissa set down the burger and wiped her face.

"I take it you're enjoying your first bison burger?" the waitress asked.

"That's an understatement," Carissa said, eyeing the second half. The restaurant would be a perfect addition to the retreat, but she wasn't sure if the small place could accommodate everyone. "Do you ever serve large parties?"

"Like catering?"

Hmm... I hadn't considered that. Which was surprising, since she worked with caterers all the time. "That wasn't exactly what I meant, but that might work too." At the waitress's perplexed expression, Carissa continued, "I'm planning a corporate retreat, and I've been scoping out restaurants and activities all day. The food would be a big hit, but I'm not sure we can fit everyone in here."

"I'd have to ask my boss, but we've catered events before. Maybe she'd be willing to bring the food to you." The waitress opened a notepad. "Where will you be hosting it?"

Carissa provided the details of the cabin rental location. They chatted for a few more minutes, and the waitress promised to give her boss the information.

Once she was alone again, Carissa greedily ate the rest of her burger and licked the grease from her fingers. As she sipped her beer, she promised herself she would stop back by there again for one more burger before she headed home.

Home. She sighed. The weekend was almost over, and she still had no idea what to say to Max. If she were honest, the distance from him had made the possibility of secretly dating more appealing than when he'd first mentioned it. But she couldn't quite stomach the idea of going behind

Lanie's back. Besides being unprofessional, it risked ruining any chance Max had of improving his relationship with his daughter.

And yet, keeping Max at arm's length until after the wedding was no longer feasible. After their kiss, she wanted more.

Once she'd paid the bill, Carissa headed to her cabin. When she arrived, she sat in her car and stared at Max's text. With a secret smile, she typed her response.

Chapter Twenty-Three

"I'm back in town." Carissa's voice came over the line, filling Max's chest with warmth. "Are you free for dinner tonight?"

Max surveyed his progress on the arch as he considered her question. On the one hand, he was dying to see Carissa again and catch up on how her planning was going. On the other, he'd planned to show her the arch the next time they met, but it was nowhere near ready. He'd carved one branch into a long curved archway, but he hadn't quite started on the intricate designs he was planning.

"I'd love to," he said, deciding he would show her another time. "There's a place I've been dying to take you. I'll make a reservation."

"Oh, where's that?" she asked.

Shaking his head, Max grinned. "It's a surprise."

They planned for him to pick her up in a couple of hours, and he hung up the phone. In the meantime, he got back to work on the arch. Lanie had said she needed to stay late at school for some parent–teacher conferences, and he was trying to take advantage of her absence. There wouldn't be much time to work on the arch during the rest of the week, as Halloween was the next day, then he, Lanie, and Steven were planning on spending Melody's birthday together that weekend.

He decided to focus on carving the other side of the arch. It made more sense to make sure the pieces could fit together like he wanted before starting to carve designs into the wood. If they didn't fit right, he would have to scrap one of the pieces and start over. With November just around the corner, he didn't have time to waste.

An hour later, he stood and stretched his aching back. He'd made more progress on the other side of the arch, but he'd run out of time. After grabbing a quick shower, he dressed and headed over to pick up Carissa.

His heart pounded as he parked his car in her driveway and walked to her front door. They hadn't seen each other since their kiss, and he was nervous about how she might act.

She opened the door with a smile. "Hello there, stranger."

He couldn't help grinning in return. "Long time no see."

Without another word, she hugged him. He chuckled as his arms slid around her waist.

"I've missed you," he whispered, though the words were inadequate for the depth of his feelings. In truth, he'd been going crazy and was desperate to find out where they stood.

Too soon, she stepped back, and it took a lot of willpower not to tighten his arms around her to bring her close again. But they had a lot to talk about and a reservation to get to.

He walked around to the passenger side and opened her door.

Her brow furrowed as she looked from the truck to him. "Aren't you going to tell me where we're going?"

Shaking his head, he held out his hand. "You'll see when we get there."

Her lower lip jutted out in an adorable pout, and for a moment, he was distracted by the desire to kiss her. Thankfully, she climbed into the truck before his desire got the better of him. There would be plenty of time for that later, assuming things went well that night.

Instead of heading north toward the National Harbor, Max turned the truck south. Out of the corner of his eye, he caught Carissa staring at him before she shifted her gaze to the window as if the scenery would help her decipher their destination.

"So, how was your trip?" he asked, hoping to distract her.

"It went really well, actually."

"You sound surprised."

"I am a little. I wasn't expecting everything to come together so easily, but I managed to speak to several different places about possible activities and dining." She smiled. "The event is practically planning itself."

"That's good, though, right? Less stress for you?"

"That's the goal." Her expression darkened. "But I still have to run it by Jacob."

They drove in silence for a few minutes until the landscape opened around them. A minute later, they were crossing the bridge to Solomon's Island.

Carissa gasped and turned to him with wide eyes. "We're going to dinner here?"

He nodded, proud of himself for keeping the secret. Immediately, she began naming potential places, but he refused to confirm or deny any of the options.

"Ugh, this is killing me," she whined, playfully punching his arm. "I can't believe you're not going to tell me."

"Wouldn't be much of a surprise if I did."

When they turned onto a deserted dirt road, her eyebrows pulled together. "Are you taking me to the woods to murder me and dispose of the body?"

He laughed. "Has Lanie been showing you her true-crime shows? Besides, I wouldn't need to drive all the way down here to do that." The road evened out, and a small building appeared in the distance. "This is the island's best-kept secret."

After he pulled into the makeshift parking lot, he grinned at the perplexed expression on her face. He understood her confusion. The building appeared no larger than a boathouse, with blue siding and white shutters.

"Welcome to La Vela." He jumped out of the truck and went around to open her door. "The best Italian food around."

They entered the main area, which had a bar and several small dining rooms that branched off to the right and left. Most of the tables were empty, but it was rather early and a weeknight.

After they were seated, he leaned closer to her. "I wanted something more secluded. Gives us a chance to talk."

Her smile appeared forced, and for the first time since they'd arrived, he wondered if he'd made a mistake. Maybe she preferred somewhere more public.

"I haven't been to this restaurant since they moved locations."

"Well, it is rather out of the way—"

"It's not that," she said quickly. "It's just..." She closed her eyes, and it dawned on him she was trying not to cry.

Oh no, what have I done now? "Do you want to go?"

"Give me a second," she choked out. The server placed two glasses of water on the table then hurried away as if he, too, could sense she was barely holding it together.

Once she'd taken a couple of sips, she gave him a sheepish smile. "Gosh, this is so embarrassing."

"It's okay. We can go somewhere else if you want. There's a seafood restaurant next door."

"No, this is fine, and I'm okay." She cleared her throat. "My husband often came down to Solomon's on business, and I have planned several weddings throughout the island. This was his favorite restaurant."

Oh no. He'd hoped to avoid memories of her husband after their lunch at the National Harbor, and he assumed he would be safe taking her somewhere less well-known. "I'm sorry. I had no idea."

"And why would you?" After she dried her eyes with her napkin, her smile appeared more genuine. "I've always loved this place, too, but I haven't been able to bring myself to come back here." She slid her hand across the table. "I'm glad I'm not doing it alone."

Still, he felt awful. "We should go somewhere else. I want tonight to be about... well, us. And I don't want to bring back painful memories."

"That's just it." She shook her head. "They aren't painful memories. We had a lot of good times at their old location." After giving his hand a reassuring squeeze, she opened her menu. "I want to stay."

He hesitated before opening his menu as well. Part of him wanted to ask her if she was sure, but he didn't want to keep bringing it up either. He hoped maybe tonight would give her a chance to make new memories with him.

"What's your favorite thing to get here?"

"Oh, there's so many things I like," she said. "They have pasta, but I had that the other night. I'll get their duck al vino."

The server returned to take their orders. Max gestured for Carissa to go first. When it was his turn, he ordered the filet mignon.

With a nod, the server took their menus and left. Max sipped his water to buy himself some time before he launched into the discussion they needed to have.

Taking a deep breath, he leaned forward. "Now that we have a moment alone, we should talk."

Her expression became guarded. "You don't waste any time."

"I don't mean to put you on the spot." He cleared his throat. "But it has been a few days since our kiss, and you spent several of them avoiding my calls."

She lowered her gaze. "I'm sorry about that. I wasn't sure what to say or how I felt."

His heart sank. "Then you regret it?"

Her head shot up. "Of course not." The corner of her mouth twitched. "But the timing left a lot to be desired."

"I know." He groaned. "I shouldn't have kissed you, but I couldn't seem to stop myself. I've wanted to do it for a long time."

"Me too." Her voice was almost a whisper.

He heaved a sigh of both relief and frustration. "So what do we do now?"

"I'm not sure what we can do," she admitted. "You gave your word to Lanie, and her wedding is still almost two months away."

"We've kept it from her thus far," Max said, hating himself for even considering betraying his daughter's trust. But she was the one who'd wanted him to put himself out there. And he couldn't help who he'd fallen for.

"I don't love the idea of sneaking around behind her back." Carissa frowned. "Aside from being unprofessional, we're adults, not teenagers hiding our relationship from our parents."

"The role reversal isn't lost on me." Max's chuckle was hollow. "If you want to keep trying to wait, I understand." It would likely drive him mad, but he'd already decided Carissa was worth it.

She squared her shoulders. "I don't want to wait anymore."

"I don't either." He slid his hand across the table, and Carissa grasped it in her own.

Though joy filled his chest, his stomach churned with trepidation. He imagined it was only a matter of time before Lanie found out about them. While the wedding was nearly planned, he hated breaking his word to his daughter. He could only hope everything turned out okay in the end.

An hour later, they tossed their napkins onto their plates at the same time and leaned back. The food was delicious, as always, and Max was greatly enjoying the company as well.

"Would you like dessert?" the server asked as he cleared their plates.

Max glanced at Carissa, but she gave a small shake of her head. "No, thank you. Just the check, please."

"Right away, sir."

"Are you in a hurry to get home?" Max asked.

"Not particularly."

After paying the bill, Max led her outside, and they walked along the streets until they came to the beach. The water of the Patuxent River lapped gently against the shoreline as the sun sank low on the horizon.

"We always seem to end up near water," Carissa said, taking his hand and entwining their fingers.

"It's hard to find a place in Maryland that doesn't have access to water. We're kind of surrounded by it."

"Touché."

"But that sounds like a fun challenge. I'll have to find a place away from the water for our next date."

She raised an eyebrow. "Getting ahead of yourself there, aren't you, Mr. McAllister? I haven't agreed to another date."

"It's too late for your weak protests now. You said you didn't want to wait to be together, so another date is inevitable." He brought their joined hands to his lips and kissed her knuckles. "You're stuck with me now."

Her laugh warmed his heart. "You're quite sure of yourself."

"I know what I want." Wrapping an arm around her waist, he bent to kiss her.

"And what's that?" she murmured against his lips.

"You."

He kept the kiss short, not wanting to get carried away again, especially in public. But it was difficult to let her go. As they continued along the small beach, his heart was full for the first time since he'd lost Melody.

"I've never been here at night," she said. They stopped at the edge of the beach to enjoy the sunset over the water. "Chuck didn't like being so far from home in the evening."

Normally, he might be put off by how much she talked about her late husband, but since losing Melody, he understood. It wasn't the same as being with someone who was still in love with their ex. Death gave a finality that nothing could overcome, and grief was a testament to the strength of love.

"I prefer the evenings here." A chilly breeze made her shiver, and Max wrapped an arm around her. "But we should probably get going. It's a long drive back."

"Just one more minute," she said, leaning into him. "I'm not ready for this night to end."

"Me either."

Time seemed to stop, even as the sky changed from orange to pink and then a deep purple. Her scent wafted over him with the breeze, and he closed his eyes, savoring the moment.

"Would you ever want to get married again?" she asked, her voice barely a whisper.

That wasn't a question he was expecting, and he spoke without thinking. "No."

She stiffened in his arms. He grimaced. Clearly, that was the wrong answer. It might have been the truth, at least up until recently. But despite how he felt about Carissa, marriage hadn't crossed his mind. For one thing, it felt too soon. And for another, he'd been a bachelor for so long, he wasn't sure how he would feel about having a wife again.

"Never?" she asked.

"Uh, I mean, I didn't expect to date again either. I haven't given much thought to marriage." *Ugh.* He wasn't making much sense. "I guess I haven't had much of a reason to consider marrying again, if that makes sense."

Though she nodded and smiled, there was a hint of disappointment in her eyes. "I get it."

"What about you? Do you want to marry again?"

She sighed. "At first, I didn't. I couldn't imagine ever finding what I had with Chuck again, and anything else would be a poor substitute." She gestured toward the street, and he took her hand and led her back up the beach. "But after a few years, I started thinking it might be nice. I've still got a lot of life to live, God willing. And I'd like to share it with someone."

Wanting to share your life with someone doesn't have to mean marriage. But he didn't say that out loud. A comment like that would likely ruin what had otherwise been a pleasant evening.

"It's not something I want to rush into," she continued when he didn't respond. "Right now, I want to focus on my business."

"That makes sense. Expanding it takes a lot of time and effort."

She frowned but didn't contradict him. They walked the rest of the way in silence, but it wasn't as comfortable as before.

When they arrived at his truck, he opened her door. She searched his face briefly before climbing in. As he drove her home, he wished he could find a way to salvage the night, but he kept coming up empty.

Finally, she broke the silence. "I'm sorry if I spooked you with the marriage talk."

"Not spooked," he corrected. "Just caught off guard." He glanced at her before turning his attention back to the road. "I'm not necessarily against getting remarried. It's not something I've had occasion to think about since I wasn't dating."

"I understand." She rested a hand on his knee. "I shouldn't have brought it up."

"No, I'm glad you did." He squeezed her hand. "If we're going to keep seeing each other, it's important we're both honest about what we want, now and in the future." He cleared his throat. "And it's okay if that changes, as long as we talk about it."

A little while later, he pulled into her driveway and hopped out to walk her to her door. After kissing her good night, he spent the drive to his place mulling over their conversation. Though he'd meant it when he said he'd never had occasion to think about marriage, what he hadn't told Carissa was that he'd sworn off marriage the moment the divorce decree was signed. But then, he'd sworn off love too. *And look how that turned out.*

⁓ℓℓ⁓

Halloween came and went without much fuss. Max passed out candy. Lanie and Nate went with Steven and Rose to a party at Seabreeze. As time marched into November, the pressure was ramping up for him to finish Lanie's wedding present. He needed to show Carissa the arch soon, as he hoped to get her opinion on where it might fit in the ceremony.

But first, he was meeting his children at the cemetery. It was Melody's birthday, and they had agreed to get together as a family.

As he climbed into his truck and headed to the gravesite, he couldn't help recalling how much had changed in the last year. His son was married, Lanie had moved home permanently and was soon to be married, and he'd started to open his heart again for the first time in over a decade.

"Melody," he whispered hoarsely, "you would be so proud."

Lanie and Steven were already in the parking lot when he arrived. While their significant others had offered to join them, they had decided to keep the visit between the three of them.

Lanie was already wiping tears from her eyes, and Max rushed toward her, pulling her into a fierce hug. His son held a small bouquet of flowers in one hand and an angel statue in the other.

A moment later, Lanie pulled away and forced a smile. "Let's go visit Mom."

Together, they trudged through the graveyard. The autumn wind ruffled their hair, and Max liked to think it was Melody showing them she was with them. When they reached the grave, Steven knelt and placed the flowers and the angel figurine in front of the headstone.

"Happy birthday," he said, his voice hoarse from the tears he appeared to be holding back.

Max bent and put a hand on his son's shoulder. He hated seeing his children in pain but knew there wasn't anything he could do for them except offer comfort.

"I'm getting married next month, Mom," Lanie said with a sniffle. "You'd love the dress I picked out."

"It's beautiful," Max agreed before he turned away, not wanting his children to see the tears that came to his eyes at the memory of the first time he'd seen Lanie in that dress. She looked radiant and so much like her mother, it broke his heart.

Steven and Lanie continued to tell their mom about all the things going on in their lives. Max could almost pretend Melody was sitting there listening to them.

"Why don't you tell Mom about your woodworking, Dad?" Lanie called, bringing Max back into the conversation. "She loved the furniture you made for her before..."

She swallowed, but Max could finish the sentence. *Before the divorce. Before everything changed.*

Max shifted closer to the headstone, feeling silly to be talking to a rock. "I'm working on something for Lanie, a wedding present."

"Really?" Lanie asked, her eyes lighting up. "Is it a desk? Nate said I could use the second bedroom as an office for grading papers."

Averting his eyes, Max shifted uncomfortably. Perhaps he should have considered a desk, though he supposed the vanity could double as one, especially if he made the mirror removable. But he was sure she would love the arch just as much once she saw it.

"You'll have to wait and see," he finally said.

They stayed for as long as they could stand the bitter wind, then they headed to the parking lot. After a quick goodbye, Max drove to his house, his heart light. The sun broke through the gathering clouds, and he hoped Melody was smiling down on him.

Chapter Twenty-Four

"Hey, stranger," Max said when Carissa answered her phone.

"I'm sorry I've been incommunicado for the last week." Carissa leaned back in her chair and closed her eyes. For several days, she'd been working on a proposed schedule for the corporate event. "What's up?"

"I was wondering if you could tear yourself away from work to have lunch with me today or sometime this week." When she didn't immediately respond, he continued, "I'm cooking."

"Is that supposed to entice me?" she teased.

"It's a Lanie-approved recipe," he retorted, though she could hear the smile in his voice. "I promise I won't burn it."

Carissa pursed her lips. The timing wasn't great, as she needed to get the schedule over to Colin by the close of business the next day, but she was hungry, and her eyes were starting to cross from staring at a screen. Maybe a break would do her good.

"I can be there in about an hour. Does that work?"

"That's perfect. See you soon."

After they disconnected, she stretched, working the kinks out of her back. She promised herself she would finish the schedule first thing in the morning when she was fresh and closed her laptop. Then she headed straight for the shower.

Forty-five minutes later, she put the finishing touches on her makeup. Covering the dark circles under her eyes was getting more difficult the longer she worked on the event for Imaginavigation Enterprises. But it would be worth it when the clients began pouring in next year.

After donning a heavy coat, she left her house and drove to Max's. The afternoon sun was high in the sky but did little to cut through the day's chill. Before she had even fully exited her car, the front door swung open, and Max stepped out.

"Glad you could make it," he said as he wrapped his arms around her and bent to give her a quick kiss.

But it had been too long since she had last seen him, and she slid her hands into his hair, holding him in place. He chuckled against her lips as he pulled her closer, deepening the kiss.

"I guess absence really does make the heart grow fonder," he murmured when she finally released him. "Come inside where it's warm."

The house smelled of garlic and onion, and her stomach growled in anticipation. She could get used to someone cooking for her again.

"What are you making that smells so delicious?" She slid into a chair at the table.

"Chicken parmesan." He glanced over his shoulder, and her face must have betrayed her skepticism. "It's Lanie's recipe. I'm planning on making it for her later this week for dinner. You get to be my guinea pig."

Pressing her lips together to keep from laughing, Carissa smiled. "Lucky me."

"After we eat, there's something I'd like to show you," he said. "I've been working on a gift for Lanie, and I'd love your opinion on it."

"I'm sure it'll be beautiful."

"But you have to promise not to tell her. It's a surprise."

"I promise."

He served lunch, and Carissa was pleasantly surprised by how well it had turned out. They talked about how their weeks had gone, and Carissa filled him in on the progress she'd made with planning the corporate event.

Once they were finished eating, Max cleared the table and put the dishes in the sink. His excitement about his present for Lanie was palpable.

"I'll take care of those in a bit." He grabbed her hand and pulled her from her seat. Carissa struggled to keep up with him as he led the way to the garage.

After flicking on a light, he moved toward a large object covered with a sheet. With a wink at Carissa, he removed the sheet and revealed a wooden archway. Most of the wood was smooth, but he'd started carving a design featuring roses, leaves, and vines.

Carissa fought to keep her expression neutral as she stared at the monstrosity in front of her. While the arch was beautiful, it was huge. It seemed to almost touch the ceiling of the garage, and it stood about five feet wide.

When she still hadn't said anything, Max cleared his throat. "Well, what do you think?"

Instead of answering, Carissa walked around and through the archway, studying the piece. A million questions ran through her mind. What was his intention with the gift? Did he hope Lanie would use it in the ceremony? She shuddered. *Hopefully not.* She doubted it would fit through the door of the church, let alone in the sanctuary.

Finally, she took a deep breath. "Is this piece going to Nate's house?"

"Eventually, but I hoped it could be included in the ceremony."

Carissa swallowed her horror and kept her tone as diplomatic as possible. "Did you measure the church to ensure this will fit through the door?"

The excitement in his dark eyes dimmed. "No, but the pieces interlock, so they can be taken apart if needed." He pointed at the top of the arch. "See this part here? It disconnects."

Well, at least we can get it in *the church.* She pressed her lips into a thin line as she tried to think of something nice to say.

"Aren't you going to say anything else?" he asked. "I mean, obviously, it's not finished, but I have no doubt I can get it done by the wedding."

Carissa held up her hand. "You should talk to your daughter before you continue wasting your time." The hurt in his eyes made her wish she'd chosen her words more wisely.

"Wasting my time?" he repeated as if dumbstruck.

She sighed. "I'm sorry. That came out wrong." Pinching her nose, she closed her eyes. *How can I get him to understand he's overstepping again?* She opened her eyes and tried a different tactic. "What I meant was Lanie has a specific aesthetic in mind for the ceremony." She stared at the arch. "Honestly, I'm not sure it'll fit the stage area even if we can get it in the door."

"It's a church. I'm sure we can make it work," he insisted, his tone defensive. "Besides, I know my daughter better than you do."

She didn't respond, but her expression must have conveyed her skepticism. While she didn't want to hurt him or make the afternoon any more awkward, she'd promised Lanie to help rein in her father's antics.

Before she could say anything else, Max crossed his arms and stared at the floor. "Maybe you should go."

Her heart sank. She wished she could spare his feelings, but she wasn't sure how else to convey what a terrible idea the arch was. It would be one thing if he'd run it by Lanie, even if he'd offered to make something for her ceremony and left the actual item a surprise. Though given how large the arch was, she doubted that would stave off Lanie's irritation.

Perhaps there was a way to salvage their time together. One glance at his face disabused her of that notion, and she sighed. She moved past him and went into the house to gather her coat.

He followed her. "Promise me you won't tell Lanie about the arch."

At first, she didn't respond. While she appreciated that Max wanted the arch to be a surprise, she was contractually obligated to tell her client.

"Please, Carissa," he begged, his eyes boring into hers. "It means a lot to me to be able to do this for her, and I want it to be a surprise."

"I understand that," she began. "But you don't understand the position you're putting me in by asking me to keep this a secret. Lanie has entrusted me with this event because she knows I will run everything by her, and we already saw how she reacted when I didn't tell her about the band. You're asking me to lie to her again."

His face flushed. "It's not a lie!"

She crossed her arms. "Lying by omission is still lying."

"I'll tell Lanie before the wedding, when the arch is finished."

"And when will that be?"

"I-I don't know," he admitted. "But I'll try to get it done by the end of this month. Then Lanie can decide what she wants."

They stared each other down as the minutes ticked by. Finally, Carissa nodded. "But if she finds out before then and comes after me, I'm throwing you under the bus."

"Duly noted."

She opened the door and took one last look at him over her shoulder. He refused to meet her gaze. All the warm feelings she'd felt when she'd entered the house had vanished, leaving her with a bleak emptiness. As she stepped out into the cold November day, she wondered if their relationship had ended before it really had a chance to begin.

*   *   *

Carissa didn't sleep well that night. After tossing and turning for hours, she gave up around four in the morning and tried to lose herself in event planning. Several emails and calls had come in during her lunch with Max.

Sliding her fingers through her hair, she clasped her hands behind her head and rested her forehead against the dining room table. How had such a wonderful day soured? Had she overreacted to Max's surprise for his daughter? Maybe he was right. Maybe Lanie would love it.

With a groan, she pushed back from the table and began pacing. On the one hand, Lanie had been very enthusiastic about her dad revisiting his old hobby. During some of their meetings one-on-one, she'd gushed about how talented he was. So it was entirely possible she would be thrilled to receive something he'd worked so hard on for her.

But on the other hand, it clashed with the rest of the decor. The church wood was mahogany, and the deep-brown color went well with the rich red-and-green decor they had chosen for Christmas. Meanwhile, the wood Max was carving was cherry, a much lighter brown. Perhaps that wouldn't matter to Lanie, but every time Carissa tried to picture it, she cringed. And as far as she knew, no amount of staining would make the wood dark enough to fit in with the rest of the church.

It also bugged her that he hadn't come to her about it before he started the project. While she had no idea if Lanie even wanted a wedding arch, Carissa could have at least given him pointers on what type of wood would work best, though she hadn't the first clue whether it was even possible to choose different types of wood. For all she knew, he had to work with what was available.

He'd put her in an uncomfortable position, as if she didn't have enough on her plate. Not telling Lanie felt wrong, especially since Max couldn't guarantee when the arch would be done. Which meant Carissa had no idea when he would tell Lanie.

"I didn't need this right now," she muttered as she sat back at the table and stared at her computer screen. "I wish I could trust Max to finish on time and tell Lanie."

Saying Max's name brought up other unpleasant thoughts. She wished she hadn't said he was wasting his time. It had been overly harsh and unfair. At the same time, he'd *just* gotten back into woodworking and was still honing his skills. Why would he decide to take on such a huge project when faced with a tight deadline?

And then he'd asked her to leave. An otherwise perfect day completely ruined because of a pointless argument. She wished he'd never shown her the arch. Then she would be blissfully ignorant, and any fallout between him and Lanie wouldn't land on her.

You can't put the genie back in that bottle now. Her husband's voice rang in her head with one of his favorite sayings. She hated to admit that like all the other times he'd said it, he was right. What was done was done, and what mattered was what she did moving forward.

Shaking her head, she forced herself to focus. As soon as the sun rose, Jacob would start blowing up her phone again, and she needed to address his latest "urgent" nonemergency he'd emailed and called about when her phone was off.

Two hours later, as if on cue, her phone vibrated beside her. Resisting the urge to roll her eyes, Carissa pressed the speaker button.

"Good morning, Jacob."

"I hope you enjoyed your evening off," he said by way of greeting. "Because we've got a lot of work to do."

"We have a call with the board in about an hour to give them an update, so we may have to push off whatever you're hoping to accomplish until after that call."

"Colin sent some talking points he wanted to make sure we covered during the meeting."

Carissa nodded. "I saw those, and I responded with comments of my own."

Following a beat of silence, Carissa lifted her fist in a quiet cheer to have finally been one step ahead of the irritating CEO. After her fight with Max, she needed a win.

"Color me impressed," Jacob said. "You must have been up late last night."

Or early this morning. "Something like that. Anyway, I'll forward you the email thread between Colin and me for your review, but I think we're ready."

"That's good to hear. Can you schedule a meeting with the three of us directly after the call so we can keep our momentum going once the board approves our plans?"

Stifling a sigh, she clicked into her computer calendar and started entering information into an appointment. "Sending to you now."

"All right. I guess I'll talk to you in an hour."

"Sounds good. Bye." She tried and failed to keep the smugness out of her tone. *Score another point for me.* If only she could keep it up.

The next day, Carissa had a meeting with Lanie, Nate, and their preacher at the church. Her part was simple. She was there to go over logistics, but the preacher wanted to have a deeper conversation with the engaged couple about their relationship to make sure the two were ready to enter into matrimony.

They met in the church itself, and Lanie wandered around the sanctuary, taking in all the details. Carissa stayed near the pulpit, hoping once the preacher took the two lovebirds into his office, she would be able to pull out a measuring tape and figure out where they might fit Max's arch monstrosity.

"It'll be even more beautiful when it's decorated for Christmas," Lanie said as she came up behind her.

Carissa forced a smile. "I have no doubt." She waved a hand over the banister that separated the pews from the pulpit. "With the rich red carpeting, it has a natural disposition for Christmas and likely complements the greenery."

"The only thing I don't like is the lack of a center aisle."

Carissa pursed her lips. It was somewhat odd that the church had two side aisles that branched off to pews to the right, left, and center. While it might work well to have the bridesmaids and groomsmen use the two aisles, it would be awkward to have Lanie and her father do the same. But the main door to the church was located stage left, behind the pews.

"You and your father will come down this aisle here." Carissa pointed. "And we can always encourage people to sit in the middle and left pews. That way, they won't miss out on your entrance by being too far away."

"True." Lanie cocked her head. "I don't think the guest list will require the whole room. Maybe we can set up some decorations in front of those seats to mark them as off-limits."

Carissa's mind strayed to the arch. Maybe that was a compromise Max could accept. The arch was certainly large enough to block off the aisle, then it could still be featured in the wedding, perhaps not exactly as Max had envisioned.

"What's wrong?" Lanie asked.

Carissa worked to rearrange her facial expression. "Nothing. I'm brainstorming some options to bring your vision to life."

Guilt churned in her stomach, and she glanced away, hoping Lanie couldn't see through her poor attempt at lying. Maybe she and Max should have stuck to their decision to wait until after the wedding to start dating. Then she wouldn't be faced with divided loyalties.

"Lanie? Nate?" a deep voice called from the front of the church. "Are you ready?"

"We'll be right there," Lanie said before turning back to Carissa. "You'll wait here for us? I'd like to hear your ideas of how to block the aisle."

"Of course," Carissa promised, hoping she sounded more enthusiastic than she felt.

After Lanie and Nate followed the preacher out of the church, Carissa retrieved her measuring tape and set to work. She had to guesstimate how big the arch was based on her memory, but it had stood taller than Max by at least a foot and appeared roughly four or five feet wide.

"Better safe than sorry," she muttered as she measured five feet. Working quickly in case the preacher finished sooner than expected, she measured every place she could think of putting the arch, marking the measurements on a piece of paper.

When she was finished, she slumped into a pew and put her head in her hands. If the arch could indeed be separated, it would fit in the church, but it would stand out as an eyesore no matter where she tried to put it. And if Max's intention was that they would be married *under* it, then Carissa really had her work cut out for her.

As much as she loved the idea of it sitting in the aisle to block people from entering, it would be cumbersome to set up there because of the limited space in the aisle itself. The only other option she could think of was to have it at the entrance to the church. That way, it could be used as a photo opportunity, and it could be displayed in all its glory, but it wouldn't clash with the interior or disrupt the wedding ceremony itself.

But Max probably wouldn't go for that either. With a sigh, she put her measuring tape away. *Maybe my measurements are off.* After all, she hadn't actually measured the arch itself and had relied on estimations of its size.

The door to the church opened, and Lanie and Nate came in, followed by the preacher. Plastering a smile on her face, Carissa stood.

"All set?" she asked.

"Reverend Patrick believes we are fit to be married," Lanie replied, beaming. She took Nate's hand. "But he did want to discuss your idea of blocking the right aisle."

"We have had several couples who have voiced your same concerns," Reverend Patrick began. "And I've found that strategically placed decor seems to be just the ticket to discourage guests from using the right pews without marring the beauty of the sanctuary." He gestured behind him. "Come with me, and I'll show you photographs from past weddings."

"He showed them to us already," Lanie said. "But you might have a better idea of how to incorporate what others have done into my vision."

Carissa followed the preacher. His office was small and simply set up. A wooden desk sat a few feet out from the back wall with a simple upholstered chair that had seen better days behind it. On the other side were two straight-backed chairs. In one corner was a bookshelf with several versions of the Bible, a few hymnbooks, and some devotionals.

On the desk lay several photo albums that had been opened to specific collages of weddings, and beside those was a document entitled Marriage Contract. She hid a smile. Though she didn't see it often these days, it had been more popular when she'd first started in wedding planning. The document wasn't legally binding but was meant to serve as a vehicle to talk to couples about what marriage was like and what was expected of each party. Unlike the Catholic version of premarital counseling and the agreement of a covenant, it was a symbolic gesture to demonstrate a couple's willingness to enter into matrimony.

"Have a seat," Reverend Patrick said.

She took the seat nearest the door. "Do you keep photos from all of the weddings you host here?"

"If the bride and groom are willing to donate them," he replied with a smile. "But we respect their wishes if they do not want to provide photos, and we don't take our own." Leaning forward, he pointed at a photo at the top of the album page. "Here, they strung tulle down both sides of the aisle to block the seats. While that's not exactly what you're going for, it would signal to guests to return to the main aisle." He flipped a page. "And here, they put up a simple sign asking people to sit on the other side of the church."

Both options seemed appropriate for what Lanie hoped to accomplish, but the image of the arch kept intruding on Carissa's thoughts. She studied the reverend. Max had forbidden her from telling Lanie, but he hadn't said she couldn't discuss it at all. Reverend Patrick would know better than anyone whether such a thing would work in his church.

"What about an archway that directs people down the aisle we want them to use?"

Reverend Patrick raised an eyebrow. "What sort of archway?"

A ridiculous one. But she kept that comment to herself. "A large wooden one. Roughly seven feet high by five feet wide." When he didn't immediately answer, she continued, "I can get more accurate measurements and a photo to give you a better idea."

He leaned back in his chair and tented his fingers. "Lanie didn't mention an archway."

"That's because she doesn't know." Now, she was treading on dangerous territory. Technically, if the reverend told Lanie, it wasn't necessarily Carissa's fault. However, since he knew about the archway only because of her, she doubted Max would see it that way. "Her father is a skilled woodworker, and as a surprise gift, he's decided to build an archway. He wants to incorporate it into the ceremony, but it likely won't fit at the front of the church, nor do I believe Lanie would want it there. However, if it would fit, putting it in front of an aisle may be a compromise he's willing to accept."

Pursing his lips, Reverend Patrick stared at the ceiling. Carissa wondered if he was consulting God, but she assumed he was just considering the request.

"It's hard to say without actually seeing the structure." Shifting forward, he rested his hands on the desk. "Get a picture and the precise measurements, and we'll figure out a way to make it work."

"Thank you, Reverend." She stood to leave then glanced back. "Please keep this between us. I'd hate to ruin the surprise for Lanie."

He smiled. "My lips are sealed."

As Carissa left the office, she felt like a weight had been lifted from her shoulders. At least she could say she'd done everything in her power to help Max with his surprise and maintained her client's vision. A small smile tugged at her lips. In some ways, she supposed she'd left the situation with God.

Chapter Twenty-Five

Despite his attempts to throw himself into carving the arch, Max hadn't quite been able to ignore the bitter silence that hung between him and Carissa. As the days turned into one week then two, Max tried to accept that whatever had been building between them was over.

Her harsh words still echoed in his head every time he worked on the arch. *Before you waste any more time.* A few times, he'd considered leaving the arch unfinished and giving Lanie the desk she'd mentioned. He'd even started building a desk just in case. But his heart wasn't in that. The arch was not only different and unique, but it was also a symbol of the marriage he hoped his daughter would have—two halves that could stand completely on their own but worked together to make something truly beautiful.

Of course, he couldn't completely avoid any mention of Carissa. Lanie kept him informed of the wedding planning progress, and from their conversations, he learned bits and pieces about how Carissa's life was going.

One night at dinner, about a week before Thanksgiving, Lanie propped her chin on her hand. "I was thinking of asking Carissa to Thanksgiving." At his expression, she frowned. "Don't look at me like that. She doesn't have any family here, and I bet she gets lonely during the holidays. Besides, the two of you seemed to be getting along better."

"It's your first Thanksgiving since you graduated," Max said, avoiding responding to his daughter directly. "I'd rather keep it to family."

"But we always have more than enough food," Lanie protested. "I'm sure Rose and Steven won't mind."

"*I* mind," Max cut in more forcefully than he'd intended. Lanie's eyes widened, and he was filled with regret. "I'm sorry. It's not a good idea."

"Why not?"

He shoved a forkful of chicken into his mouth to buy himself some time. *Why, indeed.* He would have to tread lightly, or Lanie would get suspicious.

Since Lanie wasn't aware of their many outings together, he figured it couldn't hurt to pretend he and Carissa meant nothing to each other. "While I've tolerated her for your sake, I suspect I'm the last person Carissa would want to spend a holiday with."

"That's an assumption on your part. You don't know it for sure."

"Trust me, it's not an assumption," he muttered. The memory of Carissa's face when he'd asked her to leave flashed through his mind.

"You don't even have to talk to her. She'll sit at the other end of the table with Rose and me." She leaned forward, and her hazel eyes pleaded with his. "Please, Dad. No one should have to spend the holidays alone."

His resolve faltered. The last thing he wanted to do was have an awkward dinner on one of his favorite holidays, but Lanie was right. After the divorce, he'd spent too many holidays alone when Melody had the kids. He remembered how lonely he'd been back then, and he wouldn't wish that on anyone.

"Fine," he said reluctantly. "You can ask her, but don't be surprised if she says no."

Lanie brightened. "Thank you."

Max grumbled a response, but inside, he was a mess. His only hope was that Carissa would want to avoid an awkward family dinner as much as he did. Otherwise, he suspected the night would only end in disaster.

The Monday before Thanksgiving, Max headed to the grocery store to grab the last few items he planned to serve at the feast. Lanie hadn't mentioned whether she'd spoken to Carissa yet, and he wanted to make sure they had plenty of food.

The store traffic was light. One of the many benefits of retirement was the ability to shop on a weekday morning. After grabbing a cart, Max steered it toward the produce aisle.

"Hello, Max," a familiar voice said behind him.

Max froze. Squeezing his eyes shut, he held his breath. As if he could make Carissa disappear. Or at the very least, make himself invisible. But when she tapped her foot, he realized his actions were futile, and he slowly turned to face her.

"I haven't heard from you in a while," she said when he didn't speak.

"I could say the same about you." His back was ramrod straight, which made him appear even taller than normal. Some people might be intimidated by his height, but Carissa didn't seem to notice.

At the sight of her, a wave of emotions ripped through him. Her gray hair was pulled back from her face in a messy bun, and her eyes seemed duller than usual, like she hadn't been sleeping well. His hands ached to touch her, but he crossed his arms to keep from giving in to temptation.

"That's fair." She bit her lip. "I'm sorry for how I reacted to the arch."

"Did you tell Lanie about it?" he asked, cringing at how desperate he sounded.

"Of course not." Her eyes rose to meet his. "I promised I wouldn't."

For a moment, they stood in uncomfortable silence. He knew he should ask her about Thanksgiving, but he couldn't quite bring himself to do so. When he couldn't bear her presence anymore, he slipped behind the handle of his cart and aimed it at the other end of the aisle.

"Wait," Carissa said, so softly that he thought for a moment he'd imagined it.

He glanced back at her. His hands tightened on the plastic handle, causing it to squeak under the pressure. "Yes?"

"I spoke to the reverend at the church." Her hands fiddled with the plastic on a bag of bread sitting in the top of her cart. "We're trying to figure out how to incorporate the arch into the ceremony."

"You told him?" Max's heart sank. The more people who knew, the more likely Lanie would find out and the surprise would be ruined.

"He promised he wouldn't say anything," she said as if reading his mind. "But I was wondering if it would be okay if I stopped by to measure it. We need an accurate understanding of how much space is required."

Max hesitated. That moment was simultaneously the perfect opportunity to ask Carissa to join them for Thanksgiving and the worst possible time to do so. They were barely able to speak to each other. Spending more time with him was clearly the last thing on her mind.

And yet... Seeing her there, he realized how much he missed her. While her initial reaction still stung, realizing she'd spent some of their time apart brainstorming ways to blend his gift into Lanie's vision of her wedding touched his heart. Perhaps olive branches came in unexpected ways.

"Max?" Carissa prompted.

"That would be fine." He cleared his throat. "How would you like to spend Thanksgiving with the McAllisters?"

Her eyes widened with what he hoped was surprise. "I wouldn't want to intrude on your holiday."

"It's no intrusion. We would love to have you." Lanie's words came back to him, and he repeated them to Carissa. "No one should be alone for the holidays."

Her lips curved into a tentative smile. "Thank you for thinking of me. I would love to."

Though her response lacked the enthusiasm she'd had the last time he'd invited her over, Max's chest warmed. "Great. Dinner is at five."

She chewed her lower lip, and Max was distracted by the movement. Desire swam in his belly at the thought of kissing those lips again, but he forced himself to refocus.

"Do you need me to bring anything?"

"Only if there's something you'd like to bring." He gestured to the cart. "We've got the rest covered."

"Sounds great. I'll see you then."

On Thanksgiving Day, Max was up with the sun to start preparations for the feast. Every year the kids were with him for the holiday, he and Lanie had the same routine. The day before, she would make deviled eggs and pumpkin pie. In the morning, Max would get up and set the turkey out to rest on the counter while he made pumpkin pancakes for breakfast. Then, once the turkey was in the oven and breakfast was cleaned up, they all gathered in the living room and watched the Macy's parade.

After the parade, he planned to spend the rest of the afternoon helping Lanie in the kitchen. She made the rolls from scratch, while he made the other sides. He had a buffet server Crock-Pot that he used to make slow-cooker macaroni and cheese, green beans, and stuffing. When the turkey was almost done, Lanie would boil sweet potatoes and make a casserole. The minute the turkey came out of the oven, the casserole and the rolls would go in. They were like a well-oiled machine.

Of course, last year, Lanie hadn't come home. With Rose's help, he and Steven had tried to recreate the tradition, but it had turned into a huge mess. Somehow, the turkey was both burnt and undercooked, the sweet potatoes exploded in the oven, and each boiled egg had ripped apart when he tried to pull the yolk out. Max was glad Lanie was back and hoped things would go more smoothly.

As he removed the turkey from the fridge, a door opened upstairs. A moment later, Lanie appeared in the kitchen doorway, rubbing her eyes.

"Have you started on breakfast yet?" she asked with a yawn.

"Was just about to." Max set the turkey on the counter and preheated the oven. "If you want to start frying the bacon, that would be great."

With a sleepy nod, Lanie poured herself a cup of coffee before setting up the griddle on the stove. As he worked quietly next to his daughter, a sense of peace washed over him. Thanksgiving was his favorite holiday for many reasons. Although Christmas was also a family holiday, he found the rampant consumerism associated with it off-putting. In contrast, Thanksgiving was a more relaxed get-together.

He chuckled to himself. *Well, if you don't count the stress of cooking and the cleanup.* Still, the expectations were different, and people tended to linger, whether because they were too full of the feast or simply able to enjoy the company of family.

Just as he flipped the last pancake, the front door swung open. Steven's voice carried through the house as he and Rose made their way to the kitchen. Rose carried an apple pie, and Steven had several grocery bags in his hands.

"Lanie asked me to pick up a few things," Steven said as he set the bags on the floor. He sniffed the air appreciatively. "Did you make enough for us?"

"Of course." Max carried the plate of pancakes and set it on the table next to the bacon Lanie had made. "There's fresh coffee in the pot."

"Don't mind if I do." Steven poured mugs for Rose and himself and took them to the table. "No Nate this morning?"

"He'll be by later." Lanie passed him the butter. "He planned to visit his parents first."

"And he didn't invite you?" Rose asked.

Shaking her head, Lanie took a bite of pancake. "He did, but I told him I have too much to do here." She turned to Max. "This is delicious, Dad."

"Don't act so surprised," Max grumbled, though he couldn't help smiling.

After finishing one pancake, Steven reached for another. "Is it just the five of us, then?"

Instead of answering, Max lifted his coffee and drained the liquid. Lanie bit her lip, and Max wondered if she hadn't had a chance to talk to Carissa.

"Um, we might have one more," he finally said.

Rose tilted her head. "Who?"

Keeping his eyes on his food, Max answered, "I asked Carissa to join us."

While Lanie's eyes lit with a happy surprise, Steven exchanged a wary look with Rose. "You two are spending quite a bit of time together."

"I've been making an effort to get along with her," Max said. "For Lanie's sake."

"You two seemed pretty cozy when we were at the festival." Rose gave him a secretive grin that suggested she knew he wasn't being entirely truthful.

"We're just friends," he insisted, though he wasn't even sure that was true anymore. But Carissa had agreed to join their holiday festivities, and that gave him hope.

Before anyone could further comment on his and Carissa's relationship, he stood. "I, uh, need to start on the dishes if we want to watch the parade."

Thankfully, his children didn't push him on the issue, and the rest of the day went as planned. As the clock ticked closer to five, his stomach began tying itself in knots. The meal was on schedule, and everything had turned out beautifully, thanks to Lanie, but Max couldn't help worrying about what might happen when Carissa arrived. Would they be able to move past the arch-shaped elephant that stood between them?

A few minutes before five, the doorbell rang. Max wiped his sweaty palms on his jeans and prepared to answer the door, but Lanie got there first. He stood in the hallway as his daughter wrapped Carissa in a warm hug.

"Happy Thanksgiving!" Lanie cried.

"Happy Thanksgiving." Carissa's voice was more subdued as her eyes met Max's. "I brought a pecan pie and homemade cranberry sauce." She shifted her weight to her other foot. "I hope that's all right."

"Homemade cranberry sauce?" Steven turned in his chair in the living room and raised an eyebrow. "Doesn't everyone eat the kind that comes in a can?"

Carissa gave a nervous laugh. "It's my mother's recipe."

"I'm sure it'll be delicious." Lanie took the bags from Carissa and led her into the kitchen. "I'm glad you were able to make it."

"Thanks for inviting me." As she stepped into the kitchen, Carissa's eyes widened. "Wow. That's a lot of food." Her gaze found Max's again. "You really go all out."

"We haven't eaten since breakfast," Max explained. "We save our calories for the meal. Did you want something to drink?"

"White wine if you've got it."

Max removed the bottle from the fridge and poured Carissa a glass. He was thankful to have an excuse to turn away from her. She looked absolutely radiant in a simple blue dress with a matching jacket. Her hair was pulled away from her face with a clip, showing off her high cheekbones. It had taken everything in his power not to reach for her the moment she set foot in the house.

As he handed her the glass, their fingers brushed, and a jolt of electricity shot up his arm. He wished he could have a moment alone with her, to hash out what was wrong between them as well as to kiss her senseless.

She stared at him, and the same yearning he felt was reflected in her eyes. The beep of the oven timer broke the spell, and they glanced away from each other.

"That's dinner!" Lanie removed the sweet potato casserole and rolls from the oven and set them on the counter.

Grateful for a distraction, Max rushed to help her carry the food into the dining room. Steven and Rose came in from the living room and took their seats on one side of the table with Lanie and Nate on the other. That left Carissa and Max to sit at opposite ends.

A flash of memory shot through Max as he realized no one had occupied that seat since Melody. Seeing Carissa sitting there caused an avalanche of emotions to come crashing through him all at once. Sorrow at what he'd lost after his divorce. Joy at seeing the seat filled once more with someone who had stolen his heart. Hope that Carissa's presence was the promise of something new and beautiful. And fear that he had already screwed it up.

"Dad?" Lanie prompted, bringing him back to the present. "Are you going to carve the turkey?"

With a gruff nod, he picked up the carving knife and a fork and began slicing the meat from the bird. Everyone passed their plates and called out whether they wanted light or dark meat. Once everyone had turkey, other sides were passed around. Max finished carving the last of the turkey and tossed out the bones.

His children and their partners had already begun digging into the food when Max finally had a chance to fill his plate with the rest of the sides. As he lifted his fork, he caught Carissa staring at him.

"Everything all right?" he asked.

She glanced at the two couples sitting on opposite sides of the table before clearing her throat. "Do you not say grace?"

"Um…" Lanie set down her silverware. "Not usually, but we can if you'd like."

Steven smiled. "Our tradition is to say what we're thankful for after the meal."

"But Carissa is our guest." Rose gestured to her. "Would you like to say grace?"

The way Carissa's eyes widened suggested to Max she was wishing she hadn't said anything. He had opened his mouth to save her when she nodded.

"Dear Heavenly Father." She bowed her head. "We give thanks for this bountiful feast prepared by loving hands. We give thanks for this time with our family and friends. We ask that you bless those who are gathered here and those we have lost but still hold in our hearts. Amen."

As Max raised his head, he fought back the tears Carissa's words had brought forth. Despite being raised Catholic, he'd never been a religious man. But the simple prayer Carissa had offered reminded him so much of Melody that for a moment, it'd felt like she was still in the room with them. Her faith, even at the end, had been steadfast.

Everyone began eating again, but a much more somber mood filled the room. Carissa gave him an apologetic smile, but he shook his head. Her prayer was beautiful in its simplicity. And it made him realize that while he missed Melody terribly, there was no doubt in his mind he was ready to take a second chance at love—and all that came with it.

Chapter Twenty-Six

After dinner, Carissa offered to help with the dishes, but Steven and Nate shooed her and everyone else out of the kitchen.

"Since we didn't help with the cooking, the least we can do is the cleaning," Steven said as he filled the sink with soapy water.

Rose and Lanie claimed the couch and talked excitedly in low voices. While Max sank heavily into his recliner, he kept his gaze on Carissa.

"Take a load off," he said, gesturing to the other recliner.

But she couldn't sit still. As happy as she was not to have to spend another holiday alone, she couldn't ignore the last time she'd been in that house with Max and all the things they'd said. They needed to talk.

"I need to burn off some calories," she said with what she hoped was a lighthearted smile. "Want to go for a walk with me?"

To her surprise, he jumped out of his chair. "Absolutely."

She started for the door. *Don't be rude.* With a sinking heart, she turned to Lanie and Rose. "We're going for a walk. Do you want to join us?"

The two women exchanged a glance then looked at Max. Their eyes widened, and they shook their heads as if Max's expression had made their decision for them. But when Carissa glanced at him, he had a pleasant smile on his face.

"Shall we?" he asked.

They grabbed their coats and headed out the front door. Once they were safely on the sidewalk, Max tentatively took her hand.

"I'm glad you came tonight." He kissed her cheek. The slightest peck, but it sent shivers down her spine. "I don't like how we left things the last time."

"Me either," she breathed, momentarily forgetting her apprehension about the evening.

"I should have reached out." His eyes were filled with sorrow. "Our first contact after the argument shouldn't have been in a supermarket, though I hope to make it up to you."

Her heart fluttered. "What did you have in mind?"

A slow smile stole over his face, but he shook his head. "We'll get to that later. For now, we should probably talk."

"I'm sorry for what I said about you wasting your time with the arch," Carissa began. "I'm concerned we either won't be able to fit it into the church or it won't be done in time to do so." She frowned. "I wish you had told me before you started working on it. I could have helped you."

Max sighed. "In retrospect, I should have included you in my plans. I was so focused on keeping it a secret from Lanie, I didn't think about the impact it would have on your work."

"I appreciate that." They strolled through Max's neighborhood, and Carissa took a deep breath of cool air. "Before I leave tonight, I'd like to get the measurements of the arch. I can take them to the church tomorrow."

"As long as we can wait until Lanie is otherwise distracted, that sounds fine."

She gave a short nod. While she appreciated how much Max wanted-ed to surprise his daughter, logistically, he couldn't keep it from her for much longer. For one thing, he was storing the arch in their garage, and it wouldn't take much for Lanie to stumble upon it. Then there was the fact he'd promised to tell Lanie before the wedding, and as they were approaching the end of November, time was running out.

Carissa supposed she could come back on Monday when Lanie would be at school, but the longer she put off measuring the arch, the less time Max would have to make something else. Though at that point, she wasn't sure he *could* do something else even if he wanted to, which he clearly didn't.

When they got back to the house, Lanie and Nate were already cutting into the pies. Steven and Rose sat at the table, enjoying a glass of wine.

"Welcome back," Lanie said as Carissa and Max entered the kitchen.

Carissa detected a hint of suspicion in Lanie's eyes, but she only asked, "Pumpkin, apple, or pecan?"

"Apple," Max said without hesitation.

"I'll try the pumpkin." Carissa had never been a fan of apple pie.

After Lanie handed them their plates, they took their seats at the table and dug in. The pie was the perfect blend of sweet and savory. She was surprised at how quickly she gobbled it up considering she was still full of dinner.

When everyone had finished their desserts, their little group began to break apart. Steven and Rose said their farewells and headed home. Lanie and Nate finished cleaning the last of the dishes.

As Carissa left the kitchen, Max took her hand. "Perhaps now is a good time for you to measure the arch."

She allowed him to lead her into the garage. The moment he removed the sheet from the arch, she gasped at the progress he'd made. One side was almost finished, with intricate roses and vines. The only part he hadn't carved was the top of the curve.

Without a word, he handed her a tape measure, a notepad, and a piece of paper. She got to work measuring the arch and comparing it to the measurements she'd taken at the church.

"So, what's the verdict?" Max leaned against one of the finished night-stands.

She flicked her gaze back and forth between the measurements she'd scrawled on the paper and the ones from the church. It didn't look good.

He raised an eyebrow. "Does it pass muster?"

To buy herself some time, she remeasured a few sections just in case, but they only confirmed what she already knew. Her mind raced through different tactful ways she could explain her concerns.

"I need to go to the church to measure the doors and one other area where it might work," she began before shaking her head. "But I can tell you that even if we can get the pieces inside the church, it's not going to fit."

"Even though the pieces can be separated?"

"It's too wide." She handed him both the paper with the arch measurements and the church measurements. "The church's aisles are narrow. It would fit near the handicap entrance, as that is wide enough for a wheelchair, but that's on the other side of the stage from where the ceremony will take place."

He waved a dismissive hand. "I'm sure we'll find a way, but I'm happy to come to the church with you to troubleshoot."

"That won't be necessary," she said quickly. "Besides, it might look suspicious if we're both there. Wouldn't want it getting back to Lanie and ruining your surprise."

His eyes narrowed in apparent suspicion, but he nodded. "Fair enough. Let me know what you find."

"I will. I promise."

⁓ele⁓

Carissa wasted no time getting to the church the next day to compare the measurements. The church was empty when she arrived, though she assumed most people were Black Friday shopping. She'd called ahead to Reverend Patrick to make sure the building was open, and she'd hoped she could get in and out without too much fuss.

After setting her purse on a pew, she walked to the railing that separated the sanctuary from the congregation. At Steven and Rose's wedding, they had stood on one side of the railing in the center, and Reverend Patrick was on the opposite side on the slightly elevated platform.

Lanie wanted to be married at the small opening to the right of the elevated area near the choir loft, but Carissa might be able to convince her to move to the center. *Best to measure both to be safe.*

After surveying the measurements and looking at the spaces, Carissa determined the arch would fit better nearer the congregation, but it wouldn't leave much room in the front pew for people to sit. As she'd suspected, the only other place it would fit was near the handicap entrance, which would allow it to be in the church but not part of the ceremony.

On the other hand, if Max could narrow the arch, it would fit in that small opening by the choir. The preacher could stand on the step, and the arch could be placed where Lanie and Nate would stand. She tilted her head. *Though they might have to stand in front of it if it's too narrow.*

With a sigh, she headed to the back of the church and measured the entryway just to be sure. The moment she began measuring, the door to the church opened, and in walked Lanie.

"Carissa, I'm glad I ran into you. I want to—" Her eyebrows pulled together. "What on earth are you doing?"

"Uh, I-I needed to measure the church."

"For what?" Lanie asked, her frown deepening.

Carissa's mind raced, but she couldn't come up with a lie fast enough. Besides, she didn't *want* to lie to her client, even if it meant breaking her promise to Max. Her reputation was built on being forthright and honest no matter the circumstances.

Lowering her arms in defeat, Carissa took a deep breath. "I'm not supposed to tell you this, but I imagine you'll find out soon enough anyway." She gestured to a pew, and Lanie sat, her bewildered expression growing more pronounced.

"Your father is building you a wedding arch." Carissa sank into the pew beside Lanie. "I tried to talk him out of it, but it's a surprise wedding gift for you." She then explained why she was there and what she was doing by measuring the church.

"And he didn't think to discuss this with me?" Lanie's face reddened.

"He was going to tell you when he finished it." Carissa put a hand on Lanie's shoulder. "I'm sorry. I shouldn't have told you."

"No, you did the right thing." Lanie's eyes flashed as she glared at the front of the church. "Of course he would pull something like this. First, he bullies his way into paying for Steven's rehearsal dinner. Then he has to put his two cents into everything we're doing, despite repeated requests from both of us that he back off. And now, he's completely changing the decor of my wedding without even asking me." She scowled. "Clearly, we need to have a come-to-Jesus meeting."

"He's not going to be happy I told you," Carissa warned.

"Is he working on it in the garage?"

"Yes. He covers it with a sheet, but its height is impossible to miss."

"Then it's easy enough for me to happen upon it myself." Lanie glanced at Carissa, her expression softening. "He never needs to know you told me."

At first, Carissa breathed a sigh of relief, then she shook her head. "No, it's better if you tell him the truth. I'll deal with any fallout later."

With a nod, Lanie stood. "All right. Well, wish me luck."

Carissa blinked. "You're going now?"

"I'm hoping to catch him in the act." Without another word, Lanie spun on her heel and stalked out of the church.

Lord help us. Bowing her head, Carissa sent up a prayer she hadn't just blown up two relationships. But she wasn't holding out much hope.

Chapter Twenty-Seven

Max was meticulously carving a heart into the side of the arch when the door from the house to the garage swung open. His heart stopped when he caught sight of his daughter's face.

"Lanie, wha—" Although he knew it was too late, he threw the cover over the arch in a half-hearted attempt to hide it.

"It's true, then?" she demanded as she rushed into the room and yanked the sheet away. "You've been building this behind my back?"

"H-how'd you find out?"

Instead of answering, she took a deep breath as if to calm herself. "Does it matter? The fact is, I know, and I don't appreciate you trying to make such a major change to the layout of the ceremony without consulting me."

Max held his hands up. "Now, hold on. I'm doing something nice for you." He touched the wood. "It's a gift."

"That you decided to create without any forethought into whether it would fit into the church, let alone with the rest of the decor?"

Something about the way she spoke sounded suspiciously like Carissa. He narrowed his eyes. "She told you, didn't she?"

"Again, it doesn't matter how I found out, though I would love to know why you told her and not me." Lanie crossed her arms. "But we'll deal with that later. Right now, we're talking about *you*. What were you thinking?"

"I wanted to do something nice for my daughter," he retorted. "Though I didn't realize how ungrateful she would be to receive it."

"Ungrateful?" Her eyes widened in disbelief. "This isn't like a table or chair Nate and I could incorporate into the wedding and then use in our future home." She held up her hands to try to capture the sheer size of the arch. "How are we supposed to fit this in Nate's house, let alone the church?"

Pain stabbed in his gut at her sharp words. Of all the reactions he'd expected Lanie to have, he'd never expected that one.

When he didn't say anything else, she let out an exasperated sigh. "Why couldn't you have at least talked to me before you went to all this trouble? I love what you've done with the pieces you recently finished. I would have been happy to have something similar as a wedding gift."

"But I wanted to be part of your big day," he blurted out as he spun around. The realization of what he'd said hit him, and he hurried on. "I mean, I wanted *it* to be part of your day. The arch."

The flush of anger on her cheeks faded as she bit her lip. "You didn't need to make anything to be part of the day." She moved toward him and placed a hand on his arm. "You're walking me down the aisle and dancing with me at the reception."

"I know," he said gruffly, shaking her off. "I wanted to give you something that showed how much I love you." He glanced at the arch. "I could try to make it smaller—"

"It won't work, Dad," she said sharply. But he must have flinched because her face softened. "I'm sorry to be harsh. This isn't what I envisioned, and it doesn't go with the rest of the aesthetic."

"Fine." He threw the cover over the arch and stomped out of the garage, calling over his shoulder, "I'll figure something else out."

But his attempt to get away from her was thwarted when she followed him. "Why did you tell Carissa and not me?" She grabbed his arm. "Is something going on between you two?"

He froze before slowly turning to meet her gaze. "Why do you ask that?"

She frowned. "Something Rose said at Thanksgiving, that you two would make a cute couple. Then you went for a walk alone at dinner, and you were gone for a while." She studied his face. "There is something, isn't there?" Tears sprang to her eyes as the realization fully hit. "You're dating? After I specifically asked you not to?"

"You wanted me to put myself out there," he mumbled, shoving his hands into his pockets.

"With anyone but her!" Lanie's hands balled into fists at her sides. "I can't believe you did this to me. I thought we were getting closer. I thought—"

"It doesn't matter anyway because clearly, she and I aren't going to work out." He was unable to keep the bitterness out of his tone, but at least it masked the pain.

"Great." Lanie put her hands on her hips. "The whole reason I asked you not to date her was to *avoid* making things awkward at the wedding. So thanks for ruining that plan."

"Well, you won't have to worry about that," Max said, his anger getting the better of him. "Because I'm not going to your wedding!"

The words came out before he could stop them. Lanie's face crumpled, and without another word, she fled the room. The front door slammed, and a moment later, an engine started.

Max leaned against the counter and buried his head in his hands. The arch was supposed to be symbolic, a way to bridge the divide between him and his daughter.

Congratulations, old man. You just burned that bridge.

⁓ℓℓ⁓

An hour later, Max had stewed in his emotions long enough. He grabbed a coat and headed out into the chilly autumn air to confront Carissa.

On the way to her house, he rehearsed what he wanted to say. But the more he recalled her betrayal, the angrier he became. By the time he roared into her driveway, he was practically spitting fire.

He didn't even make it to the front door before she swung it open and came out. Her hands were lifted, whether in surrender or to fend him off, he couldn't tell.

"I'm sorry," she said quickly. "I ran into Lanie at the church, and I couldn't lie to her about why I was there."

"Why not?" he demanded. "There are a million reasons you might be at that church that had nothing to do with her. Why couldn't you have said you were there for another bride? Or you needed to check in with the reverend about something?" He glared at her. "You promised me you wouldn't tell her."

Instead of cowering under his berating questions, she lifted her chin. "Lanie is my client. She is paying me to assist her with her wedding. It's one thing to ask me not to say anything to her, but it's quite another to insist I lie when directly questioned."

"So it's okay to lie to me, then?"

Carissa's eyes flashed. "I didn't lie to you. I did everything in my power to keep your secret." She crossed her arms. "But it was a fool's errand to expect Lanie wouldn't find out about the arch. You live with her for goodness' sake. You don't think at some point she might have grown curious about what you were working on in the garage?"

Warmth rushed to his cheeks, but Max shook his head. "She hasn't yet, and I've been working on the arch for over a month now."

"And we've still got about a month until the wedding. A lot can happen even in that short amount of time."

"Well, count me out."

Her mouth fell open. "What is that supposed to mean?"

"I'm done with it." At Carissa's bewildered expression, he continued, "All of it. If my work isn't good enough for her wedding, then clearly, neither am I."

Carissa pursed her lips. "Did Lanie say she didn't want you in her wedding?"

"She might as well have." Max ignored the heaviness in his stomach. It wouldn't surprise him in the least if Lanie decided not to have him at her wedding after the way he'd behaved. But Carissa didn't need to know that part.

"Give her time," Carissa said. "I'm sure you both said some things you didn't mean and—"

"Don't lecture me about how to handle my daughter."

Her mouth turned down. "I'm not." She gestured behind her. "Look, why don't you come in, and we can talk about—"

"No, thank you." Max straightened his spine. "As you said, Lanie is your client, and it wouldn't be appropriate." He headed to his car.

"Max, wait!"

But he didn't stop. As he drove away, he tried to hold on to his anger to counteract the pain.

When he returned home, he wasn't surprised to find Lanie wasn't there. She would probably stay the night with Rose and Steven. Guilt needled his belly, though he tried to ignore it.

His phone vibrated. At the sight of Carissa's name, he almost turned it off, but the beginning of the text message caught his attention.

FYI, the arch won't fit in the church. Not sure it matters at this point, but here are the measurements.

When he tapped the message, he saw that the arch was about two feet too wide. He sighed and leaned his head back against the seat. She was right. It didn't matter now.

For a moment, he considered burning the arch. Then he imagined chopping it into smaller pieces and using it for firewood. He climbed out of his truck and went into the house as visions of destruction danced in his head.

Though it was nearing dinnertime, he wasn't hungry. And he'd had more than his fair share of cooking for one after his divorce. He headed into the garage and leaned against the wall, allowing his eyes to move from the arch to the desk and back again.

The desk likely didn't need half as much work as it would take for him to remove two feet of wood from the arch. But even if he hadn't blown up two relationships in one afternoon, he couldn't quite bring himself to work on the desk. While Lanie was right in that the desk would be useful beyond the wedding, it didn't feel big enough for what he wanted to do.

A car door slammed on the other side of the garage door, and Max rushed into the house with his heart in his throat. The crushing disappointment was only slightly buoyed by the sight of his son.

"Steven," he said. "What a nice surprise."

A muscle feathered in Steven's jaw as he entered the house. "I'm afraid it's not a social call."

Max's smile faded, and he gestured for Steven to go ahead of him into the living room. "I assume Lanie visited you."

"Well, she came to talk to Rose," Steven corrected. "But I closed the office for Black Friday, so I was home." With a sigh, he sank onto the couch. "Dad, what were you thinking?"

Crossing his arms, Max prepared to dig in his heels once more. "I wanted it to be a surprise."

"I'm not talking about the arch, though I'll get to that in a minute." Steven leaned forward. "I mean telling your only daughter you don't want to be at her wedding. She's already struggling with the fact that one parent *can't* be there, and now the other parent is choosing not to be."

A lump formed in his throat. In all his righteous anger, Max hadn't once considered how hard planning a wedding must be for Lanie without her mother. Melody had had such grand plans for her children's weddings, including a dance with both of them.

"I didn't mean it," he said. "Her reaction upset me, and I spoke without thinking."

Raising one eyebrow, Steven shook his head. "That seems to be your MO lately."

"What's that supposed to mean?"

"Exactly what it sounds like." Steven raked a hand through his hair. "You could have talked to me about the surprise you were planning. I would have been happy to steer you in a direction that would have both fit her wedding theme and served a functional purpose in her new life." He rolled his eyes. "I've heard more about floral arrangements and color coordination than I ever expected to in my young life, but it's all she and Rose talk about."

"I didn't want to tell people because I was afraid Lanie would find out," Max said, feeling like a broken record.

"And I would have kept your secret. You could have even stored it at my house."

"What if Rose found out and told her?"

Steven's expression darkened. "First, I don't appreciate your lack of faith in my wife. And second, I have my hiding places. Rose rarely goes into the basement because she thinks it's creepy."

"But my tools are here," Max protested feebly. It became clearer with each passing moment that he wasn't going to win the argument.

"All I'm saying is you could have handled this differently." Steven's eyes softened. "You and Lanie haven't always had the best of relationships, and I understand why you wanted to do this for her." He took a deep breath. "But a true gift shouldn't be about you and your desire to fix things. It should be about the person receiving the gift." A quiet chuckle. "Believe me, I learned that the hard way with Rose. I almost worked myself into an early grave trying to give her what *I* thought she needed rather than letting her tell me about her needs in her own way."

"It's a bit late for that now," Max grumbled.

"It's never too late to fix a mistake. Take Rose and me. It took her breaking off our engagement for me to see reason, but I did." Steven smiled. "And now we're married."

As much as Max hated to admit it, his son had a point. Still, Steven had had an easier time mending his relationship with Rose. They'd been together only a few years, and the conflict they faced was a recent development. In contrast, Max's relationship with Lanie had been steadily deteriorating for over a decade.

"And what's this I hear about you and Carissa?" Steven asked when Max didn't respond.

Pressing his lips together, Max stared at the floor and refused to answer. But if his son's groan was any indication, he didn't need to.

"I'm glad you're dating again, but I don't understand why you couldn't tell me everything."

With a sigh, Max raised his head and met his son's stare. "I promised Lanie I wouldn't date her wedding planner, and honestly, when I made that promise, Carissa was the last person I ever considered dating. But... things happened."

"Is it safe to assume you blew things with her as well?"

Max crossed his arms. "Only because she broke her promise not to tell Lanie about the arch."

Steven stared at him with wide eyes. "Are you for real? She's employed by Lanie. It's her job to keep the bride up to date about the goings-on of her wedding. You literally asked her not to do what Lanie is paying her for. If she'd lied to Lanie, she would have risked her position over it. Her livelihood."

"A text message warning me Lanie was on the warpath would have been nice."

"Perhaps, but you aren't her client. She's under no obligation."

"But we're in a relationship. Shouldn't that count for something?" The argument sounded worse out loud than it had in Max's head.

Steven grimaced. "Well... You *were* in a relationship."

That's enough hard truths for one evening. Max made his way to the kitchen. "Since you're here, would you like something for dinner?"

"I could eat."

Grateful to have something to distract him, Max removed some leftover turkey from the fridge and diced it. Once the turkey was cut up, he mixed it with a can of cream of chicken soup and frozen vegetables. After assembling the mini turkey potpies in the muffin pan, he placed the pan in the oven and left it to cook.

While he waited on the potpies, he stepped outside for some fresh air. The little mourning dove was eating at one of the bird feeders. When it saw him, it flew to the railing.

"Hello again."

She cooed in response and cocked her head as if she understood him. Her gray feathers ruffled in the cool evening breeze.

"I've really done it this time." Lifting his face to the heavens, Max closed his eyes. *If Melody were here, she'd know what to do.* A soft chuckle bubbled up in his throat, and he opened his eyes. "If Melody were here, she'd probably tan my hide for treating Lanie so poorly."

The bird cooed as if in agreement, and the chuckle developed into a laugh. Max turned to look at his feathered companion.

"You have the right idea, staying single and true to your love for your lost mate." He shook his head. "Relationships are more trouble than they're worth."

Shaking its wings, the dove suddenly took flight, startling Max. A moment later, another dove joined it. They circled each other before swooping into the nest he'd seen the other day.

"Well, I'll be," Max said as the birds nestled down together. "I guess you moved on after all."

He'd never felt so alone.

Chapter Twenty-Eight

"I WANT TO THANK you for all your hard work on this," Colin said as they finished their virtual meeting late Monday evening. "I couldn't have done it without you."

"We make a good team." Carissa leaned back in her chair and rubbed her temples, grateful that Colin didn't force her to turn her camera on when it was just the two of them. Her love life might have blown up in her face, but she was kicking butt at planning the retreat. It helped that Jacob had been caught up with another project in his office and hadn't joined the last few meetings. Working with Colin was easier when the CEO wasn't breathing down his neck.

"If you can make the latest changes to the schedule, I'll forward our slides to Jacob for approval." Colin sighed. "And then maybe you and I can take a well-deserved break for the holidays."

Her heart panged. The last thing she needed right then was a break. Staying busy kept her mind off the problems with Max. They hadn't spoken since he'd shown up at her house on Friday, but Lanie had a dress fitting the next day. She was torn between hoping Max would show up and praying he'd stay away. She wasn't sure she was ready to see him again.

"I'll get those over to you by close of business tomorrow," Carissa promised. As she disconnected from the call, she put her head on the table, promising herself she'd rest for only a moment.

The buzzing of her phone woke her, and she blinked bleary eyes into the bright morning sun. Her neck and back ached from being hunched over the table all night, and her throat was bone dry. With a groan, she stretched and glanced at her phone.

"Oh no." She was late for Lanie's fitting.

Be there in twenty, she texted. Then she ran upstairs to take a quick shower. When she left the house ten minutes later, her hair was damp. The cold wind blew the wet strands against her bare neck, making her shiver. As soon as she started the car, she cranked up the heat and prayed her hair wouldn't form icicles on the way to the dress shop.

Minutes later, she raced into the bridal shop, where Lanie stood on the pedestal in front of the mirror. Only Rose and three of Lanie's other friends sat on the benches by the pedestal. Max was nowhere to be seen.

"I'm sorry I'm late," Carissa said. "I overslept."

"That's all right. You have a lot going on." Lanie smoothed the satin skirt of her white dress. It had a sweetheart neckline with off-the-shoulder lace sleeves. "What do you think?"

Carissa put her hand to her heart and smiled. "It's perfect." Tears sprang to her eyes, and she dashed them away. *What on earth is wrong with you?* She never cried when seeing a bride in her dress.

"Should we shorten the hem?" Lanie asked, oblivious to Carissa's sudden onset of emotions. "I don't want to trip."

"Maybe just an inch?" Rose suggested as she lifted Lanie's skirt. "If you go too much shorter, it might look awkward."

The seamstress pulled Carissa aside. "We've got the bridesmaids' dresses ready for final fittings as well. Did you want us to bring those out?"

"Since the bridesmaids are here, we might as well. It'll save us a trip later." Carissa clapped. "Ladies, your dresses are ready. If you're game, we can have you try them on now to determine if there are any additional alterations needed."

"Oh, that's wonderful!" Lanie cried, hugging herself. "I can't wait to see them."

The seamstress beamed at her. "While they're changing, let's pin up your hem."

Once the room had emptied of all of Lanie's friends, Carissa sat heavily on one of the benches. Her neck and back still ached from sleeping at the table, and she wished she'd had time to grab a cup of coffee.

"I'm glad to have a moment alone with you," Lanie said. She glanced at the seamstress. "Well, semi-alone, I suppose."

"Oh?" Carissa asked, immediately on high alert. "Something on your mind?"

"I wanted to talk about my dad."

Keeping her eyes on her own reflection, Carissa nodded. "What about him?"

Lanie sighed. "We haven't spoken since he said he didn't want to go to my wedding, and now, I'm worried I won't have anyone to walk me down the aisle."

"I'm sure he just needs to cool off." Carissa tried to sound more confident than she felt. A memory of the anger and pain in Max's face flashed through her mind, and she winced. "He wouldn't miss your wedding."

"Turn, please," the seamstress said.

"You don't know how stubborn my dad is." Lanie shifted to her right.

Carissa snorted. "I have a pretty good idea."

"Would it be weird if I asked Steven?"

With a sigh, Carissa shook her head. "It wouldn't be weird, but you should give your dad some time. The wedding is still a few weeks away."

"But we're not even speaking," Lanie said mournfully. "I have no idea what to say to him anymore. He hasn't apologized for what he said, which makes me think he's stubborn enough not to attend my wedding." She sniffled. "And that really hurts."

"Maybe start with how you feel." Carissa moved beside Lanie, taking her hand. "He needs to know how this is impacting you."

"What if he doesn't care?"

A laugh bubbled up in Carissa's throat. "The man built you a seven-foot arch. Actions speak louder than words, and that action tells me he cares."

Lanie rolled her eyes. "Is it really that tall?"

"I've got the measurements right here." Carissa patted her purse.

That brought a grin to Lanie's face, but it quickly faded. "I'm struggling to get past him not telling me about the arch or the fact that you two are dating."

Carissa squeezed her hand and worked to keep her emotions in check. "For my part in that, I'm sorry. I should have kept things more professional until after your wedding was over. As for your father, give him a chance to apologize. If he won't come around, we'll figure out a contingency plan for the wedding." Her eyes filled with tears for the second time that morning. "Just know there's no replacement for your father."

The truth of her words hit her harder than she'd expected. There was no replacement for Max for her either. He'd touched her heart in a way she'd never expected, and she wished they could find a way to mend what they had broken. But at that moment, it seemed hopeless.

"All done," the seamstress said as she stood.

Lanie turned in the mirror, checking her reflection at all angles. "What do you think?"

"You look beautiful."

Chapter Twenty-Nine

MAX FELT LIKE HE'D gone through all five grief stages since his confrontations with both Lanie and Carissa. But at least he'd made progress with Lanie. She'd agreed to have dinner with him that night, and he was determined to mend things between them.

Carissa was a different story. Every time he tried to see things from her point of view, his emotions got all mixed up again. He understood why she hadn't wanted to lie to Lanie, but would it have killed Carissa to give him a heads-up?

Steven's words echoed in Max's head. Lanie was Carissa's client, and Max was not. In the last few days, he'd realized he would always come second to her business, and he wasn't sure how he felt about that.

Her branching out into the corporate world would only make things worse. Her business was her priority. If she was successful, how long would it be before she had no time for him? *Better to rip the Band-Aid off now, forget her, and move on.*

Unfortunately, that was easier said than done. Despite how upset he was, he missed her. And the pain of missing her was sharpened by each day that passed when they didn't speak.

All those thoughts were running through his head as he parked at the supermarket to buy ingredients for his dinner with Lanie. As much as he hated to admit it, he half hoped to run into Carissa. But every time he went down an aisle, he was met with another wave of crushing disappointment.

With a sigh, he finished his shopping and headed to the checkout. Since the weather had taken a turn for the worse, a nice hearty meal of shepherd's pie might help thaw his daughter's frosty countenance toward him. He suspected Lanie had accepted his invitation only because Steven had encouraged her to.

After he checked out, he scurried to his car, anxious to get to the house. Aside from getting dinner started, he'd been splitting his woodworking between the desk and the arch. Perhaps he was a glutton for punishment, but he wasn't ready to give up on the gift he'd intended for Lanie.

Besides, Carissa's measurements had given him renewed purpose. If he could narrow the archway, it would fit in the church right where Lanie and Nate would stand. He hoped to discuss the possibility with his daughter over dinner—after he apologized profusely, of course. But since the arch was no longer a surprise, he could get her perspective. And if she hadn't warmed to the idea, then he would force himself to let go of his plans and focus on the desk instead.

When Max arrived home, he still had a few hours before he needed to get dinner started. He headed into the garage and continued his efforts to decrease the width of the archway. Inch by inch, he'd been shaving the wood on both pieces where they would meet in the middle. Once he was sure he'd narrowed the arch to the correct size, he planned to carve two heart pieces that would interlock when placed together.

As he worked, his mind kept returning to Carissa. *Wouldn't kill her to send a text.* The smooth, rhythmic movement he used to shave the wood morphed into a frenzied back-and-forth motion as his mind raced.

After all, I'm *not the one who broke the trust in our relationship.* He frowned as he recalled the way her lips had twisted when he accused her of breaking her promise. The argument was reminiscent of several he'd had with Melody during their marriage.

That was the trouble with women, and his own daughter was no exception. They seemed to think they could do no wrong, and when called out on their behavior, they flipped things around to paint the man as at fault.

Not this time. It would be a cold day in the devil's house before he would take the blame. All he'd tried to do was create something beautiful for his daughter. Max's conversation with Steven had convinced him he hadn't handled things well, but it didn't change the intent of his gift.

Max's renewed fervor paid off when he stepped back an hour later and surveyed the arch. He'd shaved off a foot on each side. After checking his measurements against Carissa's, he smiled for the first time in days. The arch was the right size. All that was left was to finish the intricate designs and the interlocking hearts.

But that would have to wait. He needed to start dinner. He headed into the house to get cleaned up. After washing his face and changing clothes, he went into the kitchen and drizzled oil into a skillet then set it on the stove to heat. Then he filled a pot with water and placed it on a burner to boil. While he waited, he chopped an onion.

Just as he'd added the onion to the pan, the front door opened. Max frowned as he stirred the onion. Lanie was early.

Her heels clicked on the linoleum in the hallway. A moment later, she peered around the wall of the kitchen and sniffed the air. "What's for dinner?"

"Shepherd's pie." Max glanced at her and stifled a sigh at the way her shoulders seemed to hug her ears. The tension in the air between them grew. *Maybe this is a bad idea.*

But he was determined to make things right with his daughter. For too long, they'd had an arm's-length relationship. He'd tried many different tactics to grow closer to her, but they all seemed to blow up in his face. He cringed whenever he recalled their dinner at The Muddy Oar when Lanie was still planning to go back to California. And he'd come to accept that her decision to stay in Cedar Haven had had nothing to do with him. If anything, his actions had almost sent her running back to the West Coast.

"Seemed a decent meal for a cold day," he continued when she didn't respond. "I'm a bit behind, though. I wasn't expecting you until later."

"I can leave if you want."

"That's not what I meant," he ground out then closed his eyes. Taking a deep breath, he opened them and turned to look at her. "I had simply hoped to have things set up by the time you arrived."

Her expression softened. She nodded at the potatoes he'd set on the counter. "Want me to peel those?"

"You don't have to," he said. "I can manage."

"Nonsense." She went to the sink and washed her hands. "I'm here now. Might as well put me to work."

"Thanks," he said. They worked together in silence. Once the onions were ready, Max added the lamb and the herbs, sautéing the meat mixture on the stove. The water in the pot began to bubble.

"Shall I add these now?" Lanie held out the peeled and chopped potatoes.

Max couldn't help the smirk that came over his face. "You don't have to ask. You probably know how to cook this better than I do."

Her tentative grin took him back in time. She looked so much younger when she smiled like that, and when her hazel eyes lit up, he could almost see the little girl he remembered.

Once she'd added the potatoes to the pot, she stepped back. He finished browning the lamb before draining the grease. Then he added the rest of the ingredients to the meat, stirring to combine them.

"So, how's school?" he asked, hoping to fill the silence.

"It's going well. The first couple of months were a bit of a struggle. A lot of the students didn't remember me from my brief time with them in the spring. They missed Mrs. Carlisle. But we're finding our groove now."

"That's good." He leaned against the counter and smiled. "I'm glad that all worked out."

"I've had to get up earlier than usual, though, since Steven's house is farther away." She gave him a pointed look.

"You're welcome to come back anytime. You know that."

She arched an eyebrow. "Do I?"

His face flushed. "I'm sorry for what I said—about not wanting to go to your wedding." He ran a hand through his hair. "I didn't mean it."

"It sure sounded like you meant it."

The pain in her voice cut through him, and he sighed. "I'm sorry I didn't tell you about the arch." He finally met her gaze. "It's just... You and I haven't always had the easiest relationship."

She snorted. "That's the understatement of the century."

His chest tightened. "Ouch." She opened her mouth as if to respond, but he shook his head. "No, I deserve that. But that's why I was building the arch. I wanted it to be something meaningful to you in hopes it might show you what I've always struggled to say."

"I know you love me, Dad." She gave a rueful smile. "Sometimes, you have a strange way of showing it, but I know you do, in your own way."

A splash sounded from the stove, and she hurried over to lower the burner heat for the potatoes. When she turned away, he impulsively pulled her to him in an awkward hug. She stiffened, clearly surprised by the contact, but she shifted slightly to face him and wrapped her arms around his waist.

"I hope you know I do appreciate the thought behind the gift," she mumbled into his shoulder. Too soon, she moved away. "I wish you would have talked to me about it, and your feelings for Carissa. It might have saved us both a lot of heartache."

His face must have changed at the mention of the wedding planner's name because Lanie's eyes narrowed. "Have you spoken to her?"

Max vigorously stirred the meat mixture, hoping Lanie would drop the subject. But he knew his daughter better than that.

"Aren't you being a little unfair?"

"I don't want to talk about her," Max grumbled.

"All right. I won't press."

Spinning around in surprise, Max gaped at Lanie. She gave a one-shoulder shrug before testing the potatoes but didn't volunteer anything else.

Soon, both the potatoes and the meat were ready to be combined. Lanie drained the water before mashing the potatoes with some sour cream, butter, salt, and pepper. After Max poured the meat into the casserole dish, Lanie dolloped potatoes on top. Then he slid the dish into the oven.

"Want something to drink?" he asked.

"Wine would be nice."

He poured Lanie a glass of wine and got himself some ice water. They sat on opposite sides of the table and sipped their drinks. The silence was stifling, and Max struggled to find a safe topic of conversation.

"So, what are you working on these days?" Lanie asked.

So much for safe subjects. Max braced himself for her reaction. "Well, I've been splitting my time between working on a small desk and... finishing the arch."

Her throat moved as she swallowed her wine and stared at him. A fire lit behind her hazel eyes, but she took a deep breath. It bothered him that she seemed to be carefully choosing her next words.

"We agreed the arch wouldn't work."

If things hadn't been so tense between them, he might have laughed. After all, from where he was sitting, there was no "agreement." Lanie—and Carissa, for that matter—had *told* him to ditch the arch idea.

It was his turn to take a breath and measure his words. "While I understand your concerns about the size, I've taken Carissa's measurements into account, and I'm altering the arch to fit the parameters of the church." When she opened her mouth, presumably to start yelling at him again, he held up a hand. "But I'm also working on the desk. If you don't like the arch, you can use that instead."

That seemed to catch her off guard. "You're giving me a choice?"

"I didn't want to leave another project unfinished, but I also don't want to force you to incorporate something you don't like into your wedding."

Her eyes became misty. "Dad... I—thank you."

The conversation was becoming too emotional for his tastes. "See there? I do listen..." He gave a sheepish grin. "Well, sometimes."

Her laughter warmed his heart. Then the oven beeped, and he rose to remove their dinner. He set it to rest on the counter, and Lanie grabbed dishes and silverware. As she slipped by him to set the table, she put a hand on his shoulder and squeezed it. And for the first time in a long time, he believed things were going to work out after all.

Later that evening, Max sat in his living room, reflecting on the conversation he'd had with Lanie. She'd been open to the idea of incorporating the arch into the ceremony, but she'd insisted that Carissa be part of the process. Her reasoning had left him doubtful and suspicious.

She'd requested that Carissa view both pieces to determine which would work best. That way, they could still salvage some of the surprise, as Lanie hadn't seen the desk yet, and she hadn't viewed the arch since that day she found out about it.

Though he wasn't thrilled at the idea of Carissa coming to his house again, he'd agreed. He'd also reluctantly promised his daughter he would reconcile with Carissa, at least as far as the wedding went. The last thing he wanted was to cause Lanie more stress before her big day. They'd left things on good terms, with Lanie promising to move back home that weekend. He suspected that had more to do with the distance between Steven's house and Lanie's job than anything else. Still, he would take what he could get.

Something Lanie had said at dinner nagged at him. She'd danced around his issues with Carissa, but at one point, she'd told him she missed the happiness he'd shown after he started spending more time with Carissa.

"I can't remember the last time I saw you so..." She seemed to struggle to find the right word. "Content. Carefree."

The words had stuck with him because they weren't ones usually associated with him. *Grouchy, grumpy, irritable, pigheaded, and stubborn. That's what most people say about me.*

After she'd said it, he'd thought back to before the whole arch drama. Things with Carissa had been simple, easy. Mixed in with that heady feeling of a new relationship was an unexpected familiarity. *Almost like coming home.*

In all his righteous anger at Carissa for breaking his trust, he'd pushed aside those feelings to protect his heart. He'd developed that defense mechanism during the final years of his marriage. He found it easier to stay mad, which served only to push him further from what he really wanted—love and acceptance.

His ex-wife's voice echoed in his head. *I told you so.* But there was no malice or anger behind it, only gentle teasing.

"You were right." He smiled sadly. "And now I'm about to make the same mistake twice."

Oh, your count is much higher than that. He could almost picture her making that retort while her hazel eyes, so much like their children's, flashed, her hands on her hips. Then he imagined her face softening. *You never understood how to be vulnerable. Always had to be the strong one, even when you were falling apart.*

Max shook his head, and the image of Melody's ghost faded. Yet the ache in his chest remained. Melody had warned him that his lack of emotional availability would cause his downfall. She'd meant it regarding his relationship with their children, but he now understood that it applied to other aspects of his life too.

For the first time since their fight, he began to understand Carissa's perspective. In his quest to save his relationship with his daughter, he'd put Carissa's professional reputation at risk. Although he couldn't imagine that Lanie would have bad-mouthed Carissa or her company, he recognized why it concerned Carissa.

Her reputation and business are important to her, but what about me? That was the one question he couldn't answer. They hadn't spoken since he'd blasted her after she told Lanie about the arch. While he could, begrudgingly, admit his mistakes and contribution to their falling out, he needed to know if there was space in her life for him.

With a groan, he stood and stretched before heading upstairs to get ready for bed. Lanie had said she requested a meeting with Carissa sometime that week. Her plan was to have Carissa stop by the house and assess the two pieces to determine which one would work for the ceremony.

And then, I'll know if my arch and my relationship with Carissa have a future.

Chapter Thirty

When Carissa entered Bea's, Lanie was waiting for her. To Carissa's surprise and immense relief, the man sitting beside Lanie was Nate, not Max. Still, she covertly searched the rest of the restaurant to make sure he wasn't lurking somewhere.

"Good morning, Lanie. Nate." Carissa smiled. "I'm sorry I couldn't meet sooner, but my schedule has become rather busy as of late."

"It's fine," Lanie said, her voice higher pitched than normal.

Immediately, Carissa was on high alert. Something, or perhaps someone, was making Lanie nervous. Carissa took another cursory glance around the diner but saw no sign of Max.

"We wanted to discuss revisiting the arch," Nate said, bringing Carissa's attention back to the conversation.

"Oh?" Carissa's stomach flipped. The only thing worse than having Max attend the meeting was talking about that blasted arch. If she never had to think about wedding arches again, it would be too soon.

"I had dinner with my dad last night, and we had a long talk," Lanie said, and Carissa was relieved to hear her voice return to normal. "While he still hasn't shown me the arch, he said he's working with your measurements to make sure it fits in the church." Lanie took a deep breath. "But he's also been working on a desk that we can use for the ceremony in case the arch won't work."

"How accommodating of him," Carissa said, unable to keep the sarcasm out of her voice.

Lanie stiffened. "I know you aren't on good terms."

The talent of understatement must be a family trait. Carissa waved a dismissive hand. "That's not important right now. What matters is what *you* want for *your* wedding."

Lanie and Nate exchanged a glance.

"Well, that's the thing," Lanie said. "We want to keep the final arch a surprise." She gave a nervous laugh. "I mean, I saw it in its unfinished monstrosity when everything came out the other day, but Dad's keeping both the smaller version and the desk under wraps until the big day."

A silence fell over the table as Carissa digested their words and what they likely meant. Her lips parted, the *no* on the tip of her tongue.

"And so," Nate hurried on before Carissa could say anything, "we were hoping you would view them both and decide which one would work best."

"I don't think—"

"As our wedding planner, your opinion matters." Lanie gave her a meaningful look. "And you would know best what works with our vision."

Carissa stifled a groan. What Lanie hadn't said was they were paying Carissa to bring their vision to life, which meant she needed to view the arch to determine whether it would work.

Still, she wasn't about to give in without a fight. "I would suggest you forgo adding any unnecessary distractions to the ceremony space. The church is beautiful as it is."

Lanie frowned. "But my father wants to be a part of the day—"

"Which will happen without including his hobby." Carissa hated herself for being so cold, but she didn't want to spend any more time alone with Max McAllister than was absolutely necessary.

Nate's eyes vacillated between Lanie and Carissa, and he shifted uncomfortably in his seat. It was clear he wanted to be there even less than Carissa did. But she presumed Lanie had insisted he attend to present a united front.

Is avoiding Max worth upsetting a client? The thought came unbidden to Carissa's mind, but she pushed it away. She saw no reason they couldn't continue with the wedding without such an unnecessary hiccup.

Then Lanie bit her lip and lowered her gaze. "He won't say it, but he misses you."

A knife to the heart would have been more subtle. Carissa took a calming breath in through her nose and released it through her mouth. "I appreciate your concern, but my relationship with your father is not up for discussion."

"That's fine," Nate said suddenly, catching both Carissa and Lanie off guard. "But as your clients, we are telling you we want one of Max's wood pieces in the wedding ceremony." He slid an arm around Lanie's shoulders. "It's important to her that one of her father's handcrafted pieces be a part of our day, which means it matters to me, and it should matter to you."

Darn it. How could she argue with that? While she'd never fully bought into the saying about the customer always being right, in the current instance, he was. Were they any other clients, she wouldn't have even blinked at such a request. She had to admit that the only reason she was resisting was because of Max.

Stifling a sigh, she nodded. "You're right. I'm sorry. This is unprofessional of me." Though the words burned her throat, she continued, "I will contact Max and set up a time to see the pieces. Then I'll get back to you with my recommendation."

Lanie's eyes lit up. "Thank you. We really appreciate it."

"Now, let's talk about the seating chart," Carissa said, desperate to change the subject. "While we're still waiting to hear from a few people, we have a pretty good guesstimate of the head count."

⁓ℓℓ⁓

Though she tried to put off calling Max for as long as possible, by Thursday, Lanie had begun sending her daily text messages asking for a status update. While Carissa could try to blame it on Max, his daughter wouldn't buy that since she'd probably seen Max since the meeting.

Carissa planned to call him that afternoon, once she'd finished her weekly grocery shopping and tied up a few loose ends with the retreat. Fate must have had other plans because when she turned the corner to the bread aisle, she almost ran smack into Max.

His eyes met hers, and several emotions flashed through them. Some, she expected—anger, resentment, and even fear. But as all of the other reactions faded away, a look of longing stayed.

Her heart skipped a beat, and she put a hand to her chest. "S-sorry. I didn't see you there." Spinning the large cart around in the aisle was no easy feat, but she tried to make as hasty a retreat as she could.

"Carissa." Her name on his lips felt like a caress, and she squeezed her eyes shut as if she could make him disappear.

He shifted forward and put his hand lightly on her arm. "We need to talk."

She shook her head, stepping away from him. "Not here."

"I can come by your place—"

"No," she said quickly, opening her eyes. The last thing she wanted was that man in her personal space. Besides, she'd promised Lanie and Nate she would assess the arch and desk. "Let me drop off these groceries at home, and then I'll come to you."

There was a beat of silence, and she held her breath. Part of her hoped he would say it wasn't convenient, which was stupid since he'd just offered to meet at her house.

"All right," he finally agreed. "I'll see you soon."

The words were said kindly, but it felt like a threat nonetheless. Once she was sure he wasn't going to add anything else, she tore back down the aisle. Not wanting to risk running into him several more times, she abandoned her cart and rushed out of the store.

Instead of heading home, she drove twenty minutes across town to another store. She felt silly for going to all that trouble to avoid him, but she needed time. Seeing him there had shaken her more than she wanted to admit.

The relief she felt at entering the new store was palpable. But as she shopped, she was reminded why she never went there. Their selection left a lot to be desired, and everything was overpriced.

Oh well. At least I can get my groceries without a side of drama. She lingered over each item on her list. The longer she stayed in the store, the less time she would have to spend in Max's presence.

Yet even as she dreaded the moment she would have to abandon the pretense of shopping and head over there, she also yearned for it. In their brief meeting, she'd realized that the longing she saw in his eyes was reflected in her own. The simple fact of the matter was she missed him.

When she finally ran out of stalling tactics, she checked out and went home. It took her no time at all to put everything away. Taking a deep breath, she grabbed her keys and purse before forcing herself to walk to her car.

The drive over seemed to simultaneously last forever and end in the blink of an eye. To her surprise, the garage door was open, revealing Max's woodworking shop in all its dusty glory. As she climbed out of the car, she steeled herself for another argument.

At the sound of her car door slamming, Max stepped out of the garage and waved. "Come on in. I've got the arch uncovered and ready for your inspection."

She followed him into the garage, and as he'd promised, the arch was unveiled in all its glory. Even without closer inspection, it was clearly narrower than the first time she'd seen it. After digging in her bag, she removed her measuring tape and her phone. Then she refreshed her memory on the measurements of the church and measured the arch.

"I took about a foot off each half at the top," Max said. His voice shook, and Carissa breathed easier, knowing he was having a rough time with her visit too.

Once she finished taking measurements, she leaned back and pursed her lips. As he'd promised his daughter, Max had managed to alter the arch to fit into the church. But it was still a huge inconvenience.

"And the desk?" she asked, keeping her tone professional and detached.

"It's here." He gestured to a small rectangular table.

She hesitated, not wanting to be in such close proximity to him. As if reading her mind, he took a few steps back.

Goodness, this is awkward. But she kept her emotions in check as she examined the table. To her, it made the most sense for the wedding. Lanie and Nate were having a unity candle ceremony, and the piece was just the right size to hold the two individual candles that would join a flame on a large candle in the center.

And yet... Turning back to the arch, she could understand why Max had insisted on creating it. The piece was striking, with intricate leaves and flowers carved into the wood. Though it didn't go with Lanie's aesthetic, it had enough indentations and curves to make it easy to decorate with garlands and other Christmas décor.

"We could drape it with cloth to make it less one-dimensional," Max suggested. He lifted the cover and twisted it to demonstrate what he meant.

"Flowers and garland would work better." Carissa pressed her lips together. She hadn't meant to say that out loud. Until she'd determined which option was best, she didn't want to give him false hope.

He tilted his head as he surveyed the arch. "I could see that."

Glancing back at the table, she leaned closer. "Unfortunately, we'd be covering much of the design on this with a cloth to protect it from the wax."

"Oh." He frowned. "I hadn't thought of that."

A small smile pulled at her lips. "That's why I'm here." He gave her a tentative smile in return, which made her heart flutter. "At the same time, I'm still not sold on the arch. It does appear to fit the measurements I gave you, and I believe it will physically fit into the church, especially since it's in two pieces." She tilted her head. "But it's going to be difficult to transport, and we'd have to move it in and out of the church the day of the wedding."

When Max didn't immediately respond, she risked a glance at him, expecting to find his face flushed with anger. Instead, he stared at the arch as if assessing it from a different perspective.

"What if I take full responsibility for moving it?" he asked. "It'll fit in my truck, and I can get Steven to help me carry it the day of the ceremony."

Carissa tapped her chin. "I hate to ask this, but could you haul it over to the church now? It would help me to visualize how it would look the day of the wedding."

Max's face lit up. "I can get it in my truck and bring it over."

"Uh, maybe find someone to help you lift it," Carissa advised with a rueful smile.

He pulled himself up to his full height. "I'm stronger than I look."

"Be that as it may, I don't want to have to tell Lanie you won't be able to walk her down the aisle on her wedding day because you threw your back out." She began typing on her phone. "I'll ask Nate if he can spare a few guys once I get the go-ahead from the pastor to stage this in the church."

"Sounds like a plan." Max shuffled his feet. "Do you have a minute? I can make us a cup of coffee."

Her immediate instinct was to say no, but something about his demeanor made him appear more vulnerable and open than she had ever seen him. Against her better judgment, she nodded.

Max moved toward the entrance to the house and pushed the button to close the garage. Then he led her out of his workshop and into the kitchen. He indicated a seat at the table while he made the coffee. A few minutes later, a piping-hot cup was placed in front of her.

"Thank you," she said, keeping her eyes on the steam swirling out of her mug.

Sinking into the chair opposite her with a sigh, Max set his mug on the table and wrapped his hands around it. Neither of them said anything.

"I'm sorry for the way I acted after Lanie found out about the arch," Max said, breaking the silence. "I didn't handle the situation well, and I said a lot of hurtful things to both you and Lanie."

"I appreciate your apology," Carissa said.

He seemed to wait for her to say more, and when she didn't, he continued, "But it doesn't change anything?"

She met his gaze. "I didn't say that."

A spark of hope flashed in his eyes. "I'd like to start over—"

"I'm not ready for that."

He frowned. "Why not?"

Why not, indeed. A war waged inside of her, and she had no idea which would win—her head or her heart. On the one hand, she missed Max. When she lost Chuck, she expected to spend the rest of her life alone. But the more time she'd spent with Max, the more she wondered if it was possible to have two great loves in her life.

On the other hand, Max was stubborn and set in his ways. While she was glad he and Lanie had made up, they were family, and kin tended to overlook shortcomings because of the whole *blood is thicker than water* belief. Carissa wasn't sure she could get past the things he'd said and the way he'd treated her.

She chewed her lip as she debated her next words. Max was laying his cards on the table. It made sense for her to do the same.

"I'm not sure you fully comprehend what could have happened as a direct result of your actions." She leaned forward. "Lanie may just be one client of many, but she's a pillar in this community. The wedding side of my business is based mostly on word of mouth at this point. I enjoy the privilege of not having to reinvest my profits into advertising dollars, which has freed that money up for the expansion into corporate events." She shook her head. "One bad review from a client can devastate small businesses like mine, and by putting me in the middle of your relationship with your daughter, you risked that livelihood."

He put his head in his hands. "I realize that now, and I'm sorry." But when he raised his head again, she recognized the stubborn lines forming around his mouth. "At the same time, it might have made more sense for you to tell me that you couldn't keep the secret from Lanie rather than going forward with seeing the arch."

That was a fair argument. She had no excuse for why she hadn't refused to keep the secret when he'd asked. Perhaps things would have worked out differently if she'd insisted on telling Lanie from the start.

"I understand your work is important to you," Max continued. "Sometimes, I wonder if you had the right idea in the beginning."

Although she could guess what he meant by that, she wanted clarification. "I don't understand."

He sighed. "About holding off on any sort of relationship until after Lanie's wedding. If we weren't dating, I wouldn't have roped you into seeing the arch surprise, and maybe we could have started with a fresh, conflict-free slate. But what's done is done, and now I must ask if there's room in your life for anything beyond your expanding business."

She blinked. "What is that supposed to mean?"

"It means I want to be with you." He gestured between them. "You and I have a good thing going here, or at least, we did until everything blew up. I understand how important your business is to you. I need to know if that's always going to be your priority."

"Like I said, it's my livelihood."

His forehead wrinkled as if he was struggling to find the right words. "Can you see yourself building a future with me?"

That caught her off guard, especially given his reaction when she'd asked about marriage. "We've only been on a few dates."

He laughed. "I'm not proposing." His expression turned serious. "But I'm also not getting any younger, and, well, I want to give us a real shot."

If he'd said something like that over the summer, she would have laughed. The Max she'd known then was not like the Max she'd come to know since. He'd opened up to her, shown her his vulnerabilities. And there he was, asking her not only to forgive him for his mistake for his daughter's sake but also to give their budding romance another chance.

She sipped her coffee to buy some time. As much as she'd missed him, she wasn't sure she could trust him. He might be questioning her priorities, but she'd already seen how he put family before anyone or anything else.

"I need time," she murmured, pushing back from the table to leave.

The disappointment in his eyes almost made her reconsider, then he nodded.

"Take all the time you need."

⁓ℓℓ⁓

As Carissa had expected, the rest of the month leading up to the wedding was filled with hectic last-minute plans. Unlike Rose and Steven's wedding, which had been planned for two years, Lanie had given Carissa less than six months. That she had been able to pull it together at all still felt like a miracle. The McAllisters had even come through with their cookie plans. Lanie and Rose had dropped off the homemade favors the night before.

But they'd finally made it. It was the day before the wedding, and Carissa was getting dressed for the rehearsal. The pastor had agreed to let them set up the arch and desk that afternoon, and Carissa was excited to see Lanie's reaction.

After Max had taken the arch to the church, Carissa had finally been able to envision what it would look like on the day of the ceremony. The moment he'd set it up at the front of the sanctuary, all her objections died on her lips. The piece was truly beautiful.

While Carissa had suggested they wait until the day of the wedding to allow Lanie to get the full effect with all her guests, Max had insisted that his daughter see it beforehand in case she wanted to make any changes. His care and concern for Lanie's happiness had helped dissolve Carissa's remaining doubts about him. She couldn't wait until the wedding was over because she hoped to give their romance a second chance.

Once she was dressed, she headed to the church. She wanted to get there early to make sure everything was set up for her bride-to-be.

As she climbed out of her car, she grabbed a small bouquet of fake flowers she always used for brides during their rehearsals. A lone familiar truck sat in the parking lot near the church entrance. She climbed the stairs, anticipation building as she entered the doorway.

Max sat alone in a pew, staring at the arch. She quietly crept down the aisle and slid in beside him. If he was surprised by her sudden appearance, he didn't show it.

"What are you doing here so early?" she asked.

"What do you mean early?" he scoffed. "I never left after the guys helped me bring in the arch."

"Why?"

He shrugged. "Lanie wanted the house to herself for her and her brides-maids. I didn't want to be in the way." His gaze slid to her. "Besides, I figured you'd come before everyone else and we'd have a moment alone."

"Something on your mind?"

"Just you," he said simply, turning to face her. "And a question you asked me once."

"Oh? What's that?"

"Whether I'd get married again."

She stiffened. His reaction to her asking that question hadn't endeared him to her. While she understood him better now, his immediate rejection of the idea had stung at the time.

He covered her hand with his. "I was wondering if I could change my answer."

She swallowed, unsure of what to say. "Um... Sure?"

"After my divorce, I swore off relationships entirely. I didn't want to even date, let alone consider marriage again." His eyes searched her face. "Maybe it was watching my children find their own joy in matrimony. Or maybe it was spending this time with you, but I would like to get married again." He smiled. "Someday."

The emotions coursing through her were overwhelming. She tried to lighten the mood. "You'll have to let me plan your wedding."

"Hmm, I was thinking more of a destination type of deal."

"Really?" She raised an eyebrow. "To where?"

"Well, I'm not one for traveling, as I hate flying. But maybe somewhere drivable." A sudden gleam came to his eye. "Deep Creek, perhaps?"

Her heart in her throat, she opened and closed her mouth but couldn't find the words. She was saved from responding by laughter outside the church door. Taking a deep breath, she tried to calm her pounding heart.

"Oh my goodness!" Lanie squealed from the back of the church. "It's gorgeous." She rushed to their pew.

Max gave Carissa's hand a squeeze before he released it and stood to greet his daughter. Together, they stepped out of the pew, and Lanie threw her arms around her dad's neck.

"Thank you, Daddy. I love it."

"I thought you would," Carissa said with a smile. Her mind still whirled from what Max had said, but she had a better handle on her emotions. "I ordered a few garlands and poinsettias from that silk flower site you sent me. We could wrap them around the arch to make it more Christmasy."

Lanie nodded with enthusiasm. "That sounds perfect!"

Several people filed into the church with Nate, Steven, and Rose leading the way. The wedding party and some out-of-town guests Carissa had yet to meet moved toward the arch.

"Wow, Mr. McAllister," Nate said. "That's quite a talent you've got there." His dark eyes examined the arch with appreciation.

"Isn't it about time you called me Max? You're about to be family, after all."

"Would 'Dad' be too forward?" Lanie teased as she stepped away from her father and grabbed her fiancé's hand.

"Let's not push it."

Then the pastor came through the side door. "Welcome, everyone." He gestured to Lanie and Nate. "Are you ready to begin?"

Lanie exchanged a glance with Nate then nodded. "Let's do it!"

For the next hour, the pastor and Carissa worked together to line up the processional and walk through the ceremony. They went through it all a couple of times to ensure everyone knew when to enter and where to stand.

"All right. Everyone appears to have a better idea of what to expect tomorrow," the pastor said. "I'll open the church around eight in the morning for decorating, but please tell me if you need anything between now and then."

Before everyone dispersed, Carissa clapped. "Bea is holding several tables for us at her diner. Please make your way there as soon as possible."

She waited until most of the party had left before grabbing her things to leave as well. While Bea's was not her first choice for a rehearsal dinner, Lanie and Nate had insisted. It held sentimental value from their many dates there as teens.

When she came out of the church, Max was sitting on the stairs, hunched over seemingly to protect himself from the bitter December cold. He looked up at the sound of her footsteps.

"You didn't have to wait for me."

He shrugged. "I wanted one more moment alone with you before everything gets crazy."

They descended the church stairs together and went out to the parking lot. She opened her car door and put away her wedding binder before facing him. "I have an answer to your question."

His eyebrows pulled together. "My question?"

"About whether I could see a future with you."

"Oh." He swallowed. "And?"

Her heart pounded as she took a deep breath. "I want to *make* room in my life for a future with you."

The way his whole face lit up caused her stomach to flip. Without a word, he leaned forward and cupped her cheek. Then he brushed his lips gently against hers. Warmth spread from her face, down her neck, and to the tips of her toes.

Too soon, he pulled away, but he didn't release her face. "I was wondering..."

She raised an eyebrow. "Yes?"

"How would you feel about me tagging along on your corporate retreat in October?"

Her mouth fell open in surprise. October was months away. Why was he thinking so far ahead?

"Um... It shouldn't be a problem, but I expect I'm going to be very busy. We may not be able to spend much of that time together."

"That's okay. I'd just like to be there with you, and for you. To help where I can."

Her heart melted. "That would be lovely."

He kissed her again before stepping back with apparent reluctance. "We'd better go."

As he turned to leave, she called out to him. "Save me a dance tomorrow."

"I'll save you all of them."

⁓ ℓℓ ⁓

As much as Carissa loved working with her brides and planning their big days, she tended to hate the wedding itself. The planning was fun because everyone was usually relaxed and excited. But the day itself never failed to cause her a big ball of stress. Something always went wrong, and she had so much to keep track of, she sometimes felt like she momentarily had gone insane.

Lanie's wedding was no exception. Carissa had gotten to the church early with a few volunteers to start decorating the church. Another team, mostly Nate's friends, worked in the reception hall. Thankfully, the caterer was overseeing that, though Carissa would swing by before everything got started.

Meanwhile, the bride and groom were in their respective homes, getting ready. Max had texted multiple times, complaining about the level of

260

estrogen in his house. He'd begged to assist Carissa, but she kept telling him he needed to be there for his daughter. Based on his grumpy replies, that wasn't what he wanted to hear.

The morning passed quickly as Carissa ran around making sure everything was perfect for her clients. For a few moments, she forgot it was Christmas Eve. Usually, it was one of her favorite holidays, but she'd barely had time that month to go shopping let alone enjoy the holiday season.

Luckily, the church was already decorated for Christmas with a large tree covered in gold and white ornaments. A swag with pine cones and red ribbons adorned the pulpit, while green garland with red bows wrapped around the altar railing. But Carissa had added more greenery to the arch itself as well as red roses, white lilies, and holly berries.

Before she knew it, it was half past two. The wedding was due to start at three. Nate and his groomsmen milled about the church as guests arrived. There was no word on the bride yet, but Carissa had told Max to keep Lanie at the house until the last minute to avoid any opportunity for the groom to sneak a peek before the wedding.

As the clock ticked closer to three, Carissa suggested the groom and groomsmen get into place. Her phone buzzed in her pocket with a text from Max confirming he, Lanie, and the rest of the wedding party had arrived. The time had come.

The guests were ushered into their seats, and the pastor entered the church through the side entrance, just as he had the night before. At his nod, Carissa headed to the back of the church to begin the processional.

As she stepped out into the bright afternoon sun, she lifted her hand over her eyes. Lanie stood at the bottom of the staircase with one of her bridesmaids fussing about her train. Her blond hair was pulled up on the sides and curled in the back. A simple lace veil cascaded gently over her curls.

Carissa put a hand to her chest. Seeing a bride for the first time on her wedding day always brought a tear to Carissa's eye. But something about that particular bride stuck with her. Perhaps it was her involvement with the family, having planned Steven and Rose's wedding as well. Or it could have been her feelings for Max and what she hoped the wedding signified for their future. Whatever the reason, it took her a moment longer than usual to compose herself, but once she had, she descended the stairs.

"Lanie, you look beautiful." Carissa allowed her gaze to sweep over the rest of the bridesmaids. As the maid of honor, Rose wore a stunning green gown with cap sleeves and a V-neckline. The other bridesmaids wore similar gowns, but their sleeves were long and sheer. Each dress had a red sash to coordinate with the Christmas décor.

When Carissa finally turned to Max, her breath caught in her throat. He wore a black tuxedo with a red tie. A boutonniere of a red silk rose surrounded by green leaves and holly berries hung loose and lopsided on his lapel.

Without asking, Carissa went to him and straightened the flower before pinning it more securely. She didn't miss the way his eyes traveled over her. Glancing at her outfit, she was pleased with the way her simple red dress suit hugged her curves.

"That dress is going to put the bride to shame," Max whispered, grabbing her hand and pressing his lips to her knuckles.

"Don't say that," she scolded playfully. "Your daughter is beautiful."

"She is," he agreed, giving Carissa another once-over. "But you're gorgeous."

"You're distracting me." She addressed the rest of the wedding party. "All right, ladies. It's time to start the processional." After searching for the flower girl, she found one of Lanie's students standing wide-eyed near the bridesmaids. "Beth? Come here, please. And where is Robert?"

"Here." Robert stepped forward.

"You two are up first." Carissa handed the ring bearer pillow to Robert and a bouquet to Beth. "Are you ready?"

They nodded, and Carissa led them up the stairs to the church door. She peeked inside and signaled the pianist, who began to play the music Lanie had chosen, the traditional Irish ballad "Red Is the Rose." She gave each child a gentle push, and they began their procession to the front of the church.

Next, Carissa sent Trudy then Tocarra down the aisle. Finally, it was Rose's turn. Carissa gave her a quick hug.

"It's hard to believe only a few months ago, we were at *your* wedding."

"And maybe in the not-so-distant future, we'll be at yours," Rose quipped with a meaningful glance back at Max.

Carissa's face warmed, and she averted her gaze before gesturing for Rose to make her way to the front of the church.

Once everyone was assembled, Carissa again signaled to the pianist, and the music changed from "Red Is the Rose" to "A Thousand Years" by Christina Perri. Tears pricked behind her eyes as her latest bride began her walk down the aisle to her future. Max glanced back and winked at her before focusing on the task before him.

As the wedding continued and Lanie and Nate promised themselves to each other, Rose's words echoed in Carissa's mind. *And maybe in the not-so-distant future, we'll be at yours.* The idea of getting married again both thrilled and terrified her. It was too soon to even consider that with Max. They'd only just begun. But if the past year of spending time with the McAllisters had taught her anything, it was not to take anything for granted and to make the most of the time she had.

Epilogue

OCTOBER OF THE FOLLOWING *year*

If Max had thought weddings were hectic, he was completely unprepared for how insane a corporate retreat could be, at least for the person planning it. Luckily, the people attending the event seemed to be relaxed and enjoying themselves.

As much as he tried to help, he often felt like more of a nuisance than an aid. Carissa was like a well-oiled machine, which was no surprise after watching her handle both of his children's weddings. Still, he hoped he was at least a comfort to her if nothing else.

It was the last day of the retreat, and Carissa was run ragged. They'd just sent the group off to a restaurant for dinner. They had a few loose ends to tie up before everyone went home, but overall, it'd seemed a smashing success. Even the jerk of a CEO, Jacob, had begrudgingly complimented Carissa on her work. They planned to book future retreats with her, and she'd already had a few calls from potential clients. Between her wedding business and the new venture, she was doing well.

Max had made a point of becoming more involved. While he was often out of his element with the wedding stuff, Carissa appeared to appreciate that he provided a male perspective on the activities and ideas she had for the events. They made a pretty good team, and working together had only brought them closer.

So much so that he was hoping to find a moment alone with her before they headed back to Southern Maryland. He had a particular question he wanted to ask her, and he'd been planning how to do it for months.

After making sure she was still in the shower, he snuck the ring box out of his pocket and opened it. A brilliant solitaire diamond glinted back at him from the velvet cushion. It was simple but elegant. Truthfully, the ring had been burning a hole in his pocket ever since he'd bought it, and he'd had to restrain himself from popping the question multiple times. But the trip meant a lot to Carissa, and it seemed the perfect way to end what had been a long and exhausting road.

The shower turned off, and he slipped the box into his pocket. He'd debated asking her that night, but she'd been so tired when she got back to their cabin. Without telling her, he'd extended their reservation for one more night. He'd reserved a picnic basket and a wine tasting at a local winery for the next day. He hoped once the hubbub of the retreat was over, she would relax and enjoy their time together.

But that night, they were planning a quiet evening in. He'd bought some steaks for the grill and had already opened a bottle of red wine to breathe. As soon as she was dressed, he would get started on their meal.

As she entered the room fully dressed, her graying hair wrapped in a towel, his breath caught in his throat. She was more beautiful to him than ever before. His hand slid into his pocket, and he caressed the velvet box. *I should ask her now.*

He shook his head, pushing the thought from his mind. *Not yet.* Everything needed to be perfect. Her eyes met his, and she smiled.

"You look like you're struggling with something."

He swallowed and waved a dismissive hand. "No. I was caught off guard by how beautiful you are."

She scoffed. "I look like death." After walking over to the mirror, she unwrapped her hair and began towel drying it. "As happy as I am with the success of this week, I'm glad it's over. I need a vacation."

"I can't give you a whole week, but I extended our stay by another night. We leave Sunday."

She spun around, eyes widening. "What? Why didn't you tell me?"

"I wanted it to be a surprise." He moved toward her and wrapped an arm around her waist. "You worked hard this week, and you could use a day to relax before returning to the realities of home."

"Wow." Her face lit up with a smile. "A whole day here with just you." The smile morphed into a smirk. "Whatever will we do with ourselves?"

He laughed and kissed her briefly. "How does an afternoon at a winery sound?"

She closed her eyes and drew a deep breath. "Like heaven."

The urge to ask her bubbled up inside him again, and he forced himself to step back and put some space between them. "You hungry? I've got the steaks ready for the grill."

Opening her eyes, she nodded. "Famished."

He made his escape, carrying the steaks with him. After firing up the grill, he waited for it to get hot before he tossed the steaks on with a few vegetable kabobs and closed the lid. Drinking in the cool autumn air, he tried to clear his mind.

A moment later, Carissa joined him with a glass of wine in each hand. She handed one to him then clinked it with her own.

"To the best unexpected assistant I've ever had," she said with a wry grin.

"To us." His eyes never left her face.

She sipped the wine and frowned at him over her glass. "Something's gotten into you."

His heart skipped a beat, and he almost blurted out the question, but he bit his tongue to keep from speaking. When he recovered, he raised his hands.

"I don't know what you mean."

After setting her glass on the table next to the grill, she crossed her arms. "You've been jumpy all week. At first, the stress seemed to be getting to you, but the retreat is over. Everyone goes home tomorrow." Her lips quirked in a smile. "Well, except us."

"It was more stressful than I expected."

She raised an eyebrow. "There's more to it, though, isn't there?"

Lie. Tell her you're tired or missing the kids. But if the whole arch debacle had taught him anything, it was that he shouldn't hide things from her.

"I have something I want to ask you," he began.

"So ask me."

He sighed. "It's not something you just blurt out."

A light of understanding dawned on her face. "Oh."

Darn it. There goes the surprise. He grimaced and turned to the grill to check the steaks.

Then she leaned closer and took his hand. "I don't need some big romantic gesture."

He rolled his eyes. "You might not *need* it, but I want to give you one." He harrumphed. "Or I did, but once again, my surprise is ruined."

Cupping his cheek with her other hand, she held his gaze. "It's still not something I was expecting. And you know my answer is—"

Before she could continue, he dropped to one knee. *No way is she going to beat me to the punch.* With a shaky but determined breath, he removed the box from his pocket and opened it.

"Carissa Owens," he began. If nothing else, at least he could give the darned speech he'd been practicing for weeks. "I can't say we had love at first sight." Her laughter urged him on. "Or even second, third, or fourth sight. But it's been a long time since I felt this way about someone. I never saw myself getting married again, but then I fell in love with you, and I can't imagine spending the rest of my life without you." His voice cracked. "Will you marry m—"

"Yes!" she squealed before throwing her arms around him and sprinkling sweet kisses all over his face.

"You didn't even let me finish the question," he protested, sliding his hands into her hair and pressing his lips to hers.

She pulled back just far enough to look at him, a twinkle in her eye. "I wanted to prepare you for what a lifetime with me will be like."

He narrowed his eyes, hoping to appear stern but mainly to keep from laughing. "You mean you plan to ruin all of my surprises?"

"Pretty much."

She stepped back and helped him stand. Then he slipped the ring onto her finger. It was a perfect fit. While she admired her ring, he flipped the steaks then gazed toward the lake. He blinked. Sitting on the picnic table across from him was a pair of mourning doves. One of the birds cocked its head at him before preening its mate. A slow smile spread across his face.

"Looks like we both found someone," he whispered.

"Did you say something?" Carissa asked.

Max cleared his throat. "Uh, do you have a date in mind?"

She moved beside him, a mischievous grin on her face. "What about a West Virginia wedding? They have a drive-through service."

A laugh bubbled up in his throat. "That's not quite what I had in mind for a destination wedding." When he glanced at the birds, they took flight, soaring above the deep orange and red hues of the leaves on the trees as the sun set in the distance. His heart felt lighter. "But I could see getting married here."

"Hmm." Her brow furrowed. "Same time next autumn?"

He kissed her again. "Let's do it.

Enjoyed this story? Honest reviews of my book can help bring them to the attention of other readers. Please consider leaving a review (it can be as long or as short as you want) on the Goodreads page.

Finished The Love Birds series and ready for what's next? Read on for a sneak peek at my next book, The Tides That Bind. Coming Spring of 2025.

The Tides That Bind

If sibling rivalry was an Olympic sport, the Gallaghers would be gold medalists. Loyal Emily, the eldest, puts family and work above everything else, including her happiness. Ambitious Peter wants nothing more than to finish his doctorate. While their free-spirited younger sister, Cassie's, goals change on a whim.

When they are called home to save their family's flailing pub, the siblings' disagreement over the pub's future tests their bond. Emily teams up with a hotel heiress to rebuild tourism in the town, but there's more to their relationship than just business. Peter wants to sell the pub, but his attraction to an interested buyer clouds his judgment. Cassie jumps in with Emily's plans, but her attention is torn between the local mayor and her childhood crush.

And when Cassie suffers a life-threatening accident, the fate of the pub isn't the only thing hanging in the balance. The siblings must put aside their differences and choose a course of action before they lose the pub, their bond, and a chance at love.

The Tides That Bind — Sneak Peek

AROUND EIGHT IN THE evening, things were slowing down. Cassie took advantage of the lull in customers to wipe down the bar. It would make closing easier if she started cleaning early. The door to the pub opened and a light breeze followed a new customer. She looked up as he approached the bar. A baseball cap covered his head and obscured his face, though strands of blond hair peeked out from the sides.

"What can I get you?" she asked as he sat down.

"You're new," he said, raising his head and giving her a quick once-over.

"Actually, I'm not," Cassie said. "I'm filling in. My family owns the place."

He did a double take. "You're a Gallagher? Emily or Cassie?"

Wow, personal much? Cassie took a giant step back as she folded her arms across her chest. "Who are you?"

He gave her a sheepish grin. "My apologies. I'm Ryan Caulfield. I'm the mayor of Blue Heron Bay, thanks in large part to your father." He held out his hand, and she hesitated before she took it. "Your dad meant a lot to me, and I like to stop by and check on the place whenever I can."

She worked to swallow past the lump that still formed in her throat whenever someone spoke of her father. Her father mentioned working on a local campaign, but as she'd never much cared for politics, she hadn't paid attention to who the candidate was.

"I'm Cassie," she said. "The youngest of the Gallagher brood."

"It's wonderful to meet you. Did you move back?"

Cassie shook her head. "My siblings and I came home to help our mother, but I'll be leaving at the end of the summer."

"That's too bad, though I'm glad your mother found help." He folded his hands on the bar. "I was afraid I'd asked too much of her when I told her about the hotel group I've pitched to build here."

Cassie nodded absently. She vaguely recalled Emily talking about a hotel during their FaceTime the other day, but truthfully, she'd been more focused on the time off from work than the reason it was needed.

"Now that you're here, I hope to make the most of your time," Ryan continued with a wink.

She blinked, unsure what to make of it. Was he flirting with her? She, of all people, should be able to tell, especially after spending much of the evening flirting herself. But he was different, more sincere, more... purposeful, like he had set a strict path for himself and refused to deviate from it.

"So, can I get you anything?" Cassie asked again.

"Sorry, yes, I'll have a Sam Adams."

She nodded and grabbed a glass before heading over to the taps. The weight of his gaze followed her every move, and she shifted from foot to foot. Not that there was anything wrong with him, but he wasn't her usual type. For one thing, he appeared much older than her—maybe mid-thirties?

"Thank you," he said as she set the glass in front of him. "Are you planning to go to the town's Memorial Day parade?"

Cassie gave her one-shoulder shrug. "I'm not sure. I only arrived today."

"And you're already working?" he asked with raised eyebrows.

"I wanted to," Cassie said. "Besides, it was a long drive. Feels good to move around."

"How far away are you?" Ryan asked.

She stared at him. *Again, with the personal questions.*

As if he read her mind, he hurried on. "I mean, if you don't mind my asking."

"I'm right outside of D.C.," she said, not wanting to give out too much information. A girl could never be too careful, regardless of his connection to her late father.

"Wow, that's quite a change of pace from here. Do you prefer the city?"

"Usually," Cassie said, the tension in her shoulders releasing. "I love being able to walk most places and there's so much life there. Every day, I meet new people. But I do miss the ocean."

"What do you do?"

Cassie rolled her eyes. Of course, the inevitable professional question. Sometimes it seemed like that's all that mattered to some people: a job, a profession, a neat and tidy box into which they could categorize someone.

"I'm sorry. Did I say something wrong?" Ryan asked as his brows furrowed.

"Not exactly," Cassie said with a sigh. There wasn't much point in explaining it to him. He struck her as a stuffed shirt, and he was clearly established in a career path if he was mayor. He wouldn't understand. "I'm a paralegal."

His face cleared, as Cassie expected it would. Now that she fit into a box in his mind. Typical. And before he spoke again, she knew exactly what he was going to ask.

"Have you ever considered going to law school?"

There it was. She'd known his type from the second he walked in, and he hadn't disappointed. This was the question she was most often asked by business professionals. The question had been the bane of her existence since she'd finally finished her legal studies degree. Everyone wanted to know what her next move was, her career goals, her ambitions. The truth was, she didn't have any. Why did everyone else adhere to a strict timeline of events for their lives: college, career, marriage, then family? Cassie swallowed another sigh.

"Probably not," she finally said. "I barely finished my bachelor's, so the idea of more school doesn't appeal to me."

Instead of pressuring her, as people often did, he laughed. "I don't blame you. I've thought about going for a J.D. with a focus on tax law, but I don't need to take on more student loan debt."

She couldn't help wrinkling her nose. "That sounds incredibly boring."

Ryan grinned. "It is, but it's also very lucrative." He took a swig of his beer before setting it back on the counter. "I like to keep fallback options in mind, especially since politics is hardly a stable career."

Stability wasn't really a word with which Cassie was well acquainted. She flew by the seat of her pants and this method hadn't failed her thus far. The idea of having a fallback option more boring than her current job was about as appealing as getting a root canal.

"It was nice to meet you," she said as she moved away. "But I better check on my other customers."

He nodded. "I'm sure I'll see you around while you're in town."

Cassie wasn't sure if that was a threat or a promise.

Also By Katie Eagan Schenck

A Home for Christmas
A Marine has just one wish this Christmas: a home.
Available at all major retailers.

—ℓℓ—

The Love Birds trilogy
When Cardinals Appear, When Swans Dance, and *When Doves Lament*
Available at all major retailers.

About the Author

Katie Eagan Schenck writes sweet romance and women's fiction that warms the heart and gives all the feels. She has an MFA in creative writing from Queens University of Charlotte. When she's not writing she's either drafting regulations for the federal government, baking delicious treats, or binging Hallmark movies. She lives in Maryland with her husband, daughter, and their three cats. Connect with Katie on her website at keschenck author.com, instagram: @keschenckauthor, or Facebook: @keschenck

Acknowledgements

As always, I want to start by thanking my mother, who encouraged me to pursue my dream of writing from the tender age of eight. I want to thank my husband and daughter, who have provided me with so much love and support throughout the whole process. My deepest thanks to my father and step-mother, who have supported me for the past several years through all the ups and downs of my life and who served, at least in part, as the inspiration for this book! A huge debt of gratitude to my sister and sister-in-law who have helped spread the word about my books! Much love to my brother and his partner who cheer on my writing from across the country.

I'd be remiss not to thank Rashida and Angela McRae at Red Adept Editing for their assistance with making this story shine! I also want to thank Kathleen Sweeney and the amazing staff at Book Brush for the beautiful cover.

Finally, thanks to all my friends who have offered feedback on my writing over the years, especially those of you who were unfortunate enough to read my angsty teenage poetry. They say it takes a village to raise a child, and I think it takes at least that, and so much more, to raise a writer.